IDLEWILD

IDLEWILD

a novel

JAMES

FRANKIE

THOMAS

THE OVERLOOK PRESS, NEW YORK

Library of Congress Control Number: 2023933935

ISBN: 978-1-4197-6914-6
eISBN: 979-8-88707-079-7

Printed and bound in the United States

1 3 5 7 9 10 8 6 4 2

Abrams books are available at special discounts when purchased in quantity for premiums and promotions as well as fundraising or educational use. Special editions can also be created to specification. For details, contact specialsales@abramsbooks.com or the address below.

ABRAMS The Art of Books
195 Broadway, New York, NY 10007
abramsbooks.com

for Shapiro

O, is it all forgot?
All school-days' friendship, childhood innocence?
We, Hermia, like two artificial gods,
Have with our needles created both one flower,
Both on one sampler, sitting on one cushion,
Both warbling of one song, both in one key,
As if our hands, our sides, voices and minds,
Had been incorporate.

—*A Midsummer Night's Dream*, III.ii.204–211

We're an empire now, and when we act, we create our own reality.

—attributed to Karl Rove

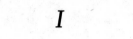

I

F&N, 2002

Somehow a year has gone by. Idlewild is a Quaker school, which means it values consensus, which means there was an Upper School Meeting yesterday to discuss what to do about today. Should it be a designated day of sadness, or would that be letting the terrorists win? Our class resolved that the best way to honor the anniversary would be to cancel school and stay home. Our class was then informed that this was not a legitimate option. In Quaker tradition, the Meeting ended with a half-assed compromise: today will be a normal school day in every way except that the morning Meeting for Announcements will be replaced by a special Meeting devoted to somber contemplation of the anniversary. That Meeting starts in five minutes, which is why we two, we happy two, we the F&N unit are standing in the Peace Garden outside the side door of the Meetinghouse, furiously fellating the green plastic straws of our caramel Frappuccinos as we review the rules of Guess Who's Gay.

F: "Walk me through the math one more time."

The two of us have a neat division of labor: N is good at numbers and homework, while F is good at having big tits and being the boss. Both of us are good at musical theater, reading each other's minds, staying up till five in the morning reading slashfic on the Internet, and Socratic dialogue—viz.:

N: "Okay, so, percentage-wise, how many people in the world are gay?"

F: "Ten percent, supposedly, though if you adjust for the closet it's probably more like, I don't know, a hundred."

N: "Sure. But for our purposes, one out of every ten people is gay."

F: [*Socratic*] "Yes, quite so."

N: "And how many people are there in the senior class?"

F: "Like, two."

N: "Time-out. I'm non-Socratically asking. What are we down to now, fifty-ish?"

Fifty-five of us began our freshman year here in the fall of 1999, but since then our numbers have dwindled. Last year alone saw three casualties:

1. Andy Edelson moved away because his whole family freaked out and fled to the suburbs after the event that today is the one-year anniversary of.

2. Samantha Kerrigan "transferred to Simon's Rock," which is a euphemism for "flunked out but has very rich parents."

3. Jacob Teifer got busted with weed and had to go before StuDisc, i.e., the Student Disciplinary Committee, i.e., the Narc Club, which reached consensus that he should be expelled.

F: "Forty-eight, I think."

N: "We'll round up to fifty. So if there are roughly fifty kids per grade, which is roughly two hundred kids in the Upper School, and one out of every ten people is gay, then . . . ?"

F: ". . . you like to fuck boys. In the ass."

N: "What?"

F: "Because you're Socrates. Know thyself, homo."

The point, though, is that there must, mathematically speaking, be twenty gay Idlewilders among us. We the F&N unit count ourselves as one single gay unit, which leaves us with nineteen probable homosexuals in the Upper School—most likely dudes, statistically speaking; and most definitely cowards, objectively speaking, since they have not yet revealed themselves to us. Having thus reached the limits of science, we must identify them using magic, which we perform twice a week at Meeting for Worship.

Meeting for Worship, which happens every Tuesday and Friday morning, is when the entire Upper School gathers in the Meetinghouse and sits for twenty minutes in Silence. You're allowed, if the Holy Spirit moves you, to stand up at any point and speak spontaneously in front of the whole school on any topic you wish. When you've finished speaking, you sit back down and Silence resumes. People who don't attend Quaker schools often remark, upon learning about Meeting for Worship, that speaking during Silence sounds like a terrifying prospect. They are correct, which is why, in practice, most Meetings for Worship consist of twenty minutes of unbroken Silence. When someone stands up to speak, it's like bumping into Ethan Hawke and Uma Thurman at the video store on West Twenty-second Street: you have to play it cool, but there's no denying it's the most interesting thing that will happen all day.

At some point last year, we the F&N unit decreed in secret that speaking during Silence turns you gay. The decision was arbitrary but binding. Regardless of what you say—whether you're describing a poignant cartoon you saw in *The New Yorker*, mourning the late Shel Silverstein, or pondering the true meaning of Passover—if you speak, you're automatically gay for the day. Congratulations! (Your sexual orientation resets at 3:15 p.m.)

But because today is a Wednesday and this is a special Meeting for Worship devoted to somber contemplation of the anniversary, the rules require some circumstantial addenda:

1. The first person to cry is gay.

2. The first person to laugh inappropriately is so gay that he or she will be counted as *two* gay people.

3. If a Quaker standoff occurs—that is, if two people accidentally stand up and begin to speak simultaneously—then those two people are gay for each other.

4. Telling the story of how you personally experienced the events of this day last year—as if it were an interesting anecdote belonging to you and you alone, as if we all weren't fucking *there*—disqualifies you from ever being gay again in any future game of Guess Who's Gay.

5. To raise the stakes: if we get a crier within the first ten minutes, F is entitled to one (1) triangular half of the peanut butter sandwich in N's backpack.

N: "But I'll give it to you either way."

F: "Funny, that's what your mom said to me last night."

It's time to go in. We have to throw away our Frappuccinos because no food or drink is allowed in the House of God. There's no trash can in the Peace Garden. There's not much of anything in the Peace Garden, which is really just a walled courtyard. It's outside, but direct sunlight is blocked by the four-story school building, so the only plant life is a dense dark-green bed of ivy where the brick walls meet the ground. A mural decorates the walls. It was painted by Lower Schoolers, and you can tell. It's a nightmare orgy of rainbow daisies, wonky-eyed doves, and—taking up one whole wall—stick-figure children holding hands in a chain around a not-to-scale planet Earth.

We toss our sticky Frappuccino cups onto the concrete and kick them into the ivy. The cups vanish under the rambling tangle of vines. We enter the Meetinghouse through the gray-painted side door.

On the inside the Meetinghouse looks like an old-fashioned church but gray all over, from carpeted floor to high vaulted ceiling. Upper Schoolers, backpacked and baseball-capped and still blurry with sleep, spill in through the Peace Garden side entrance and the East Fifteenth Street front entrance. They trudge rumbling through the aisles and shuffle onto gray-painted benches. The benches, whose wood is smoothed out by two hundred years' worth of Quaker butts, are arranged in a square of rows: the senior benches face the freshman benches, the sophomore benches face the junior benches, and teachers scatter themselves non-hierarchically among them. Skip and Trudy—he's the principal of Idlewild, she's the head of the Upper School—always sit with the freshmen, directly facing the seniors. That means that we the F&N unit spend every Morning Meeting in their line of vision, but Skip and Trudy don't scare us. You can't really get in trouble at Idlewild, except by peer consensus.

We the F&N unit claim our favorite spot in the back row. Last year our favorite spot was on the radiator by the big window that looks out on East Fifteenth Street. It's weird to see two unfamiliar juniors occupying it today. They look too young to be juniors. The freshmen look too young to be sentient beings.

N: "Were we ever so young?"

F: [*Norma Desmond voice*] "We *are* big. It's the freshmen that got small."

Silence falls. No one ever calls for Silence: it simply comes over us, like a cloud. It starts out thin, but within the first couple of minutes it thickens. It holds us. The air is warm from the sunlight streaming through the big windows, whose old glass has a squiggly bubbled-up texture because glass is a liquid or something. Skip has his eyes closed, head bowed, hands folded in his lap. It looks pious when the principal does it, but we wouldn't dare try it for fear of looking like we're asleep. You'd expect people to fall asleep all the time during Silence, but it never seems to happen.

A stirring. A collective creaking of wood as all butts shift in their benches in search of the source of the sound. Two rows ahead of us, the F&N unit, a boy is standing. We know him by the back of his round head, his round ears that stick out, and the overall roundness of his teddy bear body. It's the boy we call Bottom, because he played Bottom in *Midsummer* last year, and also because he is a total bottom even if he doesn't know he's gay yet.

He speaks.

"It was such a beautiful day." With his rich resonant voice and perfect diction, everyone in the Meetinghouse can easily hear every word. He's played the male lead in every show we've ever done, and we adore him for it. "I think even if nothing happened that day, I'd still remember it now as one of the most beautiful days I've ever seen."

That's it. He sits.

An acceptable contribution to Meeting for Worship. Bottom, not for the first time, is gay for the day.

Silence knits itself back around the hole Bottom poked in it and slowly re-envelops us. The big clock on the opposite wall shows that ten minutes have passed and no one is openly weeping, so N wins the bet, though we'll share the peanut butter sandwich anyway.

Another stir of movement, another mass creaking of benches and craning of necks. Another senior. No surprise there: at this early point in the school year, seniors and teachers are the only ones confident enough to speak during Silence. He's directly in front of us. From the back of his blond head, we know it's Oliver Dicks.

Yes, Oliver Dicks. No, we never make fun of his name—nobody does. Oliver Dicks is, like F, an Idlewild lifer, which means he's been here since kindergarten, when his classmates were oblivious to his name's hilarity. To point it out after knowing him for so many years would be tantamount to admitting that one was too naïve to notice it before, and then the joke would be on oneself, not on Oliver Dicks. Ninth grade brought an influx of transfer students (including N) who cautiously followed the lead of the lifers. To this day, when Oliver Dicks says he hopes to become president of the United States, no one dares suggest that his name might be an impediment. Irrespective of his name, however, we the F&N unit consider him a smarmy-ass prep. He's been on the StuDisc committee since freshman year—need we say more?

"I'll always remember where I was when I first heard the news," says Oliver Dicks in his you-forgot-to-assign-us-homework wheedle of a voice.

"I was right here, actually, in the Meetinghouse for Morning Meeting." (Yes, we know that, Oliver Dicks, because *we all were*.) "At first I thought it was some kind of weird accident . . ."

No, no, *no*. Fuck Oliver Dicks. Fuck him up his stupid preppy-ass ass. Who does he think he is? We hereby disqualify Oliver Dicks from being gay for this or any future day; we hereby disqualify him from life itself.

". . . and, I dunno, I guess up until that day I'd never really thought about America's place in the world. I didn't know there were people who hated us. I didn't know there could be . . ."

He will not stop talking. We the F&N unit exchange a panicked glance. We have no available distractions; we are powerless to stop him.

"I kind of think of it like, America lost its innocence that day . . ."

We stare at our knees with denim-bleaching, fabric-ripping rage; we stare at our sneakers with lace-fraying, aglet-cracking panic; we look around the Meetinghouse in search of anything to stare at other than this stupid butt-sucking prep who thinks the story of this day last year is the story of his own bad day—

". . . that nothing will ever be the same. The view outside my kitchen window is changed forever, and *I'm* changed forever, and America—"

And then someone farts.

But the word *fart* is insufficient for the sonic event that interrupts Oliver Dicks. No onomatopoeia would do it justice. It is a mighty tuba blast, sustained for what must surely be five full Mississippis, with the timbre and crescendo technique of a true virtuoso. Furthermore, the blurry acoustics of the Meetinghouse make it difficult to locate the origin point of the sound, leaving open the possibility that Oliver Dicks himself is the culprit, which lends an extra layer of sadistic delight to the situation.

Screw Silence: it would be downright immoral *not* to laugh. The Meetinghouse erupts. People are screaming. People are clapping. Teachers quake with a visible effort to suppress their mirth as they shush the students in their vicinity. Even Skip, who manages to keep his eyes closed and his head bowed throughout it all, allows himself a smile. If the first person to laugh inappropriately is gay, then we are all flaming homosexuals on this fine September morning.

Oliver Dicks stands frozen in place for a few seconds before giving up and shrinking back onto the bench, the back of his neck scarlet with the blood of defeat.

To whom do we owe our lifetime debt for this act of heroism? We the F&N unit scan the Meetinghouse crowd. Our gaze lingers on a boy in the sophomore benches. He's pale, slight, dark-haired—inconspicuous but for a certain smirking serenity in his laughter, as of the cat who swallowed, et cetera.

Him, we think for one instant. But then we're not sure.

Silence resumes.

NELL

Today, for the first time in years, I saw the Meetinghouse. I work at the VA clinic on East Twenty-third, so I'm always kind of in the neighborhood, but I usually manage to do a pretty good job avoiding Idlewild. It would be an exaggeration to be like "I haven't laid eyes on the place in *fifteen years*," but only a slight one. I've never gone to a reunion. I go out of my way to avoid the stretch of Fifteenth Street between Second and Third Avenue. If a taxi takes me past it, I close my eyes so I can't see it, and I shield my face with my hand so no one can see me. Even at night. I won't take chances.

But despite being fifteen years out of Idlewild—despite being a thirty-three-year-old nurse practitioner who knows all kinds of things she didn't know in high school—I still don't know how to say no to a girl when I want her to like me. So I saw Idlewild today, and it was all because of my Tinder date. Her name was Hannah. I didn't get her last name. I'm not even confident on her hair color—that's how mentally present I was during this date. She'd texted offering to meet me outside the clinic when my shift ended so we could walk together to an udon restaurant in Union Square. I'd been on my feet for eight hours and would have preferred to go home first and shower and change out of my scrubs, but instead of saying so like a normal person, I texted back, *Perfect!*

At six o'clock we met up on the corner of Twenty-third and First and started walking downtown. It was one of those clear sunny days with the kind of objectively perfect weather that always gives me uneasy flashbacks. She was a fast walker, faster than me, so I was struggling to keep up with her and trying really hard not to let it show because I wanted to come off as the good kind of fat person, not the kind of fat person who gets winded walking down the street. I kept asking her open-ended questions—"How long have you been living in New York? What do you think of it? What are your favorite and least favorite things about it?"—so she would do most of the talking and I could breathe.

On Fifteenth Street, she turned right and I couldn't think of a way to stop her. I trotted quietly and miserably after her, keeping my eyes down.

She stopped in the middle of the sidewalk. Even with my eyes fixed on the ground, I knew exactly where we were standing.

"Oh, cool," she said. "Look at that building."

Reluctantly, I lifted my head and looked.

"I wonder what it is," she said. "It's so pretty."

It was—exactly as pretty as it was twenty years ago when I saw it for the first time and decided on the spot, without knowing anything else about the school, that I wanted to go there. The Meetinghouse is red brick and shaped like a child's drawing of a house, pitched roof and all. It looks totally incongruous on a Manhattan city block, surrounded by boxy modern apartment towers. It's always reminded me of that picture book about the little red house in the countryside whose anthropomorphic house-face grows increasingly forlorn as a big city gets built up around it. (That book confused me as a kid. What's so bad about a big city?) Today, in the golden light of sunset, its red brick walls and big casement windows looked radiant and inviting, almost enchanted.

"It's called Idlewild," I said.

"Idlewild? Like the old airport?"

"No. I mean, yes, but it's even older. This building—it's a Quaker Meetinghouse—it was built in 1860. So it's older than, uh . . ." My mind blanked on any phrase except *not-slavery.* "It's super old." I started to walk on, hoping she'd follow me.

She didn't. She was examining the wrought iron fence that wrapped around the Meetinghouse. "I love old buildings," she said. "This fence is so picturesque."

"See how the tops of the fence posts are kind of blunted and uneven?" I said, a little desperately, like I was negotiating my release in exchange for some fun facts. "There used to be decorative spikes there, but the Quakers sawed them off during World War I because they looked too militaristic and Quakers are pacifists." The fence had been repainted, I noticed. I remembered it being chipped and rusty, but now it was glossy black all over. "And now the fence is weird-looking forever."

She ran her fingers over a blunted fence post. "The gate is unlocked." She turned to me with this manic-pixie-dream-girl grin that would have been charming under literally any other circumstances. "Let's go in!" She reached toward me like she was going to grab me by the wrist and lead me through the gate.

I dodged away from her hand.

Then her face did fall. "Sorry," she said. "I should have asked if I could touch you."

"Oh, god, no," I said, horrified. "No—I'm so sorry—it's just—I went to high school here." Why the fuck hadn't I said so right away?

She looked confused. Understandably so. "It's a school?"

"It's attached to a school. That four-story building next door"—I gestured upward in a Muppety flail—"that's the school part. But we had Meeting every morning in the Meetinghouse, so, you know, it's *full of memories*." I said it with a sarcastic inflection, hoping she'd mentally fill in the blanks with clichés—snooty cheerleaders, bullies shoving nerds into lockers, whatever traumatizes lesbians at normal non-Quaker high schools. "No one wants to go back to high school, right?"

"So you're Quaker?" she said uncertainly. I could see her adjusting her idea of me based on whatever she knew about Quakers, which she was possibly confusing with the Amish—picturing me dressed like the guy on the oatmeal box. That's happened before.

"No, Jewish," I said. "Most of us were Jewish, actually. I don't think anyone there was actually Quaker."

"But then why . . . ?"

"I applied to a bunch of high schools. That was the best one I got into." I shrugged self-deprecatingly. "It's kind of a second-tier private school."

"Oh," she said, and I saw her understanding of me shift yet again.

"But I transferred from public school." I internally cringed at my use of the word *but*. Whatever I was trying to imply about myself, it probably wasn't true. "I was on partial financial aid, and my grandparents covered the rest of my tuition as a gift. Most of the other kids were much richer than me." I searched my mind for a colorful example, but it was surprisingly hard to come up with one on the spot, because that wasn't really

how Idlewild operated. Flaunting your wealth went against Quaker ide-
als, plus Idlewild parents tended to be shabby-chic trust fund artists, so
it was often hard to tell who was really rich. There were signs, but they
were subtle. And as a teenager I had been bad at picking up on them.

But Hannah nodded knowingly. "I gotcha," she said.

To my relief, she started walking again. I fell into step beside her.

"So you were an outsider," she said. "You must have been so lonely."

I decided right then that I didn't want to see her again. I did go to dinner with her, and the udon was good, and so was the conversation—but
the whole time, I was just waiting for it to be over. All I wanted was to
be where I am right now: sprawled on my bed, scrolling Facebook on
my laptop, ignoring the text Hannah just sent me (*That was really fun!
Thanks for the neighborhood tour*, emoji of a face blowing a kiss). I knew
right then on Fifteenth Street, my certainty growing with every footstep
I took away from the Meetinghouse, that there was a distance between
me and Hannah—between me and the rest of the world, really—that I
didn't know how to bridge. I can't talk about Idlewild. If you weren't
there, you wouldn't understand.

For my first two years at Idlewild, I had no friends. I didn't mind it much.
I appreciated that no one paid attention to me, that I could move through
the school unnoticed. It meant that I could have a whole secret routine.
Every morning I showed up ten minutes early so I could lurk outside the
East Fifteenth Street entrance to the Meetinghouse—leaning against the
sawed-off wrought iron fence, listening to music on my Discman—and
wait for Fay Vasquez-Rabinowitz to show up. Once she appeared, I'd
follow her (from a safe distance) into the Meetinghouse and hover creep-
ily in the aisle, waiting for her to choose a bench, so I could choose my
own seat accordingly. I didn't want to sit next to her; I wanted to sit
behind her, at a slight angle, so I could spend all of Meeting looking at
her in profile, studying the outline of her boobs and clenching my vaginal
muscles until I brought myself, hands-free, to a wet, motionless, stone-
faced orgasm on the gray wood bench.

As a crush object, Fay was kind of an odd choice. I was convinced I was
the only one in the whole school who recognized her beauty, although I'm
sure that was just a self-flattering fantasy. There must have been plenty
of boys ogling her too. Not even just her chest: she had a striking face,

with dramatic dark eyebrows. I wouldn't have been attracted to her if she hadn't been attractive. Still, she seemed to go out of her way to downplay her looks. Her thick dark hair was chopped short, and sometimes it looked like she hadn't brushed it or even washed it in a while. Her clothes were so baggy that at the time I didn't yet know the full extent of her Jessica Rabbit proportions. There was no hiding those boobs, but she didn't wear a bra, so they were always flopping around—arousing, but also a little grotesque. Even if you'd given her the full *Breakfast Club* makeover, she wouldn't have been anything close to the most beautiful girl in our class. Lily Day-Jones had the claim to that title.

Despite that, Lily Day-Jones never captured my imagination like Fay. Lily's beauty was a public asset, like Central Park, made for red-blooded boys and Shakespeare festivals and modeling scouts from *Teen People* magazine. Beautiful girls belong to the world. But Fay—scruffy, slouching, fast-talking Fay—Fay belonged to me.

I'd had my suspicions about Fay since day one. Part of it was the outfit she wore to freshman orientation: green army jacket, combat boots, cargo pants. For context, though, lots of girls were wearing cargo pants in the fall of 1999. Plus, I had similar suspicions about every girl I found attractive, including Laura Prepon on *That '70s Show*, Laura Prepon in real life, and Daria Morgendorffer, a literal cartoon character on MTV. It was all wishful thinking. I had no idea what signs to look for, so every girl on earth was Schrödinger's lesbian.

Soon, though, Fay gave me more to work with. We had freshman English together, and during class discussion, she was always bringing up gay shit. Like, *always*. We read *The Iliad*, and she wouldn't shut up about how Achilles and Patroclus were boyfriends. We read *The Great Gatsby*, and she physically thrashed and squealed in front of everybody when we got to that weird party scene where Nick Carraway ends up in bed with some dude in his underwear. We read the freaking Bible, and I resigned myself to a dry spell for gay shit—but I hadn't counted on David and Jonathan in the Books of Samuel.

"Ms. Caputo!" she cried out, raising her hand with such force that her boobs flopped around and her armpit hair peeked out of her T-shirt sleeve. Whenever she raised her hand like that, all the other kids in class snickered and rolled their eyes like, "There she goes with the gay-shit conspiracy theories again." (Even with *Gatsby*, where the gay shit was textual.)

"HoYay," she said, stabbing her fingertip against the passage she'd highlighted in her Oxford Study Bible. "There is *so much* HoYay between David and Jonathan."

Well, I knew from my gay corner of the Internet that "HoYay" stood for "Homoeroticism: Yay!" If Fay knew this too, then she must have been visiting the same gay corner of the Internet. Which meant . . . *which meant.*

On the other hand, she never had anything to say regarding LezYay, not even when it came to Ruth and Naomi, the Bible's most obvious dykes to watch out for. Fay's interest in gay shit appeared completely limited to guy-on-guy. So the jury was still out. Maybe she was just twice as heterosexual as most girls.

At least that's what I tried to tell myself. The truth was, from the moment I first heard her say the word *gay* in class, I would have thrown myself in front of the M23 crosstown bus for Fay Vasquez-Rabinowitz. Day after day I sat in the desk next to hers and studied her handwriting and crossed my Z's the way she did. Night after night I typed "Fay Vasquez-Rabinowitz" into the Yahoo search bar, finding nothing, of course, about this random fourteen-year-old girl in the year 1999. One day I overheard an art teacher mention that Fay's dad was a Mexican artist who was kind of famous—in the art world, anyway—so I switched to searching his name, over and over, until I became a sort of accidental expert on him. (Ask me anything about his multimedia installation in the 1983 Whitney Biennial.) From his 1984 *New York Times* wedding announcement, I learned that Fay's mom was a garment-business heiress who did charity stuff; from black-and-white society party photos in the Sunday Styles section, I learned that she was dark-haired and busty like her daughter.

I created a LiveJournal blog just to keep track of all this research. Its privacy setting was "friendslocked," meaning no one could read it unless they were on my list of approved LiveJournal "friends." Since I had no friends, on LiveJournal or anywhere else, the blog was essentially unfindable, which freed me to go fully nuts in it. Every day, I went home and blogged about Fay: where she lived, according to the school directory (Twenty-third Street, just like me, but we were on opposite ends); what she'd worn to school that day (the green army jacket, always, over a T-shirt); what her Starbucks order was (tall caramel Frappuccino); what books she surreptitiously read under her desk (Sherlock Holmes, *Dorian*

Gray, Rimbaud poetry); who she hung out with after school (no one, apparently).

Did I ever talk to her? Ha. Back then I was too shy to talk to anyone at school unless they talked to me first, which Fay never did. At home, though, I talked about Fay nonstop. I never officially "came out" to my mom, but my crush was so humiliatingly obvious that my mom grew concerned. One day I came home crying like a little bitch because I'd caught Fay looking at me with a facial expression that I interpreted as pure contempt for me and also I was on my period and my entire body felt like one giant sob. "She hates me," I wailed. "Why does she hate me?"

My mom, who is herself a therapist, which was why I'd been in therapy since second grade, said, "You should bring this up in therapy."

So I did. In my next session with Dr. Rothstein, I described a recent non-interaction with Fay and asked, "What do you think it means?"

Dr. Rothstein, a middle-aged lady with the longest hair I'd ever seen on a middle-aged lady, replied placidly, "What do *you* think it means?"

"I think," I said, "I'm a lesbian."

Although I'd known this about myself since middle school, that was the first time I'd said it aloud, and it felt so unexpectedly intense that I burst into tears as soon as the words were out of my mouth.

Dr. Rothstein frowned, no longer placid. "You're only fourteen," she said. "You don't need to label yourself right now."

I grabbed a handful of complimentary Kleenex from the table next to me and buried my face in it. "I'm pretty sure," I said in a small voice that got swallowed by the wad of tissues and the white noise machine.

"You know," she said, "it's very common for girls your age to develop 'crushes' on other girls." (Trust me, I could hear the quotation marks around *crushes*.) "But it doesn't have to mean anything about your sexuality."

I realized she'd misunderstood my tears: she thought I was crying about being a lesbian, that I wanted reassurance that I wasn't a lesbian. In reality, I was fucking psyched about being a lesbian. But I didn't know how to say this to Dr. Rothstein.

"Don't lock yourself into an identity, okay?" she said gently.

I nodded and made a mental note not to bring this up with her again.

All this angst and HoYay and bad therapeutic advice continued, more or less, through sophomore year. Fay did all the plays and musicals, so I did too. That helped with my shyness a little—by the end of sophomore year I was on friendly terms, if not real friends, with a handful of fellow theater kids—but it didn't bring me any closer to Fay. Which was okay with me, honestly. I was fully prepared to graduate without ever having spoken to her. I was happy to adore her from afar.

But one morning at the beginning of junior year, everything changed.

I was at my usual post on East Fifteenth Street—leaning against the wrought iron fence, listening to a CD on my Discman—when I spotted Fay standing just a few feet away. Not walking or reading or listening to music, just standing on the sidewalk in a patch of sunlight. She caught me looking at her (heart attack), smiled (double heart attack), and spoke (RIP Nell Rifkin, dead of three consecutive heart attacks). I saw her lips move but didn't hear what she said because of the music blasting through my headphones (I wish I didn't remember this, but it was Blink-182's album *Enema of the State*). I pressed pause on my Discman, took off the headphones, placed them around my neck, and spoke my very first word to Fay.

"What?"

"It's such a beautiful day," she said.

I must have said something in reply. Probably an expression of agreement. It *was* a beautiful day.

"I just want to stay out here forever," she said. "Preferably in a bikini."

I looked very quickly at the ground so she wouldn't notice me having any kind of facial reaction to the idea of her body in a bikini. The universe rewarded me by showing me a shiny quarter on the sidewalk. Childishly, I went, "Hey, a quarter!" and knelt down to pick it up.

Fay asked, "Old or new?" The government had recently started to roll out new quarters whose tails side depicted, instead of an eagle, the iconography of a particular state. They were still a collectible novelty at the time. My favorites were Georgia, which had a peach, and South Carolina, which had a little bird.

I inspected it. "New," I said. The tails side said LIVE FREE OR DIE. "New Hampshire," I said—and then, impulsively, "You can have it." By the time I realized what a weird and desperate gesture that was, it was too late: I was already holding it out to her.

"Oh, I couldn't possibly," she deadpanned.

"No, take it," I insisted, feeling like I now had no choice but to commit to the bit. "As a token of my, uh . . ."

"Chivalry?"

"Esteem," I said at the same time. "No, chivalry. That's better."

By then everyone else had gone into the Meetinghouse. Rather than argue, Fay took the quarter and shoved it into the pocket of her cargo pants. We walked inside—not together, exactly, but the junior benches were mostly filled up, which meant that Fay and I had no choice but to sit together. She sat down. I sat next to her. My butt touched her butt. I mean, we were basically having sex.

Seriously, it was dizzying to be so physically close to her. I could smell her. It wasn't a pleasant or unpleasant smell, it was just recognizably the smell of her body, but compared to the cucumber-melon chemicals that wafted off other girls, it was like seeing her naked. I didn't know what to do with myself.

I looked at the big clock on the wall. We had almost a full minute before Silence fell. Had we exhausted the topic of the weather? I remembered that we were in the same English class again, American Lit. I asked, "What do you think of *The Scarlet Letter* so far?"

She began to answer—but it was right at that moment that Eddie Applebaum squeezed his way onto the bench beside us. Eddie was always late for Meeting, which was just one of his many daily public embarrassments. Another one was that he was fat. Not, like, unusually so—there were plenty of other fat kids at Idlewild, including me—but it was Eddie Applebaum whose name was tauntingly invoked in a thousand games of Fuck/Marry/Kill and who died a thousand hypothetical deaths as a result. What's more, he had a naturally high-pitched voice and an emotionally expressive face, both of which made him seem gay, and that was often the subtext of the teasing. But only the subtext. Idlewild kids didn't have a problem with gay people. They just had a problem with Eddie Applebaum.

And I was no exception. Sometimes I felt sorry for him, but that morning, when he interrupted my conversation with Fay, I hated his needy round face. I hated his stupid Yankees cap, which he was supposed to take off in the Meetinghouse. I hated his squeaky voice as he leaned in close to us and said, "Guess what I just saw."

I ignored him. "Sorry, Fay," I said. "What were you saying about *The Scarlet Letter?*"

She began again. "I haven't—"

But Eddie Applebaum was persistent. "You *guys*," he said. "I just saw a plane crash into the World Trade Center."

Fay reached into the pocket of her cargo pants and pulled out the New Hampshire sidewalk quarter. "Here," she said. "Call someone who cares." She flicked it at Eddie's face. He flinched, and as the coin bounced off his nose and onto the gray-carpeted floor, Fay glanced at me. It was a really quick glance, the way you'd fake-casually glance at your reflection in a storefront window, almost impossible to catch—but I caught it. She was hoping to make me laugh.

And I did. I laughed and laughed. Silence was falling, but I couldn't stop. The happiest year and a half of my life started right then.

FAY

I saw Nell today.

She didn't see me. I've spent years cultivating the art of seeing Idlewild without being seen. I keep to the opposite side of the street. I face forward, resisting the flowerlike instinct to turn my face toward the Meetinghouse. To walk briskly is key. So long as I appear to be going somewhere in a hurry, no one looks at me long enough to notice that I'm going in circles, turning the corner and reappearing a minute later like a background extra in a shoestring street scene (see *The Truman Show*, 1998, dir. Peter Weir). As I tell students, one can mask a lot of weakness—in a thesis statement, in the transitions between paragraphs, in the conclusion or lack thereof—with the illusion of forward momentum. I never stop or slow down to drink in the sight I wish to see. I allow myself to glimpse it only in my peripheral vision.

It was in my peripheral vision, then, that I glimpsed Nell. Despite this, and despite the fifteen years that had elapsed since I'd last seen her, I recognized her with an alacrity that preceded thought or even surprise. For an instant, it felt perfectly ordinary to see her in front of the Meetinghouse. In that instant, I might have turned, waved, cried out *Nell! Hey, Nell!*

In the next instant, I thought I might be dreaming.

All my dreams take place at Idlewild. I dream, like anyone, of the test for which I haven't studied, the class I've forgotten to attend all year, the

play for which I haven't learned my lines. But even in the dreams the-
matically unrelated to school, Idlewild serves as the perpetual backdrop,
the same set repurposed for every show, as though hamstrung by the
cheap production budget of my unconscious. My dreams recreate Idlewild
with a mind-numbing degree of architectural accuracy, never adding a
classroom or deleting a corridor or taking any Escherian liberties with
the stairs (see *Inception*, 2010, dir. Christopher Nolan). The Idlewild of
my dreams is every inch the real Idlewild. Or, rather, the real Idlewild
circa 1990–2003, which no longer exists except in my dreams.

A good twenty feet past the Meetinghouse, I ducked behind a lamppost
and peered around it. Yes, it was Nell Rifkin herself, accompanied by a
tall string bean of a woman; their combined silhouette put me in mind
of Ernie and Bert. The two of them stood very close together, facing the
Meetinghouse as they conversed, as though their intimacy was such that
they didn't need to make eye contact. It was the same pose Nell used to
strike with me.

All this passed through my mind in several seconds. Then Nell and her
friend (her girlfriend?) began to walk away, west toward Third Avenue.
In a trancelike state, I followed behind. I kept a careful distance, but the
street was sparsely populated; there was no crowd into which I could
blend. Had Nell looked back at any point, I would have been caught—but
I knew, somehow, that she wouldn't look back.

Nell appeared, at a glance, exactly as I remembered her. The sand-
colored hair. The shoulders slightly hunched upward, as if braced for
a blow. Even her outfit was oddly familiar. In school she favored a T-shirt
worn over a long-sleeved shirt, a look that's long since fallen out of
fashion, so it puzzled me to see her wearing the same thing today. Then
I saw that what I'd taken to be a T-shirt was part of a set of matching
scrubs, which I'd failed at first to recognize as scrubs because they were
a tasteful, un-medical shade of maroon. Of course: I knew, from
Googling, that she was a nurse. It was a warm day, too warm for lay-
ered shirts, but I imagined the chill of hospital air-conditioning; I pictured her wearing a long-sleeved shirt under her scrubs every day, even
in summer.

Then, as if this thought had broken a spell, I saw how Nell had changed. Her hair was shorter than ever, shaved at the sides and back in a men's taper fade. I wondered if she went to a salon or a barbershop. I imagined someone (I did not imagine myself) coming up behind her and tickling her bare neck. Something in her demeanor made me think that she would not giggle or shriek, as she would have in our Idlewild days, but spin around in unamused indignation. She was not a puppyish teenager. She was, like me, thirty-three years old.

Sunset dimmed to dusk as I stalked Nell and her companion (her girlfriend, I was increasingly certain) up Fifteenth Street, across Third Avenue, and farther west still, into the open space of Union Square. I followed them, dodging skateboarders and a chanting Hare Krishna horde, across the park's broad concrete steps on which Idlewilders used to sit after school and on which teenagers still sat now. I followed them through the greenmarket's evening stragglers, briefly losing them in the crowd surrounding the She Wolf Bakery booth, spotting them again at a stall that sold bundles of dried lavender. I was prepared to follow them as far as they walked. Had they walked into the Hudson River and swum to New Jersey, I'd have been twenty feet behind them the whole way, so long as I could remain hidden.

But my pursuit, in the end, lasted no more than ten minutes. Having sniffed the lavender to their satisfaction, Nell and her girlfriend crossed the avenue and disappeared into a Japanese restaurant on Sixteenth Street.

I came back to myself, as it were, disoriented on the western edge of Union Square. I cast my glance in the downtown direction, saw the tripod-mounted spire of the Freedom Tower glittering in the sunset sky, and knew I was awake.

I had a six-thirty meeting with a student at a Starbucks whose East Village location I had selected for its proximity to Idlewild, but now, having walked so far in the opposite direction, I would be quite late. I had forgotten the appointment, forgotten the time, forgotten everything but

Nell. So overcome was I at the sight of her, and so consumed with the task of remaining unseen, that only now—alone in my apartment with all the lights off, drinking my midnight whiskey by the blue glow of my laptop screen—do I pause to consider the obvious questions.

1. What was Nell doing at Idlewild today?

I can only assume she wanted to show her old school to the woman she loves.

2. What has Nell told this woman about me?

Perhaps nothing at all. Perhaps Nell never thinks of me.

A year and a half, after all, is but a blip in time. Our friendship was a brief and strictly binary thing, never passing through any intermediate stages like *casual acquaintance* or *theater buddy*. We were strangers to each other; then, suddenly, we were best friends; a year and a half later, just as suddenly, we were strangers again.

3. How did that come to pass?

It's a long story, and there are parts of it I struggle to explain even to myself. We grew so close, so quickly, and I still don't entirely understand why.

As with so many dramatic social changes, though, 9/11 played a role.

4. Why did I approach Nell on the morning of 9/11?

Anyone who was in New York that morning, anyone who stepped outside even for a moment, surely remembers what a pure and sparkling day it was. In the clear sunshine, something in me unfurled. I wanted to share the beauty; I needed someone else to see what I was seeing, feel what I was feeling. I saw Nell outside the Meetinghouse. I thought she might understand.

5. Why Nell?

Three months prior, there had been an incident in the computer lab.

Idlewild's computer lab was a stiflingly hot little room at the end of the fourth-floor hallway. The school computers had Internet capability, so theoretically the computer lab should have been packed during lunchtime, but the close quarters and wide Power Macintosh G3 screens conferred zero physical privacy—so that if one wanted, say, to read Sherlock Holmes slash fiction, one had to read Sherlock Holmes slash fiction in full view of everyone in the room, including Jimmy Frye the IT guy. In practice, then, the computer lab was a ghost town but for a handful of Idlewild's inveterate nerds. This included Nell, but not me. I was more of a library dweller. Certain corners of the Idlewild library were so secluded from view that I occasionally masturbated there.

One day at the end of sophomore year, I paid a rare visit to the computer lab to print out my final paper for British Literature (thesis: Iago is a closeted homosexual whose villainous actions are motivated by his secret desire for Othello). I logged into my Idlewild intranet account and navigated to the alphabetical list of folders, one for every Idlewild student. Under normal circumstances my personal folder, labeled FVasquezRab03, was easy to spot, being the only one whose icon was not obscured by a forbidding little padlock icon signifying inaccessibility. On that day, however, some kind of glitch had occurred in the system: there were no padlocks anywhere. All the student folders were temporarily open and available for anyone's viewing pleasure. This was a major security breach and a once-in-a-lifetime opportunity to snoop. My heart raced as I scrolled in search of NRifkin03.

An onlooker might have been surprised, given the choice of so many interesting Idlewilders, that Nell was the classmate whose secrets I coveted. Nell never drew attention to herself. She and I had never spoken. We sat next to each other in British Literature, but she was so taciturn both in and out of class that I knew almost nothing about her.

Except, of course, that she was a lesbian.

6. How did I know that?

I'd suspected it from the very beginning. While I was a "lifer"—an Idlewild student from kindergarten onward—Nell transferred from public school in the ninth grade, so it was in freshman orientation that I saw her for the first time. She had the kind of hair that I've now come to associate with teenage proto-butches: long, almost down to her waist, a length that suggested not vanity but accidental neglect. I kept my own hair cropped short, but it was out of a similar apathy toward my physical appearance, so I recognized it in her.

As freshman year went on, I began to notice the way she looked at me, and by sophomore year there was no doubt in my mind that she had a crush on me. She wasn't subtle about it; I could almost feel the pressure of her eyes on me in Morning Meeting. It preoccupied me.

7. Pleasurably so?

Not in the way one might assume. I didn't find her attractive. I didn't find any girls attractive. That was one reason I avoided her. Perhaps it was also the real reason I avoided the computer lab.

But here I was now. I cast a covert glance around the lab—and there was Nell, hunched in a corner, her gaze fixed on her own computer screen. I was intoxicated by the prospect of perusing her private documents, right in front of her, without her knowledge. I double-clicked to open her file.

My excitement faded as I scrolled through the alphabetical list: *canterburyessay.cwk, canterburyresponse.cwk, chemstudyguide.cwk.* Of course it was all homework. No one used one's school account for anything else. What had I expected?

The bell rang, and in my peripheral vision I saw Nell rise to leave. I scrambled to return to my original purpose, busying myself with the print job. Nell's straggly long hair tickled my shoulder as she walked behind me. Consumed with the pretense of not noticing her, I opened *othelloessay.cwk* and selected Print. The printed pages arrived facedown in the printer tray, and in my haste, I didn't look at them closely.

We all handed in our papers at the beginning of class. As the teacher, Devi, inspected the stack on her desk, she frowned. "Nell," she said. "I have two copies of yours."

In the desk next to mine, Nell shrank slightly from the attention. "Sorry," she said. "Maybe it printed twice." Her voice, which I'd rarely heard before, was lower pitched than mine.

"And Fay," Devi continued, "I'm missing yours."

Surely no one in the classroom deduced on the spot that I had snooped in Nell's private account, distractedly mistaken it for my own, and printed out her paper instead of mine. Nonetheless, I couldn't have felt more exposed if Devi had torn off my shirt to reveal my braless chest. Aware of Nell's eyes on me, I did my best to project imperious boredom. "That's because I didn't give it to you," I said. "I didn't have time to print it out."

My impertinence was somewhat out of character, and the gentle Devi was visibly thrown by it. "The last week of school is a busy time," she said uncertainly. "Just get it to me by the end of the day, okay?"

I shrugged, feeling Nell's gaze upon me as one feels sunlight through glass.

I never did hand in that paper. Nor did I ever tell Nell about my computer lab blunder. Over the course of the summer, though, I ruminated on the memory, and then on the very fact of Nell. By the time junior year began, the version of Nell that existed in my head felt so real, I'd all but forgotten we'd never spoken in real life.

F&N, 2002

Skip breaks Silence in the traditional way, by reaching over and shaking Trudy's hand. The Meetinghouse stirs to life as everyone follows suit and shakes hands with their neighbor, then disperses for first period, still aglow over the already-legendary Great Meetinghouse Fart of '02.

Despite the ongoing efforts of our teachers to separate the F&N unit, we've managed to get most of the same classes this semester. Wednesday first period is Slavery, Capital, and Empire: Rethinking the American Experiment, taught by Glenn Harding.

"Okay, settle down," he intones, as if he's bored by us rather than terrified of us. No one is fooled. He is twenty-three years old. His monotonous delivery is a protective mechanism, as is his slouch, his scruff, his emo glasses, and his ironic trucker hat. According to our informant Jimmy Frye the IT guy, he moonlights as lead guitarist for a local band called Automatic Caution Door. *Ergo*: we the F&N unit have the right—nay, the duty—to haze the shit out of him.

F: "You're gonna have to be more assertive than that, Glenjamin."

N: "Come on, Glennifer, speak from your diaphragm!"

Idlewild is a Quaker school, which means we call our teachers by their first names. There are exceptions, like Mr. Prins and Ms. Caputo, who earn their honorifics by exuding authority. Glenn obviously hoped to be one of them. On the first day of school he slouched at the front of the room and mumbled, "I'm Glenn Harding. You can call me Glenn, or Mr. Harding . . ." in a studiedly casual way that simultaneously (1) made it clear that he keenly hoped we'd opt for Mr. Harding and (2) ensured that he would never, ever be called Mr. Harding. Indeed, he's lucky if we call him Glenn.

F: "You can do it, Glennothy!"

N: "We believe in you, Glennifred!"

"Whatever," he mumbles, like this isn't crushing him inside, and turns to the blackboard to write something about the British East India Company.

Losing interest, we the F&N unit survey the classroom. The girl sitting to our immediate left—the girl whose name is Lily Day-Jones but to whom we refer to as Daylily Jones because that's obviously better—is crying.

We harbor complex feelings toward Daylily Jones. Her defining personality trait is her beauty, and if you don't believe that physical beauty is a personality trait, then you've never met anyone as beautiful as Daylily Jones. With her porcelain skin, plump lips, and cascading waves of glossy hair (naturally chestnut, lately tinted with a raspberry sheen) down to her waist (a white sliver of which is currently exposed between her tank top and her jeans), she's beautiful like a rose or a sunset or a swan. As a result, she's widely mistaken for a talented actress. In the last three years Daylily has appeared on the Meetinghouse stage as Titania, as Perdita, as Ophelia (in *Rosencrantz and Guildenstern Are Dead*, but still). In *eighth grade* she landed the role of Philia in the Upper School production of *A Funny Thing Happened on the Way to the Forum*—and she can't even fucking sing.

Yet try as we might, we've never been able to hate her: she's just too nice, in the way that extraordinarily beautiful people tend to be, because the world is always smiling at them. When you look like Daylily Jones, the world leaves flowers in your locker on Valentine's Day. It throws in a free blueberry muffin with your Frappuccino. It comes up to you on the street and asks you to model for *Teen People*, and when you show up at the fashion shoot, it does not turn out to be a sex trafficking scam and you really do appear in the January 2002 issue of *Teen People* looking, if anything, a notch *less* beautiful than you usually do, because professional makeup and airbrushing can only gild the refined gold that is your face. When you look lovely, everyone is lovely toward you, and thus life has never given Daylily Jones a reason to be anything but lovely toward everyone in return. This is also why she's not funny.

So it is with a mix of concern and curiosity that we the F&N unit collaborate on a handwritten note—*Are you OK?*—and paper-airplane it her way.

She reads our note and looks over at us all dewy-eyed and trembly-lipped, her complexion rosy with sorrow. (Okay, sometimes we do hate her.) Glenn is droning on about commodity fetishism and the birth of consumer culture, and teachers never reprimand Daylily anyway, so she replies to us aloud in a sob-choked stage whisper.

"I don't think today should be a normal school day."

We nod sympathetically, as anyone would at the sight of Daylily in distress, though we are not necessarily in agreement with her.

"I can't believe it's been a whole year," she says. A single tear actually slides in slow motion down her cheek, which we thought happened only in the movies.

So Daylily is our first crier of the day. We failed to anticipate that the first tear would not be shed until *after* Meeting for Worship, so it's unclear whether the amended rules of Guess Who's Gay are still in effect. Is Daylily Jones gay for the day?

We the F&N unit call an emergency meeting (location: N's notebook) to adjudicate the question.

F: *NOT GAY. Too pretty. Rules don't apply*

N: *Lesbians can be pretty!!!*

F: *Not like DLJ*

N: *I'd do her*

F: *I'd do your mom*

Glenn has the temerity to interrupt us. "Fay, can you give us another one?"

F: "What?"

"Another one of the main British imports. We've already got cotton and tea on the board. What else?"

F: "Homosexuality."

The class laughs, which buys time as N flips through the textbook to refresh her own memory. This is our elegant system for textbook-based classes: only one of us buys the book, and we share joint custody of it. This saves money but also means that only one of us can do the reading on any given night. Usually N.

Glenn is getting passive-aggressive. "This was all in last night's reading."

N surreptitiously writes down *sugar* and flashes the page to F under the desk.

F: "Sugar."

"Good one," says Glenn. "Really important. We'll talk a lot more about the sugar industry next week." He writes SUGAR on the blackboard. "What else? Lily, can you give us one?"

Daylily looks at him like she's Bambi and he just shot her mom. And even though we both know in our hearts that she *is* too pretty to be gay, for this or any other day, we make a split-second decision to treat her as one of us. Our hands shoot skyward.

F: "Hey! Glenningrad!"

N: "Glenntropy!"

F: "United Colors of Glennetton!"

N: "Glennifer Glaniston! From the hit TV show—"

F&N: "*GLENNDS!*"

"Jesus Christ." Glenn looks to be on the verge of psychic collapse. "What is it?"

We have no idea, but it doesn't matter; Glenn has lost any semblance of control over the room. The class is cracking up, not because they find us funny—we the F&N unit operate on a higher comic level than our peers can appreciate—but because it's fun to watch a teacher get bullied and they appreciate us for fulfilling this necessary role in the Idlewild ecosystem.

As Glenn tries and fails to restore order, Daylily casts a grateful glance our way. We return to our scribble meeting.

F: *Never mind, she's totally gay for us*

N: *She'll be eating our collective box by the end of the day*

We are joking. Even if Daylily were gay, she would never go for either of us, because we are, on principle, absolutely disgusting. We have matching short haircuts, unbrushed. We shorten our fingernails by chewing them and leaving little Hansel-and-Gretel nail trails behind us. We cut the sleeves off all our T-shirts to let our armpits breathe, and we grow our armpit hair thick and fluffy so we can absentmindedly stroke it like a pet during class. Our classmates may be grossed out, but the joke is on all of them, because we have freed up our precious minds to contemplate important gay shit, like whether or not Daylily Jones is gay for the day. The question is still unresolved when the bell rings.

As luck would have it, she's in our next class: Freud, Jung, and the Uses of Enchantment, one of the senior English electives. We the F&N unit signed up for it because the teacher told us that our ongoing quest for homoerotic subtext would be not only welcome but encouraged.

Once again we find a seat beside Daylily, who resumes shaking with photogenic sobs. Now would be a great time for us to think of something consoling to say.

F: "At least it's a beautiful day, right?"

N: "Just like last year. Only windier."

F: "Good thing it wasn't this windy then, right?"

N: "Oh, shit, good call. Imagine all the . . ."

Together we ripple our fingers to convey ashes blowing through the air. Daylily continues to weep at her desk. The uncharitable thought is beginning to enter our shared mind that she is perhaps overdoing it just a little.

F: "Don't you think the skyline looks better without the . . . ?"

N: "Totally! They were an eyesore."

F: "It's a shame it had to happen this way, but . . ."

N: "Gotta look on the bright side."

Enter Juniper Green. Her real name is Jennifer, but we the F&N unit refer to her as Juniper so we can complain about her while she's in earshot. We do hate Juniper Green, uncomplicatedly. She's loud and obnoxious in a way that only extremely petite girls can get away with. A fat girl with her personality would get her ass kicked, even at a Quaker school.

Juniper's defining personality trait is that she's a slut, or at least she wants you to think so. Her AIM screen name is Strumpet19, because (as she explains to everyone, unbidden) nineteen was the number of guys with whom she'd hooked up at the time of her AIM account's creation—although (she always adds) if she were to create it today, she'd be Strumpet[19 + x, with x being the updated number of people up-with-whom she claims to have hooked since then]. Last year, as we stood backstage waiting for the curtain to go up for *Midsummer*, Juniper asked us, "Any guys in the cast you want to hook up with? I can make it happen at the cast party. I know all the tricks. Pick a guy, any guy."

We the F&N unit were forced to issue a clarification.

F: "We don't go to parties."

N: "Plus, Fay's into gay guys only."

F: "And Nell is a lesbian."

In response to which Juniper was speechless for a record-shattering few seconds before exclaiming, "I hooked up with a girl once!" and launching into a tedious anecdote involving a summer program at Skidmore.

She recounted it at a volume that swiftly attracted the attention of every guy in the play. At the cast party, she made out with all of them. Or so she claims.

Now we watch in distaste as Juniper Green flings herself upon Daylily Jones and smothers her with cheek kisses, hair strokes, and repeated murmurs of "Sweetie! *Sweetie!*"

"I don't think today should be a normal school day," Daylily says again.

"I know," says Juniper, petting her like a dog. "I know. Let it all out, girl."

Daylily, melting into the embrace, allows herself to sob into Juniper's (surprisingly ample) bosom.

F, *sotto voce* to N: "Gross."

N, *sotto voce* in return: "Get a room, lesbos."

Enter our English teacher, Devi Saxena. Her punk aesthetic—kohl-rimmed eyes, pierced septum, curly black hair dyed magenta on only one side—belies her true nature, which is so gentle and conflict-averse that we the F&N unit call her Devi the Dove. Of all the teachers at Idlewild, Devi the Dove is the biggest pushover. She opens today's class not by urging us to settle down, nor by telling Juniper to get off Daylily's lap, nor even with any reference to last night's reading (Act II of *Oedipus Rex* and a selection from Freud's *Interpretation of Dreams*)—but instead by asking, "How are you all feeling today? Be honest with me: are you okay with us having a normal school day?"

Daylily sniffles. Juniper seizes Daylily's hand and raises it into the air with her own.

"Devi," says Juniper. "Lily and I are *not* okay. May we be excused?"

"Of *course*," says Devi, pinking with pleasure at this public display of vulnerability, and possibly also at the grammatically correct "Lily and I" construction. "I really appreciate your honesty. Anyone else?"

A few others rise and scatter, hardly believing their luck, but we the F&N unit can't bring ourselves to do it. We don't need any favors today. We're tough enough to spend forty-five minutes half-listening to Devi the Dove talk about dream symbolism.

At least this is our initial stance. But halfway through class, N scribbles to F:

Bathroom meeting—NOW

Devi the Dove is the kind of teacher who allows unlimited bathroom breaks (we have actually heard her utter the words "When you gotta go, you gotta go!"). She does not protest when we the F&N unit get up and walk out together.

In the bathroom:

N: "You know where Juniper and Daylily went, right?"

F: "To smoke in the park, probably."

N: "No! To the Witch's office."

Wanda the Witch (we mean the epithet as a compliment, though we'd never say it to her face) is the drama teacher. Juniper and Daylily are Wanda's favorite students, making her their favorite teacher. These things do tend to go both ways, especially when said teacher has reliably cast said students as the female leads in every play since the eighth grade.

N: "You're the Witch, okay? Daylily and Juniper show up in your office all sad and crying. What's the one surefire way to cheer them up?"

F: ". . . *Fuck*."

It's so obvious: those assholes have pulled a fast one and now they're off getting advance intel on what the fall play is going to be. The fall play of our *senior year*—the play in which we're all but guaranteed the best roles of our high school acting careers.

F: "Those meretricious little *fuckers*."

N: "We can still catch them."

So we end up cutting English after all, without even returning to the classroom to retrieve our backpacks—there will be plenty of time later to worry about our notebooks and wallets and shared Discman and peanut butter sandwich. For now, we run. We run down four flights of stairs, leaping over the last two steps at each landing; we run outside across the noonday-bright Peace Garden to the gray-painted side door of the Meetinghouse; we body-slam it open and run through the empty Meetinghouse and up the creaky wood back stairs to the Meetinghouse Loft, where Wanda keeps her office and all her secrets.

Halfway up the creaky wood stairs we intercept Daylily and Juniper, accompanied by Bottom, on their way down. The three of them are beaming. They know exactly why we're here. Before we can ask, they cry out to us in chorus.

"*Othello!*"

We the F&N unit repeat: "*Othello?*"

They confirm: "*Othello!*"

And the five of us jump and scream. What a day to be alive!

NELL

I have to leave the room when people start casually swapping where-were-you-on-9/11 stories. I loathe it for all the reasons you'd expect, but also because it's a game I'm cursed to lose. Even though I was physically there, I didn't see it in real time, not even on TV. After first hearing the news from Eddie Applebaum in Morning Meeting, Fay and I had Ms. Caputo's American Lit class. There was no TV in the classroom. (Why would there be, right? But I've heard so many people talk about watching it on TV at school. Did kids at non-Quaker high schools just watch TV all day?) But someone did have a radio, and Ms. Caputo let us listen to the live news broadcast. Like it was World War II or something.

We could have just gone outside to see it for ourselves. It was only two miles downtown. But you have to remember that we were all assuming it was just a weird accident, and we had all day to check out the aftermath. What was the rush?

Then the second plane hit—which, again, we saw only in our imaginations as it was described on the radio, even though we'd have had a perfect front-row view of it if we'd just walked to the corner of Fifteenth and Third—and the radio guy started screaming *oh my god oh my god oh my god*, and I noticed Samantha Kerrigan crying silently and mouthing *my dad my dad my dad*, which was disturbing because Samantha Kerrigan was usually all punk rock and cigarettes. When the screaming radio guy abruptly lost his connection, and a different radio guy came on to report the this-just-in about the Pentagon, the whole classroom exploded into chaos.

But Fay was calm, quietly scribbling in her notebook. Ms. Caputo noticed this and seized on it. "Everyone, look at what Fay is doing," she said. "She has the right idea. You should *all* be writing down what's happening."

I was sitting right next to Fay, so I was the only one close enough to see that she wasn't writing down what was happening. She wasn't writing at all. She was drawing a dick.

"Take out your notebooks," said Ms. Caputo. "Create a written record of this moment."

Paper rustled and fluttered as everyone scrambled to obey, relieved to have instructions. "It's like fucking *Independence Day*," I remember Kevin Comfort saying, with a nervous laugh.

"They're probably gonna go for the UN next," Oliver Dicks replied knowingly.

That was the first time I felt real fear. The United Nations International School—not the UN itself, just the school, but still—was just two blocks from where I lived. I sat frozen with my pen posed above my notebook, wondering if there was any point in creating a written record if we were all about to get razed anyway.

(That's something I never hear about in other people's stories: we had no idea how many more planes or bombs to expect. For all we knew, this was the end of New York City. There's no way to say that now without sounding melodramatic, but at the time it didn't feel that way. During those first few hours, I felt, along with the fear, something almost like resignation—like, "Oh well, we had a good run." And as the day went on and it became clear that nothing more was going to happen, I was too giddy with relief to feel much of anything else. For years, actually. I was in college when the horror first started to sink in. I think in some ways it's still sinking in.)

By second period, the teachers had given up on teaching. Flailing toward some vague idea of safety, Skip and Trudy decided that no student would be permitted to leave the Idlewild building without a parent or guardian, so the entire Idlewild student population formed a line for the pay phone in the lobby. (No one had a cell phone. That was the last day in history that no one had a cell phone.) In the crush of kids, Fay and I got separated from each other without saying goodbye, and I was so upset about this—I'd come *so close* to befriending her, and then *this*—I actually started crying. Luckily, if there was ever a day I could get away with crying at school, it was this one.

When it was my turn to use the pay phone, I called my mom at her office on the Upper West Side. By then all the streets were closed to traffic and the subways had stopped running, so she'd have to walk downtown to come get me.

I figured I'd kill the hour it would take her to get there in the computer lab, but for once, it was crowded to capacity. Kids were emailing their parents, I guess, or maybe reading the latest news, not that there was any news we couldn't see for ourselves by looking out a fourth-story window. So I went to the library instead, and that was where I found Fay.

She was sitting cross-legged on the carpeted floor, reading *Film Comment* magazine with her back against a bookshelf. I went up to her, planning to pick up where we'd left off that morning—but then I noticed she was crying. Not like actively boo-hooing, just kind of red-eyed and blotchy and, frankly, ugly in a way that turned me off but also emboldened me. I sat down on the floor beside her and asked, "What's wrong?"

As the question left my mouth, I heard how monumentally dumb it was. I broke into helpless giggles. Fay did too. "Oh, it's nothing, really."

"Just one of those days, right?"

"Sunny days and Tuesdays always get me down. It's actually not what you think," she said. "I have no attachment to the South Tower. It didn't even have a spire."

"If we had to lose one," I agreed, "I'm glad it wasn't the one with the spire."

(Neither of us knew yet that the North Tower had fallen too.)

"So it's not about that. It's just that my mom's out of town." She wiped her eyes on the sleeve of her army jacket. "Usually I spend Tuesdays with her, but she's in Utah this week for a music festival, so I'm on my own at my mom's house until tomorrow when I switch to my dad's. And my dad didn't answer the phone when I called just now, and Trudy won't let me leave by myself because she's a total fucking cunt." Seeing me flinch at the word, she added, "It's okay. I've reclaimed the word *cunt*."

Did she really stay all alone at her mom's? I was amazed but pretended not to be. "What time does your dad usually get home?"

"Oh, he's home now," she said. "Working on his art, with the phone unplugged. He gets really mad when he's interrupted. Especially on his days off from me."

"He unplugs the *phone?*" I couldn't imagine my mom doing that. She didn't even like me using the Internet before 10:00 p.m. because it tied up the phone line. "What if there's an emergency?"

Fay laughed grimly. "Well, indeed."

We sat in silence for a moment. Through the library window, I heard ambulance sirens wailing down Second Avenue.

I worked up my nerve and said, "Come home with me."

That embarrassed her. "No, that's okay," she said. "I'll call again in a few—"

"You don't have to do it for real," I said. "My mom will tell Skip and Trudy you're staying with us tonight. Once we're a safe distance away, you can peel off and go home by yourself."

Fay looked impressed. "That's actually not a bad idea."

"Yeah, I'm a criminal mastermind," I said, and it was a funny joke because it was already so clear that my role in our friendship was to be the dumb one. Even when I came up with something smart, it was only in the service of my dumbass golden retriever love for Fay.

So Fay and I left school together with my mom. Everything was closed to traffic, so we could walk right in the middle of the street. At Second Avenue we got swept up in a huge crowd of people walking uptown. If those people hadn't been caked in white dust, you'd have thought we were at a street fair, or a parade. It was so beautiful outside, the sky such a pure sparkling blue, and my heart lifted guiltily as I realized that Fay was still walking beside me. She wasn't going home by herself. She was staying with me, for real.

FAY

Nell's building was part of a complex of featureless brown-brick residential towers in the East Twenties. On first seeing them, I assumed Nell lived in *the projects*, a misconception that makes me laugh now. I suppose Peter Cooper Village *is* a housing project in the most technical sense: it was originally constructed to provide housing for returning World War II veterans. Special preference was shown to those who were white, and as of the 2000 census the neighborhood remained over 80 percent Caucasian (Beveridge, Andy A. "Stuyvesant Town and Peter Cooper Village, Then and Now." *Gotham Gazette* 14 September 2006). Those white veterans included Nell's grandfather, whose name was still on the apartment lease, though he and his wife had long since retired to Florida. Nell's apartment, though I failed to grasp this at the time, was my first encounter not with poverty but with the middle class.

It was just Nell and her mother and two tabby cats, Willow and Winnicott, crammed into a two-bedroom apartment with a view of FDR Drive. (As far as I could tell, there was no father anywhere in the picture—not deceased, not divorced—and I puzzled over Nell's apparent parthenogenesis.) Just as Nell and her mother weren't really poor, their apartment wasn't really unsanitary; Nell's mother was assiduous about maintaining the litter boxes and lint-rolling the cat hair off every claw-scratched surface. But the cats made it easy for me to project filth and squalor onto the Rifkin residence, justifying my instinctive aversion to it. After that first night, I got out of future visits to Nell's home by pretending to be allergic to cats.

On that Tuesday in 2001, though, neither Nell nor her mother questioned the gingerly way I moved through their apartment. It was a gingerly situation all around, and not just because of the obvious. I hadn't had a sleepover in recent memory, and from the way Nell's mother struggled to contain her excitement at my presence, it was clear that Nell was not in the habit of receiving guests either. Within my first five minutes in the apartment, Nancy Rifkin had offered me the following:

1. use of the telephone, to call my father and assure him of my safety

2. use of the computer, to email my father when he did not answer the phone

3. my very own guest towel, almost entirely devoid of cat hair, in case I wanted to shower off whatever white dust had accrued to my skin on the walk over

4. the right to help myself to anything in the kitchen

5. a glass of wine, on the grounds that I "deserve[d] it. Today, we all deserve[d] it."

This last offer I declined, as did Nell.

"Sorry about Mommy," Nell said once we were alone. (Yes, she really did call her mother *Mommy*.) "If she had her way, she'd still be calling other moms to schedule playdates for me."

I raised my eyebrows. "Playdates, you say?" Back then I often spoke in sexual innuendo. It was an act of aggression, intended to throw people off-balance so that I could win the interaction, if you counted terminating it as winning it, which I did.

Nell blushed—literally reddened. It was mesmerizing. I'd never seen anyone so inept at concealing the contents of her heart. She made me feel, by contrast, as coolly opaque as a secret agent.

All evening, Nell's mother watched the news on the living room television. For a while, Nell and I watched with her. It was the easiest way to structure the time that loomed intimidatingly before us. But the tone of the television coverage was wholly unsuited to the mood in which Nell and I found ourselves, a mood one might call *the giggles*. When the president appeared on the air (Bush, George W., "Address to the Nation on the Terrorist Attacks," 11 September 2001), I laughed in anticipation of the humorous malapropisms we could always count on him to provide. At one point, I recall, he stumbled over the word *appropriate*—pronouncing the adjectival form as though it were the verb form, as in *to appropriate the experiences of actual survivors* rather than *hand over every terrorist to the appropriate authorities*, before correcting himself—and I cackled as though it were a Bushism on par with "Is our children learning?"

But then I saw footage that disturbed me—not the fire or gore or weeping survivors, but a brief clip of people somewhere in the Middle East. I didn't catch (I didn't care) which nation; I still don't know. All I saw was that they were celebrating—laughing, chanting, looking into the camera and wiggling their tongues in apparent mockery.

"What are they doing?" asked Nell.

"It's called ululation," said her mother.

I had never heard that word before, but I recognized its root from the werewolf chapter of my middle school Latin textbook, and its meaning was onomatopoeically self-evident. As I watched those wiggling pink tongues mocking me from half a world away, a dizzying lust for retributive violence surged within me, and for the first time I understood the appeal of bombing a foreign city.

"I've never even heard of this Osama bin Laden guy," said Nell.

Redirecting my fury onto her, I asked, "Do you, like, not read the newspaper?" I had never heard of bin Laden either, but I did read certain sections of the *New York Times* weekend edition, so I felt entitled to this point against her.

Self-deprecatingly, she replied, "I mostly just read fanfiction."

What a marvel she was! I would never have dreamed of admitting aloud that I read fanfiction; I was too intellectually vain to admit it even in that moment. Still, I was so disarmed as to be reduced anew to giggles—at which point Nell's mother suggested in a tear-choked voice that we relocate this conversation to Nell's bedroom, a suggestion we sheepishly heeded.

And there we remained until morning: Nell in her bed, I in a pristine sleeping bag on the floor. Neither of us slept. Even if we'd been tired, the emergency sirens would have kept us awake. FDR Drive had been closed to all vehicles except ambulances and fire engines, every last one of which in the city was now careening back and forth between the wreckage and the hospitals. All night long, as the sirens shrieked beneath us, we talked into the dark.

What did we talk about? I wonder about this in general. Nell and I effectively spent a year and a half talking to each other nonstop, face-to-face by day and on AOL Instant Messenger or the telephone by night—but all I can think of now is what we *didn't* talk about. What did we actually say to each other?

That night, for what it's worth, we must have discussed Nell's parental situation. (Her mother, it turned out, was a celibate career woman who took the sperm donor route at the age of forty. Nell was raised with the support of her grandparents, retired lawyers now subsidizing her Idlewild education.) If we discussed hers, we must have also discussed my own. (My parents had separated when I was thirteen, and though I referred to them for the sake of convenience as "divorced," they were technically still married; the state of New York had not yet legalized no-fault divorce, and in any case my father would have been a bona fide starving artist had he lost his access to my mother's inheritance.)

But I have no recollection of these disclosures. All I've retained from that night is an interlude during which our conversation turned to the recent film *But I'm a Cheerleader* (1999, dir. Jamie Babbit).

"It's my favorite movie of all time," said Nell. "I've rented it like four or five times already. Have you seen it?"

I stiffened in my sleeping bag. I knew what she was really asking. Even then, I understood *But I'm a Cheerleader* to be a bad movie that young lesbians have to pretend to like, so they can invoke it to each other as a sort of mating call.

"I hated it," I said.

"What? *Why?* It's so good!" She added, foolishly, "I love the bright colors."

"The bright colors are symptomatic of the movie's central failing," I *Film Commented*. "It's so exaggerated and cartoony, how are we supposed to take it seriously?"

"It's supposed to be campy," she said.

"Is it?" I'd spent a lot of time thinking about this; I, too, had rented the film multiple times. "I think it has no idea *what* it's supposed to be. In some scenes it's campy, but then in the very next scene you've got soft romantic music playing over this really earnest sex scene, or Natasha Lyonne doing that stupid cheer routine, you know, the whole *Two, four, six, eight, I want you to be my mate!*"

"I do hate that scene," Nell admitted. "It's embarrassing."

Her assent egged me on, as her assent always would. "Besides," I said, "how is something *supposed* to be campy? Have you read Susan Sontag's 'Notes on "Camp"'? She says the whole point of camp is that it's trying to be serious, and then later on, gay people decide it's funny. So if something is *supposed* to be camp, doesn't that automatically preclude it from being camp?"

The word *camp* had fully defamiliarized in my own ears. Nell was silent in her bed for such a long time that I wondered if I'd put her to sleep. Outside, sirens screeched and honked.

"I guess you're right," she murmured.

I never did let her know that *But I'm a Cheerleader* had forever changed the way I rinsed out my mouth after brushing my teeth. Ever since my first viewing of the film, instead of using a glass, I cupped my hand under the faucet and slurped the water straight from my palm, the way Clea DuVall does in the montage where Natasha Lyonne is watching her and falling in love. I still rinse out my mouth this way. I did it that very night, washing white dust off my face in Nell's unfamiliar bathroom, half-hoping Nell was watching me through the open door.

F&N, 2002

Daylily Jones was right: today should *not* be a normal school day. We the F&N unit should be allowed to spend it strategizing how to get ourselves double-cast in the same role—a *good* role—in *Othello*.

Alas: class. We are cruelly separated for third period (French for F, Latin for N), fourth period (a free for F, Calculus for N), and fifth period (Senior Astronomy Seminar for F, Advanced Physics for N)—then joyfully reunited for sixth period Chorus in the Meetinghouse Loft.

There are only nine people in the chorus. The baritone section is just Bottom. We the F&N unit sit together, despite singing in different sections, and pencil notes to each other on the blank side of our Xeroxed sheet music for the "Fair Phyllis" madrigal.

N: *Which role do you want to share?*

F: *There are only 2 good ones for girls*

N: *Desdemona + Emilia?*

F: *We might have to murder DLJ & JG*

N, drawing an arrow pointing toward the initials *"DLJ"* and circling them: *After she eats our collective box*

Suddenly our note is snatched off our shared music stand by the teacher. "What's this?"

F: "Sorry, Dorothy."

N: "We're paying attention, I swear."

She squints at our note, deciphering our handwriting. Then she narrows her eyes at us. "Meet me in my office after class."

Her name is Dorothy Schneider, but we the F&N unit refer to her as Ms. Spider because she looks scary but is actually a useful friend in the Idlewild ecosystem. Indeed, she's our most reliable ally amongst the faculty. What Wanda the Witch is to Daylily and Juniper, Ms. Spider is to us. Secretly, Ms. Spider never gets mad at us; she just pretends, to maintain her tough reputation.

She dismisses Chorus a few minutes early and leads the F&N unit into her office, a tiny room just off the rehearsal space of the Meeting-house Loft. She shares it with Wanda the Witch, who isn't here right now. We look around hopefully in search of some *Othello* clues that Wanda might have left lying around—a tentative pre-audition cast list, perhaps? But our view of Wanda's side of the room is blocked by the clutter of Ms. Spider's desk. When Ms. Spider sits behind it—"Oy, my knees," she groans as she lowers herself—even her frizzy auburn-dyed head is barely visible through the stacks of sheet music and lipstick-stained coffee cups.

"You want some candy?" She proffers a clay ashtray full of Tootsie Rolls. We help ourselves to several handfuls. Ms. Spider leans back in her chair. "Let's talk *Othello*."

We explain to Ms. Spider, through mouthfuls of Tootsie Roll, that there are two things we know beyond a doubt.

1. Bottom is a lock for the eponymous role. (Wanda obviously selected the play as a showcase for the talented black guy in the senior class.)

2. Daylily Jones has Desdemona all wrapped up.

F: "Unless you think there's some way we could override Wanda's, you know . . ."

N: ". . . raging boner for Lily?"

"Wild horses couldn't override that," says Ms. Spider.

Ms. Spider is approximately one hundred years old. This is her last year before retirement, hence her increasing disregard for propriety, a disregard to which we the F&N unit can deeply relate.

We consider the remaining options.

1. Fight Daylily for Desdemona, hoping for the best-case scenario wherein the role is double-cast with Daylily in the Friday night show, leav-ing second-string Desdemona relegated to the poorly attended Thursday night show. (Idlewild shows perform only twice, opening on Thursday and closing on Friday. It's a drawback of our performance space, the Meetinghouse, doubling as a public house of worship: the set must be struck by Sunday morning.) We the F&N unit would prefer to share a role with each other, so this scenario is unideal. On the other hand,

neither of us has ever died onstage and Desdemona has a death scene to die for, so we won't rule it out.

2. Set our sights on Emilia, which will place us in direct competition with every other girl who auditions, including Juniper Green, who might also go for second-string Desdemona but tends to have the edge when Wanda is casting the soubrette role.

3. Settle for Bianca, a role minor enough that Wanda will likely reserve it for us if we call dibs on it—but damn it, we're seniors! We deserve *leads*!

"Think bigger," says Ms. Spider. She leans over her desk conspiratorially. "We all know there's only one boy at Idlewild who can handle a major lead, and he's gonna be Othello. Wanda's gotta be open to cross-casting the other male roles. Why not audition for Iago?"

We the F&N unit giggle and squirm as if she just correctly guessed the person on whom we have a crush.

F: "We *really* like Iago."

N: "He's gay."

Ms. Spider laughs at us. "Is he, now?"

F: "I wrote a whole paper about it sophomore year."

N: "It was a *really* good paper. A-plus."

Ms. Spider regards us skeptically. "Devi gives grades?"

F: "Well, not as such."

N: "But just objectively, it was an A-plus paper."

F: [*reciting from memory*] "I lay with Cassio lately . . . In sleep I heard him say, 'Sweet Desdemona, / Let us be wary, let us hide our loves.' / And then, sir, would he gripe and wring my hand, / Cry 'O sweet creature!' and then kiss me hard . . . then laid his leg / Over my thigh, and sighed, and kissed—"

"Now, hang on a minute," says Ms. Spider. "Cassio is dreaming he's kissing Desdemona, right?"

F: "Yes, but Iago says *I lay with Cassio lately*, and if you look at contemporary Elizabethan writing, you can see that 'lay with' had sexual connotations—"

Ms. Spider flings up her hands. "Uncle!" she says. "I'll take your word for it."

Which is a relief, because we're doing a terrible job explaining why Iago is gay. It's not just that he lay with Cassio, although, to be sure, this is objectively true; it's not just that he homosexually wishes to get fucked in the ass by Othello, although F proved this definitively in her paper as well. What we mean to say, but what Ms. Spider is not equipped to understand, is that Iago is gay in the way that all the best fictional murderers are gay—Norman Bates, Tom Ripley, the titular Third Man—and he was the original. Iago is gay like a black leather whip, like Paris in the 1920s, like calling non-food things *delicious*. Iago is gay like cold eyes and bony hips, like a pearl-handled pistol tucked in one's suit pocket, like delicate fingers that could play a Chopin prelude or crush a throat with equal grace. Iago is gay in the way that we the F&N unit aspire to be gay, but it's harder for girls.

The telephone rings on Ms. Spider's desk. She answers it. "Oh, hi, Skip," she says, rolling her eyes at us to indicate her dislike for the principal. (According to Jimmy Frye the IT guy, our informant, the dislike is mutual.) She cups her hand over the mouthpiece and whispers. "I gotta take this. Wait for me at the piano."

We exit Ms. Spider's office and reenter the gray-carpeted rehearsal space of the Loft. Seventh period is Senior Musical Theater Seminar, the so-called "class" that Ms. Spider conned the administration into approving this year so that we the F&N unit could get academic credit for singing show tunes with her. The only other person in the class is Bottom.

Early as usual, Bottom stands at the piano with ramrod-proper posture, his hands clasped as though he's already singing. A shaft of sunlight shines through the big window and hits him at a painterly angle, illuminating him like an angel.

F&N: "Hey, Othello!"

"Oh, come now," he says mildly. (That's how he talks—like some kind of elderly headmaster or wizard.) "Let's not jinx it."

We the F&N unit laugh. Bottom is one of the only black kids at Idlewild, and the only black guy who does theater. He's the best actor we have, but he could pee his pants during auditions or skip them altogether and still be guaranteed the role of Othello.

"I mean it," he says. "Let's talk about something else." His eyebrows crinkle with seriousness. "How are you bearing up?"

We have no idea what he's talking about.

"I can't believe it's been a year," he adds.

Whoops: in all the excitement over *Othello*, we totally forgot what today is.

N: "We really liked what you said in Meeting this morning."

F: "Way better than what Oliver Dicks said."

Bottom bats this away with a modest flutter of the hand. "Please," he says. "It's not a contest."

We're not sure how he pulls it off, but somehow—despite talking like this all the time, despite his goody-goody choirboy carriage, even despite being on the StuDisc committee this year—Bottom is *not* a smarmy-ass prep. The difference between Bottom and Oliver Dicks is that when Bottom says smarmy shit like "It's not a contest," he actually seems to mean it. The other difference between them is that Oliver Dicks *volunteered* to be a narc on the StuDisc committee, whereas Bottom was nominated by his peers because everyone trusts him to be fair and just.

Actually, we the F&N unit were the ones who nominated him. Actually—he doesn't know this—we the F&N unit ripped up our scrap-paper ballots into smaller pieces and wrote his name on all of them and stuffed the ballot box for him. He's our favorite person at Idlewild, after ourselves.

Enter Ms. Spider. "Settle down, class," she says, which is a joke, since there are only three of us. "I have a surprise for you."

She sits on the piano bench. The three of us cluster expectantly around her.

"I just got off the phone with Skip," she says. "He's approved funding for a Senior Musical Theater Seminar field trip." She grins. "Wanda and I are taking the three of you to *La Bohème*."

We the F&N unit shriek. We think even Bottom might have just shrieked, though we're shrieking too loudly to know for sure.

F: "The Baz Luhrmann one?"

N: "On *Broadway*?"

"It'll be in December," says Ms. Spider. "Consider it my Hanukkah gift to you."

Bottom looks overcome. We the F&N unit know this present is mostly for him. We all love Broadway and Baz Luhrmann, but Bottom is an honest-to-God opera buff. "I wanted to see it so much," he says, "but tickets were so expensive, I never . . . I figured it was . . ." Suddenly he bursts into Rodgers-and-Hammerstein song. "*Impossible*," he booms, his baritone rich and deep and magnificent. "*Impossible!*" Ms. Spider begins to play along on the piano, and Senior Musical Theater Seminar officially commences.

At the bridge of the song, Bottom generously stops singing and gestures to the F&N unit, encouraging the two of us to take a turn. We the F&N unit sing in unison, harmonizing at the end: *"And because these daft and dewy-eyed dopes keep building up impossible hopes, impossible things are happening every day!"*

We the F&N unit share everything. As gay God is our witness, we will share a role in *Othello*.

The day is almost done. Wednesday eighth period is Activity Period, an unstructured forty-five minutes during which all student clubs meet. Bottom heads off to join the narcs in StuDisc. Other Idlewilders disperse for yearbook, newspaper, lit mag, chess, squash, anime, and the surprisingly popular Idlewild branch (headed by the surprisingly popular Juniper Green) of the Communist Party. We the F&N unit relocate to the library.

F: "I call this meeting of the Invert Society to order."

N: "Roll call! President Fay?"

F: "Present."

N: "President Nell? Present. Good, everyone's here."

This is all the fault of our English teacher Devi the Dove. Last year she was the faculty advisor for Idlewild's so-called Gay-Straight Alliance, which was always a bit of a college-résumé-padding shell company even before its erstwhile president graduated and left the organization leaderless. With no remaining students willing to step in and run the GSA, Devi the Dove turned to the F&N unit as Idlewild's best hope of forging an A between G and S.

"You don't have to be gay to be in the GSA!" was her unpersuasive pitch.

On the one hand, we the F&N unit had no wish to take on any responsibility whatsoever. On the other hand, we were intrigued by the promise of official institutional sanction for hanging out and talking about gay shit. Plus, N's mother was riding her ass on the college résumé issue. So we the F&N unit came up with a stone that would kill all these birds at once: we agreed to be the co-presidents of the GSA—and then, once sworn in, we transformed the club into something so unappealing that it all but guaranteed no additional members.

F: "First order of business: our name. Are we still wedded to the Invert Society?"

N: [*consulting her notebook*] "According to the minutes from last week's meeting, we've narrowed down our alternatives to The Diogenes Club, The New Mattachine Society, and Ass-Fuckers Anonymous."

F: "I hereby cast my vote for option three."

N: "Petition to table this vote."

F: "Petition granted. Second order of business: promotion and recruitment."

Our mission, now that a new school year has begun, is to promote our club in such a way that no teacher could rightfully accuse us of keeping it a secret, but also that no student in his or her right mind would want to join it. That's where the fliers come in.

N: "If we go to the computer lab, I can whip something up right now."

F: "No need. I took care of it during my free." [*producing a stack of papers from her messenger bag*] "Jimmy let me use the faculty printer."

Idlewild's student printers are black-and-white only. But thanks to our backroom deal with Jimmy Frye the IT guy, our fliers are printed in multicolored ink, each word a different color in ROYGBIV order, so garish as to be barely legible.

Calling All Inverts, Perverts, and Omi-Palone:
Fay Vasquez-Rabinowitz and Nell Rifkin cordially invite you to join
THE INVERT SOCIETY
A shirt-lifting, pillow-biting, and Polari language study group
Activity Period in the library
WARNING: HEAVY READING LOAD

F: "The font is called Party LET."

N: "It's beautiful, boss."

We the F&N unit tack the fliers to every bulletin board in the Idlewild building. Once finished, having earned ourselves a chocolate milkshake, we step outside.

The air is so pure, the sky so blue, it makes us gasp. The sparkle of the sunshine feels almost violent. All beautiful days hold a certain horror now. We walk west down Fifteenth Street, wishing for a storm.

NELL

When I was younger I had trouble thinking of myself as a *real* lesbian. For one thing, I had zero experience, sexually and romantically speaking. I was studying to be a lesbian from books and movies and TV, which made the process seem straightforward: befriend a gorgeous girl (Annie in *Annie on My Mind*, Clea DuVall in *But I'm a Cheerleader*, Mischa Barton on *Once and Again*), share a spontaneous kiss with her, have a brief identity crisis, and then be her girlfriend forever. I knew I liked girls, but if I hadn't arrived at that knowledge via soft tender girl smooches, did it even count?

So that was part of it. But I continued to suffer from lesbian impostor syndrome even after I got older and racked up some lesbian experience points. The *real* lesbians—as I kept thinking of them—had suffered for it in a way I never had. Especially my now-ex, Kiley, who grew up in the Walmart headquarters city in Arkansas. When I told her I'd been "out" in high school, she was so incredulous, I thought she might even be angry with me. I tried to backpedal. "I wasn't, like, *out* out," I said. "I didn't really talk about it. People just kind of guessed." By *people* I specifically meant Fay, but I didn't say so.

Kiley was still wary. "But they didn't give you a hard time about it?"

In that moment I would have traded my entire Idlewild experience for a one-sentence sob story that would be relatable and legible to Kiley.

"No," I said. "I guess I was lucky."

And in the beginning, I really did feel lucky.

After our 9/11 sleepover, Fay and I started Instant Messaging every night. Looking back now on the fall 2001 archives of my old friendslocked

LiveJournal, I can see it evolving from a Fay research file to a Fay-and-Nell Instant Message archive. Here's one conversation we had on September 28, 2001, posted to my LiveJournal under the heading "A good sign or a bad sign?"

> OmiPalone212: Nell, old sport.
> Auto response from m k fantastico (5:37:01 PM): MY FAVORITE SHOW IS ON!!!!!
> m k fantastico: j/k I'm here!!! ignore the away message
> m k fantastico: I'm turning off the tv cuz talking to u is way more fun!!!
> m k fantastico: u still there?

(I want to reach through time to throttle sixteen-year-old Nell and yell at her to dial it the fuck down.)

> OmiPalone212: I don't want to interrupt your *favorite show*.
> m k fantastico: it's ok! it's a rerun
> m k fantastico: I've seen it before
> OmiPalone212: Wait, don't tell me what it is.
> OmiPalone212: I want to guess.
> OmiPalone212: Your favorite show is . . .
> m k fantastico: *doo doo doo doo, doo doo doo*
> m k fantastico: (that's me doing the Jeopardy tune)
> m k fantastico: (I'm not just randomly saying poop)
> OmiPalone212: Buffy?

It wasn't a tough guess. My screen name was a *Buffy* reference. Still, to flatter Fay's ego, I pretended to be blown away.

> m k fantastico: DUDE
> m k fantastico: that's AMAZING
> m k fantastico: how did you know?? are you psychic???
> OmiPalone212: I bet I can guess your favorite characters too.

I froze in my computer chair. If she guessed Willow and Tara—the lesbians—that would be obvious code for "I know you're a lesbian, Nell." And if she'd guessed it because she recognized the reference in my screen

name (Miss Kitty Fantastico was Willow and Tara's kitten), then she must
have loved Willow and Tara too. And if *she* loved Willow and Tara . . .

OmiPalone212: Willow and Tara, right?

My heart exploded into a cloud of butterflies. No longer needing to
fake my excitement, I typed my reply with such enthusiasm I messed up
my exclamation points:

m k fantastico: YES!!1
m k fantastico: they're my OTP
m k fantastico: yours too??

"OTP" was a fandom expression. It stood for One True Pairing. If two
characters were your OTP, that meant you wanted them to be together
more than you wanted anything else in the whole world. That was how
I felt about Willow and Tara. Maybe Fay felt the same way. Maybe we
could become Willow/Tara shipping buddies—watching the latest episode
together every Tuesday night, co-writing Willow/Tara fanfic, posting it
together on the Kittenboard forums. We could dress up as Willow and
Tara for Halloween. I would even let her be Willow.
　　Then Fay's reply came.

OmiPalone212: No.
OmiPalone212: I've never seen Buffy.
OmiPalone212: I don't watch TV.
OmiPalone212: Have you read that David Foster Wallace essay about
how TV is malignantly addictive?

I remember physically flinching from the computer screen, whiplashed
and wondering if I'd failed some kind of test. I scrolled back up the
message window, reading closely in search of clues I'd missed. Maybe
I'd overdone it with my whole "are you psychic???" bit. Maybe she was
punishing me for being a phony-ass suck-up. Maybe I deserved it.
　　I began to cry, right there at the computer. I was alone in the apartment, so I could really let loose with it, and I was openly sobbing as I
typed my reply:

m k fantastico: LOL

m k fantastico: yeah my brain is probably rotted by now :)

I copy-pasted that whole conversation into my LiveJournal so that I could keep analyzing it for data on how Fay really felt about me. That was always my mindset around Fay (around everything, really)—that I could study my way out of feeling shitty.

At school she was less mean and less cryptic, but also less friendly—less everything. During our sleepover, she'd laughed till she shrieked, but at school she never reacted to my jokes with anything more than an approving nod. She spoke in a monotone, mostly about neutral school-related stuff, and rarely looked me in the eye. This confused me. It would have been one thing if she just iced me out; I would have left her alone (and, you know, died of heartbreak or whatever). But Fay was actively choosing to hang out with me in school. If anything, she was clinging to me. She sat next to me every day in Meeting, in American Lit, in Chorus, in *Midsummer* rehearsal. And it was Fay's idea, one sunny October afternoon when we didn't have rehearsal, to go out for burgers at Joe Junior, the diner on the corner of Sixteenth and Third.

The two of us sat at the counter, side by side on lox-orange vinyl and chrome stools. Along with burgers, we ordered chocolate milkshakes. They came in trumpet-shaped glasses with a tall metal cup full of extra milkshake, the way diner milkshakes always do. As we ate, I thought about how we must have appeared through the window: like a wholesome young couple on a date in the 1950s, except we were both girls, and also we were avoiding direct eye contact with each other for some reason.

"I hate all the American flags everywhere now," said Fay, eyeing the one on the wall.

I hated them too, so much that I didn't know how to talk about it. I made a joke instead. "It's like the whole city is reminding me to do my American Lit homework."

"I also hate American Lit," said Fay.

"Me too. I haven't even started on my *Scarlet Letter* essay yet." All of this was a lie; I didn't mind the class, and I'd already written the intro-duction and first body paragraph.

"I'm gonna one-up you." Fay spoke to the limp pickle spear in her hand. "I haven't read *The Scarlet Letter* at all."

I wished I could take a bite of something to hide my shock, but I'd already eaten everything on my plate. "How do you pass the reading quizzes?"

"I don't." She bit into the pickle.

"What about the reading journal?"

With her mouth full of pickle: "I haven't been keeping it."

"Ms. Caputo's gonna collect it," I started to say, but stopped myself before I went full Oliver Dicks. Fay sucked at her straw, noisily slurping the dregs of her shake, and stared across the counter at the cake display case or the American flag or nothing.

Once again, the simplest explanation—that Fay was, like me, shy and awkward and struggling with the whole friendship thing—didn't occur to me. In class, onstage, online, she was so unfailingly cool and in control. I thought her face-to-face standoffishness had to be deliberate, a riddle she was waiting for me to crack. And suddenly I had an idea for how to crack it.

"You might actually like *The Scarlet Letter*," I said. "It's kind of gay."

Her head snapped toward me. "Really?"

"Totally," I said. "This guy Chillingworth is obsessed with the Reverend Dimmesdale." I didn't really stand by this theory, but it didn't matter. Fay was looking me right in the eye.

"I thought he was obsessed with what's-her-name," she said.

"That's what Ms. Caputo wants you to think," I said.

The old Greek waiter brusquely slapped our bill onto the Formica countertop. Fay and I put down a handful of cash (a burger and a shake were like six bucks plus tip, God bless Joe Junior) and walked out of the diner.

"How do you know he's gay for Dimmesdale?" Fay asked. "What's your textual evidence?" She began to cross Third Avenue, heading west, which was the diametric opposite of the way home for me. I followed her anyway.

"There's this one part," I said, "where he goes into Dimmesdale's room while he's sleeping." I'd just re-read that chapter while outlining my essay, so it was fresh in my memory. "It's a little unclear, but I think Chillingworth touches him under his shirt?"

"He *what*?"

We crossed Union Square Park, and then the Union Square farmers' market. We kept walking down Seventeenth Street and crossed Fifth Avenue. I accepted that I'd be late coming home, wondered if my mom would freak out, and decided I didn't care enough to stop at a pay phone and call her. We crossed Sixth Avenue, Seventh Avenue, and still Fay kept leading me west. It was looking increasingly like we were going to her house, but I didn't want to scare her off with any hint of inviting myself over. I just kept bullshitting about Chillingworth and Dimmesdale, and the longer Fay listened to me, the less it felt like bullshit.

When we reached Ninth Avenue she said, "I have to make a stop at the video store," and we turned north. At Twenty-second Street, she led me into a tiny storefront whose flickering red neon sign said CALVIN'S CAVERN.

When I remember Calvin's Cavern now, I picture it in black and white—partly because everything was gray with dust and age, including a dust-gray cat that rubbed itself against my ankles as I walked in, and partly because it seemed to deal exclusively in black-and-white movies. While my local Blockbuster sorted videos into categories like New Releases, Romantic Comedies, and Action-Adventure, the shelves here were marked with handwritten signs with unfamiliar names: Deborah Kerr, Betty Hutton, Agnes Moorehead. A black-and-white movie was playing on the store monitor. Behind the counter was a bald dude whose gray beard matched the rest of the store—presumably the Calvin whose cavern this was.

He greeted Fay by name, which impressed me, and asked, "What'll it be today?"

"*Rope*," she said.

"Again?"

"Again. And for Gareth . . ." She picked up a tiny yellow pencil from the counter, took a slip of paper from a Halloween candy bowl full of paper scraps, and wrote something down. I peeked: *Leather Obsession 6.* Calvin took the note and disappeared into the crowded shelves behind the counter.

I giggled. "*Leather Obsession 6*? That sounds like a gay porno."

"It *is* a gay porno," said Fay. "It's for my dad's friend Gareth. But he'll let me watch it with him."

I wasn't sure I'd heard right, and I didn't want to ask her to repeat herself, so I didn't react at all. I pretended to examine the dusty empty video cases on the Ann Miller shelf until Calvin came back with Fay's videos and we left the store.

As we turned left on Twenty-third Street—I couldn't believe Manhattan stretched so far west—Fay said, "I just really like the idea of two guys together." She spoke in a low, tentative voice, different from her usual professorial patter. I wondered why. It wasn't like this was a secret. "Two dudes doing it," she said. "It's like . . . my *thing*."

"Everybody's got a thing," I said. "Or so Stevie Wonder has led me to believe."

I don't think she got the reference. "Yeah?" she said. "Do you have one?"

I did a half-assed Bill Clinton: "I guess it depends on what the meaning of *thing* is."

She stopped, and I stopped beside her, in front of a dingy white town-house with an old-fashioned Narnia-style lamppost by the stoop.

Have you ever stood on some random street and felt, for no particular reason, like you were home? That's how I felt in front of that little building. That whole area west of Ninth Avenue was pretty deserted back then, pre–High Line; I'm sure Fay and I weren't literally the only two pedestrians on Twenty-third between Ninth and Tenth, but that's how I remember it. There was a chilly wind blowing in from the Hudson, carrying the thrumming growl of a passing helicopter and the faintest smell of saltwater. I thought it smelled different from the East River wind where I lived. Wilder, somehow.

"Come on," said Fay. "I told you my thing."

In a burst of bravery, I decided to tell her.

"Chicks," I said. "Dames. *The ladies*. That's my thing."

"I know," said Fay. "But I'm talking about something more than just being a lesbian."

I was light-headed, my heart pounding in my ears. I couldn't believe I'd actually said it, and that it was no big deal to Fay. I wanted to make a huge gesture for her, like get down on my knees or die heroically saving her from a fire.

"I have *The Scarlet Letter* in my backpack," I said. "I can give you a dramatic reading of the HoYay."

She fished her keys out of her messenger bag. "What about my PreCalc homework? Can you make that gay too?"

I was goofy with gladness. "With our powers combined," I intoned, "we can make the whole world gay."

She laughed—a real, full-throated laugh. Because of me, I thought dizzily. Well, not me *personally* so much as me talking about the abstract idea of gay shit—but if that was what it took to make Fay happy, I'd play along forever. If I couldn't give her flowers or jewelry or orgasms, at least I could give her this.

"This is where I live, by the way," she said, gesturing with her thumb toward the white townhouse. She unlocked the front door and let me inside.

FAY

In a certain sense, Nell brute-forced her way into being my best friend. The first time she entered my home, she did so uninvited after following me there, puppylike, all the way from school. What was I to do, close the door in her face?

Well, to be candid, I considered it. I never had friends over (I never had friends), and of my two parental households, my father's would not have been my first choice to show to Nell. But I could hardly turn her away after she came out to me as a lesbian. As she followed me downstairs into my father's basement apartment, though, it struck me that she had now volleyed the coming-out ball into my court, and my heart sank.

I hung up my army jacket on the brass coatrack in the foyer. Nell draped her jean jacket on the same hook, covering mine. "Um, quick question," she said. (I tensed up. *Are you a lesbian too?*) "Can I use the bathroom?"

I did the requisite sarcastic "No," then directed her to it. This bought me some time, but she was sure to ask the real question any minute now. How ought I respond to it? Too preoccupied even to turn on the lights, I stood in the dark foyer and considered the available options.

The sob story: "In the seventh grade, back when you were still in public school and Idlewild social circles were configured differently, I attended an all-girl slumber party in celebration of Jennifer Green's birthday. At one point we played Truth or Dare, and as is developmentally appropriate for middle school slumber parties, every Truth question was some variation on *With which boy in our class would you most like to 'do it'?* By the time my turn arrived to pose a Truth question, it seemed to me that this avenue of discourse had been exhausted, and so I decided to mix it up a bit by asking, *With which* girl *in our class would you most like to 'do it'?* This was, as it turned out, a faux pas of socially suicidal proportions, and the resultant ostracism continues to this day, which is why I am currently hanging out with you, Nell, rather than with anyone else at Idlewild. Why don't you ask one of *them* if I'm a lesbian?"

The Drama of the Gifted Child (**Alice Miller, 1979**): "My liberal artist parents tolerate all forms of sexual divergence from a humorous, half-admiring distance that would be compromised were I to claim a divergent sexual identity for myself, so it's not worth the trouble."

The Foucauldian cop-out: "What *is* a lesbian? Is it a stable or coherent category? Can human sexuality be taxonomized at all? I am so very intelligent."

Nell emerged from the bathroom. I regarded her across the foyer—her Discman headphones dangling around her neck, her Jimmy Eat World T-shirt worn confusingly over an additional long-sleeved shirt, a shy smile on her face—and thought of another option.

The stab in the heart: "Until this very moment I thought I might be a lesbian—but here you are now, a girl nakedly yearning for me, and I feel nothing at all."

Aloud I said, "Do you want a glass of water or seltzer or something?" I was stalling for time, as another dilemma had just occurred to me: where should we sit? Taking her into my bedroom felt dangerously suggestive. But the living room carried a risk of running into Gareth, who lived and slept there. It would have to be the bedroom, I decided, filling two glasses with bottled seltzer.

I led Nell into my room and lowered myself onto the Persian rug, pointedly far from the bed, drawing my knees up to my chest. She joined me on the floor, sitting cross-legged at a safely unerotic distance, and produced from her backpack a heavily annotated copy of *The Scarlet Letter* (Nathaniel Hawthorne, 1850).

"You're gonna love this." She flipped to the middle of the book and began to read aloud in a jokingly lascivious voice. *"So Roger Chillingworth—the man of skill, the kind and friendly physician—strove to go deep into his patient's bosom, delving among his principles, prying into his recollections, and probing everything with a cautious touch, like a treasure-seeker in a dark cavern . . ."*

Something stirred within me. Almost against my will, I pictured it: the old doctor cautiously approaching the young minister and, careful not to wake him, cautiously fingering the exposed skin of his chest. "Is there more?"

Nell grinned, flipped the page. *"The physician advanced directly in front of his patient,"* she read, *"laid his hand upon his bosom, and thrust aside the vestment, that, hitherto, had always covered it even from the professional eye. Then, indeed, Mr. Dimmesdale shuddered, and slightly stirred. After a brief pause, the physician turned away. But with what a wild look of wonder, joy, and horror! With what a ghastly rapture, as it were, too mighty to be expressed only by the eye and features, and therefore bursting forth through the whole ugliness of his figure . . ."*

"Oh my god," I said, my pulse quickening. I took a deep breath and was conscious of how audible it was. "He totally just ejaculated."

"I know, right?" Nell exclaimed. "Like, what else could that mean?"

As she read on, it dawned on me that she was laying the groundwork for a different question: *Why are you so obsessed with two dudes doing it?*

The central research question of my life. My fellow Idlewilders had been asking me some version of it for years, but in a teasing manner easily dismissed as juvenile homophobia. It was only recently, thanks to my father, that I'd begun to consider it in earnest.

I was fourteen when my father's twelve-step friend Gareth took up residence, temporarily and then indefinitely, on the living room couch. A film buff, Gareth often commandeered the television to watch movies. One evening he rented *Velvet Goldmine* (1998, dir. Todd Haynes). I happened to enter the living room just in time to catch the eighteen-second kiss between Jonathan Rhys Meyers and Ewan McGregor, and I was instantly mesmerized with something almost closer to religious awe than sexual arousal. Gareth noticed and rewound the tape so we could watch the whole film together. After that night, he took it upon himself to introduce me to gay cinema. The curriculum eventually expanded to include the pornographic, and one night my father wandered into the living room during an onscreen blowjob. "Fay," he said, "what do you get out of this?"

"Why do straight boys like lesbian porn?" Gareth countered. "Same thing. She wants to join in."

I appreciated Gareth coming to my defense, but he was mistaken: the idea of *joining in* had never once occurred to me in the hundreds of hours I'd spent in contemplation (via film, fanfiction, or fantasy) of two dudes doing it. "No," I said. "I don't want to join in."

"Interesting," my father said. "So in your wildest dreams, you're merely a voyeur?"

That wasn't quite right, either. "No," I said. "In my wildest dreams, I'm not there at all."

Gareth shushed us, pointing out that the onscreen intercourse was now in transition from oral to anal. I excused myself, as I always did at that point, and retreated to my bedroom computer for gentler visions of assfucking involving Holmes and Watson. Still, my father's question lingered in my mind.

It resurfaced as Nell read to me from *The Scarlet Letter*. Why *did* I love gay shit so much? Why, in particular, did two-dudes-doing-it uniquely do it for me?

Over the years, I've approached this question through various theoretical lenses.

Feminist theory: Heteropatriarchal society conditioned me to associate female sexuality with violence, such that I could achieve arousal only by envisioning sexual scenarios in which women were absent.

(But this framing sells short the intrinsic hotness of two dudes doing it—the stark clarity of the boner as a barometer of want; the emotional gratification of seeing manhood rendered vulnerable, objectified, receptive; the taboo thrill, which no amount of political progress can quite diminish, of the guy-on-guy kiss.)

Intersectional theory: The appeal of two dudes doing it is located not only in their dudeness, but also in their whiteness, their able-bodiedness, their cis-ness, even their apparent straightness; my fantasies were really working toward a vision of sex utterly divorced from politics, a meeting of two culturally "generic" bodies in a state of perfect neutrality.

(But how dull.)

Psychoanalytic theory: I was in denial about my secret preference for my own sex, and my fantasies of male homosexuality were an act of displacement.

As a teenager, I preferred this explanation. There was something comforting in the idea that my real sexuality existed elsewhere, somewhere so remote and well protected that it was inaccessible even to me. It even accounted for my inconvenient lack of interest, romantic or otherwise, in my fellow girls—I was just that good at repression. My fixation on male homoeroticism was a defense mechanism that I was sure to outgrow once I embraced my attraction to women.

But Nell's presence in my life, and now in my bedroom, was rather forcing the issue.

"*After the incident last described,*" Nell read, "*the intercourse between the clergyman and the physician, though externally the same, was really of another character than it had previously been.*" She lowered the book onto her lap and looked at me expectantly.

I giggled. "Intercourse," I said.

"Intercourse," she agreed, and then we doubled over with laughter. Nell knocked over her glass. "Oh, shit!" Seltzer puddled on the Persian rug, fizzled and frothed and went still, and we laughed harder.

I stood. "Want to watch *Rope*?" I asked. "It's my favorite movie."

Nell peered up at me uncertainly from the rug. "Is it a gay porno?"

"Basically," I said. "If you use your imagination."

"Okay," she said, and I understood then that she wasn't going to ask me any question at all. I knew, as surely as if I could read her mind, that she would never ask anything of me that I couldn't give to her. An odd bitterness gripped me. What a pussy, I thought cruelly; what an incurious coward she was.

But that passed quickly, leaving in its place a buoyant sense of possibility. If I couldn't manifest homosexuality in myself, I would instead locate it everywhere else. If Nell and I couldn't be gay together, we could—we would, we did—create for ourselves a separate world in which gayness was ambient and immanent and unrelated to us.

That was the tacit arrangement to which we came on that afternoon in the fall of 2001. It held—remarkably well, in retrospect—for one whole year.

F & N, 2002

Sound the trumpet, roll out the red carpet, lock up your daughters and so forth—today is *Othello* audition day!

Two dozen aspiring Idlewild actors have gathered upon the Meetinghouse's creaky wood back stairs, which groan and squeak under the weight of so many bodies and backpacks. To rise above the crowd, we the F&N unit have hoisted ourselves, with some effort, onto the big windowsill at the top of the stairs. From this lofty overlook we sit side by side, swinging our legs, the afternoon sun shining through the window on us and us alone. Any minute now, Wanda the Witch will emerge from her office and summon the first auditioner into the Meetinghouse Loft rehearsal room. In the meantime, we the F&N unit are an oasis of serenity.

Or we would be, if the underclassgirls at the bottom of the stairs would shut the fuck up. There's a cluster of them standing in a circle on the downstairs landing. At the center of the circle are two boys: one sleek-haired and small, the other curly-haired and tall. They're angled away from us, so we can't see their faces. Nor can we hear their voices, due to all the underclassgirl screaming with laughter. "Do me!" cries a girl who hasn't bothered to take off her Rollerblades. She wheels around in place, and the other girls shriek their agreement, popcorning up and down. "Do her! Do her!"

The girl-crowd parts slightly. The smaller boy turns, and from our windowsill perch, we the F&N unit see his face for the first time.

Except it's not the first time. Pale, sharp-featured, a certain cat-who-got-the-cream smirkishness to the mouth—he's the sophomore boy upon whom our eyes fell during last week's anniversary Meeting for Worship. The boy who looked so suspiciously composed after Oliver Dicks was defeated by the Great Meetinghouse Fart of '02. Our potential savior. Or possibly just some random boy who doesn't deserve our attention. Regardless, he has it now.

"Look at me," he says.

An unnecessary command: all eyes in the stairwell are trained on him. But he says it a second time, and then a third—"Look at me. Look at *me*"—and each time he says it, his voice alters, tightens, like a thin guitar string being tuned. "Look at me! I'm . . ." He looks expectantly at the girl on Rollerblades.

"Maddy," she says.

"*Maddy*," he echoes, his voice now a squeaky parody of hers. "Ooh, look at me. I'm Little Maddy Two-Shoes. Tra-la-la!" He begins to prance in place—the wood floor wails at the impact of his sneakers—and to fluff imaginary pigtails on either side of his head. "Now where's my gosh-darned shepherd stick? I've got some gosh-darned sheep to herd!"

In reality, there's no hint of the shepherdess to this girl's outfit or demeanor; her hair isn't even pigtailed. The boy's performance, apart from being unflattering to Maddy, has essentially nothing to do with her—yet we the F&N unit can see from all the way upstairs that her face is flushed with pleasure as she laughs, protesting.

"Excuse me, kind sir," the boy continues in Maddy-character to his taller friend. "Have you any gosh-darned sheep for sale?"

The tall boy replies, "Little girl, this is a RadioShack."

"I will take two dozen of your fluffiest sheep!"

"We don't sell sheep at RadioShack."

"Then I will take twenty radios . . . and twenty shacks."

The scene continues in this surreal vein, much to the merriment of the underclassgirls. We the F&N unit turn to each other, perplexed.

N: "Who the hell are they?"

F: "The shorter one's like a little Marble Faun."

N: "Like from *Grey Gardens*? Or like a literal statue of a goat guy?"

F: "I don't know. I just like saying Marble Faun."

Who else might have intel? Juniper Green is closest to us, sitting on the floor of the upstairs landing, leaning against the wall right beneath the windowsill. Her hair, recently bleached to a brittle Barbie-doll blond, is tied up in a high ponytail conveniently within our reach. We lean down and yank it.

"Ow!" She turns and glares up at us, rubbing her scalp. "What the fuck?"

N: "What's the deal with those boys?"

"No clue," says Juniper. "But they're being obnoxious as shit." She turns around and resumes studying her printed-out audition monologue (unlike *some* superior talents who have bothered to memorize their).

"Do Glenn," another girl yells.

"Okay," says the Marble Faun. He says it a few times—"Okay. Okaaayyy. O*kaaayyy*"—with increasingly *Fargo*-ish intonation, developing a Minnesotan accent that the real Glenn Harding does not have. "Oh, jeez. Has anyone seen my pants?" Off the girls' laughter: "Class, class, please don't make fun of me, okay? If we work together as a team, we can find my pants."

The character is not, by any means, our history teacher (who is from Maryland and has never once, to our knowledge, parted with his pants). But he's also not the boy playing him, whoever that may be. All comedic judgment aside, that's what's compelling about his impressions: not their accuracy, but the effortless totality of his transformation. It's almost eerie, as though he can switch off his soul and summon another at will.

Which has major implications for the Idlewild theater community, and for the F&N unit in particular.

F: "Do you think he'll try out for Iago?"

N: "I don't know, boss. He's a wild card. Maybe he'll go for, like, Bianca."

F: "Or Othello, even."

N: "Yeah, maybe he can turn himself black."

Bottom's deep voice replies from out of nowhere. "Anything's possible in the theater."

Abashed, we look down from the windowsill and see that Bottom and Daylily Jones have joined Juniper on the floor.

N: [*to Bottom*] "That was obviously a joke."

F: "You're the only Othello in our eyes."

"You're too kind," says Bottom. "But let's not count our Othellos before they hatch."

Daylily pokes his arm and says, "One"—counting him, you see, before he hatches. She giggles at her own wit. Since it's Daylily, he rewards her with a warm smile.

From the bottom of the stairs comes the Marble Faun's regular voice again. "Who should I do next?"

And Daylily Jones, who is always nice to everybody because everybody is always nice to her, waves her pretty arm. Her bracelets clatter. "How about me?" she calls down the stairs.

"Oh, Lils, don't encourage him." Juniper buries her head in her hands.

Up till this point, we the F&N unit have been unsure whether to feel irritated, threatened, or amused by the Marble Faun and his sidekick. But now, thanks to Juniper, the answer is clear: any enemy of Juniper Green is a friend of ours. We begin to chant loudly, banging our fists on the windowsill.

F&N: [*chanting in unison*] "Do Lily! Do Lily!"

The rest of the crowd in the stairwell joins in. "Do Lily! Do Lily!"

The Marble Faun climbs the stairs to get a closer look at her. His sidekick follows him. Crouching Idlewilders scrunch up and flatten themselves against the stairway wall to make way for the two boys. Someone hisses "Ow" as an unguarded hand is stepped on.

At the top of the stairs, the Marble Faun stands above Daylily, inspects her from various angles. He rocks back and forth on his feet, preparing his impression.

Daylily giggles. "I'm getting a little scared."

Beside her on the floor, Bottom murmurs to the boys, "Keep it kind, please."

The Marble Faun doesn't seem to hear him. The Marble Faun is closing his eyes, shifting his body, straightening his spine, lifting his hands into the air—becoming someone else.

He opens his eyes, which suddenly look dewy and long-lashed. "Oh!" His voice comes out breathy, pure. His hand flies to his heart. "Oh, I prithee—fare thee well—but soft!"

People laugh. Even we the F&N unit have to laugh. It's not a bad impression of Daylily.

The Marble Faun sighs. "Ay, me!" He cups a delicate hand against his delicate cheek. His entire body has somehow gone light and delicate and lovely, just as some boy in Shakespeare's acting troupe must have gone light and delicate and lovely to play Juliet the first time anyone ever played her. "O, Romeo, Romeo! Wherefore art thou Romeo?"

Throughout all this, his tall curly-haired sidekick has been standing on the stairs, waiting to be conscripted into the scene. Now, at last, the Marble Faun turns to him.

"Good pilgrim," says the Marble Faun, "you do wrong your hand too much, which mannerly devotion shows in this!" The Marble Faun stamps his foot—so lightly, so delicately, the wood floor doesn't even creak. "For saints have hands that pilgrims' hands do touch, and palm to palm is holy palmers' kiss." He raises a hand toward his sidekick, palm open, as if soliciting a high five.

The sidekick has very large, very round eyes, which lend his face a sweet if rather bovine look. He climbs the stairs to join the Marble Faun on the landing. Their palms touch.

From the floor, Daylily Jones calls out encouragingly, *"Have not saints lips, and holy palmers too?"* (Of course she has *Romeo and Juliet* memorized. Probably just because of the Baz Luhrmann movie.)

The sidekick repeats the line, uncomprehending: "Have not saints lips, and holy palmers too."

"Ay, pilgrim," says the Marble Faun. The two boys' palms are still touching in midair. "Lips that they must use in prayer."

They're losing their audience. The time seems long past for some sort of punchline; heads are turning away, and distracted chatter begins to echo through the stairwell. But we the F&N unit continue to watch the boys intently.

The Marble Faun takes a step toward his sidekick. "O, then, dear saint, let lips do what hands do!"

"Hey, that's not your line," Daylily complains from the floor.

The Marble Faun rolls his eyes, then grabs his sidekick by the shoulders, pushes him against the closed door of Wanda's office, and—

Are they *kissing*?

Is anyone else seeing this? Digging our nails into the windowsill, we the F&N unit lean forward, forward, so far forward we're almost falling off the windowsill, desperate to get a closer look—

But no—it's just a stage kiss. The Marble Faun has the palm of his hand pressed against his sidekick's mouth; he's kissing the back of his own hand. He's kissing the back of his own hand and his other hand is running through his sidekick's curly hair and—

The knob turns on Wanda's office door.

The boys stumble as the door opens behind them. They leap apart from each other, away from the door, and the sidekick flees downstairs, red-faced. The stairwell falls silent as Wanda the Witch, resplendent in cat's-eye glasses and dangly earrings and patterned silk scarves, steps out of her office.

"Good afternoon, my little lambkins," she trills Britishly. "How lovely to see so many of you here! May I please borrow . . ." She consults a paper list in her hand. "Theo Severyn?"

"That's me," says the Marble Faun, instantly becoming someone else again. Now a polite, eager schoolboy, he trots over to Wanda. "Thanks for letting me go first."

Wanda leads the Marble Faun—Theo Severyn—into the Meetinghouse Loft rehearsal room.

We the F&N unit watch him disappear behind the door.

Auditions begin.

II

NELL

OmiPalone212: I can't stop thinking about them.

Auto response from m k fantastico (10:41:03 PM): to faggots, lezzies, dykes, cross-dressers too

OmiPalone212: Nell, that away message is an embarrassment.

OmiPalone212: Promise me you won't sing anything from Rent when Ms. Spider and the Witch take us to La Bohème.

OmiPalone212: Nell?

m k fantastico: reporting for duty, boss

m k fantastico: sry mommy was yelling at me for coming home late again

m k fantastico: but yeah

m k fantastico: i can't stop thinking about them either

OmiPalone212: Good.

OmiPalone212: Let's think about the boys together.

m k fantastico: u mean, think together about the boys?

m k fantastico: or think about . . . the boys *together*? <grin>

OmiPalone212: Why not both?

According to my old LiveJournal, this AIM conversation took place on Thursday, September 19, 2002. That was a notable day for a bunch of reasons. For one thing, it was the day of the *Othello* auditions. For another, it was the day I started posting in my LiveJournal again.

I'd been slacking in my LiveJournaling for almost a year. After my first visit to Fay's house, I figured I no longer needed to analyze our every micro-interaction, because I'd solved the mystery of how she felt about me—she liked me! We were best friends! (And maybe one day—fingers crossed—something more. But as with a birthday wish that won't come true if you say it out loud, I didn't dare put that into words, not even on my friendslocked LiveJournal.) But even if I'd wanted to keep LiveJournaling, I wouldn't have had the time. I was spending practically every waking minute with Fay.

We quickly fell into a routine. After school, we usually had rehearsal (*Midsummer* in the fall, *Into the Woods* in the spring). After rehearsal we walked together to Chelsea, stopping at Calvin's Cavern to rent a movie (Fay's choice, always). At her house, we spent an hour or two eating snacks and reading aloud to each other from our English homework. Whatever the book was, we passed it back and forth, taking turns doing funny voices and competing to find the juiciest HoYay. (This was easy with *Huck Finn* and *Billy Budd*, challenging but doable with *The Crucible* and *Native Son*, frustratingly impossible with *Ceremony*, and absolutely worth it for the end-of-the-year payoff: *Leaves of Grass*.) Then, to reward ourselves, we watched our movie. Early on, Fay showed me the documentary *The Celluloid Closet*, and then she made a project of showing me every old movie referenced in it. She liked all of them more than I did (she got so mad when I fell asleep during *Red River*), but considering that I'll probably never have the motivation to sit through an old movie ever again, I'm grateful she made me watch so many.

I usually stayed for dinner. On Friday nights I slept over. On school nights my mom wanted me home by 9:00 p.m., but I rarely made it back before ten. I blamed the M23 crosstown bus for being slow (not a total lie), so my mom started supplementing my allowance with extra cash for taxi rides. I spent it all on Starbucks. By the end of junior year I was regularly staying at Fay's house until 10:00 p.m. on school nights. The second I got home, I went online and continued talking to Fay on AIM, switching to the telephone if we had something really urgent to discuss. We talked until 2:00 a.m., easily. Sometimes later. Even on school nights.

"This is unsustainable," my mom yelled at me one morning. She was trying and failing to drag me out of bed; I'd slept through my alarm yet again.

Still half asleep under my blankets, I shot back, "Then why don't you let me spend the night at Fay's house?"

I keep saying "Fay's house," but I should clarify: as a child of divorce, Fay had two houses. Her dad lived in the basement apartment of that white townhouse on Twenty-third Street. It was a three-bedroom, tech-nically, but the master bedroom was her dad's art studio; he slept in the medium-sized bedroom, Fay in the small bedroom, and her dad's friend Gareth on the living room couch. There wasn't much natural light, and they never remembered to turn on lamps until it was practically too dark to see, so it was always dim and kind of spooky down there. (The foyer in particular was so dark, I must have passed through it a dozen times before I noticed the painting on the wall: a colorful, larger-than-life portrait of someone's vulva.) The air was smoky, and at first I thought it smelled like weed. Later, after seeing Fay's dad and Gareth smoking regular cigarettes, I laughed at myself for believing I knew what weed smelled like. Then, even later, I learned what weed smelled like and real-ized I *had* been smelling weed.

Fay's mom lived right across the street, twenty stories up, in the penthouse of this beautiful old building complex called London Terrace. While Fay's dad's basement apartment was dark and chilly, her mom's penthouse was so flooded with sunlight it got uncomfortably hot even in the winter. The air was deliciously fragrant up there, partly because Fay's mom was big on scented candles and cut flowers and open windows, but also because the whole setup was newer—Fay's mom had left Fay's dad by moving out of the basement apartment and just straight-up buying a penthouse across the street. (You can do that, apparently, when you're a garment heiress.) Certain rooms still smelled like fresh paint. Also, sometimes, like weed.

In both apartments, I felt totally at home. Which is not to say that Fay's parents embraced me as a second daughter, or even welcomed me as a guest. In fact, I rarely saw them at all. Fay's dad mostly kept to his art studio, and Fay's mom disappeared for weeks at a time on yoga meditation retreats. When they were around, they barely noticed I was there, which was fine by me. Fay and I could get away with staying up till dawn, belting show tunes late into the night, subsisting on diner milkshakes and Quiznos subs and pints of Ben & Jerry's Coffee Heath Bar Crunch. It was paradise.

My mom was none too thrilled about any of this. Looking back, I can't blame her. During the early, shouting-it-from-the-rooftops phase of my friendship with Fay, I wouldn't shut up to my mom about Fay's homelife, and a lot of it was pretty damning: the scented candles left burning unattended in the penthouse; the fat waterbug cockroaches I sometimes saw in the basement, just chilling in the bathtub or on a wet toothbrush; Fay's parents refusing to speak to each other even though they lived so close together they could have strung a tin-can telephone between their bedrooms. Their joint custody arrangement was byzantine (Monday and Tuesday nights at the penthouse, Wednesday and Thursday nights in the basement, weekends and holidays alternating) and so sacrosanct that Fay wouldn't dream of entering the basement on a penthouse night, not even for a minute, not even to retrieve a textbook.

"How does she get her homework done?" my mom demanded.

I made a foolhardy attempt to explain our whole dramatic-gay-reading ritual.

"Okay, but what about her other classes?"

I shrugged. I did my own homework during my free periods and over the weekend; I was usually caught up in time for my Sunday evening therapy appointment. "Well, clearly," I said, "she figures it out."

My mom shook her head. "I worry," she said, which was her way of saying I *disapprove.* "There's bohemian, and then there's feral."

She was especially weirded out by Gareth. At her dad's place, Fay and I watched our movies in the living room, and Gareth became our de facto movie buddy. While I would have preferred to have Fay all to myself, I came to like Gareth. He was short and chubby and so swishy that I didn't feel threatened by his bellowing brashness, and he used old-school gay slang that Fay and I gleefully appropriated: "shirt-lifter," "pillow-biter," "rough trade," and—my favorite—"Smell *you*, Nancy Drew!" Besides, his very existence gave me hope for a long-term future with Fay. Maybe *I* could live on her couch when we were fifty.

My mom was convinced that Gareth was Fay's dad's semisecret boyfriend. For a while I thought so too, although I of all people should have known better than to make such assumptions about friendships involving gay people and blurry boundaries.

"When did your dad come out?" I once made the mistake of asking Fay.

Fay, in a classic Fay power move, played dumb and refused to correct me outright until I'd shown my full ass. "Come out of what?"

"The closet," I said.

"What closet?"

"The gay closet."

"My dad's not gay," she said, and laughed at me. "You've really gone around thinking that this whole time? You've seen Gareth sleeping on the couch, right?" I had; he snored. "Do you think my dad fucks Gareth and then, like, kicks him out to the couch? Every night?"

I guess I *had* sort of thought that, though clearly I hadn't thought about it very hard. Fay never did get around to explaining what the actual deal was, which now makes me think that she didn't entirely understand it, either. (For what it's worth, my current theory is that the arrangement was somehow drug-related. I think Gareth was there as either a supplier, a sober companion, or first one and then the other. But what do I know?)

Because I wasn't recording any of it in my LiveJournal, that whole year is a happy blur in my memory. I was so wrapped up in Fay that I lost the ability to distinguish my opinions from her opinions, my thoughts from her thoughts, and I adored her too much to bother trying. Teachers tended to give me the benefit of the doubt—they liked me, and I think they were glad I'd finally made a friend—but even so, I flunked a few quizzes. I didn't mind. Tara on *Buffy* fucking died and I didn't mind. I gained weight and didn't mind, though my mom minded enough for the both of us.

"It's a good thing your hair is long," my mom said. "It slims out your face."

The next day, Fay took me to her hair salon and introduced me to her stylist, a gay British guy named Wayne. I told him to cut my hair exactly like Fay's. As he snipped off ten inches, I could almost hear my mom screaming. But then I felt a breeze on my neck and saw a butch girl in the mirror and my head felt light enough to float away like a balloon set free.

On the night of September 19, 2002, after the *Othello* auditions, I came home from Fay's house and logged into my LiveJournal for the first time all year. I had a new research project—and this time, Fay was not my subject but my co-researcher.

OmiPalone212: Hypothesis: the Marble Faun and his sidekick are secretly a couple.

OmiPalone212: In private, they can't keep their hands off each other – but at school, they have to be more circumspect.

OmiPalone212: The only way they can "kiss" in public is under the guise of a game.

m k fantastico: i dunno

m k fantastico: i think maybe the marble faun was just being random

m k fantastico: and the stage kiss didn't mean anything to him

m k fantastico: little does he know his sidekick is in love with him!!!

OmiPalone212: But how could the Marble Faun possibly be unaware of that?

OmiPalone212: Noticing people, observing people – that's his whole thing.

m k fantastico: i thought his whole thing was NOT observing people

m k fantastico: that's why his "impressions" are funny, right? cuz they're wrong

OmiPalone212: But intentionally wrong.

OmiPalone212: You have to study people closely to get them so wrong.

Now that I was home, I could do some real research. I dug out last year's yearbook (Fay never bought the yearbook) and the current year's school directory. Holding the yearbook open on my lap and the directory in one hand, I studied them side by side, trying to match faces and names. We knew the real name of the Marble Faun because we'd heard Wanda say it.

m k fantastico: ok I found Theo Severyn in the directory

m k fantastico: but he's not in the yearbook

m k fantastico: like he's not even listed

OmiPalone212: So he's new this year?

OmiPalone212: Who transfers schools in the tenth grade?

m k fantastico: maybe his family moved to NYC from somewhere else

OmiPalone212: Or he was in Catholic school and they expelled him for being gay.

His sidekick, on the other hand, did appear in the yearbook. It took a lot of squinting at the black-and-white ninth-grade class photo, but I managed to find his face in the crowd, and then his name in the caption.

m k fantastico: Christopher Korkian

OmiPalone212: Really! I wonder if he's related to Harry Korkian.

m k fantastico: who?

OmiPalone212: The actor from the Volkswagen commercial.

m k fantastico: lol that's so random, how do you know that

OmiPalone212: Because he played Cherry Valance in that terrible 80s remake of Red River.

OmiPalone212: But that VW ad would have made him rich. Does Christopher live somewhere fancy?

I checked the address. I wasn't sure if it counted as fancy (it was on Riverside Drive, and I didn't know shit), but it was weirdly familiar. I flipped forward in the directory, cross-referenced, and gasped so loudly my mom called out, "What's wrong?" from her bedroom.

m k fantastico: FAY!!!!!1

m k fantastico: omg you're gonna FLIP THE FUCK OUT

OmiPalone212: What is it?

m k fantastico: according to the directory

m k fantastico: Theo Severyn and Christopher Korkian

m k fantastico: have THE SAME ADDRESS

OmiPalone212: They live in the same building?

m k fantastico: no dude

m k fantastico: they live in the same APARTMENT

OmiPalone212: asadf;kj WHAT??????????

Fay always wrote in full sentences with perfect punctuation, so to see that I'd reduced her to keyboard-smashing all-caps—even now, it gives me a little thrill of pride. I loved to make her lose control. As my computer chimed and chimed again with new incoming messages—

OmiPalone212: But they're not related, right?

OmiPalone212: They definitely don't look related.

OmiPalone212: Stepbrothers, perhaps?

—I wondered if I could do it again.

m k fantastico: do you think they share a bedroom

OmiPalone212: Nell, you're killing me.

m k fantastico: maybe that's where they practice kissing, lol

OmiPalone212: NELL!!!!!

OmiPalone212: Oh, I love this.

OmiPalone212: Theo initiates it, yes?

I hate looking back at these conversations. This is where it started.

m k fantastico: obviously

m k fantastico: the first time it happened, christopher couldn't believe it

OmiPalone212: There was only one bed, you see.

m k fantastico: of course theo was supposed to have his own bed but the delivery got delayed and there was nowhere for theo to sleep, soooo . . .

OmiPalone212: "Don't you want your new stepbrother to feel welcome, Christopher?"

m k fantastico: lol are we writing a fanfic

OmiPalone212: A "Faunfic," if you will.

Okay, no, I'm tapping out. There is absolutely no fucking way I'm revisiting the Faunfic.

FAY

The Marble Faun, Chapter One:
Truth or Dare[1]

The first time it happened, Christopher couldn't believe it. There was only one bed, that was the problem. Theo was supposed to have his own bed, but the delivery got delayed and there was nowhere else for Theo to sleep. "Don't you want your new stepbrother to feel welcome?" queried Christopher's dad, Harry Korkian, in his handsome movie star voice that was so hard to say no to. "It's just for one night, son."

The words echoed in Christopher's head as he lay in the bed next to Theo. *Just for one night. Just for one night.* But Christopher didn't know

---

[1] When I was growing up, the conventional wisdom was that one ought to be cautious about what one shared online, because "the Internet is forever." How wrong we were. For those of us who came of age during the AOL era, there's a Library of Alexandria's worth of missing documentation of adolescence: emails that auto-deleted after thirty days, AOL Instant Messages that vanished along with AOL Instant Messenger, fanfiction hosted on now-defunct websites, unconverted ClarisWorks files no longer viewable on any platform, data languishing in corrupted hard drives or computers too old even to turn on. Digital cameras had already begun to replace film despite the poor quality of the images and the lack of means by which to share or store them, so even photographic records are scant. (A mercy, arguably.)

It's no small miracle, then, that I've managed to hang on to the collaborative "Faunfic" project on which Nell and I worked continually throughout our senior year. To be sure, its cringe factor is excruciatingly high—but were it ever to disappear, the loss would be unbearable.

how he was going to survive this night. It wasn't just that he barely knew Theo. It was that Theo made him feel things he'd never felt before—things he was pretty sure he wasn't supposed to feel.[2]

"Are you asleep?" whispered Theo's voice next to him. The mattress was the size of mattress that's one size smaller than queen-size,[3] and even though Christopher was lying as far away from Theo as he could, the two boys were still so close together that Christopher could feel Theo's body heat.

"No," Christopher admitted. "I can't sleep."

"Me neither," Theo replied. There was a mischievous tone in his voice. "Want to play Truth or Dare?"

What was Theo planning to make him do? Christopher found himself scared yet mysteriously eager to find out. "Okay," he acquiesced.

"You go first," said Theo. "Truth or dare?"

"Truth," said Christopher, figuring he could always lie if Theo asked him a question he didn't want to answer.

"Okay, truth," said Theo. "Have you ever kissed anyone?"

Well, that one wasn't too bad. "No," said Christopher. "Okay, my turn. Truth or Dare?"

[2] Nell and I took turns contributing, via AOL Instant Messenger, a sentence or paragraph at a time. As we went along, I took it upon myself to edit our work into a cohesive document, removing our screen names and all other artifacts of our collaborative process—an aesthetic improvement I now regret.

[3] The Faunfic starts out facetious in tone and grammatically sloppy, shot through with self-protective irony—evidence of an initial discomfort that we gradually and noticeably shed as the story goes on.

"Dare," said Theo.

Christopher tried to come up with a dare. He thought of a few, but they all involved Theo leaving the bed, and he didn't want Theo to leave the bed. Because it was cold, he told himself firmly. He liked feeling the warmth of Theo's body just a few inches away, because the room was cold. That was all.

"Come on, hurry up," Theo demanded.

Before he even knew what he was doing, Christopher said, "I dare you to take off your shirt." As soon as the words were out of his mouth, Christopher felt his face get hot. He was glad the room was so dark[4] that Theo couldn't see him blushing.

But Theo was nonplussed.[5] "No problem," he said. Christopher felt a rustle next to him as Theo pulled off his sleep shirt. It was too dark to see, but just knowing that Theo was shirtless next to him caused Christopher's heart to pound even harder.

Then it was Christopher's turn again. "Dare," said Christopher, suddenly feeling bold.

"Okay," said Theo. "I dare you to touch me."

Christopher almost choked. "What?"

"You're so scared to touch me, you're practically falling off the bed," said Theo. "It's kind of stressing me out. If we're gonna share a bed,

[4] The first chapter relies heavily on the conceit of total darkness, a weak device to disguise the fact that Nell and I, having seen Theo and Christopher only once and from a slight distance, could not yet provide detailed physical descriptions.

[5] This incorrect usage of *nonplussed* mortifies me to no end.

we should just get this out of the way so it stops being such a big deal."

"I'm sorry, I didn't mean to stress you out," said Christopher.[6] So much for being cold—even the tips of his ears felt hot now. He gulped. "Where do you want me to touch you?"

"Anywhere you want," said Theo.

Even though it was dark, Christopher could imagine how Theo looked right now: naked from the waist up, sharp hip bones jutting above the waistband of his boxers, a smirk twisting his lips. Christopher was scared to touch this beautiful boy who was too perfect to touch.

"Come on," said Theo. "Don't be a pussy." His words were harsh, but Christopher couldn't help noticing a catch in his voice. "Touch me, Christopher."

Christopher's hand shook as he lowered his hand down, down, finally touching Theo's bare chest. It was warm and smooth, with hard muscle and bone underneath, and it rose and fell as Theo took a deep, shuddering breath.

"Good boy," Theo purred into the shell of Christopher's ear, giving him goose bumps. Their mouths were so close together, their lips were dangerously close to touching. "You're doing great, buddy. Truth or dare?"

Christopher was hard in his boxers and he was terrified of Theo finding out, but at the same time, just thinking about it made him even harder. He ached to be touched. Theo smelled warm and boyish and wonderful, like laundry soap and mint and something else, some-

---

[6] The apology was most definitely Nell's contribution. At that age, I would never have thought to apologize in such a situation. Or, really, in any situation.

thing uniquely Theo. "Truth," Christopher choked out, his voice thick with lust.

"Tell me the truth," whispered Theo. "Do you want me to kiss you right now?" Theo's fingers danced around the hem of Christopher's sleep shirt, flirting with the fabric, not quite touching underneath, just inches away from Christopher's throbbing erection.[7]

Christopher felt pinned in place like a butterfly. He couldn't lie to Theo, not anymore. He would answer any question Theo asked him. He would do anything Theo told him to do. "Yes," Christopher gasped. His hips bucked against his will, begging for contact. "Please," he moaned.

And then Theo's lips were pressed against his, mouths crushing together, the two boys kissing hungrily in the dark. Theo's tongue licked its way into Christopher's mouth, wet and silky, battling for dominance against Christopher's. Theo's hand worked its way into Christopher's hair, his fingers carding through the curls. Christopher let out an involuntary keening noise.

Theo pulled away, and even in the dark Christopher somehow knew that Theo was smiling.

"You're welcome," said Theo.

"For what?"

"Your first kiss."

[7] I wanted "cock" here, which embarrassed Nell; she preferred "boner," which I found juvenile and inappropriately comical. The rather clinical "erection" was our compromise.

Theo turned over, facing away from Christopher. As Christopher closed his eyes, he reflected that maybe sharing a bed with Theo Severyn wouldn't be so bad after all.[8]

---

[8] This disgraceful blue-balling of an ending, a structure that recurs in later chapters, is attributable partly to our virginal squeamishness. Nell had scored (to her great consternation) a near-perfect 91 percent Pure on TheSpark.com's Purity Test. My own sexual history began and ended with the closed-mouth kissing of a Trinity schoolboy with whom I had an eighth-grade fling during a children's theater production of *You're a Good Man, Charlie Brown*. Nell and I were fairly confident in our theoretical grasp of gay male sexuality, but we knew how treacherous the gap between theory and practice could be.

Part of it, too, was the lateness of the hour. Most of our Faunfic was written during the punchy post-midnight period when every waking second felt triumphantly stolen, albeit from no one except our morning selves, and the creative process tended to come to an end when one of us looked at the clock. It was one of the first things we discovered we had in common, this reluctance to go to bed at a reasonable hour—and what a joy it was to stay awake for each other's sake!

My bedroom in my father's basement apartment had no blinds on the windows, and those late nights were tinted sickly orange from the sodium-vapor streetlamp in front of the building. Through my window, from a certain angle, I could see nocturnal pedestrians—gay nightclubbers, I always imagined—on the sidewalk above me. If I had my bedroom light on, I was visible to them as well. They rarely took the trouble to kneel down and peer through the basement window, but every once in a while one did, and when I masturbated—as I did frenetically on those Faunfic nights, the back of my hand chafing against the rough fabric of my computer chair—it was a thrill to run the risk of making eye contact with a stranger.

To this day I'm chronically sleep-deprived for no reason except that staying up too late, past the point of exhaustion, remains a pleasurable form of self-harm. I wonder if Nell has outgrown this habit. Or if even tonight, somewhere out there in the city, she's wide-awake with me.

F&N, 2002

It's Wednesday, six days post-auditions, but the *Othello* cast list still hasn't gone up. Worse yet, we the F&N unit have hit a dead end, research-wise, on the Marble Faun and his sidekick. All we know are their names (Theo Severyn and Christopher Korkian, respectively) and address (*THE. SAME. APARTMENT.*). We can bear it no longer; we need answers. This is a job for Jimmy Frye the IT guy.

We've already sent him an email telling him we want information on Theo Severyn's transfer to Idlewild. Now it's Activity Period, our best chance to catch Jimmy in person. We cancel our Invert Society meeting and wend our way computer-labward.

Jimmy Frye dwells hobbit-like in his own little IT cave, a closet-sized office in the corner of the computer lab. Most of the Idlewild population gives it and him a wide berth, charging him with multiple counts of perviness:

1. His pungent body odor, noticeable at all times but particularly so in the cramped, electricity-warmed quarters of the computer lab;

2. His chatty chumminess with Idlewild students, which often leads him to stand in closer proximity to one's personal space than one would ideally wish (see #1); and

3. His mustache, which evokes something of the child molester.

But we the F&N unit would argue in rebuttal that

1. His body odor alone, while perceptible if you're sniffing around for it, is not strong enough to be objectionable on its own;

2. His chumminess, while perhaps overeager, would be perfectly welcome were it not for the accompanying odor; and

3. Neither of these traits would elicit charges of perviness if not in combination with his mustache—which, stereotypes aside, is evidence of nothing.

Quod erat demonstrandum: Jimmy Frye is not guilty of perviness. Or at least this is how we the F&N unit justify our friendship with him, because Jimmy Frye is our primary source of Idlewild gossip and we'll be damned if we let anything get in the way of that.

From the outside, his office looks dark. Has he left for the day, or is he merely napping? We knock on the door. Out steps a sleepy-looking Jimmy Frye.

F: "Jimmy, old buddy, old pal."

N: "We haven't hung out in *forever*."

"I see how it is." Jimmy scowls owlishly in the brightness of the computer lab. "You're too good for me until you want something from me. Then it's *oh, Jimmy, can we kiss your feet?*"

This is pretty much true, but we the F&N unit must pretend otherwise.

F: "We just wanted to take you out for coffee."

N: "Our treat!"

We know he can't say no to this, because he's poor, because Idlewild doesn't pay him enough, which is why he is, at the age of forty-six, single and living in Ridgewood with a roommate he despises. (It's amazing what some adults will tell you if you just let them talk.) Jimmy picks up a manila folder—full of information for us?—from his office desk. "You know I hate Starbucks," he says. "Might as well drink a candy bar."

N: "Starbucks? Buddy, we're taking you to Joe Junior."

F: "Only the finest for Jimmy Frye."

To the corner of Sixteenth and Third we go, and minutes later the three of us are ensconced in an orange vinyl booth by the window. We the F&N unit order a cheeseburger for Jimmy, chocolate milkshakes for ourselves, and coffee for all. As we wait for our orders to arrive, Jimmy asks, "How's the college process going? Picked out your top choices yet?"

We the F&N unit promised ourselves we'd endure up to five (5) minutes of preliminary small talk—but this is beyond the pale.

F: "Jimmy, I would rather stick this fork in my eye than talk about college."

N: "I get enough of that at home."

"I'm serious," says Jimmy. "You girls are smart cookies. Trust me, I've seen a lot of kids come and go over the years." He peers sternly at us over his round glasses. "Promise me you won't let me down."

We the F&N unit don't give a shit what Jimmy Frye thinks of our intelligence (which is self-evidently superior to his) or our college prospects (the man went to CUNY, for god's sake). But he often acts this way, like he believes himself to be our mentor. We the F&N unit are brilliant actresses, but even we aren't sure how we managed to give Jimmy such a falsely inflated sense of our respect for him.

Our food arrives. We the F&N unit pour our coffee into our milkshakes to make it potable. Jimmy picks up his burger with two hands. "Can you keep a secret?" he says. "I'm not a fan of Juniper Green's new 'do."

We regret letting Jimmy overhear our private name for Jennifer Green. He makes no secret of his interest in her and the reason behind it. He has a type, you see.

"Blond hair on an Asian girl always looks trashy," he says. "Which can be hot, don't get me wrong." He grins. "But Juniper Green doesn't need the help, does she?"

Our friendship with Jimmy Frye requires us to put up with a certain amount of this sort of thing. We force a laugh.

F: "She's only half Asian."

N: "And not, like, *from* Asia. She doesn't speak Chinese."

F: "I don't think even her mom does."

N: "Women who speak English aren't really your thing, right?"

F: "Such a turnoff, having to *talk* to a woman."

"You hypocrites," says Jimmy. "I don't make fun of *your* sexual preference." He takes a big disgruntled bite of his burger.

We the F&N unit hesitate, wondering if we just went too far.

But then he grins. "Aw, I'm just busting your chops," he says. "Let's get down to business." He holds up the manila folder. We the F&N unit reach for it, but before we can touch it, he snatches it away. "Remember, this is strictly confidential," he says. "This could get me fired. I'm putting my ass on the line for you, pardon my French."

We blather our appreciation until, finally, Jimmy relinquishes the folder. We open it and riffle through the papers inside, splattering milkshake onto them in our ravenousness to read. They're printouts of emails, mostly—we recognize the email addresses of Skip, Trudy, and Pat the school nurse—plus some phone records we can't decipher.

"There's a lot to sift through," says Jimmy, echoing our own thoughts. "I'll give you the lowdown." Wary of eavesdroppers, he leans forward and speaks in a voice so low we have to lean in even closer to hear him. (Which is so exciting we don't even mind the smell.) "Theo Severyn," says Jimmy, "transferred from Stuyvesant."

N: "Like . . . *the* Stuyvesant? The public school way downtown?"

F: "The one that got ass-fucked by the falling towers?"

"Bingo," says Jimmy. "Though if I were you, I wouldn't put it that way in front of Theo."

F: "You mean . . ."

N: "Are you saying he was, like . . ."

F&N, in unison: ". . . *there?*"

"Yup. He was in the shit." Jimmy sips his coffee mustachedly. "In fact," he says, "you might have seen him right afterward. Remember how Idlewild hosted classes in the building for Stuyvesant refugees?"

We do. Skip and Trudy made a big Quaker deal of it. The arrangement lasted a few weeks; then Stuyvesant reopened and they all went back.

"Well, after getting a taste of Idlewild," says Jimmy, "Theo decided to transfer here permanently. Take a look at this." He points to one of the printouts. "It says here that the nurse's office needs to have an albuterol inhaler *and* a nebulizer available at all times for Theo Severyn—that's for asthma. And here, it says he's allowed to have pseudoephedrine on request—that's for rhinosinusitis." He raises his eyebrows at us. "You see what I'm getting at?"

We don't, exactly.

F: "So Theo has fragile lungs like a consumptive Victorian waif?"

N: "And he transferred to Idlewild because . . . the air is better here?"

"You're partway there," says Jimmy. "I think Theo had a bad reaction to the dust from the wreckage. No surprise there—it was full of asbestos. But for Theo, it must have been pretty severe. Because he didn't just have to change schools." With a flourish, he holds up another sheet of paper. "He had to *move.*"

We study the printout. It's an email from Elizabeth Severyn (Theo's mom, presumably) to Skip and Trudy's front desk assistant. The subject line says "home address / mailing address." The email explains that

Idlewild can still send mail to Theo's home address on Hudson Street, but if they need to reach Theo personally, he's "currently staying with Christopher Korkian's family at 125 Riverside Drive, Apartment 10C."

The paper flutters in our trembling hands. We the F&N unit are vibrating so hard we're practically falling off our orange vinyl seat. This is so much more romantic than either of us dared to dream.

F: "So Theo had to move in with the Korkians . . ."

N: ". . . because if he stayed in his own apartment, he might *die*?"

Jimmy snorts. "I don't know if it's *that* dramatic," he says. "But it sounds like you get the picture." He stuffs what's left of his cheeseburger into his mouth.

But we the F&N unit don't get the picture at all. We still have so many questions.

F: "But why Christopher Korkian?"

N: "Did the school set them up?"

Jimmy's mouth is too full to answer. He shrugs.

F: "Or did they already know each other somehow?"

N: "Like from camp or something?"

"Jeez, you two," says Jimmy, gracing us with an unwelcome glimpse of burger bolus in his mouth. "I told you what I know. Enough with the questions."

From behind us booms a familiar, magnificent baritone, singing a familiar line from last year's spring musical. *"No more questions, please!"*

We the F&N unit jump. Standing directly behind us, with ramrod-proper posture and his hands clasped primly at his belt buckle, is Bottom. We freeze guiltily—how much has he overheard?—and his smile fades. "Sorry," he says. "Am I interrupting something?"

F: "Not at all."

N: "We were just talking about, uh . . ."

"College," Jimmy cuts in smoothly, having finally swallowed his bite of burger. "I'm giving some pointers on the ol' application process."

"That's generous of you," says Bottom, looking understandably confused. "Well, I just saw you through the window, and I thought you'd want to know the good news."

We the F&N unit freeze again, but this time in a good way. Bottom's smile returns.

"The cast list is up."

We the F&N unit scream so loudly that all heads in the diner turn to look at us. We fumble for F's wallet, slap a twenty-dollar bill on the table—this intel was well worth it—and scramble out of our booth without waiting for change or even saying goodbye to Jimmy Frye.

F: "Don't tell us what we got, okay?"

"I wouldn't dream of it," says Bottom. "But I think you'll be pleased—"

N: [*fingers in ears*] "La la la."

We the F&N unit would prefer to run, but with Bottom at our side we are forced to walk at a dignified pace. Fifteenth Street feels so tortuously long, the Meetinghouse entrance so cruelly distant. What did we get? What did we get?

"Did Jimmy have any useful college advice for you?" Bottom asks.

We the F&N unit scoff.

"Well, it was worth a shot," says Bottom. "At this point I'd take advice from anyone."

N: "Oh, come on, dude. You don't need advice."

F: "You don't even need college. You could be on Broadway tomorrow."

"That's sweet of you to say," he says, "but untrue. Besides, my parents would blow a gasket if I didn't get a degree."

N: "How about a theater degree?"

"That's the dream." He sighs. "But the really good programs are so competitive."

N: "You can get in anywhere you want."

F: "The world is your oyster."

What we the F&N unit mean to convey is that Bottom is so gifted and lovable, any college would be glad to have him. We do *not* mean to suggest, to his face, that any college will accept him just because he's black—but our words have come out maybe sounding that way. Chagrined, we search for a quick distraction.

N: "Are you excited for *La Bohème*?"

F: "*That's* the Broadway show you should be in."

This works, perhaps too well: he's still talking about *La Bohème* by the time we arrive at the Fifteenth Street entrance of the Meetinghouse. "Realistically, I don't have the voice for it—I consider myself an actor who sings, not vice versa—so feel free to laugh at me," he says as we walk inside, "but sometimes, on the subway to school, I listen to the CD and pretend I'm playing Marcello in a film version. Do you think Baz

Luhrmann will make one? In general, I mean—not with me. Or with me, as long as I'm dreaming! Oh, wouldn't it be wonderful to be in a movie?"

We stop hearing him as we dash up the creaky wood back stairs. There's a handful of underclassgirls standing at the top of the stairs, clustered in front of the closed door of Wanda and Ms. Spider's office. The cast list is taped to that door.

F: "Gangway, girls."

N: "Seniors coming through."

We the F&N unit shove aside the underclassgirls and behold the cast list.

Idlewild presents
OTHELLO

Directed by Wanda Higgins
Opening Night: Thursday, November 21
Closing Night: Friday, November 22

CAST
Othello – Peter Baptiste

(That's Bottom.)

F: "Duh."

N: "Still—congrats, dude!"

We turn around to high-five him, only to discover he's not there. Whoops. We must have lost him on the stairs.

We turn back to the cast list.

Desdemona – Lily Day-Jones

F: "Once again, duh."

N: "So where does that leave us?"

Emilia – Nell Rifkin (*Thursday night*); Jennifer Green (*Friday night*)

N: "Goddamn it. Thursday night *and* I have to share with Juniper? Sorry, boss. I really wanted to share with you."

F: "Wait—look—"

Iago – Fay Vasquez-Rabinowitz (*Thursday night*);
Theo Severyn (*Friday night*)

N: "Hey! Smell *you*, Nancy Drew!"

F: "Iago . . ."

N: "You should have senior privilege, though! Why did she give Friday night to a sophomore?"

F: "*Iago* . . ."

N: "Well, at least you'll go on the same night as me."

F: ". . ."

N: "Hey, and we're married to each other! That's kind of funny."

F: ". . ."

N: "Plus you'll kill me at the end. That's cool too. I guess."

F: ". . ."

N: "Boss?"

NELL

One of the first times I visited her mom's penthouse, I noticed an antique glass candy jar and asked Fay if I could take a jelly bean from it. "Help yourself," said Fay. "Whatever's yours is mine." A second later we realized her slip of the tongue—she'd meant to say *Whatever's mine is yours*—and cracked up. It became one of our running inside jokes. Whenever she wanted to borrow my pen or take a handful of my French fries, she'd fake-generously say, "Whatever's yours is mine!" while reaching for it. And whenever I offered her my umbrella or my notes for an upcoming history test, I'd say, "Whatever's mine is yours."

It was a joke, but I took real pride in sharing everything with her. Textbooks. Notebooks. The peanut butter sandwich my mom packed for me every morning. My AIM password (she gave me hers, too, and sometimes we pranked each other by logging into each other's AIM accounts and making silly away messages). My MetroCard. A description of the texture of my period blood that day, if it was interestingly gross. I thought nothing of going to the bathroom and peeing while talking to her on the phone. There was nothing I had, nothing I wanted, no part of myself that I wouldn't give to Fay.

But of course, looking back, that wasn't true. There were certain things I kept from her, certain conversational zones we both understood to be off-limits.

For a surprisingly long time, one of those things was college.

I've heard that the college application process has gone unprecedentedly crazy these days, but trust me, it was a big honking deal even in 2002. Idlewild employed a heavily perfumed lady named Deenie Mellman as the college counselor. That was literally her only job. She didn't teach any classes or counsel students on any matters that weren't college-related. She just had monthly one-on-one meetings with all of us, starting in junior year, to discuss our college plans. She was constantly saying, in a soothing tone, "It's all about finding the right fit. There are lots of good schools out there, so you shouldn't stress out about getting into a top school." The subtext there, of course, was that it was normal and expected to stress out about getting into a top school. So I did. Stress out, I mean. (My mom helped with that too.)

It was a pretty effective form of reverse psychology. Not only did it plant the idea in your head that of course you'd want to get into a "top school," but it made you feel like it was *your* idea, like you were rebelliously going against the sober professional advice of Deenie Mellman. And it worked on me. By October of my senior year, I'd already lined up my teacher recommendations (Devi the Dove and my Latin teacher Mr. Prins). I had taken the SAT twice and was doing the cost-benefit analysis of taking it a third time. I had also taken the SAT II subject tests in Writing, Literature, Mathematics, and Latin. My Common App essay had passed through so many editorial hands—Deenie, Devi the Dove, and of course (multiple times) my mom—that it was all but unrecognizable as my own writing.

All this was pretty standard for a New York private school. But as a Quaker school, Idlewild put us at an unusual disadvantage. It was such a major handicap that Deenie coached us specifically on how to address it in our applications. In the box where we were supposed to list our awards and honors, we had to handwrite a careful little paragraph, copying out a script provided by Deenie:

> To elevate one person above another is a violation of Quaker values, which hold all human beings to be equal in the eyes of God. As a Quaker school, Idlewild does not award grades, prizes, or personal honors.

Pre-Idlewild, I was a public school kid. I knew how stressful it was to test for the gifted-and-talented program, to enter a poetry contest and lose, to fuck up in a spelling bee (curse that extra M in *accommodate*) and be forced to clap for my nemesis when the trophy was presented to her. Fay was different, though. Fay was an Idlewild lifer, so she had for real never gotten a grade, let alone a prize. The competition of the college process seemed to disturb her on a deeper level than it bothered me. She was nervous, more nervous than I'd ever seen her, before her first Deenie meeting our junior year. "But how does she *know* which college I'll be a good fit for?" Fay asked me on the way to Deenie's office. "What does she base it on?"

I wasn't sure either, but I'd already had my first Deenie meeting, so I wasn't about to pass up this rare chance to be the smart one. "Well, for one thing, your SAT scores."

Fay looked uneasy. "She knows my SAT scores?"

"What do you care? They're amazing." Mine were good enough (700 verbal, 650 math after months of prep) that I didn't feel threatened by hers (800 verbal, 530 math without studying).

"So that's it?" said Fay. "Deenie just sees me as a number?"

"She looks at your extracurriculars too," I said. "She'll probably suggest colleges with theater programs. Or creative writing. Tell her you write gay stories about Sherlock Holmes."

"I'm not gonna tell her *that*," said Fay. "I've never told anyone that."

"You told me."

"You don't count."

"Wow, I'm so flattered," I said sarcastically to cover up how genuinely flattered I was.

Fay went into Deenie's office. As I waited for her in the hallway, Eddie Applebaum came over and leaned against the wall next to me. "Deenie meeting?" he said sympathetically.

"Nope." I said it curtly, without even looking at him. Then I felt bad. I didn't want to get drawn into a conversation with him, but I also didn't want to be an asshole. "What about you?" I asked. "Are you here to see Deenie?"

"Nah. I missed Meeting this morning, so I have to report to Trudy." Skip and Trudy's office was right next to Deenie's.

I made a noncommittal noise. Even though it didn't affect me at all, I was irritated by Eddie's inability to get to school on time. He made all of us public school transfer kids look bad. People would be nicer to him, I thought resentfully, if he would just get his shit together.

Fay stepped out. I was surprised. She couldn't have been in there for more than five minutes. My own Deenie meeting had lasted much longer.

"Christ," said Fay. "I need a Frappuccino after that." She was already walking down the hall. I had to trot to catch up with her.

Eddie called out, "How was your Deenie meeting?" When he yelled, his voice came out extra squeaky, especially on the first syllable of *Deenie*.

As we turned the corner, Fay coughed into her hand while muttering "*homosexual.*"

We were far enough away from Eddie that I don't think he heard us. At least I hope he didn't. Or if he heard, I hope he understood that this wasn't an insult, at least not in the way it would be an insult coming from anyone else. Anyway, I laughed really hard.

That was the closest Fay and I had ever come to having a conversation about our college plans, which is why I sort of panicked on that late September day when Jimmy Frye brought up the subject at Joe Junior. He was treading into forbidden territory.

Fay didn't know it then, because I hadn't told her, but I'd already made up my mind to apply early decision to Yale. The year before, my mom and I had taken a tour of the Yale campus, and I'd fallen in love with it at first sight. The application was due the first week of November, and I would hear back from them about a month later. If I got in, it was binding: I'd have to go to Yale, no backsies.

If you'd asked me at the time, I would have said I was following Fay's lead by keeping this a secret. After that Deenie meeting, she never brought up college, so I never did either. I got the sense that the whole topic made her uncomfortable.

And, okay, there was another reason.

Whatever's yours is mine.

If Fay knew I was applying to Yale, she might apply to Yale too. If Yale had to choose between the two of us, they were obviously going to go with smart, sophisticated, *Film Comment*–reading, Sontag-quoting Fay. And I wanted to get into Yale so fucking bad. I wanted this one thing just for myself.

After we looked at the cast list, we walked together to her dad's apartment. "I'm seriously so happy you got Iago," I said, and I meant it. She'd wanted it more than I had. I was excited to play Emilia. "You're gonna be amazing in the role."

But Fay wasn't as happy as I expected her to be. Actually, she seemed troubled. "I don't know," she said. "I wish we were sharing it."

FAY

I was so discombobulated by my first encounter with Theo Severyn and Christopher Korkian, I could barely focus on my audition. "I'm auditioning for Iago," I announced and closed my eyes, attempting to summon the soliloquy I was so confident I'd memorized. *I lay with Cassio lately*— and then, to my horror, nothing. My mind was blank but for the image of Theo slamming Christopher against the door, Theo wetly kissing the back of his own hand, pressing his palm against Christopher's mouth. I opened my eyes. "Sorry," I said. "Can I be on book?"

"Certainly, dear," said Wanda. "You didn't need to memorize anything, you know."

Naturally, my memory returned as soon as I held my printed-out soliloquy in my hand. Afterward I lingered by the door, frustrated with myself. "I just have to say," I said, "I really want to be Iago."

"That's useful to know," Wanda said warmly. "I'll bear that in mind." She peered through her cat's-eye glasses at her clipboard, ready to call in the next auditioner.

She didn't understand. I had never wanted anything as desperately as I wanted to be Iago. How could I explain? "It's just," I said, clutching the printout against my chest, "I feel like I really *get* Iago. Like, I *am* Iago."

I remember that Wanda's earrings were bunches of grapes made from pink pearls. They jingled merrily as she threw back her head and laughed.

"Goodness," she said. "That's a bit alarming, isn't it?"

I left the audition certain I'd blown it. But six days later, the cast list went up, and there it was: *Iago – Fay Vasquez-Rabinowitz*. Thursday night only, but still. I was distantly aware of Nell speaking to me, congratulating me, reassuring me. I didn't respond. All I could do was stare at my name, at the word *Iago*, at the space between the two.

On Friday afternoon, the full cast met in the Meetinghouse Loft for the first read-through. Wanda seated us all in a circle and began, as she liked to do, by asking the leads to describe their characters. Bottom went first: "When he's not on the battlefield or giving a speech, Othello is secretly very unsure of himself." Daylily Jones went second: "Desdemona is very trusting, and she always sees the best in people. If something goes wrong, her first instinct is to blame herself." That sort of thing.

"Now, Fay, in your audition," said Wanda, "you spoke a bit about feeling a connection to the character of Iago. What does he mean to you?"

As a perennial bit player, I usually considered this exercise a tedious waste of time. But now that I was a lead, I fancied myself to be under intense scrutiny from my castmates. I cast a pained glance at Nell beside me, but she looked lost in thought, no doubt preoccupied with her own impending précis of Emilia.

"Well," I said, looking around the circle of faces, "Iago is evil, for sure. But I don't think he would be evil if he lived in a time when it was socially acceptable to be gay."

There was scattered laughter.

"Seriously," I said. "He wouldn't need to fuck up Othello's marriage—"

"Please, Fay: *screw* up," said Wanda. That was what passed for school-appropriate language at Idlewild.

"He wouldn't need to screw up Othello's marriage if he could get married himself. Iago, I mean. Like, to another dude."

I was flagrantly bluffing. These were not my authentic thoughts on the nature of Iago. I did not truly believe that Iago would cease to be evil if the Venetian government legalized gay marriage—though gay marriage was itself such a pie-in-the-sky abstraction in 2002, even at Idlewild, that I invoked it mostly as a rhetorical device. Still, the shallowness of my argument embarrassed me even then. I resorted to it only because (a) I couldn't find the language to articulate precisely why I did perceive Iago as a queer character, and (b) I knew it would create sufficient discomfort to preempt any follow-up questions.

The gambit worked. With a briskness just shy of sarcasm, Wanda said, "Thank you for sharing your thoughts," and moved on to the other Iago. "What about you, Theo? Do you agree with Fay?"

"Uh," said Theo. "Not so much." He was sitting rather bizarrely in his black plastic chair, his spine twisted in a catlike contortion so that one arm remained draped over the back of the seat even as he turned to face Wanda. His legs were crossed, and one foot jiggled madly in the air, creating a slight breeze that rippled the fringe of the scarf around his neck. He was, on the whole, a strange combination of excess energy and total languor. "It's not that deep," he said. "I think he's just a dickwad."

The cast laughed. My face burned.

"That's no way to speak about your character," said Wanda. "No one is *just* a dickwad. Is there anything about Iago that you can personally relate to?"

On the chair next to Theo, Christopher Korkian (who was cast in the role of Friday night Cassio) said, "The fact that he's a dickwad."

The cast laughed. Theo pretended to be outraged. "Bitch-ass mothafucka, I'ma choke you out," he said, doing one of his character voices. He pulled off his scarf—it was a camel-colored tartan, the Burberry pattern, though I didn't know that at the time—and approached Christopher as if to strangle him with it. Christopher leaped off his chair, and Theo began to chase him around the room, scarf brandished. People giggled and shrieked and ducked for cover. As Wanda struggled to restore order, Nell muttered, "This is why you don't give leads to sophomores."

It took quite some time before we were able to begin the actual read-through, which itself was even slower going. Wanda, a strict Shakespearean constructionist, was not in the habit of making cuts for length or comprehensibility, and she was determined to read through the full text in one sitting. Apart from Othello and Desdemona, all roles had been double-cast; for fairness's sake, Wanda instructed the role-sharing actors to take turns reading alternate scenes, which was exactly as confusing and inefficient as it sounds. Through the window, the sky darkened. The cast's excitement turned to torpor. And as I read aloud my Iago lines, alternating scene by scene with Theo, distress set in.

How vividly I could visualize what I wanted my Iago to look like! How clearly I saw his wickedness externalized as telltale sissy traits that set him apart from everyone else: the effete flicks of the wrist, the lightly sibilant pronunciation, the fine dark clothing that clung suggestively to narrow hips. Eyeliner, perhaps. The image set my heart racing with joyful narcissism, a full-body epiphany that *this was it*—with "it" existing simultaneously as "the physical manifestation of what I like best about myself" and "that which I most wish to fuck."

But this queer-coded villainy relied on a gender transgression that moved in only one direction. During that first read-through, I made the sickening discovery that I could not perform effeminacy—I physically couldn't. When I flicked my wrist for emphasis, I saw myself as a hand-flapping teenybopper ditz. I pictured myself in eyeliner and realized I would be indistinguishable from Juniper Green or Rollerblading Maddy or any other average-faced girl in drugstore makeup. Tight trousers and half-unbuttoned shirts would only draw attention to my breasts and stomach and other excess flesh so anathema to the gaunt Iago of my Platonic ideal. I'd so looked forward to delivering lines like "My lord, you know I love you" and "I am your own forever," but when I did so I heard my own voice, shrill and pink, and wanted to weep over the wrongness of it.

How unfair, I thought, gazing across the circle at Theo. He had no ear for the rhythms of iambic pentameter. He mispronounced *carrack* and

hyssop and other words I'd gone to the trouble to look up in the dictionary beforehand. He rattled out his longer speeches at the machine-gun
clip that always betrays the novice Shakespearean actor (see *Romeo +
Juliet*, 1996, dir. Baz Luhrmann). And yet he was better suited to the role
of Iago than I would ever be, simply by virtue of his *boyness*—his slim-
hipped, snakelike body, twisted impossibly in that black plastic chair; his
black turtleneck and cashmere scarf and sleek hair that flopped asym-
metrically over one eye; his arm draped indolently over the back of
Christopher's seat, creating on first glance the illusion that his arm was
around Christopher's shoulders. What a waste. Theo Severyn didn't know
what he had.

After the read-through, walking west across Union Square in the windy
dark, I tried to explain all this to Nell.

"If you can't be effeminate," said Nell, "maybe you can be manly. Combat boots, dog tags. Shave your head. You're supposed to be in the military, right?"

She didn't understand, I thought. But then neither did I. "I don't know,"
I said. "I really think Iago should be pretty."

"Well, you're pretty," said Nell.

"Sure," I said. (I never thanked Nell for anything. There would come a
time, later, when I wanted to, but by then the backlog was too vast; I
didn't know where to begin.) "But a girl is *supposed* to be pretty. I want
Iago to be pretty in a way that feels creepy and wrong, so the audience
will get that he's gay."

"You think being gay is creepy and wrong?"

Of course I didn't. Did I? Unable to formulate a counterargument on the
spot, I hesitated.

"Oh my god, you're a homophobe," she said. "I see it now. You want to
turn all the gay guys straight so they'll do you." It was a joke. Nell often

defused real problems by presenting them as jokes. At the time I failed to appreciate what a talent it was.

The wind blew harder. We paused at a sidewalk kiosk selling winter accessories—cheap hats and gloves and pashminas that would no doubt unravel within hours after purchase. Nell was drawn to the newsboy caps; the surly vendor provided her with a hand mirror so she could check herself out as she tried them on. Idly, I examined the cloches, the berets, the scarves. I picked up a slate-blue scarf with a long fringe. Experimentally, I flung it over my neck.

"Hey, that looks nice," said Nell. She held up the mirror so I could see myself. Only my face was visible in it, not my body, and visibility was low in the orange light of the streetlamps. My first thought, upon seeing the reflection, was that I looked like someone else.

Another cold gust tore through Union Square. I tightened the scarf around my neck. In the mirror, I saw the fringe ripple in the wind.

"Five dollars," said the vendor, and I bought it.

From that night onward, using the scarf, I began to practice. I did it alone, after Nell had gone home for the night, or on weekend mornings after I got out of the shower. Standing in front of my bathroom mirror, I tossed the scarf over one shoulder and recited my lines, making my voice as deep as it would go. "My lord, you know I love you," I droned. "He hath a daily beauty in his life / That makes me ugly." I flipped the scarf, beheld myself from another angle. "It's not that deep," I told the mirror. "I think he's just a dickwad." I tried again, pushing my voice even lower. "Just a dickwad."

It hurt my throat to speak this way for more than a minute at a time. I figured that my vocal cords, like any muscle, needed to be trained and strengthened. Night after night I pushed them past the point of pain, hoping the exercise would pay off in time for the play.

F&N, 2002

"Gather round, little lambkins," says Wanda. "I have an announcement."

It is six o'clock on a Friday and rehearsal has just ended, so it is not without some grumbling that the whole cast settles into a circle on the gray-carpeted floor.

Wanda strides to the center, her scarves fluttering behind her. "It's my great pleasure," she says, "to share a special treat with you."

The underclassmen perk up, unaware Wanda is a serial abuser of the word *treat*.

Wanda says, "I've cooked up a new prologue for the play!"

The underclassmen try and fail to hide their disappointment.

"It was inspired," she says, "by a conversation I had recently with Devi Saxena. She told me that at the time Shakespeare wrote *Othello*, the very concept of *race* didn't yet exist! Can you imagine?" (We can, because Devi gives the same spiel to her sophomore English class every year.) "The word *Moor*, contrary to popular belief, doesn't mean *black* in the modern sense. Rather, it refers to the Muslim people of North Africa. Othello, if he were real, would be an Algerian or Moroccan fellow—quite a bit more light-skinned than he's usually depicted."

A freshgirl named Kendra Kwok raises her hand. "How come all the characters keep describing Othello as 'black'?"

"Ah, those of you who were in *Midsummer* last year should recall the answer to that. Jennifer, you were our Hermia, the 'raven' to Helena's 'dove'—can you tell us?"

Juniper Green says, "In Elizabethan England, if you called someone *black*, that just meant they had dark hair. Or, like, a tan or whatever."

"Brilliant. Now, this poses a bit of a pickle for modern audiences! How do we convey that this play takes place in a world without the concept of race? Last night—*eureka!*—it came to me. What we need is a *framing device*, so that the audience can see us *departing* to a world before race. And so I've set the prologue in the antebellum South."

We the F&N unit, having nearly zoned out, do a double take at those last two words. The rest of the cast looks similarly thrown. Daylily mouths to Juniper, *The what?*

"It will be performed in dumb show"—we the F&N unit resist the temptation to crack an obvious joke—"but it will establish the characters through *pantomime* and *tableau*. Iago is the cruel slave master, Desdemona his lovely wife. Othello is their prize slave"—her eyes shine with excitement as she reveals the twist—"and he and Desdemona are having a forbidden love affair."

She pauses for breath, overwhelmed by the drama of a situation she just made up.

"Iago comes upon them together," she continues, "and beats Othello unconscious. That's when the lighting and sound cues will tip off the audience that we're entering a dream sequence—and from that point onward, the play unfolds as written. You see, the entire play is this slave's *dream*. A dream of a world where he can be a general and marry who he wishes."

She clasps her hands together and beams around the circle.

Here's the thing: we the F&N unit don't dislike Wanda. We wish she'd favor us as she favors Daylily Jones, but everyone favors Daylily Jones, so we don't take it personally. Wanda's attention, while distributed unevenly, is always kind in nature. When we call her Wanda the Witch, it's only because we really do suspect her of possessing magical powers, especially in the moment when the opening-night curtain goes up and the previous eight weeks of chaos somehow resolve, against all reason, into something quickbright and alive. We love that she flounces around bedecked in sequins and fluttering silk scarves. We love her cat's-eye glasses and dangly earrings and many hands' worth of oversized rings. We especially love that she's British, so much that we have a half-serious conspiracy theory that she's actually just a regular American who's been faking a British accent this whole time because it commands such awe from students. But this prologue is strong evidence for her foreignness.

Daylily Jones, upon whom we can always count to miss the point, is the first to break the silence. "Wait," she says, frowning. "So Iago and Desdemona are married?"

"In the framing device, dear," says Wanda. "Not in Shakespeare's text."

"But . . . how should that inform my performance?"

We the F&N unit roll our eyes. But this question, which will surely occupy Wanda for the next five minutes as she answers it in detail in front of an entire crowd of people to whom it does not apply, gives us valuable time to assess the mood of the room.

Of the highest interest to us is the reaction of Bottom—but of course Bottom is perfectly aware of this, and being the accomplished actor he is, he manages to keep his face perfectly neutral. We can't even catch his eye.

Juniper Green, on the other hand, is employing her acting skills (such as they are) to the opposite end, her mouth agape in a theatrical mask of horror. Though this may be only because her character, Emilia, has no role in the prologue.

Daylily Jones is a vision of quizzical loveliness, her alabaster brow furrowed in confusion, but this is most likely an issue of basic comprehension.

We survey the underclassmen and make accidental eye contact with a number of them. They're likewise studying us to gauge our reaction.

Christopher Korkian is sitting across the circle from us. We're pretty sure that he's reading the GQ magazine perpetually tucked into the binder that holds his script, and that he didn't hear a word Wanda said.

And at his side, as always, is Theo Severyn. Theo sits on the gray-carpeted floor with his knees pulled up to his chest. His face is hidden in his hands, and his shoulders shake. For one confused second, it appears to the F&N unit that he is weeping. But then he looks up and lowers his hands to reveal his eyes, which triggers the following chain of events:

1. He makes direct eye contact, across the circle, with the F&N unit.

2. We the F&N unit see that he's not crying, but laughing—or, rather, trying so hard not to laugh that his face is bright red with the effort.

3. Caught off guard and vulnerable to contagion, we the F&N unit reflexively get the giggles, which we attempt to muffle with our hands.

4. The sight of us stifling our giggles causes Theo to burst out laughing.

5. This causes the F&N unit to burst out laughing.

Heads swivel toward us in perplexity. Wanda, who has been expounding this whole time, casts us a sharp look. "May I ask what's so amusing?"

We the F&N unit struggle to collect ourselves. We mutter apologies, as does Theo. "It's a cool idea," he says. His voice is calm—how did he manage to regain his composure so quickly? "Dark, but I like it."

"Well, then," says Wanda, "if there are no further questions, I suppose that wraps up today's rehearsal." She strides to the door. "If you have any character questions you'd like to discuss, I'll be in my office until half six." The door swings shut behind her.

The instant Wanda is out of the room, Juniper Green jumps to her feet. "Cast meeting!" she shrills. "Cast meeting! Um, can we talk about that prologue?"

Murmurs fill the rehearsal room as our castmates clamber to their feet and surround Juniper. We the F&N unit join them with foot-dragging reluctance. Such a cast meeting is probably a good idea, but who died and put Juniper Green in charge of it?

Bottom glances over his shoulder toward the gray wall that separates the rehearsal room from Wanda's office. In an uncharacteristically small voice, he says, "Can we have it somewhere other than here?"

Eager to undermine Juniper's authority, we the F&N unit begin to chant. "Starbucks! Starbucks!"

Theo joins our chant. "Starbucks! Starbucks!" Christopher does too, and the underclassgirls join in—"Starbucks! Starbucks!"—until, in frustration, Juniper relents.

Five minutes later the full cast of *Othello* crowds the Starbucks on the corner of Fifteenth and Third, with the leads crammed around a tiny chessboard-patterned table. There aren't enough chairs to go around, so we the F&N unit squeeze onto a single chair, tiny Juniper perches on Daylily's lap, Theo and Christopher sit on the table itself, and Bottom stands gallantly with the underclassmen.

"So," says Juniper. "That prologue is retarded, right?"

The cast replies in near-unison.

F&N: "So retarded."

Theo and Christopher: "*So* retarded."

Bottom: "Yes, I have some concerns."

Daylily: "I don't think it's so—" She corrects herself just in time. "So retarded!"

The Starbucks barista guy calls out, with a sigh of resignation, "Heywood? Heywood Jablome?"

Cackling, we the F&N unit rise to claim the venti caramel Frappuccino we have jointly ordered under a witty pseudonym. We return to find Juniper tediously holding forth. "It's so stupid," she's saying. "It has *nothing* to do with the play."

"And on a more personal note," says Bottom, "I don't think my parents will be too happy about—"

"*No one's* parents will be happy about it," Juniper interrupts. "Because it sucks ass. So what are we gonna do about it?"

We the F&N unit unwrap our straws and blow the paper wrappers in her face. Theo laughs, rocking the chessboard-patterned table.

"Can we try to focus?" says Bottom. "Wanda's only here till six-thirty. We have . . ." He checks his watch. "Ten minutes."

"We have to confront her as a group," says Juniper. "Collective action. Like that time we protested the dress code. It'll be hard for her to say no to all of us at once."

"What if she does, though?" pipes up Kendra Kwok.

"I'm sure she won't," says Daylily. "She's so nice."

"Besides," says Bottom, "we have a secret weapon."

We the F&N unit are so busy passing our Frappuccino back and forth, it takes us a moment to register that Bottom is pointing at the two of us.

N: "Us?"

F: "Why are we the secret weapon?"

"Oh, don't be modest," says Bottom. "Teachers adore you."

"For real," says Juniper. "Just use your big words and shit."

"Christopher." Theo tugs at the sleeve of Christopher's jacket. "Christopher. Go up to the counter and buy me an iced triple grande skim cappuccino with extra foam."

"Get it yourself," says Christopher.

"I'll give you five bucks," Theo wheedles.

"That won't even cover it."

"Will you guys shut up?" says Juniper. "This is important."

"Ten bucks," says Theo. "Twenty. Fifty."

"Are you haggling," says Christopher, "or just saying random numbers?"

"Seven. Zero. Nothing. It's free."

Bottom checks his watch again. "Please," he says. "It's almost six-thirty."

"Eighty bucks," says Theo, "but *you* pay *me* eighty bucks and also get me an iced triple grande skim cappuccino with extra foam."

"I'll buy you one, Theo," says Maddy, already Rollerblading her way to the counter.

"Thanks, doll," says Theo.

The wait for Theo's complicated order detains us in Starbucks for an extra few minutes, and it's past six-thirty when the cast departs and heads back east down Fifteenth Street. The sun is setting earlier these days, and the street is awash in pink dusk. The sky is so lovely, we the F&N unit pause to admire it as we drop our Frappuccino cup into a public trash can. "Pick up the pace," Juniper snaps. "Are you real New Yorkers or what?"

As the cast approaches the Meetinghouse, we see Wanda exiting through the Fifteenth Street door. She smiles at the approaching crowd. "Fancy meeting you here," she says.

"We need to talk to you," says Daylily.

"But you're on your way home," Bottom hastens to add. "If it's not a good time—"

"No, I'm delighted to chat," says Wanda. "What's the scoop?"

A second ago we were all so full of resolve, but we failed to prepare for the actual situation. We have no prepared speech, no plan at all.

Wanda's brow crinkles. "Why, what's the matter?"

Suddenly we the F&N unit feel terribly sad. Her face is so open and gentle, her body so small and bird-boned, her old-lady cheeks so soft and delicate. Right now we would sooner act out a thousand bad prologues than hurt her feelings.

"Um," Juniper begins, and we can hear in her voice that she's wavering too.

There's a clatter on the sidewalk beside us as a plastic Starbucks cup hits the ground: Theo has dropped his iced triple grande cappuccino. The plastic lid bounces off, coffee splatters, ice cubes roll, and Theo takes off running. He's heading west on Fifteenth Street, back the way we came. Christopher runs after him.

The rest of the cast watches them in confusion. After a moment, Juniper turns back to Wanda. "We just had some questions," she says haltingly, "about, um, the prologue."

Then we the F&N unit run too. We run up the street in the rose-gold dusk, chasing the figures of Theo and Christopher, their backpacks bouncing and jackets flapping—and as we gain on them, we begin to understand why Theo bolted. We hear it before we see it: a low roar in the sky. It's getting louder and closer and louder, rising in pitch until it takes on a screechy overtone. We the F&N unit look up at the pink sky and there's a plane, a low-flying plane, so close, so big, it's right over our heads—

Theo and Christopher come to a halt on the corner of Fifteenth and Third, right outside the Starbucks where we just were, and we the F&N unit skid to a stop beside them. Silently, the four of us watch the plane. It roars above us, past us, past and above the buildings—will it—no, it doesn't touch anything and keeps flying forward, eastward, seaward, and the roar lowers, softens, fades out until it's absorbed into the ambient roar of the city.

We the F&N unit pant for breath, our pulses rabbiting. Christopher doubles over, bracing himself with one hand against the brick wall of the building. Theo is still staring at the sky, his body rigid, his backpack dangling off one shoulder. Its flap is unzipped, wide open; loose papers threaten to spill out. *Are you okay?* is a question we the F&N unit might conceivably ask him right now, but what could those words even mean in this context?

The Starbucks exterior wall vent blasts us with warm gusts of sweet coffee fumes. We breathe it in and out. Everything is normal. Everything is fine.

After a moment, Theo returns to himself. He looks around the intersection of Fifteenth and Third, as if remembering where he is, and runs a hand through his wind-tousled hair. "Fuck," he says. "I lost my iced cappuccino."

"I'll buy you another one," says Christopher.

"I don't want another one," says Theo. "I want a Brownie Special with two scoops of Phish Food and rainbow sprinkles." He begins to walk again, very fast, south down Third Avenue, in the direction of Ben & Jerry's. Christopher hurries to follow him.

We the F&N unit hesitate, remembering the castmates we just abandoned. We think of Bottom, the gifted and good-hearted Bottom who is so dear to us and does not deserve to be slave-beaten in front of the whole school to gratify the artistic whims of Wanda the Witch, who is a kind lady and would likely take our concerns seriously if we made the effort to persuade her, which Bottom is counting on us, the F&N unit, to do.

Still walking fast, faster than Christopher, Theo heads toward the intersection of Fourteenth and Third. It's not his light. Cars and trucks are whizzing down Fourteenth Street in both directions, and the east-bound M14 bus is lumbering by. Theo is stepping off the curb and into two-lane traffic—

"Theo, no," Christopher yells.

We the F&N unit run toward Fourteenth Street, but we don't make it in time. Standing beside Christopher, we the F&N unit watch helplessly from the corner as Theo walks into traffic.

Cars honk and skid to a stop, their brakes screeching. Drivers bellow indistinctly and roll down their windows to give the finger. Theo walks calmly through it all.

"He has a freaking death wish," says Christopher.

The light changes from orange DONT WALK to white WALK. Christopher chases after Theo, catches up to him on the other side of the street, grabs him by the camel-colored scarf. Theo smiles at him. The orange DONT WALK begins to blink.

Right there, in the cooling twilight, we the F&N unit make a snap decision.

Running to beat the light, we follow them.

NELL

Juniper Green almost never Instant Messaged me, so when she did, it was so unusual I saved the conversation on my LiveJournal. It happened on the night of Friday, October 11, 2002. That was the day Fay and I ditched our castmates to follow Theo and Christopher to the East Village Ben & Jerry's—a decision that ended up mattering more than I ever could have predicted.

Strumpet19: where did u guys disappear to? :)
m k fantastico: oh hey! sorry about that
m k fantastico: theo saw a low-flying plane and freaked out
m k fantastico: did you know he's a Stuyvesant refugee?
Strumpet19: holy shit :(
Strumpet19: is he ok
m k fantastico: he was pretty upset but we managed to calm him down

That was a very self-flattering way of saying that Fay and I spent three hours at Ben & Jerry's with Theo and Christopher.

m k fantastico: what ended up happening with Wanda?
Strumpet19: omg so
Strumpet19: we all went to my house and talked it over for like 2 hours
m k fantastico: Wanda went to your HOUSE?
Strumpet19: i live in the east village so it was just a quick walk
m k fantastico: were your parents there?
Strumpet19: no they're away at an ethnomusicology conference in santa fe

Strumpet19: anyway she explained how the prologue ties into the bard's themes

Strumpet19: & i feel way better about it now

Strumpet19: long story short, we're all totally BFF w/ wanda now :)

Strumpet19: too bad u missed it lmao

m k fantastico: wait

m k fantastico: so

m k fantastico: we're really doing the slave-beating prologue?

Strumpet19: chillax, girl

Strumpet19: it's gonna be good :)

When I saved this conversation, I didn't make any notes about what I was thinking, but in hindsight, I'm almost certain it was about more than just the weirdness of Juniper messaging me. I know I felt uncomfortable with the prologue. I hated it—the whole cast hated it—but I don't think I fully understood it to be *racist*. I know that's hard to believe now, but I'm positive no one said the word *racist* in our cast meeting at Starbucks. Not even Juniper Green, who definitely would have said it if she was thinking it. I do remember feeling uncomfortable, at least initially, at the idea of Bottom having to play a slave. But my logic, as best as I can reconstruct it fifteen years later, went something like this: Wanda couldn't be racist, because she was nice. And if Wanda wasn't racist, then her prologue couldn't be racist. So if her prologue made me uncomfortable, then it must have been for a different, unrelated reason.

And it was easy for all of us to land on the same reason: from an artistic perspective, the prologue was just *bad*. It was cheesy and preachy and embarrassing. This was Idlewild; our plays were supposed to be better than that. If Bottom seemed especially bothered by the prologue, well, that made sense to me: of all the graduating seniors in the cast, he was the most serious actor, and Othello was his biggest role yet. Of course he wouldn't want the play to be bad.

And the prologue *was* bad—so this was a low-stakes aesthetic issue, not a high-stakes ethical one. Confronting Wanda made sense, but it wasn't a moral imperative. Whatever role Bottom had hoped Fay and I would play in talking Wanda out of bad artistic choices, we hadn't done anything *morally* wrong by flaking. In fact, when Theo freaked out and ran, it was easy to convince myself that he took priority over the play. After all, the kid had *been there* on 9/11. Like all New Yorkers, I technically had the right to claim that I was "there on 9/11," but there are different tiers of having been there on 9/11, and Theo was really, truly, top-tier in-the-shit *there on 9/11*. There was no question that Fay and I had a moral obligation to run after him and be there for him.

But I don't know. If I'd really believed, deep down, that I was doing the right thing, maybe I wouldn't have saved that AIM conversation. I wouldn't have needed to tell myself what I kept telling myself, over and over, for the rest of the rehearsal process: *It's just a play. It's just a play. It's just a play.*

The prologue opened with Bottom alone onstage. In the official performance he was supposed to be shirtless, but during rehearsals he mostly wore his usual polo shirt and khakis. I know this because I crashed all the prologue rehearsals, as I crashed all of Fay's rehearsals when my character wasn't called, watching from a scuzzy old wingback armchair in the far corner of the rehearsal room. That armchair was left over from the *Winter's Tale* set, and it was such a high-value seat that I rarely bothered to claim it even when it was vacant, just to spare myself the disappointment of getting up and returning to find it occupied. But there were only four actors involved in the prologue—Bottom as slave!Othello, Daylily as Southern-belle!Desdemona, and Fay alternating with Theo as master!Iago—so during those rehearsals I had the armchair all to myself.

At the first prologue rehearsal, there was some initial back-and-forthing about what, exactly, Bottom was meant to be doing as the lights went up.

"Picking cotton," Daylily suggested from the corner of the room. She was waiting for her cue to enter, resting her elbows on the piano. This was extremely not allowed, but no one had the heart to yell at her for it. (Ms. Spider would have, but she wasn't there.)

"Perhaps," Wanda mused, "but how would we convey that in pantomime?" She was big on theater-as-process; it was typical for us to figure this stuff out as we went along. "Othello, dear," she said to Bottom—she was also big on addressing us by our character names—"let's see you lifting a bale of cotton."

"How heavy is it?" asked Bottom. He was always asking actorly questions like that. (Also, in retrospect, maybe he was stalling.)

"It's terribly heavy," said Wanda. "Imagine you're going on holiday and carrying a heavy suitcase full of clothing."

Bottom outstretched his arms and buckled under the weight of the invisible suitcase.

"No, that won't do," said Wanda. "Let me see, let me see. You live in a garden apartment, don't you? Do you ever work in the garden?"

"Sporadically," said Bottom. "Sometimes I help my mother plant tulip bulbs."

"Tulips! How lovely! Show us how you plant tulip bulbs."

Bottom got down on his knees and dug an invisible trowel into the gray carpet.

"Marvelous! Now let's make the shovel larger."

The rehearsal room door swung open. It was Christopher, carrying a Starbucks cup in each hand. Making a big show of staying quiet and unobtrusive, Christopher tiptoed to the far corner of the rehearsal room, reached across the piano, and handed one cup to Theo.

"Extra foam?" said Theo.

"Extra foam," said Christopher.

"Don't distract the performers, please," said Wanda.

Christopher winced apologetically and lowered himself to the floor. He blew on his own Starbucks cup to cool it and leaned back against the side of the armchair where I was sitting.

"Remember," Wanda was saying to Daylily, "you'll be wearing a hoop-skirt. With every movement, you must be physically aware of it. How do you think your character would walk?"

Daylily tiptoed toward Bottom in shuffling little baby steps.

"Brilliant! What about your arms?"

Daylily held her arms out like a toy ballerina.

"Lovely, lovely. Travel just a little farther downstage toward Othello—aaand *freeze!*"

The two of them froze into a tableau: Bottom on his knees mid-shoveling, Daylily gazing down at him with ballerina arms hovering. (In the full staging, this would be accompanied by a light change and an ominous upward slide on a glockenspiel.)

"Now, unfreeze, and Desdemona will make her way over to Othello. The two of you will lock eyes and embrace."

Daylily did the hoopskirt shuffle toward Bottom. Awkwardly, she knelt down just as he was getting up to stand next to her. Both halfway between kneeling and standing, they looked at each other and then put their arms around each other gingerly.

"Let me see the *stakes* of this embrace," Wanda called out. "This is a forbidden love affair!"

They hugged. Daylily let out a breathy "Oh!"

"Silent pantomime," Wanda chided. "No talking."

Bottom's voice came muffled through Daylily's voluminous hair. "Wouldn't I be crushing her hoopskirt?"

"Oh, blast," said Wanda. "You're quite right. Let's try it another way. Why don't you tenderly take her by the hand?"

Daylily and Bottom jumped apart with obvious relief. Bottom extended a gentle hand toward Daylily. She giggled and bit her lower lip. Something seemed to be going on between the two of them—were they secretly going out? But everyone knew that Daylily had a boyfriend named Sergio who was a twenty-five-year-old grad student at NYU! (I remember that being common knowledge, but in hindsight it sounds super messed up. I hope it wasn't true.)

"Enter Iago, catching them in the act!"

Fay went first. Theo rested his elbows on the piano and watched, waiting for his turn to swap in so they could repeat the blocking with him in Fay's place.

"Iago violently pulls them apart," said Wanda. "Well done. And then he *throws* Othello onto the ground!"

"Wait," said Fay. "What am I doing in the cotton field?"

"It doesn't matter," said Wanda. "This all takes place in a heightened theatrical space."

"What does that mean?" asked Daylily.

Wanda launched into a long-winded answer. I looked at Bottom, searching for a sign that he was upset. Or, no: I was searching for a sign that he *wasn't* upset. If he wasn't upset, I could ignore my own deepening dread. With relief, I saw that he was in an unusually jolly mood, whispering laughingly to Daylily. Well, I thought, Bottom was an actor at heart. The prologue put him at the center of attention, so maybe he was getting a kick out of it.

But as I studied him, doubt crept in. Bottom was always such a professional. He never laughed or whispered or goofed off in rehearsal. This was out of character for him. Was he trying to cover up how he really felt?

Christopher was still leaning against the armchair, close enough that I could whisper to him. "Hey," I said, and he turned his head to look up at me. "Do you think he's okay?"

Christopher considered my question. His curls bounced as he glanced from side to side, worried about being overheard. Then, to get closer to me, he stood and perched on the arm of the armchair. He bent his head to whisper in my ear.

"I'm a little worried about him, to be honest," Christopher said softly. "I think he's been having nightmares since that low-flying plane."

I stiffened in the armchair, realizing that Christopher thought I was asking about Theo. I was too embarrassed to correct him—and too curious. "How do you know?" I whispered back.

"He's been living with me," said Christopher. "Did you not know that? Everyone gives us crap about it." He sipped from his Starbucks cup. I smelled hot apple cider, which I considered a really kiddie order (you know, as opposed to the adult sophistication of a caramel Frappuccino with caramel-drizzled whipped cream), which made me feel tender toward him.

"I would never give you crap for living with Theo," I said. "It was really nice of you to take him in."

"Thanks, Nell," he said seriously. "I appreciate that." He glanced again in the direction of the piano, where Theo, in a frenzy of fidgety boredom (Wanda was *still* explaining the concept of a heightened theatrical space), was peeling one end of his Starbucks straw into green plastic petals. "It's been kind of rough," said Christopher.

"Yeah?" I was trying simultaneously to stay cool and to memorize his exact words—*It's been kind of rough*—for when I told Fay about this later. "How come?"

"I mean, it's mostly fine," said Christopher. "He helps me with homework and stuff." (*And stuff.* Fay was going to like that.) "But sometimes he can get—"

"All right, little lambkins, let's take it from the *throw*-him-onto-the-ground!"

Fay gave Bottom a wimpy little shove to the chest. He windmilled his arms and fell exaggeratedly backward, landing in a sprawl. Daylily mimed a horrified scream.

"Good reaction, Desdemona! Aaand *freeze!*"

Bottom, Daylily, and Fay froze into a dramatic tableau—Bottom on the floor, Fay with her hands dangling limp-wristedly in midair, Daylily clasping her own open-mouthed face *Home Alone*–style.

It looked so fucking stupid. Theo snort-laughed, which made Christopher laugh, which made me laugh—I couldn't help it—which set off Fay into tableau-breaking giggles.

Wanda glared at me and Christopher. "If you're going to be a distraction to the players," she said tartly, "I'll go ahead and make this a closed rehearsal."

Christopher and I quickly shut up, exchanging a *yikes* look.

"Aaand *unfreeze*," said Wanda. "Now Iago begins to beat his slave."

"Do I have a whip?" Fay asked.

"No props," said Wanda. "This is all pantomime."

"Do I have a pantomime whip?"

"What about me?" asked Bottom. "Am I just taking it, or . . ."

Theo snorted again at the double entendre of "just taking it." To avoid laughing again, I turned toward the wall and buried my face in my hands. I heard some shuffling, and then Fay whispering a whipping noise: "Whi-*tshew!* Whi-*tshew!*"

"No sound effects, please. Would you mind removing your scarf?"

"But I need it to get into character."

"I'm afraid it's hindering your movement."

"I'll just untie it. Oops, I dropped my whip."

"Ah, yes, good continuity."

I turned back around to see Fay picking up her invisible whip from the floor. As she knelt, her jeans slid down her butt, exposing the plain black band of her underpants. We were living in the age of low-rise jeans, so that was a fairly ordinary sight. Still, it wasn't every day that I had an excuse to just gaze at Fay. That was a major reason I crashed her rehearsals.

"No offense," said Christopher in an undertone. He was still perching on the arm of the armchair beside me. "But your girlfriend has a nice butt."

I tore my eyes away from Fay's ass. "She's not my girlfriend," I said flatly.

"Really?" Christopher sounded surprised—maybe disappointed. "Theo was so sure."

(I wouldn't tell Fay about that part.)

"Are you ready, Othello?" asked Wanda.

Bottom was still stage-frozen in a crumple on the floor, Daylily stage-frozen above him in a pose of helpless concern. But I wasn't thinking about Bottom anymore.

It was easy to lose sight of in the gay tornado that was my friendship with Fay, but I was the only openly queer kid at Idlewild. I was stuck being gay even when it was no fun—even when it meant being undateable, unkissable, stumbling around under the weight of a crush I couldn't talk about. Still, I'd never consciously wished for a platonic gay friend, or for more openly gay kids at Idlewild. Right up until this moment, sharing the armchair with Christopher, I'd never thought of myself as lonely.

"Ready," said Bottom. "Once more unto the breach, dear friends."

Fay lifted her whip hand. Getting into character, Bottom narrowed his eyes, clenched his jaw, twisted his face into a mask of noble suffering. He really was an amazing actor.

F&N, 2002

Another opening, another show! It is 7:40 on Thursday evening—
T minus twenty minutes—and the sweat-musky pizza-greasy Thursday
night cast is jam-packed squirming and squealing into the Meetinghouse
Loft rehearsal room. On the ground floor beneath us, filing into the
Meetinghouse and filling the wooden benches, are our parents and our
teachers and perhaps even some of our classmates if we're lucky (but
the Thursday night cast is never lucky). We want to sneak out and try
to catch a glimpse of them from the creaky wood stairs, but if Wanda
catches us doing so, she will shout at us. She is shouting at us anyway.
"Will you stop singing for one bloody moment?" she is shouting specifically at us, the F&N unit, because we the F&N unit are bashing
randomly upon the keys of the piano while belting at the top of our
lungs: *"Four weeks, you rehearse and rehearse! Three weeks and it couldn't
be worse! One week—will it ever be right? Then out of the HAT it's THAT
BIG FIRST NIGHT!"*

We cannot contain ourselves, not when we look and sound and *are* so
marvelous. We're already in costume: F in an olive-green military uniform
accessorized with her slate-blue scarf; N in a sensible pinstripe skirt suit;
Bottom shirtless in ripped jeans, with his military uniform stashed backstage for a quick change; Daylily in a frilly white dress that does not have
a hoopskirt because Wanda could not procure one in time. Juniper, who
is not in the Thursday night cast, has volunteered to do everyone's stage
makeup. She sits at a makeshift makeup table that is already a powdery
Ground Zero and applies blush-eyeshadow-lipstick to the pleasure-flushed
faces of girls and boys alike. We the F&N unit already have our makeup
on. Our cheeks are dusty, our eyelashes sticky, our lips waxy. We take

lipsticky little sips of bottled water and then make Juniper retouch us just to be on the safe side.

"Does anyone want to join us in the Coffeepot warm-up?" Bottom calls out from the corner of the room, where he and Daylily have been performing noisy vocal exercises for the last half hour.

"It's from RADA," says Daylily.

"What's RADA?" no one asks, because Daylily and Bottom have been seizing every opportunity to name-drop the fancy Shakespeare camp they attended in London last summer. They have repeatedly attempted to teach the Coffeepot warm-up to the rest of us, but no one gives a shit. Now the two of them chant it alone.

"*All* I *want* is a *proper*-cup-of-coffee, *made* in a proper-copper-coffeepot! I—*may*—be *off* my *dot*, but I *want*-a-cup-of-coffee-in-a-proper-copper-*pot*! *Tin* coffeepots and *iron* coffeepots—*they* are *not* for *me!* If I *cahn't* have a proper-cup-of-coffee-in-a-proper-copper-coffeepot I'll have—no I won't— well, I may—let me think—yes-I-*will*-I'll-have-a-proper-cup-of-*tea!*"

"Or a hot apple cider, as the case may be," Bottom adds, raising his Starbucks cup.

Even though they're not in the Thursday night cast, Theo and Christopher are here too, for moral support and free pizza. Theo says to Christopher, "I told you he was gonna do the hot-apple-cider thing."

"He does it every time," Christopher agrees.

"Twenty bucks. Pay up."

"But we didn't make a bet."

"I know. This is unrelated. I just want you to give me twenty bucks."

Just for fun, they've let Juniper do their makeup too. Juniper has given Theo the *Clockwork Orange* look: heavy black makeup on just one eye, with spider legs of lower lashes drawn on in black eyeliner. Christopher's face is covered in glitter, some of which has somehow spread to Theo's face as well (!). The boys shimmer like a disco ball at the center of the room.

"I'm not giving you twenty bucks," says Christopher.

"Okay, fine. Fifty bucks."

"No."

"A hundred bucks. Ten bucks. Nothing. It's free."

Wanda swoops in. "My little lambkins!" she cries. "Five minutes to curtain! Let's all form a circle!"

We all form a circle, or a warped approximation thereof, lining the perimeter of the room.

"Go round the circle," says Wanda, "and shout your favorite line from the play!"

Gleefully, the circle ripples with a string of shouted Shakespeare, mostly of the profane or accidentally profane variety.

"Help, ho!"

"Strumpet, I come!"

"Villainous whore!"

"This is my butt!"

"He says he will return incontinent!"

"Hot, hot, and moist!"

"Pish!"

"Holla!"

"O BLOODY PERIOD!" (That's a cast favorite, and such a reliable giggle trigger that Wanda has wisely cut it from the actual performance.)

Daylily, humorlessly: "Come, how wouldst thou praise me?"

Bottom, gazing at her: "If heaven would make me such another world / Of one entire and perfect chrysolite, / I'd not have sold her for it."

Juniper: "No, I will speak as liberal as the north!"

F: "I LAY WITH CASSIO LATELY!"

N: "It doth abuse your bosom!"

Christopher: "My leg is cut in two!"

Theo: "And will as tenderly be led by the nose / As *asses* are!"

With that, we come full circle.

"Let's all join hands," says Wanda.

We all join hands—hot, hot, and moist indeed.

Wanda's voice hushes to a near-whisper. "The hour is upon us," she says. "We're about to achieve something special. Something *extraordinary*. I don't say this every year, but I truly believe it now: this is going to be the best production in the history of Idlewild."

Chills run through our costumed bodies. We believe it too.

"Let's have a quick silence," says Wanda. "I'll pass round a squeeze."

We close our eyes and wait. The squeeze comes to the F&N unit through Juniper, who squeezes the left hand of F, who squeezes the right hand of N, who squeezes the left hand of Christopher. In the ripe, humid silence, we imagine Christopher passing the squeeze to Theo. We imagine Theo kissing Christopher, Iago kissing Cassio, Othello kissing Iago, girls becoming boys who kiss boys who look like girls. We imagine how much the crowd is going to love us out there. We imagine how good we're about to be.

FAY

The Thursday night show was videotaped by an enterprising Idlewild parent, and copies were made available to the cast. Some years later, when I was working at Calvin's Cavern, I took advantage of the on-site facilities to transfer my VHS to DVD for digital posterity. It was a rare act of foresight on my part, one for which I'm grateful tonight as I insert the DVD into my laptop.

This is an indulgence I rarely allow myself. Revisiting the play always stirs up something intense and unnameable inside me, something I can't easily subdue. But whatever that thing is, it's already awake and agitated tonight. I may as well feed it.

The video quality is poor. Under stage lights, we are all so washed-out as to be nearly faceless. When the lights dim, we vanish into darkness. The carpeted, hard-angled Meetinghouse, designed for Silence rather than performance, muffled acoustics at the best of times; as picked up by a camcorder microphone, our footfalls upon the risers are thunderous, while the dialogue is often inaudible. The cameraman evinces a clear bias in favor of the underclassgirls, one of whom must be his daughter. During crowd scenes, the camera swings away from the principals and zooms in on the crowd of background actors, their lipsticked mouths forming wide black holes as they gaspingly emote in reaction to a scene we can't see.

But I've given up the pretense of watching the video for anything but glimpses of my seventeen-year-old self. She's difficult not only to see, but to watch. I flatter myself that she has a certain stage presence, but she doesn't engage with any of her fellow actors, not even Nell, to whom she is supposedly married. Fay-as-Iago doesn't touch Nell-as-Emilia, doesn't let Nell-as-Emilia touch her, doesn't even make eye contact as far as I can tell. You'd think this might be an acting choice on her part—after all, her Iago is a closeted homosexual—but if so, she's failed to infer that her Iago should transfer his erotic attentions to Othello or Cassio or even Roderigo. Instead she touches no one, stares right past everyone into the unseen audience, entirely wrapped up in her own performance.

And what a performance! It's a bizarre spectacle: mannered, false, narcissistic. The "gay" gestures, the wrist-flicks and head-tosses, are belabored and unnatural. The physical stillness reads as mere stiffness at best, nodded-out numbness at worst. And the voice, that horrible fried-out croak—I can scarcely bear to listen to it now. *Why are you talking like that?* I want to scream at her, except I know exactly why.

In Act III, the DVD begins to skip. In the middle of my scene 3 soliloquy, it freezes altogether. I remove the disc from the player, examine it for scratches, blow on it, rub it with a microfiber cloth. I Google *how to fix a skipping DVD* in case the answer has changed since my video store days. It has not. I reinsert the disc and try again. It freezes again at the same point—my face pixelated to featurelessness, my motion-blurred body paralyzed mid-gesture, my seventeen-year-old self humiliatingly stuck in time.

What do I remember, what can I convey, about the lived experience of putting on the play? Most lines were remembered; some were embarrassingly skipped or mangled. A missed entrance from Maddy would forever define the Thursday night performance in collective memory. The corner deli sold out of rose bouquets, purchased by supportive parents and presented after curtain call to various cast members, even freshman extras with no lines, who beamed radiantly with still-lipsticked mouths as they accepted their tribute. After the curtain fell on the Friday night performance, the juniors took the stage and, in an Idlewild tradition, bestowed a single red rose upon each graduating senior in alphabetical order by surname as the clock ticked past 11:00 p.m. and parental smiles in the audience grew increasingly strained. I was last. Then, just like that, it was over. Nothing would ever bring it back.

III

NELL

One Friday afternoon in early December, Fay and I were in her bedroom at her dad's apartment, doing our usual homoerotic reading of our English homework. The play had put us way behind on reading *Hamlet*, and I felt bad about it, even though Devi the Dove had given us an indefinite extension on our *Hamlet* essays. But Fay and I had finally gotten to the end. I remember that vividly, because the last scene of *Hamlet* was the most authentically homoerotic English homework we ever had.

"*O, I die, Horatio,*" Fay cried, flopping dramatically onto the Persian rug. "*The potent poison quite o'er-crows my spirit.*" She flailed around on the floor in such dramatic death throes that her *Hamlet* book flew out of her hand. In lieu of finishing her death speech, she gurgled and lolled out her tongue.

As Horatio, I knelt at her side, cradling her body in my left arm—I was brave enough to touch her only when we were in character—while holding my *Hamlet* book in my right hand. "*Now cracks a noble heart,*" I read in an exaggeratedly tearful voice. "*Good night, sweet prince!* Oh, Horatio definitely kisses him here, right?"

"Definitely," said Fay, her eyes still closed because she was dead.

I didn't kiss her, of course. "*Good night, sweet prince!*"—and then Horatio makes out with Hamlet's dead body, blah blah blah—"*And flights of angels sing thee to thy—*"

Fay's bedroom door opened. I froze in embarrassment. It was her dad's friend Gareth, holding the landline phone. "Telephone call for Miss—" he began, doing a funny butler voice, but then he took a look at us and waggled his eyebrows. "Am I interrupting something?"

"No." Fay came back to life and rolled out of my arm. "Who's calling?"

"It's for Miss Rifkin, actually," said Gareth. "Nell, it's your sainted mother."

The phone reception was terrible in Fay's basement bedroom, so I took the phone upstairs to the front door. "Hi, Mommy," I said. "We're in the middle of homework. Can I call you back?"

"You got a letter from Yale," my mom said.

My heart stopped. "Is it . . . ?"

"It's a small envelope," she said. "But that doesn't necessarily mean anything. Would you rather open it yourself?"

I thought about it. I was spending the night at Fay's, so I wouldn't be able to open the letter until tomorrow. Of course, I could change my plans and go home now. But I was having such a great time with Fay. But on the other hand, there was no way I could continue having a great time with Fay if I was stressing out about the letter from Yale.

I sighed. "Go ahead and open it."

"Are you sure?" My mom sounded disappointed. (When I look back on that call, it seems like a transparent attempt to make me cancel my sleepover and come home. Would it have killed her to let the letter sit for one day?) "I know it's not the same as opening it yourself—"

"No, I just want to know."

I heard paper tearing. There was a long silence.

"Mommy?"

"I'm reading it."

I was losing my mind. "Read it to *me!*"

"Ow! Don't yell at me."

Okay, so it was a rejection letter. I braced myself to cry.

"*Dear Nell,*" she read. "*The Admissions Committee has completed its early decision deliberations and has deferred a decision on your application until the spring.*"

My tears, like a failed sneeze, dissipated anticlimactically in the back of my throat. A deferral. Yale hadn't accepted me, but they hadn't rejected me, either. I could still get in. I just had to wait till spring to find out.

"I guess we should apply to other schools," said my mom. "I'm sorry, honey."

"It's okay," I said. In the moment, it felt like good news. Or at least not-bad news.

I hung up and went back to Fay's room. She was still on the floor, lying on her stomach now, surrounded by the spilled contents of my backpack; we'd kicked it around and made a mess during our *Hamlet* swordfight. "I'm playing with your calculator," she said. "It's so fancy."

"It's just a normal graphing calculator. You'd have one too if you took Calc." I sat cross-legged on the Persian rug. "I just got deferred from Yale."

Fay looked up from my calculator. "What does that mean?"

So I told her. I explained about early decision, and admitted that Yale was my dream school. Fay was outraged on my behalf. "They shouldn't lead you on like this," she said. "You should tell Yale to go fuck itself."

She was a great friend, I thought. I didn't deserve her.

"But where should I go instead?" I asked.

"Nowhere," said Fay. "By my calculations"—she'd gone back to playing with my calculator—"we shouldn't go to college at all. We should run away and join a pirate ship."

"Seriously, though," I said. "I have like three weeks to apply to other schools."

As I said it, I realized what I was sort of implying: we could go to college together. I'd never dared to consider that before. I'd been too hung up on the Yale thing. But suddenly I wanted to be with Fay even more than I wanted to go to Yale.

An image popped into my head: me and Fay holding hands in a rowboat. When my mom and I toured the Smith campus, I'd noticed a pond full of rowboats. Then I'd noticed one of the boats being rowed by a butch girl. Then I'd noticed another butch girl, and another, and I realized Smith was full of lesbians—*real* lesbians, not just the Schrödinger's lesbians I used to imagine when I looked at any random girl. Maybe, at Smith, Fay and I could be lesbians together.

Feeling a little exposed, I added, "What are your calculations?"

"Let me show you." She beckoned me closer.

I scooched across the rug and looked over her shoulder.

"Once there was a woman whose boobs weighed *sixty-nine* pounds," said Fay, hitting 69 on the calculator. "They were *too, too, too* big." She hit 222. "So she went to *Fifty-first* Street"—she hit 51—"to see *Dr. X*"—she hit the multiplication symbol—"who *ate* her boobs"—she hit 8—"and now that woman is . . ." She hit Enter. The screen showed 55378008. Fay turned the calculator upside down. "BOOBLESS."

I groaned. "I remember that one."

"Juniper Green taught it to me in middle school."

"So you're saying," I said, "I should apply to the BOOBLESS League. Brown . . . Oberlin . . . what other college begins with O?"

We riffed on the BOOBLESS League until the whole idea of college went back to feeling completely abstract, almost a joke, nothing to do with Fay and me.

My mom called Idlewild and arranged an emergency mother-daughter Deenie meeting that Sunday to discuss my Yale deferral.

On Sundays, real Quakers used the Meetinghouse to have real Quaker Meeting for Worship. My mom and I had to enter the building through the Sixteenth Street delivery entrance so as not to disturb the real Quakers. As we walked up the empty stairs, it occurred to me that I was the only student in the whole school.

Except I wasn't. When we turned the corner into the second-floor hallway, we ran into Bottom. He was with his mom too. They were standing right outside Deenie's office.

Bottom looked as surprised to see me as I was to see him. Unlike me, he remembered his manners quickly. "Fancy meeting you here," he said. "Mom, you know Nell. Have you met Mrs. Rifkin?"

I can't stress enough how weird and outside the norm it was to address someone else's parents by anything but their first name. Even "Ms. Rifkin" or "Dr. Rifkin" would have sounded fussy, pretentious, almost mocking— but "Mrs." was the worst possible choice. If any other kid had done it, my mom would have launched into a feminist lecture. But she had a soft spot for Bottom, so she just laughed. "For the love of God, call me Nancy," she said. "I'm not *quite* a hundred years old yet."

Bottom's mom extended her hand. "I'm Dr. Baptiste," she said, and I remembered that she was a history professor. She was a pretty lady who wore her hair in lots of little braids. Today the braids were gathered into a tidy bun, and she was dressed so formally, in a deep purple pantsuit and shiny matching lipstick, that I was a little embarrassed by my mom's jeans.

Bottom's mom gestured over her shoulder. At the other end of the hallway I saw Bottom's dad, a short, squat man in a business suit, talking on his cell phone. "I'd introduce you to my husband," she said, "but he's having a client emergency."

I could almost hear my mom chewing over why Bottom's mom had made such a point of introducing herself by her last name. To distract from the awkwardness, I piped up, "We'd love to meet him when he's done."

"Another time," said Bottom's mom. "Today he's in a bit of a hurry." She smiled tightly. "Even though he's the one holding us up," she said. "You know how dads are."

No, I did *not* know how dads were. That wasn't something I usually felt self-conscious about, but everything about this interaction was so confusing and uncomfortable, and this was one thing too many. I stepped away from the moms, leaving them to chat without my help, and made a show of studying the bulletin board. The Invert Society flier was still there.

Bottom came over to me. "What brings you to school on a Sunday?" he asked.

I kept my eyes on the flier. *Calling All Inverts, Perverts, and Omi-Palone . . .* "Emergency Deenie meeting," I said. "I got deferred from Yale."

"Yale?" Bottom perked up a bit. "I didn't know we had the same first choice."

I wondered if we were here for the same reason. "Did they defer you too?"

"No," he said. "I got in."

He said it unthinkingly, not in a braggy or smug way, but I could see how proud he was. Just for a second. Then his face crumpled up with worry, probably because of the look on *my* face.

"Oh, Nell, I'm so sorry," he said. "I didn't mean to—"

"No, no, it's totally fine," I said. "Congratulations. That's huge." I tried to smile at him, but I could barely fake it. Bottom had gotten into Yale, and I hadn't. It finally hit me—belatedly but hard—that my deferral was actually pretty bad news. It was a soft rejection, basically. Like getting cast in the ensemble.

Down the hallway, Bottom's dad whistled like a gym teacher. "Let's go!"

Ignoring his dad, Bottom looked earnestly into my eyes. "You're going to get in," he said. "We're going to be Yalies together and hang out all the time."

That confused me. Bottom and I were friendly with each other, but we weren't on "hang out" terms. Even the words sounded odd coming from him. I wondered if this was the residual cast-bonding effect of *Othello*.

Usually that kind of thing wore off after the play was over, but maybe this time it had stuck. Maybe Bottom and I were actual friends now.

His mom came up and clapped her hand on his shoulder. "You heard your dad," she said. "Let's get out of here."

Bottom hesitated. "Maybe you could leave without me," he said timidly, "and I could get lunch with Nell?"

Oh. We weren't friends—he just didn't want to go home.

"What a wonderful idea," my mom exclaimed, at the same time that Bottom's mom said, "I'm not gonna tell you again."

His dad marched past us. "I'll be waiting outside," he said brusquely. He didn't even acknowledge me or my mom.

Deflated, Bottom followed them down the stairs. I wondered why things were so tense between him and his parents. Weren't they proud he'd gotten into Yale? Maybe they couldn't afford it, I thought. Maybe their Deenie meeting was to discuss financial aid options. Then I wondered if it was racist of me to think that. Wasn't his dad a lawyer?

Deenie's office door opened. Deenie stuck out her platinum-blond head. "Nell, Nancy! Come on in." She smiled at me the way you'd smile at someone who'd just been diagnosed with something terminal, and once again I felt so sorry for myself I forgot about Bottom.

F&N, 2002

It's December eighteenth, the last Wednesday morning of the semester, and all of Idlewild knows what that means: the chorus is going a-caroling!

"You can just say 'caroling,'" says Ms. Spider.

Nope. Here we go a-caroling!—the whole Upper School chorus, all paltry nine of us, with our magnificent baritone section consisting of Bottom and Bottom alone. We will go a-caroling a cappella except for two handbells, which we the F&N unit are tasked with carrying—F gets the F bell, N the A bell—and striking periodically to keep ourselves on key.

"We used to have a C bell," Ms. Spider tells the underclassgirls, "but it broke."

We the F&N unit wisecrack in unison, "You should take it to *Bell*-vue Hospital!" and laugh as hard as we did when we made the same joke last year. We are giddy because the chorus has official permission to miss second period in order to go a-caroling. We are giddy because it's the last week of school before winter break. We are giddy because this Friday—the day after tomorrow!—Ms. Spider and Wanda will take us on our Senior Musical Theater Seminar field trip to Baz Luhrmann's *La Bohème* on Broadway.

F: "What does one wear to the opera?"

N: "Can I wear my T-shirt that looks like a tuxedo?"

"We'll discuss it in seminar," says Ms. Spider, because she doesn't want to make the underclassgirls jealous, even though making other people jealous is pretty much the whole point of going to Baz Luhrmann's *La Bohème* on Broadway.

The chorus sets out from the Meetinghouse Loft.

"Should we carol for Wanda first?" asks one of the junior altos as we pass Wanda and Ms. Spider's closed office. Wanda always loves it when we come a-caroling.

"I don't think she's in yet," Ms. Spider says and hurries us along.

We work our way down the creaky wood back stairs, a-caroling all the way. We exit through the Meetinghouse side door and stand a-caroling in the Peace Garden, our voices turning to steam in the cold. We go inside the main building and work our way up: a-caroling on the first floor outside Nurse Pat's office, a-caroling on the second floor outside Skip and Trudy and Deenie's offices, a-caroling on the third floor outside the library, a-caroling on the fourth floor outside the computer lab. Then we cross the fourth floor, a-caroling outside the Upper School classrooms to interrupt our classmates' English and history and French and Spanish and Latin and science and math. We work our way back downstairs, a-caroling outside the third floor Middle School classrooms, the second floor Lower School classrooms, the development office in the lobby, the gymnasium in the basement. Along the way, we are met with reactions running the full spectrum from revelry to rage. When we perceive that a teacher is particularly irked by the musical interruption, we make sure to linger and a-carol an extra carol, just for them.

We circle all of Idlewild and end up back in the Meetinghouse Loft.

"Let's carol for Wanda now!" says one of the sophomore sopranos.

"She's still not here," says Ms. Spider.

"Where is she?" the junior alto wonders. "She was out yesterday too."

"And the day before," says the other sophomore soprano.

"Let's circle the school one more time," says Ms. Spider.

Off we go a-caroling again! We sing songs in Latin—one that goes *Alle psallite cum luya*, another that goes *Psallite, unigenito, Christo Dei Filio, Psallite, Redemptori Domino, puerulo iacenti in praesepio*—and we don't know what we're saying, even those of us who take Latin, because this is *church* Latin, not school Latin, and Ms. Spider has beaten it into us that we must pronounce *iacenti* as *ya-CHEN-tee* rather than the *ya-KEN-tee* upon which Mr. Prins would insist. We are dimly aware that we are singing about Jesus, and under normal circumstances most Idlewilders, being a motley mix of Jews and Buddhists and atheists and Jewish atheists and Buddhist Jews, would object to such enforced Christianity in any context other than spring semester of freshman English when we're all forced to read the New Testament—but today we are glad to lift our voices in praise of baby Jesus. *Gloria in excelsis deo! Gloria hosanna in excelsis! Psallite*, whatever that means! Bottom's baritone holds us up like a mahogany throne. F's soprano skates over it like a blade on ice. N's alto flows into the gaps like bitter gold tree sap. At the end of each song, we the F&N unit flick our wrists and our handbells go *bell!* and we discover, every time, that we have somehow crept up at least a half step sharp of the key in which we began. We try to stay on pitch for the next song, but we're too excited and our voices carry us up, up, up every time.

We circle all of Idlewild, again, and end up back in the Meetinghouse Loft, again. Wanda's office door is still closed.

"Sorry, gang," says Ms. Spider, leading us back into the rehearsal room. "Looks like she's not coming in today."

The bell rings, heralding the end of second period. The chorus disperses, leaving the F&N unit alone with Ms. Spider in the rehearsal room.

Exhausted from all those stairs, Ms. Spider lowers herself wincingly onto the piano bench. "I'm not supposed to tell you this," she says, rubbing her knees through her long woolen skirt. "But I'm about to retire and I don't give a damn." She grimaces. "Wanda got fired."

We the F&N unit gasp and bombard Ms. Spider with plaintive *Why?*s. Ms. Spider won't tell us.

N: "What about *La Bohème*?"

"Don't worry, I'm still taking you," says Ms. Spider. "Wanda won't be joining us, that's all."

F: "What about the musical?"

"I'll direct it myself," says Ms. Spider. "I've already agreed to it."

We the F&N unit breathe a sigh of relief. Then our breath quickens as the implication dawns on us: with Wanda's influence removed, and Ms. Spider in charge of casting, we the F&N unit are all but guaranteed starring roles. We feel guilty getting excited about this—we wouldn't have wished for it to happen exactly this way—but we can't help ourselves.

F: "Have you chosen a show yet?"

"I'm considering a few," says Ms. Spider.

N: "Come on, you can tell us which!"

"Like hell I can." Ms. Spider looks at the clock. "Fay, I'd like a word with you. Do you have class now?"

We the F&N unit hesitate, reluctant to be parted before we've had a chance to discuss this new development.

F: "No. I have a free." (This is a lie. F has French.) "But Nell has Latin." (This is true.)

N: "It's okay. Mr. Prins won't mind if I'm late." (This is very much a lie.)

"Yes, he will," says Ms. Spider, not fooled. "Run along, Nell."

N: [to F] "Come to my Latin classroom the second you're free, okay, boss?"

F: "I'll wait at the door."

N: "No, Mr. Prins will notice. Wait for me down the hall and I'll pretend I'm going to the bathroom at . . . how about eleven-thirty?"

F: [to Ms. Spider] "Will I be out of here by then?"

"For the love of Pete," says Ms. Spider. "You girls can't survive apart for forty-five minutes?"

The bell rings again.

"And now you're late for Latin," says Ms. Spider. "If Mr. Prins sends you to StuDisc, don't come crying to me."

N, hurrying out the door: "Eleven-thirty?"

F: "Eleven-thirty!"

FAY

The rehearsal room door swung shut behind Nell, leaving me and Ms. Spider alone together. She peered up at me from the piano bench. Her face softened. "Talk to me, kiddo," she said. "What's eating you these days?"

I was surprised that she'd noticed. Even Nell hadn't noticed. It was typical, of course, to experience an emotional crash after finishing a play, especially if that play was the final fall play of one's high school career. But the depth of my post-*Othello* grief had caught me off guard.

I was still (right then, and every day) wearing my slate-blue scarf. I twisted the fringes around my fingers, a bad habit that created intractable knots. "I miss the play," I admitted. "I miss playing Iago." Embarrassed, I added, "I'll get over it when the musical starts up."

"That's exactly what I wanted to discuss with you." Ms. Spider turned to the piano keyboard, flexed her fingers, and struck a low G chord. "Let me hear you sing some scales."

I sang five notes up and down the G scale: "*Mah-ah-ah-ah-AH-ah-ah-ah-ahhh.*" I did it again in G-sharp, in A, and so on, until the middle C scale brought me to G4, the key Ms. Spider had identified as my "break" between high and low register. Then she paused, her hands posed above the keyboard, and looked up at me gravely.

"Do you hear yourself, Fay?" she asked. "Your low register is wrecked."

My throat ached from the strain of the low scales. I didn't respond.

"I know playing Iago was important to you," she said. "So I let it slide during the play. But, Fay, you *can't* keep pushing down your speaking voice anymore. You're killing your voice. *Killing* it. You're undoing everything I've taught you."

The ache in my throat sharpened. *I didn't know I was still doing it*, I thought of saying—but that would have been a lie, and Ms. Spider would have seen through it. I'd been waiting and waiting for the altered version of my voice to come automatically; it never did. No amount of practice could make it anything but effortful, false. Unnatural.

"If you go on like this," said Ms. Spider, "sooner or later you won't be able to sing at all."

This possibility had never occurred to me. I turned away from the piano and stared out the window at the winter-bare Peace Garden below. From this bird's-eye view I saw, on the ground amid the ivy, two clear plastic cups—the empty Frappuccino cups that Nell and I had kicked into the ivy on the morning of the 9/11 anniversary.

Behind me, Ms. Spider spoke softly. "I'd like to give you a lead in the musical," she said. "You and Nell, of course. I know you want that too. That's why I'm being so blunt with you."

I nodded, still unable to turn and face her. "I appreciate it," I managed to say. My voice came out small and delicate, the voice of a mouse, or a child, or that child's paper doll.

I left the Meetinghouse Loft, or rather my body did, a body from which I found myself vertiginously untethered except at the scalp, which prickled oddly all over, as if with static electricity. I felt flayed, vivisected by Ms. Spider's words. Yes, I wanted the lead in the musical. I had not been conscious, until Ms. Spider brought it to my attention, of another, incompatible desire; nor of how relentlessly I had been trying and failing to satisfy it; nor of how obvious both the desire and the failure were to the world. How many others had noticed? Had Nell?

It was only seven minutes past eleven. Not knowing what else to do with myself, I ascended to the fourth floor, intending to wait for Nell on the stair landing. It was on this stair landing that I ran into Deenie Mellman, the Idlewild college counselor. I tried to do an about-face and pretend I hadn't seen her, but I was too late. "Fay," said Deenie. "I really need to meet with you. Are you free right now?"

Under other circumstances, I might have been able to improvise an answer that would get me out of an impromptu Deenie meeting without letting on that I was really supposed to be in French class. But as it was, I could only follow her helplessly down two flights of stairs into her office.

She closed the door behind us. The small room smelled unpleasantly of perfume, or some other synthetic source of feminine fragrance. Was it meant to evoke a flower? A fruit? I wondered why women were always cloaking themselves, catlike, in the scent of another species. Then I wondered if I, in declining to do so, smelled unpleasant to women. Or to everyone.

"Take a seat," she said. I did so, on a spindly plastic chair, and she sat across from me at her desk. I hadn't been inside this office in nearly a year, though I was supposed to have been meeting with Deenie on a monthly basis since then. I'd imagined that Deenie barely noticed my absence, or even that it came as a relief to her. This was, judging by her frazzled affect right now, yet another error of wishful thinking on my part.

"Knowing you, I'm guessing you're on top of things," she said, "but I just wanted to check in. Have you mailed in your applications yet?"

I shook my head, reluctant to speak and subject myself to the shrillness of my natural voice.

"Well," she said, "regular decision deadlines are just a few weeks away, so you should get on that as soon as you can. Have you finalized your list?"

Stalling, I stared at her as though I didn't understand the question.

"Of schools," she said, impatience tightening her voice. "How many schools are on your list?"

I paused, as if counting in my head, though I was only preparing myself to speak aloud. "Zero," I said. Was that my real voice? I could no longer remember.

She laughed. "Zero? You don't plan on applying anywhere?" She said it teasingly, as though this could only be a joke interpretation of what I'd said. "You didn't visit a single school you liked?"

"I didn't visit any schools." I might have been overcorrecting now, pushing my voice too high. Or was it supposed to be even higher?

It dawned on Deenie that I was serious. "Okay," she said. She shuffled some papers on her desk, anxiously imposing order where she could. "I do encourage school visits, because it's hard to know the character of a school unless you see it for yourself. But if you already know your preferences . . ." She regarded me pleadingly.

If I could have thrown her a bone, I would have. Boneless, I shrugged. "I haven't really thought about it." Even my accent, the elongated diphthong of *thought*, sounded foreign in my own ears. "I've been busy with the play."

"Jesus," Deenie muttered. She inhaled, exhaled. "That's right," she said. "You're involved in theater." Shifting briskly into damage control mode, she pulled open a file cabinet and began to riffle through it. "Have you looked into any conservatory programs? You still have time to schedule an audition at—let's see—Tisch at NYU. Or Steinhardt, for singing."

A wave of nausea crashed through me. "Singing?" I said. "I don't know if . . ." I trailed off, not sure what it was I didn't know.

Deenie pulled out a folder with my name on it. "I have it here," she said, studying a document I couldn't see, "that you're interested in film. Do you want me to make you a list of schools with strong film programs?" Without waiting for my answer, she began to scribble on a notepad. "I'm putting Yale on your 'reach' list. As for midrange, I think you'd be right at home at Clark . . . or American University . . . and have you heard of Pitzer? And on your 'likely' list I'm putting Occidental. It doesn't have a film program, but . . ." She glanced up at me hopefully. "Can you see yourself living in LA?"

I tried. The image that came to mind was a picture-postcard pastiche— palm trees, the Hollywood sign, surfers and smoothies and sunsets (see *Weetzie Bat*, Francesca Lia Block, 1989)—with an empty silhouette at the center where I should be, like the outline of a corpse in a crime scene. "No," I said.

"Okay. Where *do* you see yourself? A big city like New York? A rural campus? A small liberal arts school, or a preprofessional one?" She was talking fast now, trying to make up for a year's worth of lost time. "Can you see yourself in any of those environments?"

I tried again. In the city, on the farm, on the leafy campus and in the slick modern video lab, in the lesbian commune and at the frat house rager, the empty silhouette floated in my place.

Up till then I had never been forced to confront my own inability—an inability so total it bordered on the neurological—to picture myself as an adult. I couldn't fathom being anything other than what I currently was. I couldn't be what I currently was anywhere other than at Idlewild.

"Um." My voice sounded, if possible, even higher than before. "I guess I haven't really thought about it."

She laughed, a little hysterically. "Well," she said, "it's time to start, girl!"

That was the precise moment at which I decided I hated Deenie Mellman. I resolved to make myself so disagreeable that she'd lose her temper with me, thus validating my dislike of her and everything she stood for. "I don't *have* to do anything," I said. "I don't even have to be here." I stood up so abruptly I almost knocked over my spindly chair. "I have better things to do."

In my memory, I see Deenie rearing up and reddening with imperious outrage. But in all probability she was merely blushing, as anyone would from the stress of navigating my needless hostility. I wince to recall this now. The poor woman was only trying to do her job.

"Fay, honey," she said. "You're running out of time."

I fled Deenie's office and ran up the stairs, so disembodied by existential panic that I couldn't even guess at my own facial expression. It was now twenty-eight minutes past eleven; Nell would emerge from her Latin classroom at any moment. Heading for the girls' bathroom, hoping to examine and modify my expression in the mirror, I turned a corner and found myself face-to-face with Theo Severyn.

Oddly enough, Theo and I had never spoken to each other without an intermediary. There had always been Nell and Christopher, or his underclassgirl entourage, or at the very least Wanda. Being double-cast in the same role, we had never even interacted onstage. For all I thought about him, Theo Severyn was a near-stranger to me. It was for this reason that I passed him without bothering to rearrange my facial expression, as one might weep openly on a crowded street.

Behind me, he spoke. "Hey."

I kept walking, pretending not to hear him.

"Don't worry, I'm not gonna ask you what's wrong because I don't give a shit." He was following me down the hall. "I just wanted to say, that caroling thing was *really* annoying."

I turned around. The two of us faced each other in the middle of the empty hallway. He seemed different, somehow, without Christopher beside him—calmer, slightly gentler, no longer vibrating with clownish energy. In his charcoal-black peacoat and camel tartan scarf, he looked almost elegant. His eyes were fixed on me, but there was a certain heavy-lidded chill to them, a bored detachment where one might expect concern or discomfort. This convinced me, more than his words did, that he truly didn't care about my distress. I relaxed.

"That was the idea," I said. I noticed that he held in his hands a clear plastic take-out box containing what appeared to be a slice of cake. "Is that your breakfast," I asked, raising my eyebrows, "or your lunch?"

"Look," said Theo. "Sometimes you just need a tiramisu." There was something faintly effeminate about his pronunciation of *tiramisu*, or perhaps it was the inherent effeminacy of a fifteen-year-old boy buying himself a single serving of tiramisu in the middle of the school day. He popped open the box's clamshell lid to show off the cocoa-dusted contents. "They sell them at the café on Fifteenth and Irving."

"Did you cut class," I asked, beginning to smile, "to buy yourself a tiramisu at eleven a.m.?"

"What, are you on StuDisc or something?" He transferred the open tiramisu box into his right hand. With his left, he reached into the pocket of his peacoat. "I dislike you, like, twenty percent less than I dislike most people," he said. "So I'm gonna teach you a trick to get out of class whenever you want, no questions asked."

From his coat pocket he produced a stick of Burt's Bees lip balm. He uncapped it with his teeth and spat the yellow plastic cap into the open box of tiramisu—a gesture so boyishly disgusting I couldn't help admiring it.

He held out the open stick of lip balm toward me. "Touch it," he said, "and then touch under your eye."

"Yeah, no," I said. As much as I was enjoying my first-ever conversation with Theo Severyn, I was not about to fall for what seemed like a transparent prank. "Nice try."

"What, you don't trust me?" He laughed. "Okay, good instinct. But this is for real. Check it out."

He raised the stick of lip balm to his eyes and swiped it under each eye, as though applying invisible eyeblack. He blinked rapidly. His eyes reddened and began to glisten with tears.

"It's the peppermint fumes," he said, his voice trembling. "It's good for, like, three minutes of crying." He held out the lip balm to me once again, looking for all the world as though he were overcome with emotion. A single tear ran down his face.

I touched a fingertip to the slick disc of pearl-white wax, then touched the soft skin below my left eye. My eye began to sting, and then to water so copiously that I had to close it in order to see the proffered lip balm. I touched the wax again and applied it beneath my right eye, which promptly began to water as well.

"If you're sneaky about it," said Theo, through sniffles, "you can really freak out your teachers. Or get out of trouble. Or"—my vision was so blurry with tears that I couldn't see his face, but from his voice, I knew he was smiling—"audition for a play and get the Friday night lead."

"You little *fucker*," I said and let out a laugh that sounded like a sob. The menthol-induced tears were functioning as a surprisingly effective release, as though I were really crying, but even better because the context absolved me from shame. There was something oddly intimate about doing this with Theo, the two of us laughing together with peppermint tears streaming down our faces, alone in the fourth-floor hallway.

We were alone, that is, until a classroom door opened at the other end of the hall. It was the door to the Latin classroom.

Blinking away tears, I ran down the hall, down the stairs, away from Theo. Away from Nell. Later, I would tell her I'd been waylaid by my impromptu Deenie meeting, and while that was a lie, I wasn't sure what the truth was. All I knew was that, in that instant, I was afraid to let Nell see me.

NELL

I ran like hell and made it to my Latin class just one minute late. We had a pop quiz, but luckily Mr. Prins hadn't finished handing it out, and I got to my desk just in time to start it along with everyone else. It was a twenty-minute pop quiz, because Mr. Prins didn't fuck around. I translated sentences from the *Aeneid* and tried not to think about why Wanda had been fired.

After the quiz, it was time for our Wednesday group exercise. "Get into your groups," said Mr. Prins in his usual robotic drone. "Turn to today's *Aeneid* passage and identify as many different ablative forms as you can. Whichever team finds the most ablatives will win . . ." (The class perked up.) ". . . nothing." (The class deflated.)

There was a brief pandemonium of desks screeching across the floor as the class broke into three-person clusters. My group was Bottom and Juniper. (Daylily, like Fay, took French.) "Howdy, partners," I said, scooching my desk around to face them.

"Partners in Latin," said Bottom, "as in crime." He flipped through his *Aeneid* book.

Juniper opened her book too, but instead of looking at it, she leaned urgently across her desk. "Do you guys know what's up with Wanda?" she asked, in what she must have thought was a hushed voice. "Like, where is she? Last night I left her a voicemail, but she didn't call back, and she *always* calls me back. I'm starting to freak out."

Bottom shook his head, eyes on his book. "I haven't the faintest."

I was psyched to be the one with the insider info. That almost never happened to me. "You don't know?" I said, really milking it. "I can't believe you haven't heard."

"What?" Juniper's eyes bugged. "What? Tell me!"

With relish, I said, "She got fired."

Juniper gasped so loudly, our classmates turned to look. Without looking up from the quizzes he was grading, Mr. Prins said, "I assume you're gasping at the abundance of ablative forms on display in the *Aeneid*."

"Yes, Mr. Prins," Juniper chirped. She leaned even farther across her desk and made a good faith effort to lower her voice. "Are you sure? How do you know?"

"Ms. Spider told me."

Juniper was puzzled. "Who?"

"That's what Nell and Fay call Dorothy Schneider," said Bottom. He picked up his pencil and underlined something in his book. "Because it rhymes with Schneider, right?"

"And because she looks scary," I said, "but secretly she's—"

"But *why* was Wanda fired?" Juniper interrupted. "She's taught here for years. What happened?"

"I think it's an ablative of material," said Bottom, raising his voice slightly.

I looked over my shoulder and saw that Mr. Prins had paused his grading to stare suspiciously at us. Quickly, I flipped the pages of my *Aeneid* book. "I can never remember the difference," I ad-libbed, "between ablative of material and ablative of instrument."

"It's a little tricky," said Bottom. "But ablative of material usually has a preposition."

Mr. Prins, hearing this, nodded approvingly and went back to grading quizzes.

Juniper looked at me and made a desperate arm-flailing *tell-me-or-I'll-explode* gesture. Just to torture her, I asked Bottom, "Does ablative of material always have a preposition?"

"Usually," said Bottom. "Not always."

"When would you use it without a preposition?" I actually knew that one, but Juniper was literally writhing in her seat, and the temptation to drag it out was too strong.

"I think there's an example in here, actually," said Bottom. "Let me find it."

He studied his *Aeneid* book. Minutes ticked by. Juniper was bouncing her knee so frantically I could feel the vibrations in my chair. Finally she cracked. "But who's gonna direct the musical?"

I grinned. I couldn't help it. "Ms. Spider," I said. "I mean, Dorothy."

Juniper's face went sour, just as I'd hoped it would. She knew exactly what this meant. She and Daylily never took Chorus. They couldn't sing for shit and they had no relationship with Ms. Spider, at least not the way Fay and I did. They were almost certainly going to lose out on the leads.

"This is so fucked-up," said Juniper. "What did Wanda even do? I mean, what was she accused of?"

It was a good question. I had a theory about it, but I felt a little awkward saying it in front of Bottom. "I don't know," I said quietly. "But I'm wondering if maybe it had to do with that prologue."

Bottom looked up from his book. "What do you mean?" he asked.

I was hoping I wouldn't have to spell it out. "Well," I said, "some people might have thought it was maybe a little . . ." I couldn't bring myself to say *racist*. "Offensive."

"How was it offensive?" said Juniper sharply, straightening in her chair like she had a whole speech prepared about why it actually wasn't offensive. She probably did.

"It certainly didn't offend me," said Bottom, with a chuckle.

"Well, obviously not," said Juniper. "You're smart." Contemplatively, she rolled her sparkly turquoise Gelly Roll pen between her fingers. "But you know who's not smart? Skip and Trudy."

"Yeah," I said, though I didn't really have anything against Skip and Trudy.

"And I could totally see them misunderstanding Wanda's vision," said Juniper. "Because it's not politically correct or whatever."

"Now that you mention it," said Bottom, "I do remember noticing them in the audience during the show. They were in the front row, so I could see their faces. They looked very disapproving." He hung his head self-deprecatingly. "I was afraid it was my performance."

Juniper swatted him affectionately on the upper arm. "Shut up! You were amazing."

"But I think your theory is absolutely right." Bottom smiled at her. "I always knew you were a genius."

Juniper sighed. "Fuck," she said. "I'm so pissed off. I hate political correctness."

"Ablative of instrument," said Bottom.

I looked over my shoulder. "It's okay," I said. "Mr. Prins isn't listening to us."

"No, there's an actual ablative of instrument here. *Quibus.*" Bottom touched the page of my book, pointing out the word.

"But doesn't *quibus* refer to a person?"

"Sure," said Bottom. "A person can be used as an instrument."

I was about to make a blowjob joke when my eye caught the time on my digital watch: 11:33. I stood up. "I have to go to the bathroom," I said.

"You don't need to, like, *announce* it," Juniper muttered. She was clearly still furious about the musical. It was so gratifying.

I opened the classroom door and stepped out into the hallway. But Fay wasn't there. Theo Severyn, of all people, was standing where Fay was supposed to be.

"Hey," I said. "Have you seen Fay?"

It was only as I said it that I noticed, belatedly, what he was doing: literally just standing there, alone. It was unusual to see him without Christopher, but that wasn't the only weird thing. Usually Theo was a hyperactive whirlwind, always fidgeting and jumping around and shredding things with his hands. Right now, though, he was standing completely still, staring down the hallway like a sniper. (That was the analogy that popped into my head, because it was December 2002 and the D.C. sniper had been in the news.)

When he turned toward me, his eyes looked completely dead. Just for a second. But then he laughed, his face lighting up in a familiar way, and the uncanny effect vanished so fast I wasn't sure I'd really seen it. "Wow," he said. "You're obsessed with her."

"No, she said she'd meet me here."

"Don't be defensive," he said. "Christopher's obsessed with me the same way. It's fun." As he walked away, he called out over his shoulder, "I haven't seen her."

I waited there for a couple of minutes, but Fay never came.

F&N, 2002

In sixth period Chorus, via handwritten notes, we the F&N unit agree to cancel today's Invert Society meeting. As soon as the bell rings for Activity Period, we hightail it not to the library but to the computer lab.

Through the glass door of his office, we see Jimmy Frye the IT guy hunched at his desk, eating some kind of big drippy sandwich. We knock furiously.

F&N, shouting in unison: "What happened with Wanda?"

From the other side of the glass door comes Jimmy's muffled voice. "Beat it."

We the F&N unit turn the doorknob and burst SWAT-style into the IT office. Jimmy bellows in protest, but he can't rise to stop us: he has a Blimpie sandwich wrapper spread open on his lap, the paper damp and precarious with crumbs and scraps.

F&N, in unison, again: "What happened with Wanda?"

"I'm not kidding," says Jimmy. "The Jimmy shop is closed for business."

We dive-bomb his desk, seizing his computer mouse.

F: "How do we access the email system?"

N: "Hey, what's this file? Asian-porn-dot-AVI? I'm gonna open it."

"Nice try." Jimmy reaches for a napkin to wipe off his hands and reclaim his computer. "That's not a real file I have."

N, hitting command-shift-N to create a new folder: "It is now."

"Oh, grow up," says Jimmy. "Step away from the desk and I'll tell you the truth."

We the F&N unit step away from the desk and regard him expectantly. Jimmy crumples up his sandwich paper and drops it in a nearby trash can.

He rises, brushing crumbs off his lap, and goes to the door—to close it, we the F&N unit assume, so as to soundproof the room.

"The truth is," Jimmy says, "you blew it. I'm not in the mood today, or ever again." He points out the door, into the empty computer lab, and fixes us with a stern glare. "Scram."

So it's one of those days. We the F&N unit switch tacks.

N: "Sorry, Jimmy. We just got excited."

F: "Can we take you out to Joe Junior?"

"That's not gonna work this time," says Jimmy. "Get the hell out of my office, or I'm calling Trudy."

With astonishment, we realize he's serious.

F: "Wait, time-out."

N: "Are you really mad at us?"

"You're damn right I'm mad at you," says Jimmy. "I put my ass on the line to get you all that dirt on Theo Severyn, and how did you repay me? You ditched me at Joe Junior with no goodbye. Did you even *thank* me?"

F: "Didn't we?"

N: "I meant to."

"You haven't even swung by to say hi since then," says Jimmy. "You know, I've always considered us friends. But friends don't treat each other the way you've treated me."

We the F&N unit have no idea what to say, so we say nothing at all. He waves us out and shuts the glass door in our faces.

We the F&N unit look at each other, flummoxed.

N: "Well, *we* can still go to Joe Junior."

F: "Yeah, I need a milkshake after that."

But we make it down only one flight of stairs. On the third-floor landing, the library door swings open, and out walk Theo Severyn and Christopher Korkian. They're negative images of each other: Theo in his charcoal peacoat and camel-colored scarf, Christopher in a camel-colored trench coat and black scarf.

"*There* they are," says Theo, seeing us.

"Where have you been?" says Christopher. "We've been waiting for you."

Still disoriented from our Jimmy Frye encounter, we the F&N unit blink.

"What?" says Theo. "I thought you were looking for new members."

"There are confusing fliers about it all over school," says Christopher. "Like that one." He points to the bulletin board on the wall behind us.

We turn to look. Our flier is faded now, the bottom half obscured by a more recent flier tacked over it to advertise the Lower School gift wrap fundraiser. But the top half is still visible, the words still legible, just barely, in rainbow ink and loopy Party LET lettering.

Calling All Inverts, Perverts, and Omi-Palone:
Fay Vasquez-Rabinowitz and Nell Rifkin cordially invite you to join
THE INVERT SOCIETY

"Did you change the location?" Christopher asks.

"Or maybe," says Theo—is that a flash of mischief in his face?—"you don't actually want new members?"

We the F&N unit bristle.

F: "Why would you think that?"

N: "It's a real club."

F: "We're just highly selective."

N: "Yeah, there's an extensive application process."

"Well," says Theo, "we want to apply."

We the F&N unit exchange a panicked glance. We have never prepared for this scenario. We have no introductory speech, no secret handshake, no initiation rite. We don't even have an excuse, off the top of our shared head, to turn away prospective new members.

What can we do? We lead Theo and Christopher into the library. For authoritative height, F climbs and sits on the bookshelf stepladder. N settles into a heavy wooden chair. Theo and Christopher take chairs as well, placing their backpacks on a nearby table.

F: "I call this meeting of the Invert Society to order."

N: "Roll call! President Fay?"

F: "Present."

N: "President Nell? Present. Okay, that concludes the roll call."

"What the hell?" says Theo. "We're right here."

F: "We'll get to that."

N: "It's on the gay agenda."

"Oh my god," says Theo. "I don't even care about your bitch-ass gay club. I just wanted to ask you why Wanda got fired."

We didn't see that coming. Juniper Green is a notorious gossip, but she must have spread this story all over school in under three hours, which has to be a new record.

"Yeah, we've heard," says Theo. He hops onto the table, pushing our backpacks out of his way, and perches on the edge of it. "Tell us what you know."

"Is it true," says Christopher, "that Skip and Trudy thought *Othello* was racist? Even though race didn't exist yet when Shakespeare wrote it?"

It appears that the story has mutated somewhat in the telling.

N: "Christopher, this is obviously about the prologue."

F: "It's just that no one went to the play, so no one knows there *was* a prologue."

"Hey, screw you," says Theo. "Lots of girls came to see me on Friday night because I'm so hot and sexual." Theo shimmies stripper-like out of his charcoal peacoat and tosses it to Christopher, who catches it in his lap. Unencumbered by his coat, Theo pretzels himself cross-legged on the table and sits like a guru. "The joke was on them, though," he adds, "since I was playing a gay dude."

F: "Maybe that was part of the appeal."

N: "I hear some girls are into that."

"I don't get it," Christopher says. Worriedly, he rubs the wool of Theo's coat between his fingers. "Iago is gay?"

"Fay talked about this on the first day of rehearsal," says Theo. "Remember?"

"I wasn't listening," says Christopher.

Theo gestures to us. "Take it away, Presidents," he says. "Why is Iago gay?"

Well, shit. We the F&N unit really need to get it right this time.

"Is it just because of the whole sharing-a-bed-with-Cassio thing?" Christopher asks. "Because Wanda told me it was normal for two men to share a bed back then."

N: [*amused*] "You asked Wanda about that?"

F: "First of all, they don't just *share a bed*. Iago specifically says he *lay with Cassio*, and if you look at contemporary Elizabethan writing—"

N: [*heading her off at the pass*] "But, anyway, it's not just about that."

F: "Right, right. Iago is gay on a deeper level than just sharing a bed with Cassio."

Christopher frowns, trying to understand. "Is he in love with Othello?" he asks. "Is that why he wants to ruin Othello's marriage?"

N: "That's part of it."

F: "But think even deeper."

"Aw, yeah," says Theo. "*All the way* deeper." He lifts himself slightly off the table and thrusts his pelvis, air-humping an invisible butt, which buys us some time to gather our own thoughts on gayness.

F: "It's like . . . for Iago, everything is a dollhouse. He's like a fancy little boy with his own fancy dollhouse full of dolls."

N: "Except the dolls are real people."

F: "But they're not real to him. Nothing is real. Everything is just a game."

N: "But it's a serious game. He's a little gay boy who takes his doll-house *very* seriously."

F: "Have you read *The Talented Mr. Ripley*?"

"I've seen the movie," says Christopher.

F: "The book is better. What about *Rope*? *Strangers on a Train*? And *Psycho* too. Nell, write down a gay syllabus for Theo and Christopher."

N: [*already scribbling in her notebook*] "Way ahead of you, boss."

Theo leans forward, interested. "So you think evil characters are gay?"

F: [*really getting into it now*] "Well, *good* and *evil* are heterosexual concepts."

N: "It's more about being, like, chaotic."

F: "Trickster gods."

"Like Puck," Theo suggests. "In *A Midsummer Night's Dream*."

F: "Right! Or Satan in *Paradise Lost*."

N: "Or David Bowie in *Labyrinth*."

F: "Or the French poet Rimbaud. Nell, add him to the list."

"What about that one guy?" says Christopher eagerly. "The guy from the seventies."

N: "What guy?"

"The guy who walked on a tightrope between the . . ." Christopher glances guiltily at Theo. "The towers."

"Or what about the D.C. sniper?" says Theo.

This pulls us up short. We the F&N unit have never considered this.

"Didn't they just arrest him?" says Christopher.

"Shut up," says Theo. "Okay, wait, better example: the Columbine shooters."

We the F&N unit can hardly believe our luck. The two of us have had this very discussion before. We never imagined anyone else joining in.

F: "Yes! We're *always* saying that!"

N: "They were *so* gay for each other."

F: "Read about Leopold and Loeb, and you'll understand. Nell, add—"

N: "*Compulsion* and *Swoon*. Got it."

"Don't bother," says Theo. "I already know all about Leopold and Loeb. They killed a kid. They were smart. They got away with it." He smiles. "I like them."

The bell rings.

Theo hops off the table. He snaps his fingers. "Christopher, my coat."

Christopher stands and holds open Theo's coat behind him, like he's his butler.

Theo laughs. "Holy shit," he says. "I didn't think you'd actually do it." He slips his arms gracefully into the sleeves. "Oh, I like this. I'm into this. Can you do it for me at home?"

Christopher's face is bright red. "I'm not gonna dress you in the morning."

Theo sighs dramatically. "Then what's the *point* of sharing a room?"

Christopher speed-walks out of the library. We the F&N unit watch, dumbstruck, as Theo chases after him.

FAY

What a maddening mystery Theo Severyn was! As Nell and I made our way to Joe Junior, we reviewed the case for his homosexuality.

Point: He asked to join the Invert Society.

Rebuttal: He rescinded the request, admitting it was only a ruse to discuss Wanda.

Counter-rebuttal: He did so only after we established our unwillingness to expand membership.

Point: He agreed with my queer reading of Iago and incorporated it into his performance.

Rebuttal: He mentioned this in the context of his heterosexual desirability.

Counter-rebuttal: He brought up his heterosexual desirability as a springboard to discuss my queer reading of Iago.

Point: He was intrigued by our extempore theorizing on the nature of fictional homosexuality—call it Iago Theory, or Dollhouse Theory.

Rebuttal: He didn't seem to have a firm grasp of it. (The D.C. sniper? Really?)

Counter-rebuttal: He was an admirer of Leopold and Loeb.

We arrived at the diner and claimed our favorite table by the window. As we settled into our seats, Nell asked, "What about Christopher?"

The question didn't interest me at all. I paused to consider why. "Christopher is just a closet case," I said. "One day he'll grow a pair and come out, and that'll be the end of that. But Theo . . ." I gazed out the window at the Third Avenue traffic. "Theo likes to keep us guessing. Is he or isn't he?"

"He could be bi," said Nell.

"Oh, grow up." Even I wasn't sure what I meant by that.

An avuncular Greek waiter appeared beside the table. "Just milkshakes again?" he asked. "Or is today a burger day?"

"Mommy wants me home for dinner tonight," said Nell. "But maybe I have time for a . . ." She looked at her digital watch and brightened. "Hey, it's 3:33! Make a wish!"

"I wish Theo were gay," I said. Just hearing myself say it aloud spiked me with adrenaline, and I giggled from the rush of it.

To the waiter, who knew us well enough to endure our digressions with patience, Nell said, "Can we have two chocolate milkshakes, please?" He left, and Nell said, "It's kind of funny how much you want Theo to be gay. Most girls, when they like a boy, they want him to be straight."

I knew full well how strange it was. It did feel like a crush, but what excited me was the thought of Theo being, by definition, sexually *unavailable* to me. I couldn't explain it; I could only joke about it. "You know I like gay guys," I said. "Just like how Jimmy Frye likes Asian women."

Nell deflated. "I feel so bad about him," she said. "We really should have thanked him."

"Whatever," I said, uninterested in this line of conversation that wasn't about Theo. "He's a pathetic loser."

"Remember when we took him out for coffee here?" she said. "He was *so* up our ass about college. Oh, by the way!" Her tone was studiedly casual; she must have been waiting for this conversational opening. "I think I might actually apply to the BOOBLESS League."

My mood darkened. I'd believed the BOOBLESS League was a joke, one that had arisen from my attempts to distract her from the subject of college. Evidently it had failed.

"Brown, Oberlin, Occidental, Brandeis, Lewis & Clark, Emerson, Skidmore, and Smith," said Nell. "Occidental and Lewis & Clark would be my safeties." She paused, as if steeling her nerves.

I knew what she was about to ask. I wanted to beg her not to ask it.

"What about you?" she asked. "Any overlap?"

"None whatsoever," I said, "seeing as how I'm not going to college."

The waiter returned and set two chocolate milkshakes on the table before us. I reached for mine, but Nell just sat there. "No, for real," she said.

I tore open the paper wrapper on my straw and blew it toward her face. It missed.

Uncertainly, she asked, "Are you serious?"

I wasn't serious—or, more precisely, I didn't know if I was serious—but it was enjoyable to exercise my power to shock her. "Yes," I said. "I don't want to go, so I'm not going."

"Are you gonna take a year off, or . . ."

She had a habit of leaving sentences unfinished. It was a pet peeve of mine under the best of circumstances, but in that moment it infuriated me almost to the point of violence. "Comma-*or*-dot-dot-dot," I said. "Or *what*?"

"You can't just *not go* to college," she said. "What are you gonna do without a college degree?"

"The usual, I guess," I said with brittle cheer. "Wind up on the streets. Suck dick for crack." I stabbed my straw into my shake and slurped from it furiously. For the next minute or so we occupied ourselves with the task of milkshake consumption, while in my head I built my case against Nell.

Point: Who did she think she was, my mother?

Rebuttal: Not that my actual mother, or father, took this level of interest in my college applications. They trusted me to handle it myself. They had no idea how deeply misplaced this trust was.

Point: My academic future was no business of hers.

Rebuttal: Except insofar as she held a personal stake in it, imagining that we could continue our friendship outside of Idlewild, that our dynamic could survive unaffected on a college campus.

Point: I should refuse to reward passive-aggressive behavior. If she had her heart set on us attending college together, she should simply tell me so.

Rebuttal: My heart raced itself sick at the mere thought of existence after Idlewild. I felt that if I looked at my own hand I would find it fading into translucence (see *Back to the Future*, 1985, dir. Robert Zemeckis), my entire existence being erased.

A mucous noise issued forth from Nell's side of the table, curbing my appetite. "Gross, dude," I said, right as I looked up and saw, too late, that Nell was crying.

Before that moment, if asked whether Nell had ever cried in front of me, I likely would have guessed in the affirmative, even without recalling any specific instances; it seemed like the sort of thing she would do, sensitive soul that she was. But the instant I saw Nell's swollen, glistening face, I knew that I had never seen it this way before. At the sight of it, I found myself almost breathless with a surge of emotion that I took, in the moment, for fury. Didn't she know that it was for her—for *us*—that I avoided acknowledging the inevitable end of our self-contained world? How selfish she was to trivialize the matter with girlish tears, making *me* look like the one who didn't care.

Our waiter stopped by our table. "How are my favorite ladies doing?"

"Fine," I said, but Nell said, "Can I get an order of fries, please?" Her voice was teary but calm. The waiter nodded and left us alone again.

I decided to give Nell the gift—I really thought it was a gift—of acting as though I hadn't noticed she was crying. For both our sakes, I would pretend it wasn't happening.

"I'm stealing one of your fries," I said. "Before you can stop me." I paused deliberately. "I'm gonna take it. I'm gonna put it in my mouth, and swallow."

Nell smiled weakly, accepted my offer. "Funny," she said. "That's what your mom said to me last night."

NELL

That night, Fay and I got an email from Jimmy Frye.

Which wasn't unusual in itself. He liked to write us emails, long ones—I'm talking multi-thousand-worders, emails that required you to scroll even if you maximized them to fill the whole screen. I didn't save any, and even at the time I mostly just skimmed them, so I only vaguely remember what was in them. Sometimes he complained about his love life (or lack thereof), but a lot of the time it was just advice—on college, on dating, on landing a good part in the spring musical, whatever he got it into his head we needed his advice on.

This email, though, was different. I'd never gotten an email like this from anyone.

    m k fantastico: ummm did you see jimmy's email?
    OmiPalone212: His screed, you mean?
    m k fantastico: i'm scared to read it
    OmiPalone212: Don't be.
    OmiPalone212: Unless you have a phobia of typos, caps lock, and the word "FRIENDSHIP."
    OmiPalone212: In which case I advise you to delete it.

But I did read it, in a state of heart-hammering fear. I wish I could recreate it in detail now, but all I remember is the gist: he was so disappointed in us. He'd thought Fay and I were his friends ("my FRIENDS"). He'd stuck his neck out for us, put his ass on the line, bent over backward to make us happy—and what for? We never thanked him. We never talked to him unless we wanted a favor. We never even wished him a happy birthday ("which was a MONTH ago, by the way"). He was heartbroken—I remember him using that word, or maybe it was "you broke my heart." But it served him right, he concluded, for putting other people before himself. He wouldn't make that mistake ever again. "HAVE A NICE LIFE."

m k fantastico: holy shit
m k fantastico: what should we do?
OmiPalone212: Absolutely nothing.
OmiPalone212: My dad gets like this sometimes. He'll get over it.

She was wrong about that, actually. I didn't know it then, but this was the last interaction we would ever have with Jimmy Frye. He never talked to us again.

I guess, looking back, this was my first experience of someone being mad at me. (Someone other than my mom, I mean.) Which is funny to think about, considering I spent so much time worrying that Fay was mad at me—but of course, I was a person whose life was ruled by the fear of making someone mad. Now my fear had come true. Granted, it was just Jimmy Frye, whose opinion I had never given a shit about, but the feeling was still unbearable. I'd had no idea he took his relationship with us so seriously. I'd always considered it purely transactional. I thought about Bottom's remark during Latin that morning: "A person can be used as an instrument." Was that what Fay and I had done to Jimmy? Were we horrible people?

Obviously, this all looks very different in retrospect. But it took me years to fully understand what a creep Jimmy Frye was. A standard-issue sexual predator would have been one thing, but in the whole time we knew him, Jimmy Frye never made any kind of pass at me or Fay. He told us multiple times that he was only attracted to Asian women. Fay and I did recognize this as creepy, and we mocked the hell out of him—to his face, even—for talking about his fetish like it was a sexual orientation. But this just made us even more confident that we could handle ourselves around Jimmy Frye. No one knew better than we did what a pathetic loser he was. We were taking advantage of him, not the other way around.

I wish now that I could go back in time and tell my seventeen-year-old self that it's extremely not normal for a forty-six-year-old man to be friends with teenage girls. But I can imagine exactly how my seventeen-year-old self would react to that. "So what?" she'd say. "*I'm* extremely not normal. I'm not like other teenage girls."

But maybe if I phrased it differently . . . "Jimmy is placing way too much emotional pressure on you and Fay," I could say. "He's a grown man. It's inappropriate."

"Since when do Fay and I care about being *appropriate*?"

Touché. I'd have to put a finer point on it. "He's sketchy," I'd say. "It's just like everyone's always saying: he's *pervy*."

No, I'd really lose her there. "Jimmy doesn't perv on us," she'd say, incredulous that older-me could have lost sight of this. "He only likes Asian women, remember?"

And then I'd have to sigh and say it. "Listen, it's messed up how he talks about Juniper Green. It's racist, and it's disrespectful, and it's wrong. Even if she doesn't know about it, she deserves better. You should stand up for her."

But this would be the most ineffective argument of all, because my seventeen-year-old self *hated* Juniper Green. Honestly, I don't even know exactly why. Juniper was annoying, for sure, but Fay and I were annoying too. I think I just got swept up in the fun of having an enemy. So I'm sure my seventeen-year-old self would say something like, "Juniper Green deserves *nothing*."

"Come on. She's only seventeen. She's hardly a real person yet."

"Are you saying *I'm* not a real person yet?"

Am I?

Well, I can't talk to my seventeen-year-old self. Even if I could, there's nothing I could say—nothing anyone could have said—that would have changed her mind about Jimmy Frye, and nothing that would have made her feel like any less of a wreck that night. I just kept imagining myself the way Jimmy saw me—selfish, immature, a fair-weather friend—and I felt physically sick about it.

m k fantastico: do you think we're bad people
OmiPalone212: Good and bad are heterosexual concepts, remember?
m k fantastico: heeeee

I remember typing that "heeeee" with no expression on my face.

From the couch, where she was watching the eleven o'clock news, my mom said, "You're so quiet."

"Just IMing with Fay," I said.

"Usually you laugh a lot when you're doing that," said my mom. "Are you feeling down about something?"

I turned around from the computer, surprised and kind of touched that she'd noticed.

She picked up the remote and turned off the TV. "Let's talk," she said. "If you want to, that is."

I turned back to the computer and typed:

m k fantastico: UGH my mom is SO ANNOYING
m k fantastico: she wants to yell at me about college shit
m k fantastico: brb

I logged off AIM and turned back to my mom, straddling my chair backward. "So," I said, resting my chin against the back of the chair, "you know how Fay and I are friends with Jimmy Frye the IT guy?"

My mom paused, thinking. "Remind me," she said.

It was possible that I'd never mentioned him to her (I sometimes mixed up what I told her and what I told my therapist), but it was more likely that she'd just forgotten. I wasn't sure where to begin. "The guy who tells us gossip," I said. "We took him out to Joe Junior that one time?"

"This is a guy at school?" she said.

Her tone was gentle, pre-sympathetic, and I knew what she was thinking: Fay liked a boy and I was jealous. "No!" I snapped. "Well, technically yes, but—"

The phone rang loudly in the kitchen.

My mom jumped at the noise. "What the . . . ? It's almost midnight." She went into the kitchen to answer it, and I was about to get pissed off at her for abandoning me in the middle of what could have been a real heart-to-heart—but then she came back into the living room and held the phone out to me, smiling.

"I think it's him," she whispered.

My stomach dropped. I shook my head, terrified.

"Nell," said my mom warningly.

This was a fight we had a lot, mostly when my grandparents called; I'd been phone-avoidant since I was a little kid. (Everyone is phone-avoidant nowadays, but I was ahead of my time.) I didn't know how to explain right then that this wasn't just my run-of-the-mill phone anxiety. Helplessly, I took the phone. "Hello?"

"I'm so sorry to bother you at this hour," said a pleasant baritone. "You weren't asleep, I hope?"

It wasn't Jimmy; it was Bottom. I laughed in surprised relief. "No way," I said. "What am I, five?"

"Oh, thank goodness," he said. "I know the etiquette is to never call anyone before nine a.m. or after nine p.m."

(I'd never heard of that rule before. It stuck with me, and I still think of Bottom whenever I have to call a patient at home.)

"But I've been trying you for hours," he went on, "and the line was always busy."

"Sorry," I said. "I was using the Internet, so I tied up the phone line. You should have IM'd me." I thought it was weird that he hadn't. He'd never called me before. Who called anyone anymore?

"Ordinarily I would," he said. "But I wanted to discuss something"—he hesitated—"of a rather sensitive nature."

I had no idea where he could be going with this. Ignoring my mom's curious smile, I got up and took the phone into my bedroom. "What's up?" I asked, praying he wasn't about to declare his love for me or something.

"First of all, I wanted to thank you," he said, "for covering for me in Latin today."

That felt like such a long time ago. "Latin?"

"I'm such a terrible liar." His voice was hushed, like he was scared of being overheard, even though he was at home. "I appreciate you playing along."

I still wasn't sure what he was referring to, but I was too embarrassed to say so. "Oh," I said vaguely. "Don't worry about it."

"Well, I *am* a little worried," he said. "I didn't expect the story to travel so fast, but it looks like the whole school knows. And I was just wondering if you told anyone about our conversation last weekend—"

"That you got into Yale?" I was still confused, but glad I could reassure him. "No, I didn't tell—"

"—when you saw me and my parents coming out of Skip and Trudy's office," he continued, overlapping with me. "Sorry—you were saying?"

"I—wait." Now I was really lost. "I thought you were coming out of Deenie's office." Had I actually seen them coming out of Deenie's office? Or had they just been standing outside it? Skip and Trudy's office was right next to Deenie's.

"Oh, good lord," said Bottom. "I thought you . . ."

I took a sharp breath as I pieced it together. "Your *parents* got Wanda fired?"

"They didn't mean to," he said quickly. "Not like this, anyway. Not in the middle of the year, in a way that would attract a ton of attention." His voice was going higher-pitched with stress. "I begged them not to make a big deal of it. Or at least wait until after graduation. But they were so upset about the play. Especially my dad." He sounded close to tears. "He walked out at intermission."

I was pacing in circles around my bedroom. I always do that unconsciously, even now, whenever I'm making a hard phone call. "I'm really sorry," I said, not knowing what else to say.

"I love Wanda," he said. "You know that, right, Nell?"

"Of course," I said. "We all love Wanda."

"I just don't want anyone to think *I* was the one who . . ." He trailed off. "It's complicated," he said. "Do you understand?"

"Completely," I said.

But I didn't understand at all. It would take me years to appreciate how complicated, in general, life at Idlewild must have been for Bottom; even now I'm sure I don't fully get it. I probably never will. Case in point: I'm realizing only right this second, as I think back on that phone call, that it might have been less sincere and more calculated than I assumed. Could he really have thought I was "covering" for him in Latin class— when I'd so pointedly speculated that "some people" might have been offended by the prologue—or was he just buttering me up? I took him at his word when he said he loved Wanda, but if he actually hated her, would he have told me so?

At the very least, though, I understood this: Bottom was freaking out. He badly needed a friend in that moment. And he was counting on me.

I stopped pacing and stood at my bedroom window, dizzy from all the circling. I studied my reflection in the glass. I widened my eyes in an expression of concern, cradled the phone lovingly between my ear and shoulder. "You can trust me," I said. "I won't tell anyone." It didn't feel like enough, so I went even bigger. "I'm on your side," I declared, "no matter what." As I spoke, my reflection in the window looked like a trustworthy girl on a TV show.

Bottom exhaled with relief. "Thank you, Nell. You're a true friend."

"It's no big deal." I was so thrilled with myself, I started pacing the floor again.

"It *is* a big deal," he said. "Thank you, thank you, thank you. I wish I could thank you a million times, but it's already past my bedtime."

I wanted to mock him for that—it was barely midnight—but now I was getting really into the whole being-nice thing. "Sweet dreams," I said, admiring my reflection in the window. "I'll see you tomorrow."

"You mean *today*," he said. "Technically. It's two minutes past midnight."

"Hey," I said. "That means winter break technically starts tomorrow."

"And even more importantly," he said, "tomorrow is technically *La Bohème*."

He was way more psyched for that than I was, but for his sake I squealed with anticipation. "*La Bohème!*"

"*Amor, amor!*" he sang into the phone.

I hung up feeling much better. Jimmy Frye was wrong. I was an amazing friend.

m k fantastico: omg
m k fantastico: boss
m k fantastico: Bottom just called me on the phone
m k fantastico: guess what he told me

F&N, 2002

It's the last day of school before winter break. No one ever falls asleep during Silence, but on this Friday morning it's a struggle to stay awake. The cloudlight that shines through the bubbled-up window glass is a pale trace of warmth, the way the melted sugar-ice puddle at the bottom of a Frappuccino is a pale trace of coffee. The Meetinghouse is a gray cocoon and the Silence is a gray cocoon inside it.

A rustling of a coat, a creak and groan of wood as someone's weight shifts on the floor—someone is rising.

Well, this is something. It's been quite a while since anyone spoke during Silence. We the F&N unit haven't gotten to play Guess Who's Gay in weeks. Who will do us the honor of being gay for the day?

"I'll never forget my first Meeting for Worship," says Theo Severyn.

We the F&N unit jolt to attention. Guess who's gay, indeed.

"As many of you know," he continues, "I'm kind of new here." He speaks at a thoughtful, relaxed pace. His voice carries well through the Meetinghouse. "When I started ninth grade last year, I was at Stuyvesant. But then . . ."

At this, the air in the Meetinghouse goes brisk and alpine with collective unease. Is he really going to talk about . . . ?

". . . I had to spend a month here," he says (and the air warms with exhaled relief—he's talking around it). "I'd never heard of Idlewild. I'd never even heard of Quakers. I thought you'd all be dressed like the guy on the oatmeal box."

Jokes are rare in Meeting for Worship. This one gets a small, surprised laugh from the crowd.

"And to be honest," he says, "I did think you guys were pretty weird at first. I mean, you called your teachers by their first names!"

This gets a bigger laugh.

"And Meeting for Worship. The Stuyvesant kids didn't go to Meeting while we were here," he says, "thanks to the whole public-school separation-of-church-and-state thing. But when I first heard about it, I thought it sounded insane. The whole school just sitting in *silence*? For *twenty minutes*? Like some kind of cult?"

Even we the F&N unit are laughing along now. He's really working the crowd.

"But at the same time," he says, "I was curious. I thought the Meetinghouse was so beautiful. Every time I passed it from the outside, I thought it looked like a dollhouse."

We the F&N unit go suddenly still.

"And whenever I passed by during Meeting for Worship, I imagined the Meetinghouse as a big fancy dollhouse full of dolls." He pauses. "Except the dolls were real people."

Is he trying to communicate something to us, the F&N unit? We try to catch his eye from across the Meetinghouse, but he's looking off thoughtfully into the distance.

"So one day," he says, "on a Friday morning, I cut my physics class and sneaked into Meeting for Worship. Just to see what it was all about, you know? I sat next to some random kid on a random bench in the ninth-grade section. Which turned out to be a fateful decision."

Glancing down at the kid seated next to him on the bench now—Christopher—Theo breaks into a quick half smile. Christopher squirms and casts his eyes downward. All this happens in a blink, but we the F&N unit catch it.

"And then Silence started," says Theo, "and . . . I felt like I was home. Like I belonged. I'd never felt that way at Stuyvesant. Actually, I'd never felt that way anywhere." He looks at Christopher again, takes a deep breath. "By the time those twenty minutes were up, I'd fall—" *Fallen in love*, he seems to be about to say, but he falters mid-word and starts over. "I knew I wanted to transfer to Idlewild."

We the F&N unit can barely hear him over the pounding of our hearts. Is Guess Who's Gay about to come true, for the first time ever?

"And now that I've finished my first semester here," he says, "I know I made the right choice. I love it here. I love calling my teachers by their first names. I love that they're not just our teachers, but our friends." He's talking faster now, getting animated. "And I still think the Meetinghouse is beautiful. Every morning, when I come in here—and every afternoon during play rehearsal, and at night when I was performing in the play— every time I come into the Meetinghouse, I still feel like I'm walking into an enchanted dollhouse. Like . . ." He shrugs, suddenly bashful. "Like anything can happen in here."

He sits. Silence re-envelops us.

We the F&N unit wilt at this puzzling anticlimax. Theo did not, after all that, use Meeting for Worship to come out of the closet. Did he intend to, and then lose his nerve? Or did he wish simply to wax sentimental about Idlewild? But waxing sentimental isn't Theo's style at all.

Before we can think about it for long, another rustle and creak breaks the Silence. This would be extraordinary in itself—but it originates from the freshman benches. People don't even bother to hide their head-swivels of amazement. Freshmen *never* speak during Silence.

It's Maddy, she of the Rollerblades. In a small but determined voice, she says, "I love it here too. I love Quaker values—like how everyone is equal, and no one is above anyone else. And for me, being in the play was when I really got what Quakers mean about everyone having an Inner Light. And I think . . ." She hesitates anxiously, then blurts in a burst of nerve, "I think it's really disappointing when Idlewild doesn't live up to its Quaker values."

She sits. The silence, when it resumes, is confused and somewhat tense. But it's soon disrupted by a *third* rustle and creak, once again from the freshman benches.

It's almost unheard of for three people to speak during one Silent Meeting, let alone three underclassmen, and the collective surprise is palpable when the speaker turns out to be little Kendra Kwok. Her voice is so soft the Meetinghouse might swallow it entirely, if all Idlewild ears weren't straining to catch her words.

"Being in the play," she says, "was the most important thing that's ever happened to me in my whole life. It made me . . . brave."

She stands there a moment longer, as if she means to say something else, but then sits back down.

Silence barely has time to descend again before it's broken by another rustle and creak—this time in the senior benches, right next to us, the F&N unit.

"Theo is right," says Daylily Jones. "Idlewild teachers aren't just your teachers. They're your friends. And the best teacher-friend I've ever had . . . was Wanda Higgins."

She pauses for so long that people begin to fidget, wondering if she's done, but she's still standing. When she speaks again, her voice is choked with tears.

"I'll always be grateful to her for encouraging me to spread my wings," says Daylily. "And . . ." She sniffs, and her next words come out in a sob. "I miss her."

She collapses back onto the bench.

All eyes, with varying degrees of subtlety, turn toward Skip and Trudy, who keep their heads bowed and their eyes spiritually shut.

Daylily's lingering sniffles are soon interrupted by another nearby rustle and creak.

"I miss Wanda too." Juniper Green's public speaking voice is unpleasantly loud, especially from two feet away. "And furthermore, I think it was totally unfair how she was treated by the administration. She was a member of the Idlewild community. Whatever happened to second chances? Whatever happened to Quaker values?"

She sits, huffily.

She's barely seated again when a rare Quaker standoff occurs: two people stand at once, Christopher Korkian and Oliver Dicks. The whole Meetinghouse titters sacrilegiously as the two of them do a little dance of deciding who should speak first, half-sitting and standing and half-sitting and standing until it is wordlessly determined that Oliver Dicks is the loser.

"I was in Wanda's freshman Drama class last year," says Christopher. "She taught us that the number one rule of acting is to always *accept the offer.*" He pronounces that phrase with a slight British accent in imitation of Wanda's. The Meetinghouse laughs again. Encouraged, he repeats it. "*Accept the offer.* I'll always remember that. I stand with Wanda."

He sits. The thwarted Oliver Dicks pops up like a blond whack-a-mole.

"I used to think Shakespeare was boring," he says. Sheepishly, he addresses the English teachers: "No offense, Devi and Ms. Caputo. I know you're big fans." He pauses expectantly. No one laughs. "But then," he says, undaunted, "I took ninth grade Drama, and Wanda taught me so much about the Bard. Did you know that he uses iambic pentameter for aristocratic characters, and prose for low-class characters?" (Yes, Oliver, everyone knows that, because everyone has to take ninth grade Drama.) "Well," he says smugly, "even my parents didn't know that. So now, thanks to Wanda, I know more about Shakespeare than my parents." Again he pauses for laughter. Again none comes. "I stand with Wanda," he says pompously, and sits.

By this point people are glancing at the big clock on the wall. It's about 9:18. Meeting is supposed to adjourn at 9:20.

Kevin Comfort, an affable stoner in the senior class, stands. "One time," he says, "my grandpa went into hospice, and in Drama I did an improv scene about a kid whose grandpa went into hospice, and it was mad healing. I stand with Wanda."

He sits. An unfamiliar freshman girl stands.

"I didn't do the play, and I never had Wanda as a teacher because I'm not scheduled to take Drama until next quarter, but I love drama. Like, as a concept. It's the most important art form. So, I stand with Wanda."

She sits. Someone else stands.

FAY

As Meeting for Worship inched into overtime and the Wanda testimonials showed no sign of slowing, I began to suspect that only the first handful—Theo and Christopher, Maddy and Kendra, perhaps Daylily and Juniper—were part of an organized effort. Theo was behind it, but he hadn't orchestrated it so much as set it in motion, domino-style. What was happening now seemed spontaneous, and therefore to lack an exit strategy.

The clock ticked past 9:20, making all of Idlewild officially late for class. I wondered if Theo was dismayed at the way his earnest little protest had spiraled out of control. I looked over toward the sophomore benches.

Theo looked back at me—not at Nell and me as a unit, but specifically at *me*—from across the Meetinghouse. I can still see him now as he was then: luminously pale against his charcoal peacoat and floppy dark hair, a black-and-white vision, like a silent-film star. His face was wry, catlike in satisfaction, just as it had been the first time I ever saw it.

And I suddenly understood that spiraling out of control was the point. This was all a game to him. Meeting for Worship was—of course, of course, he'd said so himself—a dollhouse, and he was a boy who played with dolls. Oh, my Marble Faun! How magnificent he was in that moment. How beautiful.

Theo flashed a tiny smirk, just for me, from one Iago to another.

NELL

I kept looking at Bottom. He was sitting on a bench a couple of rows ahead of us, so I could only see the back of his head, his ramrod choirboy posture. I saw him breathing deeply, slowly, just like Ms. Spider had us do in singing exercises. His shoulders barely moved because he breathed from his diaphragm. In through the nose. Out through the mouth. Nothing was visibly wrong with him. Nothing was ever visibly wrong with Bottom. He was a good actor.

I caught freshmen and sophomores and juniors looking at him—trying to do it sneakily, like their eyes just happened to pause on him as they scanned the senior benches. But as the clock ticked past 9:20 and it became clear that something legitimately nuts was happening, they got more blatant about it. Some kids were straight-up staring. Some kids, when they yelled, seemed to be yelling in Bottom's direction.

"I stand with Wanda because art is more important than political correctness."

"I stand with Wanda because I believe in freedom of speech."

"I stand with Wanda because that's what Idlewild means to me."

It crossed my mind, as people stood and stood and stood for Wanda, that I could stand up and make some kind of counterargument—like that maybe firing Wanda was the right decision, or at least that the situation was more complicated than it looked and we should try to understand the full story before getting angry. Nothing was stopping me from speaking up.

But I had never spoken in Silence before. Even under normal circumstances, the idea scared the shit out of me. And what if I was wrong and just imagining that people were staring at Bottom? After all, no one knew for a fact that he was involved in Wanda's firing—no one but me. And Fay. But she hadn't told anyone else. Right? Anyway, I'd promised him I wouldn't tell anyone. If I stood up to defend Wanda's firing, wouldn't that sort of, maybe, in a way, be breaking my promise? If you thought about it that way, it was actually morally right for me to sit there and do nothing while everybody else stood up for Wanda.

"As editor of the *Quaker Shaker*, I stand for truth and transparency. I stand with Wanda."

"As president of the Idlewild chapter of Amnesty International, I stand in solidarity with anyone who's been silenced for their views. I stand with Wanda."

Bottom breathed on his bench, slowly, evenly, in through the nose, out through the mouth, and I found myself breathing along with him, like I was breathing *for* him, like he might die if I stopped. Fay was breathing hard too; I could feel it in her body beside me on the bench. I wondered if she was breathing for Bottom too. It felt good to imagine that we were helping him just by breathing. I breathed in and out, in and out, telling myself with every breath that this was fine, this wasn't what it looked like, he loved Wanda too . . .

F&N, 2002

By 9:30 Trudy's face is twisted into a reluctant rictus of tolerance and Skip is coiled to spring, waiting to shake Trudy's hand the instant there's a split second of stillness so that he can end Meeting without interrupting a speaker. But it's hopeless. No one will let him. Either the rules of Guess Who's Gay no longer apply, or so many Idlewilders are gay for the day that we the F&N unit have lost count of them. The Meetinghouse thunders with voices.

"I stand with Wanda!"

"I stand with Wanda!"

"I stand with Wanda!"

We the F&N unit are not among them. Not yet.

FAY

The clock passed 9:35 and still Theo held my gaze. By then the speakers had ceased taking turns and begun shouting over each other. Theo trembled sweetly as he stifled a giggle. I wasn't even aware that I was smiling back until my cheeks began to ache.

None of this mattered; none of it was real. That was the truth that only Theo and I could see. That was the hilarity of it, the joy of it.

The protesters stopped shouting over each other and began chanting as one.

"We stand with Wanda! We stand with Wanda!"

With the entire row in front of me standing, my view of Theo was blocked. I stood, trying to catch a glimpse of him between bodies. He was laughing. So, uncontrollably, was I.

NELL

I couldn't see Bottom anymore. Was he standing too, or was he one of the last holdouts still sitting? Was he still doing breathing exercises? I was forgetting to breathe at all. Everyone was shouting and the Meetinghouse was shaking and my heart was jackhammering and all I could think was that I *couldn't* be the only one still sitting, I couldn't be left behind, I couldn't be alone . . .

Fay stood.

I want to believe that's the only reason I stood. But I probably would have done it anyway.

F&N, 2002

We the F&N unit stand, because all of Idlewild is standing. We the F&N unit say it, because all of Idlewild is saying it.

All of Idlewild: "WE STAND WITH WANDA!"

F&N: "We stand with Wanda."

But it is not enough now to chant. We the F&N unit watch as our fellow Idlewilders, still chanting, begin to move as one—clambering over benches, stampeding down the aisles, bursting open the side door, swarming into the Peace Garden.

FAY

There was black snow, I remember, in the Peace Garden. An unseason-
ably heavy snowstorm had hit New York the previous week, and though
the weather had warmed since then, knobs of unmelted snowbank still
crusted the ground. Coated with airborne city soot, they looked igne-
ous, noxious.

"We stand with Wanda," my classmates cried as they marched through
the garden and onward into the main building. "We stand with Wanda!"

My voice was no longer among them. Nor was Nell's. Supposing that
she, like me, had decided to shift back from a participant to an observer
role, I turned toward her to offer some remark. But she wasn't beside
me. I glanced around the garden, failed to locate her face in the crowd.
I wondered if her participation in the chant had been more earnest and
less experimental than mine; if she was at this very moment storming
the hallways, disrupting the Lower and Middle School classes, chanting
full-throatedly alongside her peers; if she was swept up in something
primal, connected to her fellow Idlewilders in an atavistic mania, while
I remained on the outside.

Throughout my life, I've found myself psychologically barred from access
to collective displays of emotion. I'd first noticed this deficiency in myself
the year before, on September eleventh, consumed with inappropriate
giggles as the city came together in shared grief, and I would notice it
again on election night in 2008, watching blankly from my window as
cheering crowds filled the streets in celebration of a victory for which I,

too, had been dearly hoping. Often at such times, my sense of existing on the outside of my own life—on the outside of humanity, even—caused me distress. Now, when I consider it as a lifelong pattern, it disturbs me.

But on that particular December morning in 2002, I observed it with detached amusement. I thought with pleasure of Christopher Isherwood's phrase "I am a camera" (*Goodbye to Berlin*, 1939). I moved to the corner of the garden, my boots crunching against black-crusted snow. I leaned against the brick wall, surveyed the chanting crowd, and marveled at my own superiority. How easily everyone—yes, even Nell—had been manipulated by Theo Severyn! Everyone but me.

The Peace Garden gradually emptied out as the Upper Schoolers completed their migration to the main building. I did not follow them. I remained standing in the corner, my back against the brick wall, with its gaudy mural of flowers and doves and childish stick figures holding hands on a not-to-scale planet Earth. I had planted myself in the most central location, as a lost child is advised to do, to maximize the likelihood that Theo, should he be searching for me, would find me in the garden.

NELL

If I'd been sitting anywhere else in the Meetinghouse, I would have been part of the mob—not because I wanted to be, but because it was impossible to move against the current of the crowd. Luckily, Fay and I always sat in the back row of the senior benches, which were just a few feet away from the staircase to the Loft. Abandoning my coat and backpack, I scrambled over the back of the benches and escaped up the creaky wood stairs.

At the top I staggered to a halt, my windpipe dry and cold from the unexpected sprint. Wheezing, I leaned for support against the closed door of Wanda and Ms. Spider's shared office—well, now it was just Ms. Spider's office. I wondered where Ms. Spider was now. I worried about her in that crowd.

It was only then that I noticed that Fay wasn't with me.

I called out, "Boss?" It turned into a cough that echoed through the empty stairwell.

Not sure what to do, I stayed there leaning against the door, listening through the window. The chanting in the Peace Garden started to lose steam. Voices dropped out, and the remaining ones grew fainter and less synchronized, overlapping at different tempos: *"We stand with—" "WE! STAND!" "—standwithWanda . . ."* There was one guy who kept stopping and starting over—*"We stand—we stand with—with—"*—trying awkwardly to match everyone else. I didn't recognize his voice, but I had the mean thought that it must be Eddie Applebaum. I couldn't tell if Fay's voice was there. What I did hear, after a moment, was a few voices doubling back toward the Meetinghouse, suddenly loud again. Very loud. Almost like they were no longer in the Peace Garden but back inside the Meetinghouse, directly under my feet—

"We stand with Wanda! We stand with Wanda!"

—and heading toward the back stairs.

Hoping to slip into Ms. Spider's office, I tried the doorknob. It was locked. My only other option was the rehearsal room, but anyone coming upstairs was headed that way too. Where would I hide, under the piano?

"WE STAND WITH WANDA!"

The voices echoed through the stairwell. The wooden stairs creaked with footsteps. Desperately, I tried the office doorknob again. It wouldn't budge.

*"WE STAND WITH—*oh, hey, Nell!"

I turned around. It was Daylily and Juniper—and right behind them, Bottom.

"Holy shit!" Juniper's voice was hoarse from shouting. "How fucking awesome was that?"

Daylily, beside her, clutched her heart. "It was beautiful," she sighed.

As Bottom joined us on the landing, I tried to catch his eye, but he ignored me. To Daylily, he said, "It couldn't have happened without your leadership."

"Oh, I didn't do anything." Daylily was digging through her backpack in search of something. "I told you, it was Theo's idea."

"But you led by example." He smiled at her. "You always do."

The whole time they were talking, I kept looking down the stairs, expecting more people. But apparently it was just the three of them. I had a vision of a teenage mob tearing through the Idlewild hallways, throwing chairs through windows and setting fire to the Lower Schoolers' drawings on the walls. Anxiously, I asked, "Where did everybody else go?"

"To class," said Juniper. "'Cause they're lame." She was bouncing up and down on the balls of her feet. "Lily, what the fuck is in your bag that's making it so hard to find your keys?"

"Patience, patience," said Bottom.

"I keep this one on a different keychain," said Daylily.

"They went to *class?*" I said. As it sank in, I started to laugh. "The whole Upper School staged a revolt and formed an angry mob, and then the mob went to class?"

That really was what happened. I found out later that most teachers threw out their lesson plans and devoted the day to heartfelt discussion,

9/11-style, about what had just gone down. It was the most quintessentially Idlewild thing ever, and when I think about it now, it seems like such a missed opportunity for the Upper Schoolers. After all, we'd just discovered that adult authority at Idlewild was only as real as we wanted it to be. The students outnumbered the teachers. There were no security guards, let alone armed ones. It would have been shockingly easy for the kids to seize temporary control of the school.

But the thing is, I doubt most Idlewild kids would have wanted to do that. Idlewild had been pretty good to them. Life in general had been pretty good to them. I wouldn't be surprised if they got freaked out when they realized how fragile and fake it all was. So they went to class, and over the following weeks, the protest got widely retconned as the kind of self-expression that Idlewild was famous for encouraging. The next issue of the *Quaker Shaker* had a front-page article about the incident with the headline "In Silence, Idlewilders Find Their Voices." Sometimes I think that might reflect even worse on Idlewild than the original incident.

Daylily dangled a key triumphantly from her finger. "Found you!"

"Nell, out of the way," said Juniper. I stepped aside, and Daylily started to unlock the office door.

Seeing my confusion, Juniper said airily, "Oh, do you not have a key to Wanda's office? She gave us one, like, two years ago."

"Jen!" Daylily exclaimed. "She told us not to spread that around."

I couldn't afford to get distracted by this new evidence of Wanda's outrageous favoritism: this was my chance to get Bottom alone. As he passed me to follow the girls into the office, I tapped him on the shoulder.

He turned around and looked at me—but not with the warmth and vulnerability he'd shown me over the phone two nights ago. From his guarded brusqueness, I might as well have been a stranger on the street asking if he had a moment for the environment. "What?" he said.

I hadn't thought past this part. "Uh . . ."

I heard a *bleep-bleep-bloop* sound coming from inside the office. One of the girls was dialing a number on the telephone.

"Are you okay?" I asked.

"How do you mean?" he replied.

Juniper's loud voice rang out from inside the office. "Hey, Wanda, it's me! You're not gonna believe what just happened in Meeting."

I gestured toward the office. In an undertone, I asked, "Do they know?"

"Do they know what?" said Bottom, with pretty convincing blankness.

He didn't really want me to say it, did he? "You know," I said quietly. "The reason Wanda got . . ."

"Wanda got fired," Bottom said evenly, "because Skip and Trudy are a couple of philistines who don't appreciate the art of theater."

He looked me hard in the eye, daring me to challenge him.

Inside the office, Juniper said (yelled), "Oh, good call, Lils! They let you smoke at Café Pick Me Up!"

Bottom continued, "And we're showing her our support." He narrowed his eyes at me. "Because that's what true friends do."

It hit me stomach-first: he blamed me.

"I didn't tell anyone," I blurted out. "I swear I didn't tell anyone." If you rounded down, I thought, it was true. I hadn't told anyone except Fay—and he must have known I would share it with her, because he knew I shared everything with her—and Fay couldn't have told anyone (who would she tell?), so it didn't count. "I didn't tell *anyone*," I said again. Each time I said it, I believed it more. "I swear to God. I would never tell anyone."

"You would never tell anyone what?" said Daylily, who was suddenly there like an apparition in the doorway next to Bottom. Juniper popped up beside her.

"About the key to Wanda's office," said Bottom. "I made her promise." I was a little unnerved by how quickly he came up with that lie.

Daylily stood on tiptoe to kiss him on the cheek. "You're so sweet," she said.

"And so hot," said Juniper. "Okay, so Wanda's meeting us at Café Pick Me Up at four. We can just hang out at my place till then." She gave Bottom a significant look. "You should come. My parents are away at an ethnomusicology conference in Copenhagen."

Bottom nodded solemnly. "I'd be honored."

Daylily closed and locked the office door. Bottom offered her his arm. She gracefully took it. Juniper took the other one, and the three of them headed toward the stairs.

"Oh, Nell?" Bottom glanced backward at me. With a girl on each arm, he looked like he was in a musical number about being a decadent wastrel. "If Dorothy asks why I'm not in Chorus, tell her I got sick and went home."

Juniper whooped. "We did it!" she bellowed. "We corrupted him!"

Daylily giggled and leaned her head against his shoulder. "I like this side of you."

In that moment, all I could think about was how fucking obnoxious Daylily and Juniper were, and how ridiculously unfair it was for Bottom to choose them over me. I couldn't believe he would hide the truth and pretend to side with Wanda just for the sake of these stupid girls. It would take me a very long time to gain some perspective about what that morning must have been like for Bottom, and what his options really were. I understand now that he wasn't doing this to insult me personally. But that was how I felt right then.

Burning with resentment, I said, "She'll know that's a lie when she sees you tonight at *La Bohème*."

Bottom looked at Daylily, then at Juniper, then back at me.

"Fair enough," he said. "Tell her I won't make it to *La Bohème*."

FAY

I had all but given up hope when at last the heavy doors of the main building opened and Theo Severyn stepped into the Peace Garden. He, too, was alone.

"Hey, bitch." His voice, soft despite the twenty-some feet between us, steamed in the cold.

"Hey, catamite." I matched his hushed tone, though there was no one but the two of us in the garden.

The dollhouse-shaped Meetinghouse cast a shadow that fell across Theo's face as he approached me. "What do you think?" he said lightly. "Can I be in the Invert Society now?"

"Is that why you did it?" Performing a parody of coquettishness—for my question was too serious to ask seriously—I said, "All for little old me?"

He came to a stop a few feet away from me. "Don't tell Christopher."

My heart was pounding. Mentally, I ran a quick experimental simulation. I visualized Theo walking up to me, placing his hands on my shoulders, leaning in, touching his lips to mine—no. Absolutely not. The mere thought caused my heart to slow in confused indifference. Kissing Theo would be like kissing the back of my own hand.

And yet, as I looked at him, I thought: *I want.* I was aflame, ablaze with want. What was it I wanted from him?

"Christopher tries to keep up," said Theo. "But he doesn't really get the whole Leopold and Loeb thing."

"That's ironic," I said. "Since he's the Leopold to your Loeb."

"Well, we haven't murdered a guy yet." Theo smiled. "If you know what I mean."

What did he mean? I couldn't ask directly, couldn't puncture the soap bubble of double entendre in which we were floating. This was flirting, I suppose, in the sense that it was an escalating and erotically charged exchange of verbal teasing that served as an indirect acknowledgment of an attraction that felt otherwise unspeakable. But it was a delicate balance we had to strike. A single false move—by which I mean a heterosexual move, on either of our parts—would have broken the spell. The flirtation was asymptotic, the attraction displaced: my object of desire was not Theo himself, but the abstract idea of Theo being gay. *That* was what I wanted. That was what was causing my heart to flutter in my chest with a mothlike fragility that it had heretofore exhibited only in response to the image of two dudes doing it—never, until now, in response to another living person.

"Also," he added, "you think I don't know what *catamite* means." He stepped over a blackened snowbank, drawing closer to me. "But I do."

"Oh?" My face felt hot. I wondered if he could tell. "Well, know thyself."

"Bitch, please," he said. "We both know *you're* the catamite."

I went mute for the next few seconds as I catalogued the various possible readings of that statement.

1. The schoolyard bluff: He didn't know what *catamite* meant but was flinging the supposed insult back at me (rubber, glue, etc.) in hope that whatever it was, it would sting.

2. The "I know you are but what am I" gambit: He didn't know specifically that a catamite was a boy kept for ass-fucking purposes in decadent Greco-Roman antiquity, but he had intuited the word's homosexual connotations and was flinging the allegation back at me in hope that it would distract from his own homosexuality, which he had yet to confirm explicitly.

3. The anal association: He knew that a catamite was by definition the receptive partner in said ass-fucking and was flinging the implication back at me on the grounds that, questions of identity notwithstanding, this particular aspect of the word *was* an insult.

Cautiously, experimentally, I said, "You should look up *catamite* in the dictionary."

"I told you," said Theo. "I know what it means."

I took a breath. "Girls can't be catamites."

He regarded me unblinkingly. "You're not a girl," he said. "You're like this weird sad pervy gay guy in a girl's body, cruising me."

4. Identification in the wild: He saw me. He understood me. He knew me.

NELL

Fay was late to Chorus. This was a problem because she was one third of the soprano section, and with Bottom absent we'd also lost our entire baritone section. The remaining seven of us sat helplessly around the Meetinghouse Loft, wondering how Haydn's *Creation* would sound without them.

"We'll have to make do baritoneless," said Ms. Spider. "Nell, is Fay on her way?"

"I don't know," I said, more snappishly than I meant to. I was annoyed—it caught me by surprise how much it annoyed me—to be treated like Fay's personal secretary. By someone other than Fay, I mean.

"Maybe she got sick too," a freshman alto suggested. "Maybe something's going around."

"Maybe we all have it," said the junior girl who was supposed to sing tenor but usually failed to find it and just sang the soprano line an octave down. "Maybe we were all delirious in Meeting."

There was nodding and laughter and chattering agreement.

"I never spoke in Meeting before today. I didn't think I ever would."

"Me neither! Look, my hands are still shaking."

"Oh my god, mine too! I couldn't even take notes in Chemistry."

It was really hitting me, as I half-listened to this back-and-forth, how adrift I was when Fay wasn't around. As I think back on this, I can't remember any of my classmates' names. It's entirely possible that I never bothered to learn them in the first place.

"Do you think it'll work? Will they bring Wanda back?"

"They pretty much have to, right? It's the will of the people and shit."

"I'm so glad I got to be part of it. It was, like, historic."

"Yeah! Fuck political correctness!"

"*Screw* political correctness," Ms. Spider chided. "All right, we can't wait around forever. Can I get a volunteer to take over Fay's angel Gabriel solo for today?"

The two underclassgirl sopranos practically knocked over their music stands with the force of their simultaneous hand-raising.

Before Ms. Spider could choose between them, the rehearsal room door swung noisily open. Fay and Theo burst in together, flushed, mid-laugh, each with a Starbucks cup in hand.

"Theo!" the underclassgirls chorused, with more energy and synchronicity than they ever displayed as an actual chorus. Theo waved to his fans.

"Sorry," said Fay, laughing. "We lost track of time."

"It was my fault, Dorothy," said Theo. "This is a token of apology." He reached over the piano to hand her his Starbucks cup. "It's just tea," he said. "But Fay says that's your favorite?"

"Bribery will get you nowhere," said Ms. Spider, but she took the cup. "Thank you, uh . . ."

"Theo," he said. "Severyn." He reached across the piano again for a handshake.

Humoring him, Ms. Spider shook his hand. "Now if you'll excuse us, Mr. Severyn—"

"Oh, can't he stay?" cried Fay. "Come on!"

The underclassgirls started chanting "Let him stay! Let him stay!" (Like they hadn't done enough chanting for the day.)

"He'll be good," said Fay. "You'll be good, won't you, Theo?"

"I'll be *so* good," said Theo, who had already made his way into the corner of the rehearsal room. He flung himself onto the scuzzy prop armchair in the corner. "You won't even know I'm here."

"Fat chance, Mr. Cellophane." Ms. Spider sipped her Starbucks tea. "On the other hand," she said, "it can be useful to rehearse in front of an audience." She smiled at Theo. "Even an audience of one."

The underclassgirls cheered.

Fay slid into her chair next to mine. Beaming at me, she whispered, "Hi."

I looked at my sheet music and let my hair fall over my face so she wouldn't see that my eyes were suddenly filling with tears.

It was the kind of crying that hits so hard and fast, you don't even know why it's happening. I knew it had to do with Bottom, but it also had to do with the way Fay and Theo were mirroring each other—laughing in unison, holding their Starbucks cups in the same loose-wristed way, speaking in this breathy twitter of a voice that was somehow a mix of Fay-ish and Theo-ish. A smile lingered on Fay's face for the rest of the period, even as she sang her solo. It was a smile I had never seen before.

"In all the lands resounds the word
Never unperceivèd, ever understood
Ever, ever, ever understood!"

A horrible thought struck me then, slithering down my neck and shoulders like someone had cracked an egg on my head: maybe this, the two of them, had been going on for a while. Maybe Fay had hung out with Theo just yesterday, and told him what I'd told her about Bottom's secret. Maybe this *was* all my fault.

A tear slid down my face and dripped onto my sheet music. Guilt, shame, anxiety, self-pity, and dread were all swirling into an overwhelming sense of aloneness. Bottom hated me. Jimmy Frye hated me. Yale didn't want me. Everyone else saw me, if they saw me at all, as that weirdo lesbian attached at the hip to Fay. And now Fay was . . . Fay had . . . Fay never smiled that way at me. No one ever smiled that way at me. Who would I be, what would I have left, if Fay—

"Stop, stop," said Ms. Spider. "What happened to the tenor section?"

As Ms. Spider went over the tenor part, yet again and fruitlessly, with the junior girl who kept singing the soprano line an octave down, Fay pulled out a scrap of notebook paper and started scribbling. A moment later she passed me a note scrawled in urgent block letters.

We talked for an HOUR

I turned and eyed her through my hair. She covered her mouth with one hand to hide her grin.

I pressed the scrap of paper against our shared music stand. With my pencil, I circled the word "HOUR" and scribbled underneath: *Today?*

She squinted at the word, puzzled.

I scribbled again: *Did you tell him about Bottom?*

She shook her head *no.* Her hand knocked against mine as she scribbled against my music stand: *MF = INVERT. Can he & Xtopher join the Society?*

I stared at her. Too shocked to write, I whispered, "He came out to you?"

She shrugged and made a hand-wavy gesture to indicate *sort of.*

I circled *"he & Xtopher"* and drew a heart, followed by a question mark.

Unconfirmed, Fay wrote. *But he implied* . . . Under her music stand, she made a circle with the thumb and forefinger of her right hand, then repeatedly plowed her left index finger in and out of the circle, symbolizing ass-fucking.

Relief flooded me, and I burst into giggles. Ms. Spider glared at me. I clapped my hands over my mouth but couldn't stop laughing. I couldn't believe how wildly I'd misunderstood the situation. How could I mistake Fay and Theo's new dynamic for a boyfriend-girlfriend one when there was a much more obvious explanation?

I cast a glance at Theo in the corner of the room. He was bouncing in the armchair, making the underclassgirls laugh by pretending to conduct the music. I turned back to the note and wrote: *you = his fag hag now?*

I knew the expression from *Out* magazine and videotapes of Margaret Cho's stand-up, and it was clearly the best way to describe Fay's whole deal, but I'd never used the phrase myself and it felt weird to write. On second thought, I added *(except not a hag)*.

Fay read the note. To my amazement, her face turned bright red. I'd never seen her blush like that before. She turned to me and whispered, "So just a . . ." She pointed to the word *fag*.

"Yeah, you're not a hag," I whispered back. "You're pretty."

She blushed harder—even her neck turned red—and giggled so hard, she grabbed my knee to steady herself. There was a hole in my jeans, and her hand made contact with the bare skin of my knee. Her hand was very warm, almost hot, probably from holding the Starbucks cup.

"Wake up, Nell," Ms. Spider called out from the piano. I'd missed the alto entrance.

"The heavens are telling, are telling
The glory of God . . ."

As I sang along with the rest of the chorus, crescendoing our way up to the big finish, a certain feeling came over me. It happened sometimes when I was singing in Chorus (and sometimes, more rarely, when doing a play), but never this intensely before. The best way I can describe it is: I felt shiny. Not in a center-of-attention way: I felt whole, but also part of something bigger than myself. Like one glittering facet on a spinning disco ball. I guess it's what Quakers call the Inner Light. You could call it lots of things, but whatever it was, it was the opposite of the aloneness I'd felt a few minutes ago. I belonged.

And it wasn't just about the music this time. It was knowing I wasn't the only gay kid in school anymore. Now there was Theo and Christopher—and maybe, just maybe, there was Fay, with her blushing neck and her warm hand on my knee—and we were all members of the Invert Society, which was a real club now.

On the spot, I made a decision.

The bell rang. As the rest of the chorus swarmed Theo, I approached Ms. Spider at the piano. "Great rehearsal today," I said.

"Would have been better with a baritone section," she grumbled, gathering her sheet music.

"About that baritone," I said. "He told me to tell you he's sick. He can't come to *La Bohème* tonight."

"*Excuse* me?" She looked up at me from the bench, nostrils flaring. "He sure as hell didn't look sick this morning," she said. "Does he know what those tickets cost? Does he have the faintest idea how many strings I had to pull to get Skip and Trudy to sign off on this? It was for *him*, damn it, he's the one who—"

"Wait," I said. "I have an idea." I leaned over the piano and lowered my voice—partly so the rest of the chorus wouldn't get jealous, and partly so it would be a surprise for Fay. "Between him and Wanda," I said, "we have two extra tickets now . . ."

Dinner is at an Italian restaurant called Puttanesca. "Do you know what *puttana* means?" Ms. Spider asks us.

Bottom might know. He's picked up so much Italian from the *La Bohème* libretto. But Bottom isn't here.

"It means *whore*," says Ms. Spider. "Puttanesca sauce is made with anchovies and olives and capers, so it smells very pungent—like a whore's you-know-what. Or so the legend goes." To the waiter she says, "A bottle of the Chianti, please, for the table."

The waiter pours a trickle of red wine into Ms. Spider's glass. She tastes it, approves, and motions for him to serve us. The waiter pours the wine into our glasses, where it glimmers lushly. We sip it very slowly; it is lukewarm and sour and thrillingly unpleasant, lingering in our mouths like the marvelous secret it is. We dip warm bread into olive oil. We order caprese, pear and gorgonzola salad, rigatoni bolognese, potato gnocchi, and of course penne puttanesca. We'll have to eat fast because the curtain rises at eight o'clock. Ms. Spider puts down two credit cards in advance, telling the waiter to charge the wine on a separate card, and we giggle conspiratorially, our lips smeared interestingly violet. She doesn't ask us to keep this a secret, which itself ensures that we'll never tell.

F: "Bolognese is my favorite."

N: "Mine too!"

Theo: [*sly*] "Really, Nell? I thought yours would be puttanesca."

N: [*firing back*] "I haven't gotten to try it yet."

Theo: "Maybe Fay will let you eat her puttanesca."

Christopher: [*oblivious*] "I thought we were all sharing."

F: [*in the voice of Laurence Olivier during the snails-and-oysters scene in Spartacus*] "*My* taste . . . includes . . . both bolognese *and* puttanesca."

N: "Not that there's anything wrong with that."

Christopher: "I don't get it."

"You guys are a riot," Ms. Spider says merrily. "I can just picture you as the sailors and their girls in *On the Town*."

We drop our bread and snap to attention: the spring musical?

"Oh, what the hell," says Ms. Spider. "Yes, it's official."

As we eat, Ms. Spider describes the show. It's World War II, and a Navy ship has docked in New York City, its sailors on twenty-four-hour shore leave. One of them, an energetic ladies' man named Ozzie (tenor), gets together with Claire (soprano), a classy anthropologist and closet nymphomaniac. Another sailor, the neurotic and naïve Chip (baritone), gets together with Hildy (alto), a ball-busting taxi driver.

Theo: "Hey! *I'm* a tenor."

"I'll be damned," Ms. Spider deadpans.

Christopher: "And I'm a baritone! I think."

N: "Will you double-cast it?"

"Hell no," says Ms. Spider. "I'm not Wanda. One role, one performer—Thursday *and* Friday. That's what you get with me."

There's a pause. Just a slight one.

"Oh, and there's one other male lead," Ms. Spider adds. "Gabey. Another baritone."

N: "Perfect! That's Bottom!"

F: "So we *all* get to be the leads?"

"No promises," says Ms. Spider in a tone that makes it very clear that this is a promise. We all clink glasses and drink on it.

After dinner we walk briskly to the theater on Fifty-third Street and sit way up in the balcony—"in heaven," Ms. Spider calls it. When that pure oboe A first rings out and the orchestra clamorously tunes up, Ms. Spider sighs with satisfaction. "That's my favorite sound in the whole goddamn world."

Christopher, on the far left: "Hey, thanks for inviting me."

Theo, on his right: "Yeah! Thanks so much for all of this."

F, on Theo's right: "Don't thank me. It was Nell's idea."

N, on F's right: "Don't thank me. Thank Ms. Spider."

The Invert Society, in chorus: "Thank you, Dorothy!"

"Don't thank me," says Ms. Spider. "Thank Idlewild."

The four of us groan.

"Hey, now," says Ms. Spider. "Idlewild is what's paying for this."

Theo: "Okay, but Idlewild owes us. Where do you think it gets its money?"

"Oh?" says Ms. Spider. "And what, exactly, do you feel you're owed?"

Theo, flinging his hands outward: "Everything."

N: "The *best* of everything."

F: "The best, the best!"

The lights go down. The curtain goes up. The opera begins.

We're so high up, so far away, we can barely see the singers onstage. But we can see from the costumes and the scenery that it's supposed to look like Paris in the 1950s. We can read the supertitles projected above the singers' heads, in a different font for each character. We recognize Party LET, the Invert Society poster font, when the goofy guy in the yellow zoot suit says he poisoned his boss's parrot. We see a lady in a baby-blue dress—no, a girl, a delicate girl with bobbed black hair and a face like the full moon. She sings that the sunshine belongs to her, the springtime belongs to her, she looks out on the rooftops through her little window and the whole city of Paris belongs to her. She and her leather-jacketed lover embrace under a big sign that says L'AMOUR. *"Amor! Amor!"* they sing to each other, and we don't need to look at the supertitles to know what that means.

We are holding hands, N holding F holding Theo holding Christopher, the four of us linked in a chain, clasping each other in wordless wonder. When the curtain goes up for intermission, how will we even speak of what's happening right now—of anything that's happened today? Red wine. Black snow. The shouting in the Meetinghouse. The standard ambient ambulance sirens wailing faintly through the walls of the theater, the way the singers just sing over it and the whole audience leans in, willing the outside intrusion to disappear; the collective breath of relief when it finally does. The fact that we have to pee, desperately, but the physical urgency of the feeling—the way it forces us to squeeze our thighs together and clench—only heightens the intensity of the aria. The floating high C of the delicate soprano in the baby-blue dress as the curtain falls on her embrace with her lover. Like if glass could sing. If the moon could sing. If *we* could sing—if we could crack ourselves open and let our Inner Light shine out, this is how the light would sound. The four of us are joined at the hand, awash in music that only we are lucky enough to hear. No one else at Idlewild. No one else in New York. No one else in the world.

IV

FAY

I was deranged with joy. I was incandescent, iridescent, bioluminescent inside. I was in a conventional dither with a conventional star in my eye (see *South Pacific*, Rodgers & Hammerstein, 1949). I was waking before sunrise, too euphoric to fall back asleep or read or do anything but cup my hand between my legs and palm the mound where my dick would have been until I came, rapturously, to thoughts of Theo at the opera, his lips wine-stained and his fingers intertwined with Christopher's; snow-chilled Theo in the garden, boyish and puckish and girlishly coy; leather-pants Theo on the lamplit street above my bedroom window, cruising and being cruised.

Theo spent the holidays in France, where his father lived, so I had no contact with him over winter break. This suited me fine: it was Nell's company I craved, not his. All throughout winter break, in person and in AIM conversations that lasted well into the dawn hours, I attempted to make Nell understand what had happened between Theo and me—an optimistic goal, in retrospect, considering that I myself didn't understand it. But Nell was as enthusiastic a listener as I was a talker, and during that winter break she indulged my Theo fixation until the mere sight of her screen name on my Buddy List (especially when affixed with that starry asterisk alerting me that she had just logged on) lit me up with Pavlovian pleasure.

On Christmas Eve, a holiday unobserved in our households, Nell and I met up on the equidistant Union Square steps and walked together to the Sunshine Cinema on the Lower East Side, a mile-long journey during which we never once departed from the subject of Theo's use of the word *cruising*. "It's kind of an unlikely word for a tenth-grade boy to know," I said as we walked down Houston Street. "I've known it for years, of course, but I learned it from Gareth. I wonder where Theo picked it up."

"Maybe he's seen the movie," said Nell.

"What movie?"

"*Cruising*," she said. "From like the eighties, remember? It's covered in *The Celluloid Closet*."

It seemed so long ago that I had shown her *The Celluloid Closet*. I hadn't realized she remembered it in such detail, and I was so pleased, I could have thrown my arms around her. I didn't, of course.

"But the real question is," I said, "why did he say it to *me*? How did he know that *I* know what cruising is? Do I look like someone who goes cruising?" As I spoke, I was aware of my volume increasing almost to a shout every time I uttered the word *cruising*. I was talking loudly enough for passersby to overhear me. I wanted them to know—I wanted the whole city of New York to know—that I was a girl unlike other girls, a girl in possession of decidedly ungirlish knowledge.

Nell said, "I think everyone at Idlewild would assume you know what cruising is."

I laughed, shriekingly. It was the most feminine sound I was capable of making, but I didn't mind, not if Nell's words were true.

We arrived at the theater having failed to decide or even discuss which movie to see. "How about *The Hours*?" said Nell.

"I want to see *Talk to Her*," I said. "It's by the same guy who did *All About My Mother*."

"Of course you want to see that one," said Nell. "Fag hag. Minus the hag."

It was right then, I think, that I made a decision.

I thought about my decision, and its implications, for the rest of the day. I bulldozed Nell into seeing *Talk to Her* (2002, dir. Pedro Almodóvar), but I recall nothing whatsoever about it, because I absorbed none of it as I sat beside her in the Sunshine's luxurious recliner-style seats, for-mulating a secret plan.

Three days later, I visited Idlewild alone.

The building looked empty, the lights shut off in every classroom window. The front door was locked. I loitered at the Fifteenth Street entrance until a janitor spotted me through a window and confusedly opened the door. "Young lady, you gotta check your calendar," he said. "Don't you know it's Christmas vacation?"

"I'm meeting a teacher," I said. "I have an appointment." And Idlewild being Idlewild, he let me in.

I walked through the empty Meetinghouse and crossed the empty Peace Garden. It had snowed again on Christmas; the snow in the garden was still pristine, and I left an incriminating trail of solitary footprints in my path. I climbed four flights of stairs, my footsteps echoing through the empty stairwell. There was a certain post-apocalyptic *unheimlich* quality to being the only student in the building. It was a relief to find a fellow human being, right where he'd promised I would find him.

"Where's the other half of you?" was Jimmy Frye's greeting.

He gestured for me to come around to his side of the desk, where he'd placed a second chair next to his. I hoped the meeting would be quick. I came around the desk and sat down, keeping my coat and scarf on to communicate that I was only passing through.

"I told you," I said. My instinct was to be harsh and imperious toward him as usual, but I wasn't accustomed to doing so without Nell to back me up, and my voice came out wavery and girlish. "Nell doesn't know about this."

"Yeah, yeah. Just busting your chops." He turned to his computer and moved the mouse around. At such close range, his body odor was harder than ever to talk myself out of noticing. "She's not still sore over my email, is she?"

"Don't worry about it." It was imperative that I remain in his good graces today.

"I know I come off gruff sometimes," he said. "But I'm a prickly pear— real soft on the inside. That's just my Scorpio nature." Over his shoulder I watched him open the Documents folder and double-click on a file called FAY_RECOMMENDATION.doc (I remember the all-caps, characteristic of him). "I've got it mostly written," he said. "Just wanted to run a few things by you."

There was little reason for him to interview me at all. Calling me into his office in the middle of winter break, as opposed to telephoning or emailing or meeting me in a diner, was an unnecessary power trip. But I resisted the urge to roll my eyes. I reminded myself that Jimmy, as a non-teacher, had surely never been asked to write a college recommendation before. If he wanted to make a day of it, who could blame him?

"First of all," he said, "just to confirm: Brown, Oberlin, Occidental, Brandeis, Lewis & Clark, Emerson, Skidmore, and Smith?"

I confirmed.

"Would you say your main interest is theater?"

"Musical theater," I said, "and the Invert Society. Or I guess, in the letter, you can call it the Gay-Straight Alliance."

"Got it." He typed. "And what made you decide to join that club?"

"I mean, it's barely a club," I said. "It's just me and Nell hanging out in a room. Although"—I smiled to think of it—"we just got a couple of new members, so—"

"Don't say *that* in college interviews," he said. "You'll be up against a lot of other kids, you know, and they're all coming from schools that give grades and prizes. Make an effort."

I was beginning to regret asking Jimmy for this favor. Two teacher recommendations were mandatory, and while Ms. Spider had been happy to oblige me on such short notice ("I thought you'd never ask," she told me on the phone), I'd been too ashamed to contact, say, Glenn or Devi and reveal how disastrously late I'd put off my college applications. Jimmy Frye was not a teacher, but at least he was an Idlewild authority figure, and I didn't care what he thought of me. I knew how to flatter his ego, and I was confident that I could count on him to honor an emailed request, sent on Christmas Eve, for a letter of recommendation due by mail in less than one week. But I hadn't anticipated the degree to which I would be putting myself at his mercy.

"Fine," I said. "I joined the Gay-Straight Alliance because . . . I wanted to serve my community."

He typed. "And what community would that be?"

"The gay-straight community." I laughed at my own joke, wishing Nell were there to hear it.

"And are you gay or straight?"

It was the first time I'd ever been asked directly. I forced another laugh.

"Just trying to get the full picture here," he said. "Who *is* Fay Vasquez-Rabinowitz? What makes her tick? What does she eat for breakfast?"

"You don't have to go to so much trouble," I said. "It can just be, like, a paragraph."

"Come on, Fay," he said. "Don't you want to get into college?"

Not really; not so much as I wanted Nell not to go. I considered leveling with Jimmy about this, but then I noticed the look on his face—a certain hardness around the eyes, a sadistic twist of the mouth—and understood that the question was a threat.

"So give it to me straight." He grinned. "Or not, as the case may be."

"I don't like labels," I ventured.

"Well, let me put it this way." He angled himself away from the computer and faced me directly. Our chairs were so close that his knees touched mine. I pulled away. "You and Nell ever . . . play around?"

He was still grinning. The smell of him was a thing I could almost hear. His office was very hot, as the computer lab always was, but now was not the time to remove my coat and scarf. Beneath my layers of coat and sweater and shirt, my armpits felt damp. I wondered if he could smell me as well.

Had Nell been at my side, I would have yelled at him—she and I would have yelled at him in unison and laughed about it afterward. How powerful we were together, Nell and I. How useless I was without her.

"Not really," I said, unable to form an unambiguous *no*.

"Not *really*?" he said, delighted. "Oh, you're not getting off that easy. I've got all day." He chuckled, resting his hands behind his head. "Give me the dirty details."

It struck me with sickening clarity that I'd brought this on myself. This was a taste of my own medicine: Jimmy was objectifying me and Nell just as I objectified Theo and Christopher. Just as I objectified all gay men. How could I sit in judgment of Jimmy Frye? I was no better: a sleazy fetishist, sweaty and predatory and pathetic. Small wonder no one could stand me once they got to know me.

No one but Nell. I couldn't lose her. I couldn't.

"Okay," I said. "There was this one time."

I closed my eyes. *Forgive me, Nell*, I thought. *This is for us.*

"It was, um, September eleventh. I had to sleep over with Nell, in her room." My body remained in the IT office with Jimmy Frye, but I spoke from what felt like a slight distance above it. "And there was only one bed."

NELL

When the cast list went up, Fay and I burst through Ms. Spider's office door screaming "THANK YOU!"

We'd landed the leads, obviously—me and Fay and Theo and Christopher. I was the butch taxi driver, and I had a bunch of solos, including a funny song where I sexually harassed Christopher. There were technically three leading couples, but it was clear that ours were the better roles. Still, Bottom's character had the most beautiful songs, so it didn't feel unfair. To our satisfaction, Daylily's character mostly didn't sing. Best of all, Juniper Green was relegated to a minor non-singing role (my character's roommate).

Ms. Spider held out her clay ashtray full of Tootsie Rolls. "How does it feel to be stars?"

It felt amazing—right up until the first read-through.

It quickly became clear that Ms. Spider wouldn't be able to get the room under control. She was old and tired, unused to directing in general, and out of practice commanding any group bigger than the nine-person chorus. The *On the Town* ensemble included Middle Schoolers as well as Upper Schoolers, so there were almost fifty people in the cast, and Theo seemed to feed off their energy. By the time the full cast had gathered in the rehearsal room, Theo was standing on the *Winter's Tale* armchair, jumping up and down and yelling, "I AM GOD. Who wants to be my first mortal sacrifice?"

The Middle Schoolers and underclassgirls raised their hands gleefully. Fay called out, "I nominate Christopher!"

"No thank you," said Christopher. "I'm an atheist."

"You have incurred my divine wrath," said Theo. "Now you must defeat me in battle." He yanked his scarf off his neck. "It's a strip battle!" He tossed it into the crowd, where Kendra caught it.

Christopher laughed. "You mean like the kind I *won* last time?"

"Yeah, in the privacy of our bedroom." Theo unbuttoned his navy blue cardigan, revealing a white undershirt. "But can you do it in front of all these people?"

Fay and I were sitting together on the tattered gray carpet. At the reference to Theo and Christopher's shared bedroom, Fay's whole body thrashed with excitement, knocking against mine. "Why were you having a strip battle in your bedroom?"

Theo shrugged. "I get bored sometimes, okay?" He tossed his cardigan into the crowd. It landed right on Bottom's head.

Bottom was sitting on the floor in front of the *Winter's Tale* armchair. With great dignity, he pulled the cardigan off his head and draped it across the arm of the armchair above him. "Why don't we declare a tie," he said, "and start the read-through?"

"No ties," Theo declared. "Only winners and losers." He hopped in place on the armchair, trying to wrest off his left shoe with his right foot.

I glanced guiltily at Ms. Spider. She was sitting patiently on the piano bench, studying the sheet music and marking it with a pencil. Apparently she was waiting for the boys to settle down on their own, but she'd been waiting—*we'd* been waiting—for forty minutes. "Guys," I said lamely. "Maybe save the strip battle for after the read-through?"

"No." Theo jumped off the armchair and lunged toward Christopher. "Pants off, bitch!" Christopher let out a gay little shriek, and Theo began to chase him around the rehearsal room, which caused all the underclass-girls to shriek too.

"Oh, for fuck's sake." Juniper Green jumped onto the armchair. She was so tiny this gave her only a modest height advantage, but her voice pierced cleanly through the crowd noise. "EVERYBODY SETTLE DOWN! OPEN YOUR SCRIPTS TO PAGE ONE!"

This actually worked. The room fell quiet. Even Theo and Christopher sat down and picked up their scripts. "You're the best," Daylily whispered as Juniper sat back down on her chair, and I was grudgingly grateful too.

But even Juniper couldn't maintain order for long. As the cast read through the script, Theo and Christopher continued to goof off, first in whispers, and then louder. Their strip battle morphed into a fashion show, Christopher catwalking around the rehearsal room with his belt tied around his left leg and his shirt tied up in front Britney-style and tucked into his hiked-up boxer shorts. "Here we have your Sunday dinner club getup," Theo narrated in a Eurotrash voice. Ms. Spider shushed them, but that just caused the fashion show to morph into a silent interpretive dance, and then a non-silent interpretive dance about Glenn Harding getting attacked by a dog. Ms. Spider didn't notice until the whole cast was giggling. In the last hour she finally forced Theo and Christopher to sit separately, but by then it was way too late to accomplish anything productive. By the time we finally made it to the end of the script, I felt like I hadn't processed any of it. I don't think anyone else had, either.

"Good first try, everyone," Ms. Spider said weakly.

Juniper Green jumped to her feet. "Okay, I'm out," she announced. "I quit."

"What?" Daylily cried. "You can't quit!"

"She doesn't mean it," said Bottom reassuringly.

"I mean it." Juniper grabbed her coat and backpack. "This is a shitshow. I have better things to do." She stormed out of the rehearsal room.

Daylily's lip trembled. "She *can't* quit. I've never done a show without her." Her eyes filled with tears.

Bottom put his arm around her. "She'll change her mind," he said. Trying to cheer her up, he joked, "I can't imagine she'd be willing to miss the cast party, can you?"

It didn't work. As they left the rehearsal room together, Daylily was sobbing openly.

From the piano bench, Ms. Spider watched the door swing shut behind them. "That bad, huh?" she said. She looked exhausted.

Fay rolled her eyes. "She's just mad because she didn't get a big part."

"Yeah, she's bluffing," I said. "Don't worry. The first read-through is always chaos." This was true, though it was never *this* level of chaos. "You're gonna be a great director." I hoped this was also true.

The rest of the cast, quiet and uneasy after Juniper's outburst, trickled uncertainly out of the rehearsal room. I wondered if Ms. Spider would stay behind to yell at Theo and Christopher, but she walked out without a word.

Then it was just me, Fay, Theo, and Christopher in the rehearsal room.

For the last hour, forcibly separated from Christopher, Theo had been quiet, almost sulky. He was still wearing just his white undershirt, his jeans, and one black sneaker. Now he got up and threw himself into the *Winter's Tale* armchair. "Fuck," he muttered.

I felt the same way, to be honest. But Theo had some nerve to act so put-upon when he was the one who'd ruined the read-through.

"I don't know why I get like this." He flung his bare arm over his eyes. "I don't want to be this way."

I assumed he was doing some kind of bit. I waited for him to say more. But he didn't.

After a long, awkward silence, Christopher walked over to the armchair. He picked up Theo's cardigan from where Bottom had draped it over the chair's arm. He touched Theo's bare shoulder. "You're cold," he said quietly. "Put this on."

Theo sat up and allowed Christopher to give him the cardigan. He pulled it on. "I just get so bored," he said distantly. "You know?"

"I know." Christopher handed Theo the black sneaker he'd kicked off. "You need to eat something."

Theo clasped his hand around Christopher's, not letting him let go of the shoe, and looked up at him from the armchair. "Can we go to Steak Frites?"

Christopher sighed. "Am I paying again?"

"You can afford it," said Theo. "Just don't tip the waiter." He seemed more cheerful already. Finally letting go of Christopher's hand, he put on his shoe. He looked across the rehearsal room at Fay and me. "Want to come?" he said. "Invert Society dinner party? Christopher's treat."

It crossed my mind that it wasn't too late to talk to Ms. Spider about recasting him. She'd probably be relieved to get rid of him.

But then I noticed Fay's smile—it was so big I could see it in my peripheral vision—and the phrase *Invert Society dinner party* echoed in my head. Maybe, I thought, this was just how it felt to have a cool gay friend group. Maybe it was always this exhausting and destabilizing. Maybe, in that sense, it was like being in love.

FAY

The Marble Faun, Chapter Seven[1]:
Strip Hangman

It started out so innocently. They were rehearsing the museum scene, and Ms. Spider was distracted trying to corral all the Middle Schoolers playing the cavemen, so the four stars had a lot of downtime (which was okay because they already knew their lines by heart, especially Fay,[2] so they didn't

---

[1] I came away from my clandestine meeting with Jimmy Frye convinced that the Faunfic was fetish porn of the basest order and that I'd repurposed it for Jimmy so cynically that the unpleasant mental association would taint it forever. I resolved to quit writing it, much as I've often resolved in the years since to quit alcohol. In all such cases, this one included, I lasted approximately one week before guiltily, joyfully relapsing.

[2] Claire de Loone, my character in *On the Town*, is an underrated role in the American musical theater canon: a rare comedic lead for a soprano, with solo and duet numbers ranging from Wagnerian pastiche ("Carried Away") to Great American Songbook poignancy ("Some Other Time"). Her character introduction takes place at the Museum of Natural History. Though the stage directions describe her as "cool and poised," she takes one look at young sailor-tourist Ozzie and shrieks with delight. "How extraordinary!" she exclaims. "In all my studies, I've never seen one like it. This is wonderful. What a lucky girl I am." Producing a camera, a tape measure, and a notebook, she subjects her perfect specimen to an impromptu physical examination. She is an anthropologist, she explains, at work on a book called *Modern Man: What Is It?* She's engaged to an older man, with whom she has "a purely intellectual relationship." At his suggestion, she's working on this "scientific study of men," trying to "get to know them objectively," so as to "get them out of [her] system." "Did it work?" Ozzie

need to rehearse that much). They were hanging out in the corner of the rehearsal room, and they were getting bored of playing hangman.

"I have an idea," Theo announced. "Let's play *strip* hangman."[3]

"What's strip hangman?" Christopher inquired warily, already noticing the familiar devilish Marble Faun glint in Theo's eyes.

"Stand right there," Theo commanded. He placed his hands on Christopher's shoulders, and though the smaller boy's hands were slender, almost delicate, Christopher felt helpless beneath their power, as though those hands could crush his bones to dust. "A hanged man should be blindfolded," Theo declared. He borrowed Fay's beautiful slate scarf[4] and tied it around Christopher's eyes.

"Ten letters," said Theo, firmly gripping Christopher's shoulders with his gracefully long-fingered yet surprisingly strong hands. "Go."

"A," guessed Nell.

"No A," Theo responded. Keeping one hand on Christopher's shoulder, he slid his other hand to the front of Christopher's body and began deftly unbuttoning Christopher's shirt. Christopher tried to squirm away. It was

---

asks. "Almost completely," she deadpans and throws herself at her specimen, kissing him wildly. (In performance, I stage-kissed Theo with my hand covering his mouth, just as he'd stage-kissed Christopher when Nell and I first met him.) In their enthusiasm they accidentally knock over and destroy a priceless dinosaur skeleton, a crisis that renders them fugitives for the rest of the show.

[3] Though this chapter embellishes greatly upon the reality of the *On the Town* rehearsal process, strip hangman was real.

[4] This is the point at which fiction and reality diverge. What actually happened was that when, playfully, I didn't immediately relinquish my scarf, Theo yanked so hard on it that he tore it in two. Later, I would cling to the memory of Theo's face in that instant—his smile vanishing, his mouth round with dismay. He was, if not sorry, at least surprised. He hadn't meant to destroy my Iago scarf. Or so I believed then, even as I lunged at him shouting, "I'll END you, motherfucker!" and Nell and Christopher chanted, "Fight! Fight! Fight!"

one thing for the Marble Faun to undress him in the privacy of their
shared bedroom, but they were in public! But despite his slight build and
weak lungs, Theo managed to overpower the taller boy and pull off his
shirt. Luckily Christopher was wearing an undershirt beneath it.

"T," guessed Fay.

"No T," Theo rejoined, and then Christopher felt Theo's hands tugging
at the hem of his undershirt. Christopher knew he should have protested,
taken off the blindfold, refused to let Theo undress him in front of so
many people.[5] And yet he felt almost hypnotized. Theo was making him
feel like a Ken doll, mute and pliable, made to be tossed around and
played with. Christopher stood there helpless as the Marble Faun pulled
off the taller boy's undershirt.

"O," guessed Fay.

"Yes," Theo affirmed. "O is the second letter." Theo's fingertips ghosted
lightly over the naked skin of Christopher's back.

"E," guessed Nell.

"Yes," Theo confirmed. "E is the ninth letter." Theo raked his nails lightly
up and down Christopher's spine. Placing his lips close to the shell of
Christopher's ear so no one else would hear, Theo husked, "You're doing
great, buddy."

---

[5] I remember ceremoniously taking off my army jacket, rolling up my shirt-
sleeves. I remember Theo counting down.
  "Three . . . two . . ."
  I don't remember what I imagined would happen next. Was I really planning
to hit Theo? Did I really expect him to hit me?
  "One."
  I didn't expect him to barrel toward me or body-check me so hard that I
stumbled, and I certainly didn't expect him to grab me by the wrists and swing
me onto the floor. I landed ass-first and pain thrummed from my tailbone up
my spine. I'd carpet-burned my elbows, too, and my wrists throbbed. This had
abruptly ceased to be fun. For one humiliating moment, I thought I might cry.

Christopher realized he was getting hard. He prayed for Fay and Nell to guess the word.

"H," guessed Fay.

"No H," Theo replied. Expertly, his fingers unbuckled Christopher's belt, unbuttoned and unzipped his fly, and Christopher's jeans fell to his ankles.

Christopher stood there blindfolded in his boxer shorts with his jeans around his ankles. He was in an agony of humiliation, but at the same time he didn't want it to stop. He was afraid that everyone could see his erection through his boxers. The fear only made him harder.[6]

"C," guessed Nell.

"There are three C's," Theo averred. "The first letter, the third letter, and the seventh letter."

"Okay, I think I can guess the whole word," said Nell cautiously.

"Me too," said Fay more confidently. "If we guess it right, you guys have to make out."

Christopher blinked behind the blindfold. "What?" he protested. "No!"

Theo's hand clapped hard against Christopher's mouth. The other hand gripped the back of Christopher's neck like how you grab a cat by the scruff. Theo's hands were very hot now, and when he breathed into the shell of Christopher's ear, his voice was soft and rough at the same time. "Hanged men don't talk."

---

[6] Theo pounced on me, pressing his whole weight upon me as he tried to pin my shoulders to the floor. His face was suddenly very close to mine, and I wondered for an instant what he saw of me. Then his hands were on me. They were on my ribs—I squealed in anticipation, thinking he was about to tickle me—and then they were on my thighs, spreading my legs apart. With his right hand, he made a fist. He punched me, hard, in the crotch.

Frantically, Christopher reminded himself that this wasn't gay. He and Theo were just putting on a show for the girls, that was all.

Fay and Nell guessed the word at the same time: "COCKSUCKER."

Theo took his hands off Christopher's body. Christopher was partly relieved and partly bereft with yearning for the smaller boy's touch—but the next thing he knew, Theo's hands were grabbing him by the back of the head and pulling him in, and the two boys' mouths were crushed together. Christopher tried to gasp for air but Theo slid his tongue into Christopher's mouth until Christopher was choking, gagging, blind and mute and helpless in Theo's arms. Christopher couldn't stop himself from bucking his hips, grinding his barely clothed erection against Theo. The two boys fell to the floor in a heap, and still they kept kissing and kissing. Theo's hands slid over Christopher's bare chest. Christopher clung to Theo's slim hips for support as he explored the smaller boy's mouth with his tongue. Christopher didn't know how many minutes had gone by when he became aware of Fay and Nell cheering them on and remembered he was supposed to be doing this for them.

In a blasé tone of voice, because she was nearing retirement and didn't give a shit, Ms. Spider called out, "Sorry to interrupt, but I need to borrow Theo and Fay again. Let's take it from the top."

Theo got up, leaving Christopher blindfolded in his underwear on the floor.[7] Nell helped him[8] out of the blindfold and back into his clothes so they could watch Theo and Fay rehearse "Carried Away." They were amazing.

---

[7] I screamed in a playful, theatrical way before I fully felt the impact of the fist on my vulva. Through my jeans, the blow was dull rather than sharp. *Pain* wasn't the precise word for the sensation, which was lingering and almost electrical in its slow, sizzling aftershocks. Whatever it was, it silenced and immobilized me.

[8] "Theo, *no*," said Nell, as though reprimanding a dog. She managed to drag Theo off me. Kneeling beside me again, she asked, "You okay?"

There was no urgency in her voice, no acknowledgment of where Theo had just hit me. I understood then that Theo had positioned himself so that the punch wasn't visible to others. Nell hadn't witnessed it. No one had. It hadn't been for show. It had been for me alone.

NELL

Juniper Green wasn't bluffing: she really did quit the show. (Her part was reassigned to Rollerblading Maddy.) I didn't miss her, exactly, but it felt weird to do a show without her. Especially because Bottom and Daylily, in her absence, seemed totally checked out of the rehearsal process. A month or so into it, they even began to miss rehearsals.

I was getting increasingly annoyed with them. Especially Bottom—I'd never known him to miss a rehearsal before. In his defense, though, he turned out to have a pretty good reason.

The first time was in February.

Every Monday morning we had Meeting for Announcements, and there was one in February that began with a special announcement from Skip, the principal. "Have you ever noticed," said Skip, "that the iron fence posts in front of the Meetinghouse are blunted at the top? Believe it or not, they used to have decorative spikes. But in 1917, the spikes were sawed off as an act of protest. Can anyone guess what the Quakers were protesting in 1917?"

There was a long pause. Fay and I looked up and tried to pretend we weren't playing hangman in my notebook.

In the bench in front of us, Bottom raised his hand. "Wasn't that when the US entered World War I?"

"That's correct," said Skip. "As a Quaker school, Idlewild has historically stood in opposition to all wars. And now that we have yet another war looming on the horizon, I want to talk to you all about filing for conscientious objector status."

My stomach jerked with fear. Everyone I knew was against invading Iraq, but I was *really* against it. Based on what little I'd read—every morning over breakfast I scanned the front page and op-ed section of my mom's *New York Times*—I fully believed that Saddam Hussein had weapons of mass destruction. I also believed that they were aimed directly at New York and he was just one bad day away from nuking us. I can't blame the *New York Times* for that one; I'm not sure where I picked up the idea, or if I completely made it up, but it weighed on me.

"What does it mean to be a conscientious objector?" said Skip. "In 1651, George Fox said . . ."

I zoned out, looking at the back of Bottom's head. He was sitting next to Daylily, who was sitting next to Juniper. I wondered if he was still mad at me for spreading the story that his parents got Wanda fired. Which I *hadn't*, I reminded myself furiously. I'd told Fay, but she hadn't told anyone else, so it rounded down to not telling anyone. I had nothing to feel guilty about.

"God willing," said Skip, "you won't end up needing this information. But if you're eighteen, or about to turn eighteen, and male—"

Daylily lifted her hand and gave Bottom's shoulder a comforting squeeze.

I leaned over to whisper in Fay's ear. (It never felt sacrilegious to whisper or pass notes during Meeting for Announcements as it did during Meeting for Worship.) "I just don't get the logic," I said, "of attacking a guy who has nuclear bombs. Shouldn't we be sucking up to him?"

That was actually what I believed. Appeasement, in general, has always been my policy. This might be my least favorite thing about myself.

"Sucking up to him?" Fay whispered back. "He's a brutal dictator."

"Yeah, but so is Bush," I edgy-teenagered.

"So's your mom," said Fay.

"Will you shut *up*?" Juniper hissed, twisting around to glare at us.

"It's a very personal choice," said Skip. "But if you decide this is the right path for you, the forms are available in the front office—"

Juniper said, "Some of us actually want to hear this, okay?"

"It doesn't apply to girls," Fay pointed out.

"They could draft women this time," said Juniper.

"—and every teacher on the faculty is committed to supporting you," said Skip, "so don't be afraid to ask for help with the application."

"There might not be a draft," I whispered. "There might not even be a war."

Mr. Prins shushed us. Juniper turned back around. Fay and I pantomimed jacking off and ejaculating onto her head.

"Whatever your decision," said Skip, "we hold you in the Light."

He sat. Trudy stood. "Thank you, Skip," she said. "Any other announcements?"

On the bench in front of us, Juniper Green raised her hand. Trudy called on her. She stood.

"Do you feel helpless to stop the invasion of Iraq? Well, you're not! Together, we can make a difference. I'm Jennifer Green. The hot babe next to me is Lily Day-Jones. We're throwing a letter-writing party, and you're all invited. We're gonna write to Senators Chuck Schumer and Hillary Clinton and let them know that their constituents are against the war. We'll supply paper, envelopes, stamps, Gelly Rolls in all the colors, actual jelly rolls if you get hungry—trust me, you don't want to miss out. The time: this Friday, after school."

Fay and I sighed with frustration: that conflicted with a full-cast *On the Town* rehearsal.

"My place," said Juniper. "Come up to me and Lily after Meeting, and we'll give you the address. Be there! Or else . . ." And then, in this absolutely repellent sexy-baby voice, she cooed, "Me and Lily will just have to play alone in my room, *alllll* by ourselves."

People giggled. Some stupid boys hooted.

"And no one wants *that*, right?" From behind, I saw Juniper lift her hand to her mouth; I think she was playfully biting her finger. On the bench beside her, Daylily giggled and covered her face with her hands.

"All right, Jen, thank you for your announcement," said Trudy. "General reminder that this is the House of God, and all presentations in the Meetinghouse should be *appropriate*."

"Hey, that's homophobic," Juniper yelled as she sat back down.

Meeting for Announcements concluded with five minutes of Silence. At 9:20, Skip shook Trudy's hand, breaking Silence and ending Meeting. Instantly, hordes of kids exploded out of their benches to mob Daylily and Juniper. "272 East Tenth Street," Juniper shouted.

"Are freshmen invited?" asked Rollerblading Maddy.

"Everyone's invited," said Daylily.

Juniper wrapped her arm around Daylily's skinny waist and pulled her in close. "There's plenty of JG and Lils to go around," she yelled. "We wanna spread the love!"

The Friday rehearsal was a lost cause. It felt good to be angry about that, instead of guilty about Bottom or terrified of war.

A week later, I told Bottom, "We had to cancel rehearsal on Friday." He and I were walking down the hall together from Latin to history. "Only like five people showed up."

"I heard," he said. "Mea culpa."

"How was the party?"

"Oh, you know how Jen's parties are."

"No, I don't." I was surprised he did. I'd never thought of him as a party guy.

"No, I suppose not," he said. "Well, this one got typically wild later in the evening once it moved to the roof. But we did write a lot of letters before that."

"I hope it stops the war," I said.

He glanced at me, unsure if I was being sarcastic. (I wasn't sure either.) "I know it's not much," he said. "But it felt better than doing nothing." He paused at the doorway to the history classroom and motioned for me to pass him. "Ladies first."

I felt bad then. I made a mental note to write my own letter to Hillary Clinton.

Fay was cutting class, so I was paying more attention than usual when Glenn made a special announcement of his own. "This weekend," he said, "there's gonna be a worldwide demonstration against the invasion of Iraq. The New York rally is at the UN. If you write me a one-page essay about your experience there, I'll give you fifty points of extra credit on the final exam."

The whole class bolted to attention. It was unusual for Idlewild teachers to offer extra credit, since the school didn't give grades and usually de-emphasized test scores. Looking back, I wouldn't be surprised if Glenn actually got in trouble with Skip and Trudy over this—not just for offering extra credit in the first place, but for tying it to something that should have been done for its own sake. It was a rookie error. (He was only twenty-three! That's so wild to think about now.)

From the back row, where she was sitting with Bottom, Daylily called out, "Some of us are going to the march in D.C. instead. Can we still get the extra credit?"

"Sure," said Glenn.

In the front row, Oliver Dicks raised his hand. "Shouldn't we get *extra* extra credit for traveling to D.C.?" he said. "It's a much bigger commitment than just walking to the UN."

Glenn sighed, clearly already regretting this, and tugged at the brim of his trucker hat. "Fine," he said. "You get . . . uh . . . five extra points for going to D.C."

"Just five?" said Oliver.

"Just for *going* to D.C.?" said Eddie Applebaum. "We don't have to write an essay about it?"

Glenn hesitated—he clearly hadn't thought it through—and the class, sensing his weakness, pounced. "That's not fair!" "This is too short notice!" "I have softball practice!" "Can we write an essay *without* going to the protest?"

Bottom's baritone projected warmly over the other voices. "If anyone wants to join us on the charter bus to D.C., let me know! The more, the merrier."

I was surprised to find myself seriously considering it. Not just for the extra credit, either. Bottom was right: it *would* feel better than doing nothing.

"You can talk to either of us after class," Daylily was saying. "Or Jen."

Oliver Dicks twisted around in his front-row desk, smirking. "Are you and Jen gonna *play in a room by yourselves* in D.C.?"

"Maybe," said Daylily mischievously. "You'll have to come along and find out."

A titillated "Ooooh!" swept the class. It was so spontaneous, in such perfect unison, that everyone except me cracked up laughing.

Egged on by the attention, Daylily added, "Maybe it won't be in a room. Maybe it'll be on the bus."

"Let's try to focus," Glenn said weakly.

But no one was even pretending to pay attention to Glenn anymore. Boys were calling out jokey questions like "Can I reserve a seat next to you?" Some of them made exaggerated sounds of horny moaning. Girls were laughing like they'd just discovered a cheat code to the boy brain. And Daylily was blushing and beaming, ever so pleased with herself.

I felt a surge of pure loathing for her. Juniper too. I couldn't believe how effective their little gimmick was, especially since it was so obviously fake. Maybe, I thought bitterly, the fakeness was what made it effective. After all, Idlewild boys didn't act like this around *me*. Not that I wanted them to. I wasn't jealous—not exactly—that Daylily and Juniper were doing a fake-lesbian act for attention. It just made me feel invisible.

No, worse than invisible—I felt ugly. I imagined how my classmates would react if I announced in the Meetinghouse that Fay and I were hooking up. They'd probably be weirded out, or altogether grossed out. Then I was mad at myself for caring. Besides, I was never going to hook up with Fay anyway.

By the time I trudged out of class, I'd made myself so miserable I couldn't even look at Daylily. I already knew I wouldn't be going to the protest. Not in D.C., not anywhere.

(I never wrote that letter to Hillary Clinton, either.)

THE INVERT SOCIETY, 2003

We the Invert Society have Thursday fourth period free, so on this freezing February day we the Invert Society meet for brunch at Joe Junior. We crowd into a booth by the window and order waffles with whipped cream, chocolate chip pancakes with bacon, French toast with sausages, corned beef hash with sunny-side-up eggs, four chocolate milkshakes and hot coffee to pour into them. As we eat, Theo does impressions, which is to say non-impressions. He does his *Fargo* version of Glenn. He does Ms. Spider, if Ms. Spider were a blaxploitation heroine instead of an old Jewish lady from the Bronx. He tries out a new one: Christopher's dad, if Christopher's dad had a wheezy upper-register Italian accent like Marlon Brando in *The Godfather*, which Christopher insists he does not.

Theo, as Christopher's Godfather dad: "Christophuh, you come to me on the day my new VW commercial comes out, and you ask me to give you money? For drugs?"

Christopher, good-naturedly playing along: "No, Dad, it's just for lunch."

Theo: "You break my heart, Christophuh. You don't deserve twelve thousand dollars."

Christopher: "I actually don't need that much for lunch—"

Theo: "Twenty cents. That's my final offer."

Christopher: "I do need more than that—"

Theo: "Nothing. It's free."

We the Invert Society are shriek-laughing and coffee-buzzing and suddenly it's been forty minutes and we are all about to be late for our next class.

N: "Shit. I don't want to go to English."

Theo: "I don't want to go to Chemistry."

F: "Let's cut. All of us."

Christopher: "We can't cut Chemistry. There's a test."

Theo: "Hang on. I'll deal with it." He puts on his coat and gloves. "Distract the waiter, okay? Argue over the bill or something."

N: "What are you doing?"

Theo: [*languid*] "Calling in a bomb threat."

F and N and Christopher watch through the window as Theo approaches the pay phone on the corner. His gloved hand picks up the receiver.

F: "He's not really doing it, right?"

Theo pulls a coin out of his pocket, slips it into the slot, dials.

N: "He's just messing with us, right?"

F: "Undoubtedly."

On the other side of the window, Theo's lips are moving.

N: "Should we, like . . . stop him? Just in case?"

F: "No! That would be letting him win."

The avuncular Greek waiter drops the paper bill on the table.

Christopher: [*to the waiter*] "Excuse me? Uh, how much were the, uh . . . waffles?"

"Four ninety-nine," says the waiter.

Christopher: [*trying not to look out the window*] "And how much were the pancakes?"

"Three seventy-five."

Christopher: "Um . . . shouldn't the pancakes and the waffles cost the same? Because . . . like . . . they're made of the same material?"

Christopher and the waiter are going back and forth on this when Theo reenters the diner. Theo slides into the booth beside Christopher.

Theo: [*to the waiter*] "Please excuse my friend. He's a bit of a penny-pincher." [*to Christopher*] "Apologize to the nice man."

This is Theo in his apple-polishing teacher's-pet mode, which often heralds trouble. Once the waiter is out of earshot, the rest of the Invert Society regards Theo with some trepidation.

F: "I assume you just wasted a quarter on a pantomime phone call."

Theo: "You assumed wrong." [*in his Marlon Brando Godfather voice*] "Hello, Idlewild front desk. I come to you to say . . . I have a bomb. It's in, uh, my shoes. Yeah. Both of them. It's gonna go off in . . . five minutes. Thank you. God bless you." He mimes hanging up.

N: "You didn't."

Theo: [*in his normal voice*] "You don't believe me? Fine. Go to class."

Theo leans back in the booth and slides an arm around Christopher's shoulders. Christopher takes out his wallet and counts out bills. By now it's tacitly understood in the Invert Society that Christopher pays for all meals. His movements are slow under the weight of Theo's arm.

Theo: "Hurry up. We're gonna be late."

Christopher places a stack of bills on the table. We the Invert Society put on our coats and scarves and head out into the February cold. We turn left on Fifteenth Street and see the kids pouring out of Idlewild onto the sidewalk.

Theo: [*innocently*] "Oh, wow. What's going on?"

We the Invert Society walk closer.

Theo: [*sweetly*] "A fire drill, maybe?"

The Fifteenth Street entrance swarms with students. With them is Devi the Dove, who should be in her fourth-floor English classroom right now but is instead directing foot traffic onto the sidewalk. In a decidedly undovelike manner, she is shouting.

"Everybody out of the building! NOW!"

FAY

Insofar as Theo's bomb threat was a gambit to get the rest of the school day off, its success was only partial. Under strict teacherly supervision, students were shepherded en masse to the nearby Stuyvesant Square Park, where we were separated by grade and forbidden to leave. In our enforced proximity to classmates and teachers, Nell and I couldn't even discuss what had happened. For two hours she and I stood in the senior crowd and shivered, taciturn, in the February chill. The initial assumption was that it was a fire drill, and collective frustration mounted as time elapsed past the standard ten or fifteen minutes. There was widespread speculation of a real fire. Then whispers began to circulate, and the frustration began to turn to alarm: "The cops are here." "You mean the fire department?" "No, the NYPD. A bunch of police cars just showed up." After an hour or so, students were informed of an unspecified "emergency situation" and encouraged to telephone their parents for permission to go home early. As on 9/11, I convinced Trudy to let me go home with Nell rather than attempt to contact my own parents. It was with great relief that Nell and I separated from the crowd at last.

As soon as we were safely out of earshot, walking east toward First Avenue, I said, "I wonder who he did it for. For whom he did it, rather. Do you think he was showing off for Christopher? Or was he trying to impress you and me?" A third possibility—that he'd done it for me alone—I held tenderly in my mind but didn't dare say aloud.

"Or does he just do crazy shit for no reason?" said Nell.

This chastened me into silence. Over the last few weeks I'd begun to worry that Nell's interest in the Marble Faun was waning—or, worse yet, that she was beginning to look askance at mine. Perhaps my obsession with Theo had become excessive even by her standards. As we walked side by side up First Avenue, hands stuffed in coat pockets and heads bent against the cold wind from the East River, I mentally cast about for words to prove that my interest in Theo was purely intellectual, not heterosexual. There was nothing I could say, I thought, that wouldn't sound like doth-protest-too-muchness. For in truth I was electric with ecstasy over Theo Severyn, so depraved and deranged, my ice-cold little Marble Faun. My imagination ran wild with the Faunfic potential of what he'd just done, and what else he might be capable of doing.

We arrived at Nell's building and stepped into the elevator, a small rickety thing whose metallic smell filled me with half-remembered dread. As the elevator creaked its way upward, Nell said, "It's funny having you over again. It feels like there's a huge disaster happening, even though I know everything's fine."

I was relieved to find my mind in sync with hers after all. "I was just thinking the same thing," I said. "I feel like I'll look out your window and see some unspeakable horror."

There was no unspeakable horror to be seen from Nell's apartment, apart from the well-used litter box in the bathroom. I tried not to look at it directly as I used the toilet. I washed my hands and looked at myself in the mirror and willed myself not to think of what I'd told Jimmy Frye about my previous visit here. I suddenly wished I were someone else.

I remember that Nell and I ordered a pizza but, still full from our Joe Junior brunch, left most of it congealing before us in its greasy cardboard box on the coffee table. I remember that Nell guiltily slammed the pizza box shut when she heard her mother's key in the door. I remember that Nell's mother greeted us not with concerned questions about the school evacuation, as I'd expected, but with a radiant smile. In her hand was a large, thick envelope.

"Special delivery!" she sang out, and offered it to Nell. "You should have seen it crammed into that little mailbox slot! It was rolled up so tight, I think I broke a nail trying to pull it out."

Nell appeared stricken. She took the envelope gingerly, angling it away from me so as to hide the return address. "Um," she said. "Maybe I should open this later."

Nell's mother clapped her hand playfully over her own mouth in a theatrical *Oops!* gesture. "Sorry," she stage-whispered, and I simultaneously understood and didn't understand. Had it not been mid-February, too early for such things to arrive in the mail, I wouldn't have been so slow to recognize what was known in the parlance of the college application process as "the fat envelope."

Quickly, before Nell could stop me, I snatched the envelope out of her fingers. She protested and yanked it back, but not before I'd spotted the logo on the return address.

Smith College.

NELL

I was therapized enough to know that big moments rarely live up to the fantasy versions of themselves, but even Dr. Rothstein was thrown when I told her, in our Sunday session a few days later, that my college acceptance was overshadowed by a bomb threat. I told her I knew it was a prank. Just to be on the safe side, I didn't tell her who did it. Instead I just said, "It was a weird day. I wasn't in the best frame of mind to get good news."

"Let's take a look at that," she said. "What was on your mind?"

"I had this sense of . . ." I searched for the word. "Foreboding. Like something bad was about to happen. Even though I knew the bomb wasn't real."

"Where do you think that was coming from?"

I made up some bullshit about how it reminded me of 9/11, because I could tell that was what she wanted to hear. I couldn't tell her—I couldn't tell anyone—that it was really about Theo.

The bomb threat itself was standard teen-boy mischief—ill-advised after 9/11, for sure, but Idlewild had plenty of dumb boys who did ill-advised things. Except Theo hadn't handled it like a dumb boy. It had seemed so spontaneous, but the more I thought about it, the weirder that felt. He did it during lunchtime, when a lot of Idlewilders' whereabouts were unaccounted for. He chose a pay phone a block away from school, so even if the call got traced, the location wouldn't suggest anything beyond the already-obvious Idlewild connection. He had Christopher distract the Joe Junior waiter, which eliminated the likeliest witness. He did the Marlon Brando *Godfather* voice, which wasn't one of the voices in his normal repertoire, and was generic enough that any boy might have thought of it. Theo couldn't have executed it better if he'd spent weeks plotting it. Much later, I would wonder if he had.

At the time, though, I wasn't really focusing on those details. It was more about Theo's demeanor. He wasn't acting in the giddy high-adrenaline way you'd expect after a big risky prank. He was so calm and collected and casual. Bored, even. It disturbed me.

But Fay and I already knew this about him, didn't we? That was the whole point of the Marble Faun character, the whole premise of the Faunfic. It was what we loved about him. Well, it was what Fay loved about him. She was thrilled by the bomb threat, I could tell. The whole afternoon, as we channel-surfed on my living room couch, I tried to tell myself: at least Fay was happy. She was happy for a disturbing reason, but still, it was nice to make Fay happy.

And then my mom came home with the fat envelope. So much for making Fay happy.

"Smith College?" said Fay, confused.

I glared at my mom, furious, even though it wasn't her fault. She had no idea I hadn't told Fay, and now she probably thought it was a whole big secret I'd been keeping, which it wasn't. (Was it?) I just hadn't meant for Fay to find out *this* way. I hadn't decided how I wanted her to find out, but definitely not like this.

My mom backed guiltily out of the living room. Then I felt piercingly sorry I'd ruined what should have been a joyful mother-daughter moment.

Fay said it again. "Smith College?"

The envelope in my hands was still sealed. Nervously, I fingered one of its corners, where there was a little air pocket. I felt the edge of a booklet inside. "Early Decision two," I mumbled.

"Early Decision *two*?" said Fay. "What's that?"

"It's a thing," I said. "It was kind of last minute. Mommy made me do it over winter break."

I cringed to hear myself: *Mommy made me do it?* It was a lame excuse, and only sort of true. Early Decision II had been my mom's idea, but I'd willingly gone along with it. Neither of us liked the idea of me sitting around for months forlornly waiting for Yale to make up its mind about me. "Let's stick it to them," she suggested. "Don't you want to be done with the whole college mishigas?" I knew my mom was projecting—*she* wanted to be done with the whole college mishigas—but she was also right.

"Why Smith?" said Fay.

Because of the pond full of rowboats. Because of all the lesbians. Because *I* was a lesbian and starting to understand how important it was to me—important enough to make major life decisions around. Though I'd told my mom it was because of the psychology program.

I shrugged. "It was kind of random."

"But now you *have* to go there?" said Fay.

I hadn't even thought about that part yet. "Yeah," I said. "That's how Early Decision works, so . . ." I laughed a nervous laugh. "I guess I'm going to Smith."

I was going to Smith.

I looked down at my knees (at the hole in my jeans where she'd touched me that one time), waiting for her to ask me why I hadn't told her. And what would I say? *I didn't tell anyone because I didn't want to jinx it*—but that wasn't the whole reason. *It didn't seem worth mentioning because I didn't think I would get in*—but that wasn't it either. *You always get so mad at me when I talk about college.* I couldn't say that. *Sometimes I feel like our brains have melded together and whatever's mine is yours. I wanted one thing that was just mine.* I couldn't even think that one, not consciously.

But Fay didn't even ask. She just said, "Smell *you*, Nancy Drew. Congratulations."

I was surprised to hear her say that, and then surprised by my own surprise. She didn't sound genuinely excited for me, but I hadn't even expected her to fake it.

I looked up from my knees. Fay was rubbing her eyes. "The cats," she said.

"Sorry," I said. "Do you need a Claritin?"

"I took one before." She flicked a white cat hair off her black jeans. "Maybe I need another one." She went to the bathroom, where we kept Claritin. I heard her turn on the faucet and run the water at full blast—her standard practice to disguise the sound of pooping. It always stressed me out to hear her wasting water like that, which ironically had the reverse effect of making me hyperaware of when Fay was pooping.

Unless, in this case, she was crying.

I felt like crying myself. I'd never meant to hurt Fay. I hadn't known I *could* hurt Fay. But that was stupid of me, I thought. She was my best friend. I'd kept a big secret from my best friend. I'd fucked up. I sat there on the couch for a long time, clutching the fat envelope and listening to the running water and stewing in shame for being such a bad friend. That was easier, in the moment, than letting myself be excited for my future far away from Fay.

But I *was* excited. I would never have admitted it then, but I can admit it now: on some level, I wanted to get away from Fay. If I hadn't wanted that, I wouldn't have made it happen. I knew what I was doing. That was the worst part of all.

FAY

Nell retrieved her mother, and the two of them opened the envelope to marvel at the acceptance letter contained therein. They telephoned Nell's grandparents in Florida to deliver the good news, putting them on speakerphone so that the whole family could participate in what Nell's grandfather called "plotzing and kvelling"—"Our little Smithie!" and so forth. I remember much joking to the effect that Nell and her grandmother, who had attended Mount Holyoke, were officially "rivals," and some ribbing about Nell's risk of becoming a Republican, given that both Nancy Reagan and Barbara Bush were Smith alumnae. "If they ever come to campus," said her grandmother, "give them a big kick in the pants from me."

Throughout all of this, I remained seated on the living room couch, perusing one of the enclosed pamphlets that accounted for the envelope's fatness. As part of the BOOBLESS League, Smith was among the schools to which I had secretly applied, but I had never considered the reality of following Nell *there* specifically. Now the prospect filled me with a pain so pervasive that I couldn't, in the moment, trace it to its source. I was jealous, perhaps, but not of Nell's success. I was afraid, but not of my own potential failure. I was repelled, resistant, internally howling *I don't want*—but what was it I didn't want?

I ran my fingers over the pamphlet's glossy paper, streaking pizza-grease trails across photographs of girls, girls, girls—teams of ponytailed athletic girls in numbered white tunics and basketball shorts, science girls in white lab coats frowning through goggles at beakers held aloft, butch and femme girls lolling in harmony on a verdant lawn. Women, I suppose one must call them. Women only.

"We should really let Nell go," said Nell's mother. "She has a friend over."

From the speakerphone, Nell's grandmother said, "You're having a pajama party? What fun!"

Nell laughed. "*Pajama party* makes it sound like we're having, like, pillow fights," she said.

Shame surged through me, hot and nauseous, as I half-remembered the hackneyed slumber party scenario I'd fabricated for Jimmy Frye. "Actually," I said, "I should get going."

"Wait, don't leave!" said Nell. "Grandma, Grandpa, I have to go." She stepped away from the phone, back toward the couch.

At her approach, I flinched involuntarily.

She sat down on the couch beside me and spoke in a low voice; her mother had resumed the phone conversation. "Sorry."

I forced a smile. "You're sorry you got into college?"

"No, I'm sorry for being on the phone so long," she said. "I didn't mean to leave you alone."

She had no idea of the lengths I had gone, the lengths I was willing to go, to prevent her from leaving me alone. Worse yet, I had no idea whether she would do the same for me. I had been ignoring this thought for months, but the possibility existed—I could no longer deny it—that she would not be pleased to find me following her to Smith. Having to ask her, not knowing how she'd answer, was unbearable to contemplate.

"Fay?" said Nell. (When had she stopped calling me *boss*?) "You okay, dude?"

I was not okay. I was newly uneasy in the presence of Nell. It was not, as it had once been, the bracing tension of finding myself the object of a crush. Rather, it was a stinging new awareness of how much she meant to me. I needed her, suddenly, so much more than she needed me.

NELL

I didn't like to think of myself having anything in common with Skip and Trudy, but we shared the same philosophical approach to the aftermath of the bomb threat: the less said about it, the better.

It was so blatantly a prank, I don't know if they even bothered trying to trace it. The administration's official line was something like this: "The safety of our students is our top priority. Out of an abundance of caution, Idlewild was evacuated following a prank phone call. After a quick and thorough investigation, the NYPD issued an all clear, and classes will now resume normally. We thank you for your cooperation, and we hold you in the Light." Skip and Trudy delivered variations of that line over the phone to everybody's parents, over email to our Idlewild email addresses that no one ever checked, and in the Meetinghouse the next morning—and then they never acknowledged it again. I don't know if they were worried about sowing panic, or about copycat prank calls, or just about looking dumb. Whatever their reasoning, it backfired. The rumor mill went insane.

The third Saturday in March was load-in day for the *On the Town* set. Idlewild art teachers gave class credit for designing and building the theater sets and props, and the two seniors in charge that day were Kevin Comfort and Nirvana Cavendish-Epstein. Kevin was a talented burnout who was always cutting class to smoke weed in Stuyvesant Square Park and draw photorealistic charcoal portraits of passersby. Nirvana, his girlfriend, was distinctive for her red fishnet stockings and fuzzy blondish dreadlocks. (Yes, she was white.) She was the first vegan I ever met, and in freshman year she was one of my Schrödinger's lesbians, but I could never bring myself to crush on her because I couldn't get past the dreads. She was nice, though. Which was maybe another reason I never crushed on her.

When Fay and I arrived at the Meetinghouse, Kevin and Nirvana put us to work right away on painting flats. This was an important job, arguably too important for non-artists like Fay and me, but within a few minutes it became clear why they wanted us nearby.

"So is it true?" Kevin asked. "About Wanda Higgins."

I kneeled onto the tarp-covered floor and dipped a paintbrush into a can of pink paint. It seemed like an odd choice of backdrop color for a show set in 1940s New York City, but for some reason that was Nirvana's vision. "What about her?"

Nirvana said, "People are saying she threatened to blow up the school."

"In vengeance," Kevin said somberly.

Next to me, Fay burst out laughing. I wanted to laugh too, but I also didn't want to look like I had more information than they did. "I don't know," I said. "It's hard to picture Wanda doing that."

"I don't believe it either," said Nirvana. "I didn't really know her, but she always seemed so nice."

"Word," said Kevin. "She was mad nice when my grandpa went into hospice."

I dragged the paintbrush over the plywood. The pink paint distributed so stickily and unevenly, I knew I must be doing it wrong. "Probably just a rumor."

A voice above me said, "Yeah, it's bullshit." It was Theo. I turned around to see him and Christopher standing behind us. Theo continued, "The call had to be from someone who *goes* to Idlewild. Or works here currently."

"How do you know?" said Fay. *Don't encourage him*, I thought.

"Because the call was placed from the pay phone on the corner of Sixteenth and Third," said Theo. "Right outside Joe Junior."

Nirvana twisted around to look up at him. "Where did you hear that?"

"I have my sources," said Theo.

Next to him, Christopher shifted from foot to foot. I wondered if Kevin and Nirvana were picking up on his nervousness. "I've heard so many different rumors, though," said Christopher.

"My source is *very* trustworthy," said Theo.

"Paint much, Nell?" said Kevin, noticing what a shitty job I was doing.

"Sorry," I said. "Maybe you should reassign me." I hoped it wasn't too obvious that I just didn't want to be in this conversation anymore.

"No worries." Nirvana handed me an unfinished prop. It was a paper-towel-tube-sized PVC pipe stuck into a round, not-very-well-sanded wooden disk. "This is gonna be an old-timey telephone," she said. "It's called a candlestick phone. I already primed it, but it needs to be spray-painted black. Do it outside, obviously. The spray paint is in the Peace Garden."

I took the prop out to the Peace Garden. Fay stayed inside the Meetinghouse with Theo, but Christopher followed me outside. "Is it okay if I hang out here with you?"

"Sure," I said, a little confused. It was the first time he'd shown any interest in hanging out alone with me. I dug a can of black spray paint out of a cardboard box.

"Don't get any on me," he said. "I'm wearing Sevens."

I shook the can. "What are Sevens?"

"Seriously? They're designer jeans. How do you not know that?"

I tested the nozzle, aiming downward and spraying black paint onto the black asphalt. "Why did you wear designer jeans to load-in day?"

He gave me a tentative, sheepish glance. "Theo says they make my butt look good."

I laughed. I knew Fay would lose her mind when I told her about this later—but at the same time, I was suddenly glad she hadn't come outside with me. I squatted on the ground and sprayed paint onto the prop's wooden base. The aerosolized paint smelled nice, harsh and sweet.

"It's college acceptance season, right?" said Christopher. "Have you heard back yet?"

"Yeah, early decision. I'm going to Smith."

"Hey, congrats."

"Thanks. It's gonna be, like, all lesbians."

"You must be psyched for that." He paused. "Or maybe it'll feel weird," he said. "Like you're not special anymore."

That was surprisingly insightful of him. Even my therapist hadn't picked up on that.

"I do think about that," I admitted. "And I worry about fitting in. What if I say something un-PC and the lesbians get offended?"

"You're a lesbian," he said reasonably, "and you're not like that."

"I'm talking about *real* lesbians."

"What are you," he said, "a cheap knockoff lesbian from Canal Street?"

I laughed. I was surprised at how easy it was to talk about this with Christopher. "Seriously," I said, "I've never, like, *suffered* for being a lesbian, you know? Idlewild is such a boringly tolerant place."

"And your family?" he said. "They're accepting?"

I started to nod. But then I didn't. I looked over at Christopher—his big brown cow eyes, his bouncy curly hair. Everything about him was so rounded and gentle and soft.

"I used to think so," I said. "My mom's super liberal, and she has gay friends and shit. But there was this weird thing the other night."

I hadn't planned to share this with anyone. Not Fay, not my therapist. I couldn't believe I was saying it out loud now.

"I picked up the phone to call Fay," I said. "But my mom was on the other extension, in her room, talking to my grandma. I was about to hang up, but then I realized they were talking about me."

"Oh, you have to listen in when that happens," he said. "It's okay to eavesdrop if they're talking about you."

"Exactly," I said. "And it didn't even feel like eavesdropping at first. They were just talking about me going to Smith, the logistics and stuff. But then . . ."

I stared at the Peace Garden wall mural, remembering. It had come up, somehow, that Smith girls have to wear white dresses for graduation, and my mom laughed and said, "Good luck getting Nell into a dress." And then my grandma asked, "Is Nell a lesbian?"

Just like that. I remember being struck by how simple it sounded. She didn't seem worried or judgmental, just curious. But not even *that* curious—it was like she assumed the answer was yes, she just didn't know if it was official yet. As I held the phone against my ear, trying not to breathe so they wouldn't hear me on the call, I wondered if my grandma had quietly understood me all my life.

"Oh, God, no," said my mom, still laughing. "Of course not. She's just a tomboy."

"Really?" My grandma sounded confused. "I've always thought . . . who's that little friend of hers? That girl she's always going on about."

"Fay," said my mom. "But you know how intense girls' friendships can be at that age." Then she changed the subject by asking about Lillian, an old friend of my grandma's. I listened in for a few more minutes, hoping they would circle back to me, but they didn't.

I hung up and stood there alone in the kitchen for a while. I stared out the window at the traffic on FDR Drive. I told myself it didn't matter. I opened the freezer and found a frost-furred carton of store-brand mint chocolate chip ice cream and ate the whole thing directly out of the carton even though it tasted bad and I wasn't hungry and I already felt fat. I was polishing it off when my mom came in. "Is that Atkins-friendly?" she teased—she was trying to get me to go on Atkins—and I blurted out, "Why did you tell Grandma I'm not a lesbian?" She got mad at me for eavesdropping, and it turned into a big tearful fight. In the end she managed to convince me that she was just looking out for me because Grandma wasn't "ready." "I love you *so much*," my mom said firmly, "and we have all the time in the world to work on Grandma and Grandpa." We hugged and cried and I went to bed emotionally exhausted and fully intending to forget this embarrassing incident forever.

It was only now, recounting it for Christopher, that I realized how much it was still bothering me.

"But that's stupid, right?" I said. "There are gay kids out there whose parents beat them, or kick them out, or send them to *But I'm a Cheerleader* camp to make them ex-gay."

"At least those parents are being honest, though," said Christopher. "Instead of acting all supportive but then being homophobic behind your back."

I was already feeling guilty for complaining about my mom and my knee-jerk instinct was to defend her, so I started to say that I didn't think she was being *homophobic*, exactly—but Christopher was still talking.

"That's why I like Theo," he said. "He's an asshole, but he's an asshole to your face."

(I managed to bite back an asshole-to-your-face rimming joke.)

"Like, you know," he added, "Theo doesn't hide anything."

I looked over at Christopher, genuinely curious. "You don't think Theo hides *anything*?"

Christopher looked back at me, his huge brown eyes way more serious than I expected. "I mean . . ." he said.

Someone screamed from inside the Meetinghouse.

"That sounds like Fay," said Christopher, obviously chickening out on whatever he'd been about to say. He ran into the Meetinghouse through the Peace Garden entrance. Frustrated, I followed after him.

The art kids had formed a circle. I couldn't see what they were looking at—but Fay's army jacket, abandoned in an army-green heap on the floor, was a dead giveaway. By now, every rehearsal eventually devolved into this.

"Nell," said Nirvana. "Fay and Theo are, like . . . wrestling or something?"

"Yeah, they do that," I said.

"Quaker fight club," said Christopher. That was what we'd started calling it.

"That's not chill, man," said Kevin Comfort. "This is the House of God and shit."

I shoved my way through the crowd of art kids. Theo had Fay in some kind of upside-down headlock. "Theo," I said, "let her go."

"She loves it," said Theo—and he wrapped his hands around her throat.

I was pretty sure he was just pretending to choke her, but it still made me nervous. "Theo, stop."

Theo didn't stop. He tightened his hands. From underneath him, Fay looked at me silently, her face reddening, her short hair spiking out in every direction like she'd been electrocuted in a cartoon. Her eyelids fluttered shut.

I gasped. "Theo, *please*, she's passing out!"

Hearing this, the art kids screamed.

Christopher stepped forward and knelt down. He touched Theo's upper arm, gently, and whispered something in his ear. Whatever he said, it worked. Theo let go and rolled off Fay.

Fay opened her eyes right away, totally fine. "Gotcha," she said, looking right at me. "Did I scare you?"

Everyone groaned. The art kids went back to work.

Theo and Fay were still sprawled on the floor. He reached out and brushed her hair off her forehead—which, considering what her hair looked like in that moment, was the grooming equivalent of rearranging the deck chairs on the *Titanic*. "There," he said. "That was driving me crazy."

Fay giggled. Her fucked-up hair bounced. Her boobs too. I looked away.

Theo got up and brushed himself off. "I'm tired," he said. "Christopher, take me home." He fluttered his eyelashes dramatically. "Put me to bed."

As the boys left the Meetinghouse, Christopher shot me a glance—worried, embarrassed, maybe guilty—and I remembered what I'd asked him a moment ago: *You don't think Theo hides anything?* What a dumb question. Of course Theo wouldn't hide anything. You could torture someone way more effectively by putting it all out there and refusing to explain what it meant. I knew that better than anyone.

FAY

The Marble Faun, Chapter Nine:
Blackout[1]

The boys' shared bedroom was dark, so dark that Theo didn't know if his eyes were open or closed.[2] There was black cloth on the windows, but if you pushed it aside you still wouldn't be able to see anything, for the whole city was dark too. The Iraqian army hadn't dropped any bombs so far,[3] but the night wasn't over yet.

Christopher's shirtless body, warm and solid and reassuring, pressed up against him. It seemed like only yesterday that the two of them were sharing this bed for the first time. But that was two and a half years ago, and the boys had grown since then. Christopher's arms were hard with muscle. They tightened around Theo, who was still the smaller of the

---

[1] Nell and I co-wrote this chapter on the final Saturday night before tech week. Inspired by *On the Town* and contemporary world events, it was ambitiously conceived as the first installment of an extended wartime storyline.

[2] This chapter marks our first attempt to write from Theo's point of view—my suggestion.

[3] In our defense, I don't believe we were actually under the impression that the Iraq war, should it come to pass, would take the form of Blitzkrieg-inspired air raids on New York City. I like to think that the Faunfic takes place in its own distinct fictional universe. That being said, our grasp of modern warfare was tenuous in the extreme. At the time of this chapter's composition, I looked forward to writing a future love scene in a trench.

two. Christopher's face stubble scraped across Theo's cheek as he nestled in closer.

"Are you awake, Theo?" Christopher questioned softly.

Theo stiffened. "I am *now*, asshole," he snapped.

There was a time, not so long ago, when that retort would have made Christopher cower and apologize, tremblingly desperate to please Theo. How easy it used to be to bring the taller boy to his knees, worshiping Theo, begging for mercy, eager and willing to do anything he was told. Christopher was breathtakingly beautiful that way, though Theo would never tell him that.

But things had changed. And they were about to change even more.

"I can't believe this is our last night together," Christopher sighed. He held Theo against his chest so Theo could feel his heartbeat beneath the hot smooth skin. "I can't believe I'm leaving for basic training tomorrow."

Christopher had gotten drafted the day he turned eighteen. Theo got a draft notice too, but he failed the physical exam because of his weak lungs. Of the two of them, only Christopher was strong enough to go to war.

Theo didn't care. He didn't.

Christopher carded his fingers through Theo's hair. "I'm going to miss your hair," he whispered softly.

I'm going to miss *your* hair when they shave it off, Theo thought to himself. No! He didn't care. He began to shiver, though the bed was warm. "You better not talk like that in basic training," he said. "Don't ask, don't tell. Remember?"

"You're shaking," said Christopher concernedly.

Theo willed himself to lie still. None of this was real, he reminded him-self ferociously. Life was a dollhouse and Christopher was just a doll he could play with. A beautiful doll that belonged to him.

"You're smothering me," said Theo, making his voice as cold as ice, or marble. "Let me sleep."

"Are you sure?" Christopher queried in that soft, anxious tone that Theo liked best. "This is our last night together. Our last chance to . . ." He trailed off.

Good. Theo had the upper hand again. "Our last chance to *what?*" he taunted, smirking in the dark. He felt his dick begin to harden.

Christopher was silent for a long, charged moment. Even after two and a half years, the two boys never discussed the things they did together in secret.

"Our last chance," Christopher stammered, "to . . . do stuff."

Theo laughed. He was fully hard now. He rolled over to face Christopher, reached down, and discovered to his satisfaction that the other boy was hard too. "I want to hear you say it," Theo hissed, stroking the taller boy through his boxers.

Christopher swallowed. "Theo, I . . ."

"Say it, bitch."

"Touch me," Christopher gritted out. "Please."

"Oh, I'll *touch* you." Theo hooked his thumbs into Christopher's waistband and pulled off the boxers. He felt in the dark for Christopher's erection, wrapped his hand around it, and held it with a teasingly light grip. "Like this?" said Theo. "Is that what you want?"

Christopher moaned, desperate for more. "Come on," he begged. "Please."

"What?" said Theo, mock innocent. "You told me to touch you."

"I need . . ." gasped Christopher, writhing with desire. Precum was gushing from the tip of his dick, dripping all over Theo's hand.[4]

"You need me," said Theo commandingly. "Tell me you need me."

In a hoarse, broken voice, Christopher moaned, "I need you, Theo."

"Yeah you do," breathed Theo. His own dick was achingly hard, but he ignored it, wanting only to punish Christopher. "Look at you. You're pathetic. You're desperate." He bent his head down, down, until his breath was warming Christopher's cock. "You're nothing without me," he said, and licked a wet stripe up from the base to the tip.[5]

Christopher let out a keening noise.[6]

"You're mine," said Theo. He took Christopher all the way into his mouth. Christopher's hips bucked involuntarily, shoving his cock down Theo's throat. Theo gagged.[7]

---

[4] I'm surprised this sentence made it into the edited version. Precum is vastly overrepresented in slash, which tends to portray sex between men as a very wet experience, with a great deal of anatomically implausible dripping and leaking and weeping. It's a slashfic cliché over which I was constantly battling Nell; I considered it an egregious amateur error betraying both vagina and virginity. I took pride in my superior porn-derived knowledge of the male body. Now, however, I wonder what I was trying to prove. If slash fiction serves a purpose, that purpose is not the literal representation of cisgender male sexuality, but the fulfilment of an authorial fantasy. I'm rather wistful that my own was so constrained by my teenage idea of realism.

[5] I was testing Nell here. I knew she hated the word *cock*, and our Faunfic sex scenes had never heretofore gone past handjobs. I Instant Messaged her this paragraph and braced for her reaction.

[6] This was her response. I took it as a go-ahead.

[7] I took things a step further.

"Sorry," said Christopher.[8]

"No," said Theo hoarsely. "Do it again."[9]

"Are you sure?" said Christopher worriedly. "I don't want to hurt you."[10]

"Fucking *do it*," said Theo. "You can't hurt me. I can take anything." He took Christopher into his mouth again. Christopher thrust into Theo's mouth, fucking his throat, choking him. Theo gagged. He could hardly breathe. Tears began to stream down his face. And even still he wanted more of him inside him. He wanted to swallow him whole, he wanted him to fill him up entirely until nothing of himself remained.[11]

Little did Theo know that tears were in Christopher's eyes too. Christopher was going to miss Theo so much.[12]

[8] Nell parried.

[9] I persisted.

[10] Oh, Nell.

[11] I typed this paragraph in a frenzy and hit Enter before proofreading it. My regret was instantaneous. I had lost control, and it showed (note the comma splice, the profusion of ambiguous pronouns). I saw, beneath my screen name, my most private and primal wish, and I knew that Nell was seeing it too, that it couldn't be undone and we would never again exist in a world without the image of me gagging on a cock, the fictional Theo Severyn standing in for me, choking as I was choking on my desire to inhabit his body and use it to gag on a cock, even as the scene was also very much about the real Theo and the very real desires that he'd awakened in me. I was certain that Nell, who never failed to understand me, understood all of this. What had I done? I sat paralyzed with shame in my computer chair, imagining Nell's look of disgust. Or, worse yet, Nell laughing at me. Or, worst of all, Nell pitying me. When AIM finally chimed with her incoming response, I closed my eyes, afraid to read it.

[12] I dared to read it, and then I read it again, and again. I burst into the kind of laughter that I permitted myself only in the middle of the night, alone in my room, unafraid of being overheard.

But I was overheard: Gareth happened to be passing my bedroom on his way to the bathroom. He stuck his head through my half-open door. "My word. Have you got a boy in here?"

"No," I said. "Nell just said something funny."

"Funny, my ass," he said merrily. "That sounded like *une petite mort* if I ever heard one."

When he was gone, I slipped out to the darkened living room and did something that Nell and I occasionally did in the middle of our AIM conversations, though rarely at such a late hour: I grabbed the phone, took it into my bedroom, and called her at home. She answered on the second ring. "It's three in the morning, dude," was her salutation. "If you just woke up my mom, she's gonna kill me."

"Dude," I replied, "that was the girliest thing I've ever read in my entire life. I've been reading slash for years and you just outgirled all of it. You are the girliest girl who ever girled."

For the next few minutes, I mocked her over the phone. I mocked her sentimentality, her clumsy point-of-view shift from Theo to Christopher, her jarring juxtaposition of fluffy romance against my hardcore erotica. I performed a dramatic reading of the passage and laughed until, like her unrealistically girly Christopher, I was in tears.

"Fine," said Nell flatly. "Delete it. I'll write something else."

"No, don't," I said. "We should go to bed."

"I don't mind staying up," she said. "I'll fix it."

"Nell," I said. "*Stet.*"

"What?"

"You take Latin and you don't know what that means? *Let it stand.*"

And so we did.

The Faunfic, maddeningly, ends there.

THE INVERT SOCIETY, 2003

It's tech week and *On the Town* is everything. The world revolves around the rickety splintery paint-sticky set that shudders and groans when the dancers dance on it. Everything is pins and screws and sawdust, swishy taffeta and sailor suits, candlestick phones and dinosaur bones, the sleek arms and box-stepping doll feet of nymphet chorines in character heels. Everything is five-dollar dinner from the corner deli: chicken cutlet sandwiches wrapped in warm foil, flaccid fries (freedom fries!) steaming from Styrofoam boxes, shocking-pink raspberry Snapple in stippled glass bottles with fun facts printed on the caps—the smallest county in America is Manhattan, the most sensitive part of the body is the fingertips (but what about the clit?), it's impossible to tickle yourself (but what about the clit?), 50 percent of Snapple Facts are made up (no one's ever seen that one with their own eyes but we believe it). We eat sitting on the creaky wood stairs because no food in the Meetinghouse. We try to play Porn Star Names, your first pet plus the street you grew up on, but it doesn't work if you grew up on a numbered street, which most of us did. We play hangman with Christopher as the hanged man and stump the Middle Schoolers with COCKSUCKER. We play rock-paper-scissors and keep choosing the same weapon at the same time because our minds have melded together.

Final dress rehearsal runs late into Wednesday night. It's almost 11:00 p.m. when we drag our tired asses upstairs to the Loft to change out of our costumes. We're still putting on our jeans and sneakers and shirts and spring jackets when Ms. Spider enters the rehearsal room and claps her hands to get everyone's attention.

"I just got off the phone with Skip," she says. "School is canceled tomorrow. Bush just announced on TV . . ." She sighs. "We're going to war with Iraq."

The cast freezes in place.

"So Idlewild won't be having classes," says Ms. Spider. "Go to a protest instead."

Daylily Jones calls out shakily, "If you want to go in a group, let us know." She's a little hoarse, and not just from tears; it's been a problem all week. Ms. Spider keeps telling her it's because of the protests she's been going to—all that chanting and shouting is straining her vocal cords.

Bottom nods and points to himself and Daylily. He's even hoarser than Daylily, and at Ms. Spider's insistence, he's on vocal rest; he rehearsed tonight in half voice.

F and N and Theo and Christopher, in semi-unison: "What about the show?"

"I'm still negotiating with Skip about that." Just the look on Ms. Spider's face goes against Quaker principles of nonviolence. "Cross your fingers," she says. "The show must go on."

NELL

I stayed over at Fay's, since it suddenly wasn't a school night anymore. It was too late to walk, so we took a taxi. The driver was playing the news on the radio. I remember hearing snippets of Bush's speech, his horrible little pinched voice saying, *We will defend our freedom. We will bring freedom to others.*

I was scared. At first it was my usual fear: that Saddam Hussein would strike back and New York City would get bombed off the face of the earth. But the radio news guys didn't seem to share that fear. The subject didn't even come up. (Almost as if the weapons of mass destruction didn't exist and the media always knew it! But I was too exhausted and distracted to make that leap.) By the time we'd arrived at Fay's dad's building, I had shifted my anxiety to the musical.

"Skip and Trudy won't actually cancel it," I said, trying to convince myself as we climbed the stoop of the dingy white townhouse. The Narnia-style lamppost was turned on for the night. It glowed golden.

"If they do," said Fay, fumbling tiredly through her messenger bag in search of her keys, "I'll kill myself."

That startled me. Fay and I joked about a lot of dark stuff, but she didn't sound like she was joking right now. *Don't say that*, I wanted to say. "Logically it can't happen," I said instead. "The parents would freak out. It would be a whole thing."

Fay found her keys and unlocked the front door.

"At the very most," I said, following her into the vestibule, "they'll postpone it."

"To when?" said Fay. She paused at the front left corner of the vestibule, where there was a row of aluminum mailboxes. She shoved a little key into the Apartment A box. The metal frame rattled and clanged. "Next week, when the war is over?"

"Well, even if they do try to cancel it," I said, "we can just do it anyway. Who's gonna stop us?"

Fay yanked open the mailbox. Mail spilled out. Her dad often forgot to pick up the mail, so his mailbox was always overstuffed by Wednesday when Fay checked it after spending the first half of the week at her mom's. Sometimes I wished there were some kind of final Fay exam I could take, something where I could use up all the knowledge I'd crammed into my brain over the last four years and maybe make room for something else.

"We could sneak into the Meetinghouse and do it like a heist," I said. "*Ocean's Eleven*–style. Ocean's Four, in our case. Ocean's Five if you count Ms. Spider. I guess we'd be Spider's Five—"

I stopped. I saw it before she did, I think. By then I would have recognized the Smith logo anywhere. I recognized it right away on the corner of an envelope sticking out of the mail pile. A small envelope.

I looked at the envelope. I looked at Fay. She looked at me. She looked back at the envelope. I looked back at the envelope too.

"You applied to Smith?" I said.

She ran her finger under the envelope flap, tearing it carelessly open, and unfolded the letter inside.

From where I stood it looked like mostly white space, not much text. I leaned in and saw the words *regret to inform you*.

A rejection. Not even the waitlist. Fay applied to Smith and they flat-out rejected her.

What did I feel right then? I'm trying to call it back up now, but it's hard to identify and even harder to explain. I'd been so anxious, and seeing the letter made me less anxious, but at the time I couldn't have told you why. The full implication, the finality of it, would take a while to sink in, so there was only the faintest pang of sadness. There was also an ugly spark of smugness. On top of all that, though, there was anger. I was angry that Fay thought she could just waltz into Smith and meet me there like it was a Starbucks, angry that she hadn't told me, angry that she never even asked me if I wanted to go to college together. That anger, I think, is what motivated me to say what I said next.

"Well, it's for the best," I said. "You wouldn't fit in there anyway. It's all lesbians."

When I try to remember Fay's reaction to that, I picture her face looking blank, her expression unchanged. But that might be a made-up memory. I think I was still looking at the letter, not her face. Either way, I didn't see it coming at all—I had no warning signal, no time to brace myself—when she hit me.

FAY

I arrive now at an incident that I strenuously think *around* when I think of Nell. All night long, from the moment I spotted her on the street, I've been avoiding the memory. I've been avoiding the memory for fifteen years. My hope, I suppose, is that if I go long enough without thinking of it, I'll eventually forget it. But I doubt I ever will.

If she remembers it (of course she remembers it), she most likely misunderstands it. I had just received my Smith rejection in front of her, which she might reasonably assume flooded me with shame and jealousy, but she would be wrong. Reading the letter, I felt neither shame nor jealousy. I felt nothing at all. Or I felt feelings so disparate and conflicting—affront, embarrassment, guilt, relief, unwillingness to let any of this show on my face—that it was easy enough to round them down to nothing. I would most likely have continued to feel nothing, had Nell not said what she said next.

"You wouldn't fit in there anyway." She half-laughed. "You're not gay, so . . ."

All the rage I had ever carried in my body sharpened itself to the pinprick point of that unfinished sentence. "Comma-*so*-dot-dot-dot," I said. "So *what*?"

And then I hit her.

I struck her upper arm, just barely redirecting the impulse to slap her in the face—for I truly wanted to hurt her, emotionally if not physically. I hated her. I hated her only for an instant, but I hated her intensely enough to derive catharsis from the impact of my palm on her body, the resounding smack of resistance through her jean jacket sleeve. Then, just as swiftly, the rage passed, leaving in its wake a sick self-horror.

The pause that followed couldn't have lasted more than a second or two, though what a slow second or two it was. We were standing in the vestibule of my father's building. I envisioned Nell refusing for the first time to follow me down the stairs, Nell turning and walking out the door and hailing a cab to go home. I don't know if anything in her demeanor suggested this intention. I have no memory of her face in that moment. Perhaps I couldn't bring myself to look at her. More likely I looked at her and failed to see her.

I forced myself to smile. In an affectedly breathy voice I lilted, "Bitch-ass motherfucker, don't *even*." I wasn't imitating ebonics so much as a white gay man's imitation of ebonics—which is to say that I was imitating Theo, and thereby implying that I was also imitating Theo when I hit her, and that the correct response was to laugh.

Nell laughed, or pretended to. "You've been spending way too much time with Theo."

"You're right." It may have been the first time I ever said those words to her. It was certainly the first time I said them in a spirit of anxious appeasement. "When the musical is over," I said, ignoring its looming cancellation, "we'll go back to normal."

I placed my hand upon her shoulder, right above where I'd hit her. I rarely touched Nell, and certainly never touched her with gentleness, so the gesture felt at once momentous and false. I clasped her shoulder through the stiff denim, as though rehearsing my blocking for a play in which I'd been miscast. "Come on," I said. "Let's go in."

I was desperately grateful when she complied. As we descended the stairs, I realized I'd felt increasingly desperate around Nell for some time now. She was going to Smith. I was going to lose her. And now, insanely, I had pushed her further away still.

My father's apartment was dark. On the living room couch, Gareth snored. Nell and I quietly hung up our jackets and tiptoed to my bedroom. I closed the door.

Nell sank to the floor, taking her usual spot on the Persian rug. She rested her back against the wall and settled into a cross-legged position. "I'm so tired," she said. Her eyes fell shut.

At the sight of her closed lids I was seized with panic, an almost infantile sense of abandonment. She was telling me, I thought, that she would prefer to be unconscious than in my company right now. That was how thoroughly I had wrecked things.

Or she was simply tired. God knows I was.

I lowered myself to the floor beside her—right beside her, closing the careful distance I usually kept from her body. I was acting on instinct, refusing to think about what I was doing or why I was doing it. "Me too," I said. "I'm just gonna take a quick nap on you, okay?" Theatrically, I fell sideways to the floor.

I positioned my head so that it landed on her thigh. Her flesh squished under the pressure of my face. The rough fabric of her jeans chafed against my cheek. I closed my eyes, shifted slightly, let the full weight of my head settle onto her.

It was the closest physical intimacy I'd ever had with Nell. It was the closest physical intimacy I'd ever had with another girl. It was the closest physical intimacy I'd ever had with anyone. I could tell, by the smell emanating from between her legs, that she was on her period. It was not a smell I found pleasing. Under other circumstances I'd have pulled away from it. Instead I tried not to notice it, tried not to be in my body at all. I wanted her to touch me. I didn't want her to touch me. I closed my eyes and held my breath.

After a long pause, I felt her hand upon my head. She stroked my hair—a single stroke, so light and gentle it was almost unbearable, like the tickle of an insect on the skin. In the clenching of her thigh under my cheek, in the warmth of her crotch-sweaty lap, I was relieved to feel my own desirability radiating back at me. That would be enough, I thought, to make this endurable. I was beautiful to her. I would not fade into translucence, not so long as Nell loved me.

She spoke, at last, in a strangled voice. "You're hurting me."

Trying to interpret this as a direction rather than a rejection, I stiffened my neck to support my head and lessen its weight on her. "How's this?"

"Get up."

"I can't." I kept my eyes stubbornly closed. "I'm stuck."

"I have to pee." She shifted and rolled her way out from under me.

Something tore open inside me. *Come back*, I nearly cried out as she opened the door and left my bedroom. I was still lying on the floor. I was cold. In the absence of Nell—I was certain of it—I would never be warm again.

NELL

I've never told anyone that Fay hit me.

It sounds so dramatic. I guess it *was* dramatic, but not in the way you'd expect. It was just on the upper arm, so it didn't really hurt, but it was *hard* and it came out of nowhere. At first I was too surprised and confused to have any reaction at all. My first thought, actually, was that Fay had seen a cockroach on my arm (it was a real possibility in her dad's building) and was doing me a favor. But then Fay said, in a Theo-ish voice, "Bitch, don't even"—and I realized she was mad at me. Mad enough to hit me.

In theory, this was the thing I dreaded more than anything else in the world. But now that it was happening for real, I felt weirdly calm. I had gotten into Smith, and Fay hadn't. Fay was jealous, embarrassed, out of control. The thought made me giddy, so giddy I actually laughed. It wouldn't sink in till much later that Fay had fucking *hit me*.

As we walked downstairs to her dad's basement apartment, Fay—who never touched me—put her hand on my shoulder. "You're probably right," she said. "I bet Skip and Trudy won't cancel the musical."

So we were just going to act like the last few minutes hadn't happened? Fine. I could play along, for now. "We can make a case to them that it's an antiwar musical," I said. "Somehow. Even though it's a happy musical about Navy guys during World War II."

"Do you really think it's a happy musical?" Fay unlocked the apartment door. Inside, it was dark. Her dad and Gareth had already gone to bed (not together, probably). She lowered her voice. "I think it's tragic," she said. "Because the sailors have only twenty-four hours in New York. Then they have to go and get their heads blown off."

"Whoa," I said. "You think they *die* after the show is over?"

"It's implied."

Normally I would have gone along with this. But now I pushed back. "There's literally a whole song," I said, "about how Chip and Ozzie are gonna see Hildy and Claire again, *some other time.*"

"But the song is so sad," said Fay. We entered her bedroom. "They keep saying *some other time,* but the music is sad because they know it's not true."

I wondered if I was supposed to interpret this as a metaphor. Maybe she was fishing for reassurance, trying to get me to say that *we* wouldn't die after Idlewild, that we would still hang out all the time even though I was going to Smith and she wasn't. Or maybe not. Or maybe who gave a shit? I was sick of constantly guessing what Fay wanted from me.

I sat cross-legged on the floor, the way I always did. "I'm so tired," I said.

"Me too," she said. I expected her to go to the kitchen and get us glasses of seltzer, the way she always did. Instead she closed the door, walked across the room toward me, and sat down on the floor near me. She yawned and stretched out across the rug like a cat.

Then she put her head on my lap.

I stared down at her, waiting for her to say something, to tell me what the fuck she was doing. But she just lay there with her eyes squeezed shut and her cheek smushed against my thigh.

My instinct was to freeze, as if a wasp had landed on me. I clenched all my muscles to hold myself still. Time stretched on and Fay just lay there with her head in my lap, her eyes closed, like she was willing to sleep there all night.

Or like she was waiting for me to do something.

My heart pounded so hard I could feel it in my hands. My whole body was shaking, and only partly from the muscle strain. Even through my jeans I felt the heat of Fay's face, plus a warm spot on my thigh every time she breathed out. I looked down at her, taking advantage of her closed eyes to study her face. I'd been studying her face for almost four years, but this was my first time seeing it from this angle. I looked at her dark eyelashes and delicate eyelids, watched them twitch the way people's closed eyelids do when they're not asleep. I watched her breathing, her mouth slightly open, her chest rising and falling—just a tiny bit—with her breath. I looked at her boobs—of course I did. They looked huge from this angle. How many times had I fantasized about touching them?

I didn't understand why Fay was doing this now. But trying to understand Fay—maybe that was where I'd gone wrong all these years. Maybe I needed to stop overthinking things.

I lifted my hand off the floor. I let it hover above her chest, just an inch or two above it, like I was touching her aura.

Then I chickened out and moved my hand away.

I looked at her hair, the tangled snarls of it spread in every direction around her head. It was kind of amazing, I thought, how her hair was always such a mess even though she kept it short. Tentatively, I reached down and, with one finger, tucked a tuft of it behind her ear.

At my touch, Fay's whole body went stiff. Her eyebrows, her eyelids, the bridge of her nose, her whole face scrunched up in disgust.

At least that's what I thought I saw, and that's why I jerked my hand away like I'd been stung. In that instant I was certain, 100 percent certain, that I was seconds away from being humiliated—that Fay was gearing up to recoil from me and laugh at me and be like, "Ew, Nell, what are you doing? You know I'm not a lesbian!"

Before she could say anything at all, I started pushing her off me. "You're crushing me," I said. "Get off me."

"No." Fay stayed limply in place. "I'm stuck to you."

I managed to wrest my way out from under her. I scrambled off the floor and fled to the bathroom and shut myself in there for a long time.

I've been mentally replaying that moment for fifteen years now. I don't know why I was so certain that Fay was messing with me. Looking back, I think she really might have meant it. Sometimes I convince myself that I could have lost my virginity to Fay that night, and I blew it because I'm a big stupid gay dumbass.

But then I try to imagine the sliding-doors scenario where Fay and I did hook up that night—and I can't picture it. Literally, I try and my mind goes blank. It feels fundamentally impossible. Like even if we'd tried, we couldn't have gone through with it.

I don't know, though. I'm still mad at myself for being too chickenshit to find out for sure.

In Fay's bathroom I peed, washed my hands, brushed my teeth (I kept my own toothbrush in there), washed my face, peed again for good measure, washed my hands again. By the time I ran out of things to do in there, I was no longer sure that Fay was trying to trick me. I went back into her bedroom half-convinced that I'd misunderstood everything.

She'd turned off the lamp. Her room glowed orange from the streetlamps outside. (She had no blinds on her windows. At the time I thought that was a little weird; in retrospect I find it even weirder.) She'd also pulled out the trundle bed where I always slept and set it up with a pillow and a blanket for me. She was already in her own bed. There was no way she could be asleep, but she seemed pretty committed to pretending to be.

I crawled into the trundle bed, burning with something bigger and worse than embarrassment. Guilt, maybe, though I wasn't sure what I was guilty of.

Then Fay spoke. "It's not just Smith."

"What?"

"Smith was the last one," she said. "I got rejected everywhere else too."

I rolled over on my side and propped myself up on one elbow to look up at her. But I couldn't see her face. "Wait, seriously?" I said. "Where else did you apply?"

"Various places. All of them out of my league, apparently."

My heart was racing again, this time from sympathetic stress. "How many schools?" I asked. "What about your safety school? Did you have a safety?"

"Whatever," she said. "I guess I'm not college material."

"Oh my god," I said. "What are you going to do?"

I knew I was acting like my mom—or, worse, Deenie Mellman—but I couldn't help it. I'd never heard of this happening to anyone. I'd *worried* about it happening to me, but it was a superstitious, catastrophizing kind of worry, like my fear that New York City would get nuked by Saddam Hussein. Deep down, I never seriously believed I would get rejected from every school I applied to. I didn't think that could happen. Not to people like me. Definitely not to people like Fay, who talked like a professor and had an entire encyclopedia in her head and practically lived in the school library; Fay, the queen of extracurriculars, singing every solo in Chorus and acting in every play and creating the Invert Society out of thin air; Fay, whose teachers adored her so much they didn't even mind when she cut class.

But that was the thing, wasn't it? It struck me right then: Fay *never* went to class, unless I was there to whisper and pass notes with her. Fay never did her homework, unless I was there to turn it into a game. Even the Invert Society was just an inside joke of ours, not a real club. The no-grades no-prizes nature of Idlewild made it easy to overlook this, but Fay was a total slacker.

No, it was more than slacking. Fay didn't give a shit about school, I thought, for the same reason she didn't give a shit about her hair, or her exposed bedroom windows, or my feelings: she didn't give a shit about *anything* except being gay. And she wasn't even gay. She just wished she were.

And suddenly I knew the real reason she'd hit me. She wasn't jealous of me for getting into Smith. She was jealous of me for being gay. That must have been the reason she'd chosen me as her best friend: she wanted what I had. My superpower. If I could have shared it with her, I would have, but that didn't matter. She would always be jealous of me—dumb old me—for having the one thing she couldn't have. I didn't know if I wanted to laugh or cry.

"The musical," she said.

"What?"

"That's what I'm going to do," she said. "I'm going to star in *On the Town* with you and Theo and Christopher."

And then what? I didn't ask.

I squinted at my digital watch. It was almost one in the morning. Nineteen hours to showtime, if the show went on.

THE INVERT SOCIETY, 2003

The show will go on. The opening night curtain will rise, as planned, tonight at eight o'clock. We are called, as planned, for seven. We the triumphant Invert Society meet up beforehand, as planned, in Union Square.

But Union Square is packed with protesters. The protesters huddle under umbrellas in hard icy rain that makes rivulets of ink run down the soggy cardboard of the wet signs being waved: STOP THE WAR ON IRAQ. NOT IN OUR NAME. NEW YORKERS SAY NO TO WAR. The ground is black and glossy with rain, the crowd so dense and umbrella-obscured that we the Invert Society struggle to find each other in it. When we do find each other, we can't hear each other over the roaring and screaming and bucket-drum-thumping and so many different chants at once that you can't make out any of the words. Someone squats on the ground drawing with colored chalk on the hexagonal asphalt paving blocks—a crime-scene corpse outline in purple, a peace sign in pink—but the rain washes it away before he can finish. We try to step over it but we miss and our shoes smear wet pink chalk across wet black asphalt and the guy yells at us.

N, checking her digital watch: "Holy shit, it's 6:55."

Christopher: "We have to run."

F: "It's too crowded to run."

Theo: "It's too crowded to *move*."

On the eastern edge of the square, where we need to cross the street, there's a metal police barrier flanked by cops in long blue-black raincoats that they wear open so we can see the black holstered guns on their hips. They glower at the crowd from under the rain-beaded plastic visors of their blue-black caps.

A hoarse voice says, "You can't go that way."

We don't recognize the voice. But when we turn around, it's Juniper Green, brandishing a NO BLOOD FOR OIL sign. To her left is Daylily Jones, holding a PEACE ON EARTH sign. To her right is Bottom, carrying no sign but only a black umbrella, which he holds over the heads of Daylily and Juniper, allowing himself to get rained on.

Juniper rasps, "They've blocked off this whole side of Union Square. You can't cross."

F: "But we *have* to cross."

N: "How are we supposed to get to school?"

Daylily points with her PEACE ON EARTH sign. "You have to go all the way around. To the north end." She's even hoarser than Juniper. "If you want to wait, like, twenty minutes, we can all go together."

F: "But we have to go *now*."

N: "Call time is in three minutes."

At last Bottom speaks—or tries to speak. His voice is wrecked, a rough husk of itself. We can't even hear what he says.

N: [*horrified*] "Oh, shit."

F: "Bottom, what have you done?"

Juniper says angrily, "His name is *Peter*." She tosses her head, splattering us with her wet ponytail. "And he's been leading the chants all day."

Theo: "Nice going, Enjolras."

Christopher, heartbreakingly naïve: "Can you still sing?"

N: "Why didn't you save your voice?"

F: "Don't you care about the show?"

Bottom croaks, "Some things are more important than the show."

F: [*shouting*] "NOTHING is more important than the show!"

"It's okay," Daylily says brightly, or as brightly as she can with her ragged voice. "No one ever comes on Thursday night."

"Also, I don't know if you've heard," says Juniper, "but we just went to war and people are protesting in the fucking streets."

We the Invert Society give her the finger and shove our way back into the crowd.

We're going to put on the best show Idlewild has ever seen.

FAY

Opening night was fated to be disastrous from the start.

The protests, and the resulting traffic and road closures, caused everyone in the cast to arrive late. Despite the panicked, cack-handed haste with which we changed into our costumes and applied our stage makeup, the curtain didn't rise until twenty minutes past eight. It rose to a nearly empty house. In light of the traffic—and the fact that the Thursday night cast was, for once, identical to the Friday night cast—even the most supportive parents could rationalize skipping the Thursday night show. Waiting in the wings for my entrance, I could hear the threadbare applause, the devastating silence after every joke. It was indistinguishable from the previous night's dress rehearsal but for the inaudible voices of Bottom and Daylily, and for the pervasive feeling of doom.

When I took the stage for the "Carried Away" scene, I was blinded by the spotlight and briefly believed I was performing to a black void. Only the occasional cough revealed the presence of a sparse handful of people sitting in the Meetinghouse benches, wishing to be elsewhere. The collapse of the dinosaur skeleton at the end of the scene was a technical tour de force involving a team of stagehands on the backstage side of the flat, holding each individual bone on a string and letting go all at once. How I had looked forward to the audience reaction! There was none—save for a single sharp intake of breath, suggesting that someone had mistaken the meticulously staged accident for the real thing. Outside the Meetinghouse window I heard screeching emergency sirens. "*We got carried, just carried away,*" Theo and I sang to each other. The chagrin in my voice was unfeigned. I heard myself go sharp on the high note.

The lights went down. Theo and I exited the stage, dodging the rest of the cast as they stampeded onstage for the "Lonely Town" ensemble number. Theo and I collapsed onto a wooden bench against the wall, too demoralized even to whisper to each other.

"Lonely Town" began with a solo from Bottom, but Bottom's voice was well and truly wrecked. He was hoarsely Rex Harrison–ing his way through the lyrics, speaking rather than singing, and even that sounded painful.

I wished for Nell beside me. I wanted her to pound her fist against mine, silently telling me that I'd sounded amazing out there. She wasn't in the "Lonely Town" number, so she must have been nearby, backstage in the dark. But she didn't come to me.

Somewhere on the street outside, a car alarm went off. I mentally sang along with it, anticipating from memory each of its eight-beat movements—shrill allegro, low vivace, descending-slide moderato, ascending-slide largo, screeching adagio, two-tone lento, and back again to the beginning. Helplessly, the ensemble sang over it. *"And every town's a lonely town."*

Theo edged toward me. I edged toward him. His white sailor pants snagged against my pantyhose. He bounced his fist on my knee, silently suggesting a game of rock-paper-scissors. We counted to three on our fingers, then flung out our hands simultaneously. We both chose scissors. Or perhaps I half-consciously cheated, delaying my own choice for the fraction of a second it took me to perceive him choosing scissors so that I could imitate him and exult in our sameness.

He smiled, then slipped his hand, still in scissor formation, under the neckline of my blue rayon dress. I felt his scissor-blade fingers slide over my bra, then into my bra. He found my nipple and pinched it, hard. In my ear he murmured, "Does this hurt?"

I shook my head *no*. Onstage, the lights went down. The audience clapped feebly.

Theo pinched harder. "Does *this* hurt?"

It did. I shook my head *no*.

Character heels clacked on the risers as the ensemble girls crashed their way backstage.

Theo pinched, squeezed, twisted roughly. "How about now?"

Pain radiated through me. I pictured Theo's touch electrocuting the whole breast until it crumbled to ash. Convulsing silently on the bench, I shook my head *no*.

NELL

I wish I could blame the war, but the truth is, we were severely under-rehearsed. Bottom and Daylily fucked up their voices, and the audience was small, but we could have gotten past those problems if the rest of the production was a tight ship. It wasn't. That's all I can stand to say about it. If I hear any of the music, even now, I'll start crying. Four years ago, my mom bought me an orchestra-section ticket to the Broadway revival of *On the Town* as a Hanukkah present; I sold it on StubHub for $17 and lied to her that I'd gone. I couldn't bear to hear any of it. In particular, if I heard the "Times Square Ballet" from the end of Act One, I knew I'd remember how my whole life came crashing down.

THE INVERT SOCIETY, 2003

Theo, as Ozzie: "This town belongs to the Navy!" *A-five-six-seven-eight* and the stage flash-floods with music, girls, boys, middle schoolers, the whole ensemble breaking into the "Times Square Ballet." The six leads exit stage left, done with Act One.

We the Invert Society gather in a corner backstage. Our rayon costumes are damp at the armpits. Our stage makeup is caking at the forehead, pooling on our upper lips, dripping salty-bitter into our mouths. We hear, onstage, an unchoreographed crash—has someone slipped and fallen? The band plays on. The light in the Meetinghouse brightens, abruptly and arbitrarily: someone in the audience—probably attempting to sneak out early—has accidentally turned on the houselights. We wait for someone to turn them off. No one does. The audience coughs and fidgets in the fluorescent glare. Unable to take another second of this, we yank open the heavy side door of the Meetinghouse and flee outside to the Peace Garden.

Cold night air chills us, braces us. We breathe. The rain has stopped, for now. The dark garden glistens and drips and smells like wet dirt. Police sirens wail to the west.

Theo kicks the brick wall. His black shoe knocks against planet Earth in the mural.

Christopher: "You'll scuff your shoes."

Theo: "Fuck my shoes." He kicks the wall again. "Fuck this night." Another kick. "Fuck the protest." Kick. "Fuck Quakers." He spits onto the mural. The spit hits one of the stick-figure children right in the smiling face.

We gulp cool air. If we concentrate hard and tune out the police sirens, the saxophone solo is faintly audible through the closed side door of the

Meetinghouse. The "Times Square Ballet" is about halfway over, which means the Thursday night show is about halfway over, which means that all of this is almost over.

We the Invert Society look at each other. Nowhere in Manhattan ever gets really dark, but the Peace Garden by night is dark enough to flatter us—Theo and Christopher in crisp white sailor suits, F and N in flouncy-skirted dresses (peacock-blue and taxi-yellow, respectively), all four of us coifed and lipsticked and held together with pins. In the amber glow of the light-polluted sky, we the Invert Society are beautiful.

Theo: "Hey. What's that?"

He kneels on the wet ground, reaches into the bed of ivy.

Christopher: "Theo, your *pants!*"

Theo clambers to his feet, grinning, his white bell-bottom trousers streaked with grime and his pinned-on sailor's cap askew. In his hand he holds a wet metal can.

F: "What's that?"

N and Christopher, simultaneously: "Oh my god."

Theo points the can at the ground, presses a finger onto the nozzle. We hear a fizzling hiss. We smell a harshly pleasing chemical fume. We see nothing on the ground because the paint is shinywetblack and the asphalt is shinywetblack and the night is shinywetblack.

Theo: "Christopher, I dare you to spray a dick on the mural."

Christopher: "No way."

Theo presses the can into Christopher's hand.

Theo: "Do it."

Christopher: "No."

Theo sidles up close to Christopher, snakes an arm around his sailor-suited shoulders.

Theo: "Come on, baby."

Christopher: [*quietly*] "Don't do this."

Theo tugs on the navy-blue neckerchief tied around Christopher's neck, drawing Christopher close. He speaks in a murmur so soft that F and N can only just hear it.

Theo: "If you do it, I'll make out with you."

F&N, 2003

We the F&N unit exchange a glance the likes of which we the F&N unit have not exchanged in a very long time. This is the moment we've been awaiting for so long, finally coming to pass while we stand costumed in the grimy wet garden. There is no doubt in our shared mind where our duty lies.

F&N, in unison: "Do it."

Theo still has Christopher by the neckerchief. He tugs harder.

Christopher whispers, "You're choking me." He looks imploringly at the F&N unit.

F&N: [*chanting*] "Do it! Do it!"

Theo clasps his free hand around Christopher's, so the two of them are holding the can together. Manipulating Christopher's arm with his own, Theo makes Christopher shake the can. He makes Christopher aim it at the mural. He makes Christopher press the nozzle. It fizzle-hisses.

A black loop, only vaguely phallic, sizzles onto the painted brick wall, impressionistically attached to one of the smiling stick figures holding hands around a not-to-scale planet Earth.

Theo manipulates Christopher's hand again. The can fizzle-hisses and a second phallic loop appears on the wall, attached to the adjacent smiling stick figure. Now there are two disproportionately big-dicked stick figures, and their dicks are touching.

F&N: "Make out make out *make out!*"

Theo's left hand slithers upward and wraps its fingers around the back of Christopher's neck. Christopher closes his eyes and inhales raggedly. His fingers let go of the can; it falls, clangs upon the ground, clatter-rolls away.

We the F&N unit breathe in sync, our hearts pounding in unison.

Gripping Christopher by the back of the neck, Theo leans forward and closes his eyes and we the F&N unit watch as—

NELL

Theo kissed Christopher. Not a fake stage kiss through his hand like the first time we ever saw him—Theo actually-for-real *kissed* him, mouth to mouth. And Christopher, even though he'd seemed so reluctant a second ago, kissed him back almost immediately. And then they just . . . kept kissing. I'd been expecting some kind of squeamish peck on the lips, but Theo and Christopher were honest-to-god making out. There was tongue, I'm pretty sure. In their matching sailor suits they kissed and kissed, the muted trumpet solo of the "Times Square Ballet" wafting out through the Meetinghouse side door.

I wasn't like Fay. I didn't get turned on at the sight of two dudes together. But as I watched Theo and Christopher make out, I thought I understood for the first time what Fay got out of it. Something huge was blooming inside me, or maybe something huge was blooming in the world and I was just lucky enough to witness it. Gay kissing, right here at Idlewild! I'd thought it was impossible—I don't think I'd ever fully realized, until that moment, just how impossible it had always felt to me—and now, boom, it was happening. What else was possible now? Anything. Everything. The world had cracked wide open and you could kiss your best friend and you would still be yourselves, the music would keep playing, the show would go on.

I didn't turn to look at Fay. I couldn't tear my eyes away from the kiss. But I was as certain as I'd ever been that her thoughts were my thoughts. My happiness was too big to be mine alone—it must be coming from her, glowing off her like light. I let it fill me up, felt myself go shiny and rainbow-sparkly. I was part of that spinning disco ball again. *Finally*, I thought. *Finally, finally, finally.*

FAY

Achingly, vividly, constantly, in every possible scenario and from every possible angle, I had imagined this moment. What I expected from it, I think, was total transubstantiation. Through Theo, I would touch and be touched by Christopher; through Christopher, I would touch and be touched by Theo. I would inhabit both boys at once and experience their pleasure multiplied. I would exist only as light, as vapor, as pure elemental boy-kiss.

That was not what happened.

Theo kissed Christopher, and I stood there watching in the dark. Christopher kissed back, and I stood there sweating in my peacock-blue party dress. Theo slipped his tongue into Christopher's mouth, and I stood there itching in my disintegrating pantyhose. Christopher lifted a tentative hand to cup Theo's cheek, and I stood there sore in my character heels that wobbled on the wet concrete. Theo grunted softly and tightened his grip on the back of Christopher's neck, and I remained exactly where I stood, separate and earthbound and locked inside myself.

I thought of Iago's line in the final act: "He hath a daily beauty in his life / That makes me ugly" (V.i.20–21). Theo and Christopher were beautiful, and the togetherness of their boyness was what beauty was, and my own existence was the negative space where beauty was absent.

I'd been mistaken all along. What I wanted was not to *watch* a boy kissing a boy, but to *be* a boy kissing a boy. The former was achievable; the latter was not. There was no substitute. There was no consolation. There was only Theo and Christopher, their boy bodies intertwined in the garden, at once close enough for me to touch and untraversable light-years away.

Next to me, I heard a sharp intake of breath. Nell. If she looked at me right now, I thought, she would know. I was sure of it. Nell could always read me.

I took a step away from her, angling myself into the dark.

NELL

I don't know how long Theo and Christopher kissed, but it can't have been as long as it felt, because the "Times Square Ballet" was still going the whole time. I could hear it, muffled, through the closed side door of the Meetinghouse. The music, which had been slow and soft, suddenly got loud and fast, which must have startled the boys into stopping.

Theo was the one who pulled away, though he kept his hands on Christopher's shoulders. I studied Christopher. His sailor's cap was almost completely unpinned, dangling off the side of his head. His hair, which had been gelled to a flat helmet for the show, was so mussed by Theo's hands that it stuck out in spikes. His stage lipstick hadn't been that noticeable before, but now it was smudged across his face. I think his eye makeup was, too, but maybe his eyes were just naturally huge as he stared at Theo in . . . shock? Confusion? To me it looked a little like fear—but in the low light I wasn't sure.

Theo put a hand on Christopher's cheek and murmured something. I didn't quite catch it. It might have been "It's okay," or it might have been "You okay?" Weirdly, this felt more private than the kiss, and on instinct I averted my eyes.

I turned toward Fay, grinning, elated—but she was already walking away. She crossed the Peace Garden, opened the dove-gray side door, and slipped back inside the Meetinghouse. She didn't even turn back for one more look. That was odd, but maybe she wanted to exult with me in private. I followed after her.

As I crossed the Peace Garden, the music of the "Times Square Ballet" changed again: the drums and brass section dropped out, and a piccolo solo took over, piping out a military-march parody of the melody to "New

York, New York." I mention this because it meant the music suddenly got a little thinner and lower-decibel, and that's why my ear caught Theo talking in a low undertone to Christopher.

"—next chapter by, like, Sunday at the latest. I bet it's just gonna be the plot of *On the Town* but with the Marble Faun and Christopher."

I whirled around in the middle of the garden.

Theo was turned away, tucking the spray can back into the ivy. But Christopher saw me. He froze, guiltily, and I knew I hadn't misheard.

Christopher and I stared at each other across the garden. Just for a few seconds—during which the music grew louder and more discordant, the piccolo drowned out by brass, the brass drowned out by drums and cymbals—and then, abruptly, it was intermission.

V

FAY

I don't know how well I hid my psychological state from Nell for the remainder of the evening. If at some point she caught me alone backstage to enthuse over Theo and Christopher's kiss—and after six months of fevered anticipation, how could she not have?—I have no recollection of how I responded. I recall very little about the second act of the Thursday night show except that I piloted my body through it as if via remote control, dimly aware that my performance was flat and listless, and that I staved off all emotion with the mental repetition of the word *tomorrow*. I meant it in an optimistic sense, as in "the sun will come out" (see *Annie*, 1977, Thomas Meehan and Charles Strouse), but the effect was rather more akin to "creeps in this petty pace from day to day" (see *Macbeth* V.v.17–28). I was but a walking shadow, a poor player indeed—but the Friday night show, I told myself desperately, would be different. Everything would be different.

The following morning I elected to sleep in. I missed Meeting for Worship and first through fourth period. If there were ever a day I could get away with skipping school altogether, it was that day: I could have claimed to be at an antiwar demonstration, and any teacher at Idlewild would have excused the absence. It was just my luck, however, that that Friday at noon was the only time my mother and father had both been available for an emergency Deenie meeting. And so I dragged myself to school and spent an excruciating hour seated between my parents, the three of us facing down an abashed Deenie Mellman across her office desk. All parties involved would have preferred not to meet at all. But the straits were dire.

My mother and father were united, for once, in outrage—not at me, but at the colleges that had unanimously rejected me. Both were certain that some sort of clerical error was responsible, and reparable. They spoke of filing an appeal. They invoked the names of family friends affiliated with various first- and second-tier colleges who might exert influence on my case. They did not speak of the possibility that I, say, get a job.

"Who wrote your recommendations again?" my mother asked me. "Maybe you need better references."

"You know Fay," my father said, appealing to Deenie. "She's been at the college level for years. She's every professor's dream."

"Well," said Deenie, at last getting a word in edgewise, "it's a little more complicated than that." And she opened the file folder with my name on it.

It was then that I learned that Idlewild—for all its Quaker talk of eschewing grades, prizes, personal honors, and any other distinction that might elevate one student above another—did in fact calculate traditional 4.0-scale grade point averages. They were meant for colleges' eyes only and kept hidden from students and parents, but during that conference, Deenie disclosed mine. Unfamiliar as I was with the concept of a grade point average, the number meant nothing to me, and I've failed to retain it. I recall only that it began with a one, and that even my parents understood it to be abysmal.

I admit to being surprised. I considered myself highly intelligent, a conclusion drawn from a combination of teenage narcissism, adult feedback, and some degree of objective reality. One might hypothesize that my work ethic was stunted by this belief, that I operated within a "fixed" rather than a "growth" paradigm (see *Mindset: The New Psychology of Success*, Carol S. Dweck, 2006). But if that were the case, my across-the-board college rejections ought to have come as a devastating blow to my self-perception. Devastated, however, I was not. On the contrary, the absurd revelation of my GPA reduced me to giggles.

My mother shot me a perplexed look. "What's so funny?"

"Profound sorrow," my father said gravely, "sometimes manifests as inappropriate laughter."

Profound sorrow had nothing to do with it. I felt so buoyant—gleeful, even—that any observer might have thought I'd sabotaged my future on purpose.

My mother's wounded air suggested that she suspected as much. "But you're so smart," she said. "How did this happen?"

"Let's not make her feel worse than she already does," said my father, continuing to misread my mood.

"I think it's important to hear the student's perspective," said Deenie. "Fay, why do *you* think you stopped engaging academically?"

To stall for time, I pretended to consider the question.

(Tonight, I consider it in earnest. It wasn't precisely that I was a bad student. In a certain sense I was *too* good a student, overcommitted to my studies. The problem was that my field of study was not school, and schoolwork was one of many worldly matters I had renounced in my ascetic pursuit of knowledge. It was discipline, not laziness, that had me reading *Maurice* and *The Picture of Dorian Gray* under my desk during class, or playing hooky to catch *Red River* at Film Forum, or ignoring weeks' worth of homework assignments to read fanfic and write Faunfic. In essence, I'd spent all four years of high school studying to be a gay man. There was no college in the world that offered that preprofessional track.)

"I don't know," I said. "I guess I didn't really want to go to college."

"You could have told me that before I dropped a grand in application fees," my mother griped.

My father shushed her with a dismissive hand gesture. "So what do you want to do instead?"

The true answer: everything I'd already been doing for the last year and a half, with Nell at my side. But Nell was going to Smith. To be with the real lesbians.

"Nothing," I said. I thought of Theo and Christopher's haggling routine— *Nothing, it's free*—and giggled again.

"Well, you can't spend your whole life doing nothing," my mother said.

I perceived that my father was on the verge of a snide rebuttal disparaging my mother's lifestyle. To head this off, I joked, "I thought you wanted me to follow my dreams."

This had the bonus effect of signaling my unwillingness to cooperate, and from that point forth the adults in the room formed a crisis management plan without my input. It was agreed that I should apply to a selection of third-tier colleges with rolling admissions. Several local CUNY schools were suggested by Deenie but vetoed by my parents, who—I came to understand during that conference—considered my extended absence from their apartments a non-negotiable requirement of my college experience. Purdue made the list, I believe, as did the University of Iowa ("They have a good creative writing program," Deenie said brightly) and Loyola Marymount in California. The idea was that I'd (surely!) excel in my first year and then transfer somewhere more respectable.

"But, Fay, you have to be committed to it," said Deenie, belatedly remembering my presence in the room. "Can we count on you to be an active participant in this process?"

All adult eyes turned to me. There seemed little point in trying to convey to them what was at stake for me—that no place existed where I could make myself understood as I was understood at Idlewild. When I left Idlewild, I would cease to exist.

"Sure," I said and felt a chill, a distant door clanging shut.

On our way out of Deenie's office, my parents and I ran into Glenn Harding and Devi Saxena. Glenn greeted me and my parents awkwardly. "You should have told me you had a Deenie meeting," he said. "I would have excused your absence this morning."

Devi shot him a reproachful look. "Glenn, give her a break," she said. "She just got some really bad news." To me, she said, "I'm so sorry, Fay."

I wondered how they'd found out so quickly about my college rejections. Had Deenie told them?

"Yeah, sorry," said Glenn, chastened. "And I'm sorry I didn't make it to the show last night." To my parents: "I heard Fay was really good."

This was surely a lie, but I was too demoralized to challenge him. "Thank you," I said. "Are you coming tonight?"

Thrown, Glenn blinked behind his rectangular glasses. He and Devi exchanged a panicked look. "Oh," he said. "Um, this is awkward."

"I thought you knew," said Devi. "You haven't heard?"

NELL

I barely slept that night. I tried—I wanted to be at least somewhat rested for the Friday night show—but anxiety kept shocking me awake like a defibrillator. How did Theo and Christopher know about the Faunfic? How long had they known about it? Who else knew about it?

Did *everybody* know? Bottom, Daylily, Juniper, underclassmen, teachers, Oliver Dicks—did they all look at me every morning in the Meetinghouse and think about the Faunfic?

I kept going back and forth on whether to tell Fay. On the one hand, I didn't want to keep another secret from her. On the other hand . . . what if *she* was the one who shared it with them? I tossed and turned and obsessed and couldn't think of another explanation. But that didn't mean there wasn't one. Maybe Fay had nothing to do with it. She would never do that. Would she? If she didn't know, I should definitely wait until after the Friday night show to tell her. *Could* I wait that long? What if she knew something was wrong just by the look on my face in Morning Meeting?

That last worry, at least, ended up not coming true, because Fay wasn't there. Neither was Bottom; I figured he took the day off to rest his voice. And neither was Theo. Christopher was, though. I spotted him across the Meetinghouse from a slightly different angle and closer distance than usual, because the senior benches had been moved forward to accommodate the *On the Town* set. From this vantage point, Christopher looked about as rumpled and run-down as I felt.

For all twenty minutes of Silence, I stared at him across the Meetinghouse, just like I'd stared at him across the Peace Garden the night before. A few times he looked toward me, met my eyes, and quickly looked away. I wondered if everyone in the Meetinghouse was sneaking similar glances at me. It didn't seem like they were. In general, I thought, people ignored me. Especially when I wasn't with Fay. Or maybe all the time, but I didn't notice it when I was with Fay. What else had I failed to notice when I was with Fay?

Skip shook Trudy's hand to break Silence, and everyone bustled out of the Meetinghouse for first period. As I crossed through the Peace Garden on my way to Latin, I saw people crowding in front of the wall mural, pointing and giggling. I was so preoccupied about the Faunfic, I walked right past them without bothering to check out what was going on. I was in the Latin classroom before I realized they must have been looking at the spray-painted dicks. I'd almost forgotten.

With both Fay and Bottom absent, second period Chorus was barely a chorus at all—just me plus six very tired underclassgirls. "Can we just have a free?" one of them asked. "You know, to rest up for the show tonight."

Ms. Spider was usually so strict with the chorus, and this particular girl, who was supposed to sing tenor but kept singing the soprano line an octave down, was extremely not her favorite. But Ms. Spider looked as exhausted and dejected as the rest of us. "Fine," she said. "The hell with it. Get out of here."

The underclassgirls gathered their things, looking more disturbed than pleased. If Ms. Spider was too depressed to teach, we must have really blown it at the Thursday night show.

There was no point to a free period without Fay. Hoping I could just hang out here for a while, I took a slow detour to the window, which looked out over the Peace Garden. From four stories up, I saw a couple of maintenance men putting up a blue tarp over the defaced mural. I turned away guiltily.

The door swung shut behind the last of the underclassgirls. Ms. Spider exhaled loudly and slouched a little deeper on the piano bench. "Oy."

"Oy," I agreed. I waited for her to say something comforting, but she didn't, so I tried to do it myself. "Tonight will be better, though, right? The audience won't be dead, and Peter and Lily will have their voices back, and the Middle Schoolers will remember their blocking in the museum scene, and no one will accidentally turn on the houselights . . ."

Ms. Spider patted the piano bench to indicate that I should sit next to her. "Okay, kiddo," she said. "Let's talk turkey."

I perched beside her. The old wood creaked under my butt. Self-conscious, I tried not to rest my full weight on it.

"I just spoke on the phone with Peter's parents," said Ms. Spider. "He woke up with laryngitis—his voice is *gone*. No wonder, the way he pushed it last night. He's on vocal rest now, but these things generally don't resolve in a day."

My mind raced for a solution. We didn't have understudies, obviously. This was Idlewild. We barely had an ensemble.

"There have been a couple of times," she said, reading my mind, "we've managed to pull a ringer from the ensemble. But Peter would be pretty hard to replace."

"Can we postpone the show?"

She shook her head. "You gotta reserve the Meetinghouse a whole year in advance, you gotta strike the set before Sunday morning—there's so much red tape with those Quakers. Speaking of which . . ." She grimaced. "Skip and Trudy are none too thrilled about Idlewild doing a happy war musical, under the circumstances."

"It's *not* a happy war musical," I protested, even though I'd made the exact same point to Fay two nights ago.

"Yeah, yeah. But the thing of it is, this lets us save face. We can blame Skip and Trudy, and the Quakers, and that goddamn son of a bitch in the White House. No one has to know . . ." Her shoulders sagged. "The show just wasn't ready."

My eyes filled with tears. It was true. In a way, it was a relief to hear her say it. "I'm sorry."

"No, *I'm* sorry. I let you down. I thought I could take over for Wanda, but I was out of practice. I've been out of the game too long, and God knows I'm no spring chicken anymore."

I wished I could say something to reassure her, but she wasn't wrong on any count. Also, I was still kind of holding a squat over the piano bench and my quads were starting to burn and that was all I could think about.

"Poor Fay," she said. "This is going to crush her."

I jumped up, to the relief of my quads. "Oh my god," I said. "She's not even here today."

"I'll give her a call at home."

"She's at her dad's," I said. "He unplugs the phone during the day." I ignored the amazement on Ms. Spider's face, though under other circumstances I would have loved to get into a whole conversation about it. "But you could email her."

Ms. Spider looked up at me pleadingly. "Could you do it?" she said. "I'm such a dodo on the computer. Just tell her to call my office extension, if you don't want to be the bearer of bad news."

I hesitated. I hadn't been to the computer lab since my falling-out with Jimmy Frye. He was the last person I wanted to see right now.

"I'm sorry," said Ms. Spider. "That's too much to ask."

Those were the magic words that got me to say reflexively, "No, it's okay. I'll do it."

I left the rehearsal room and trudged down the fourth-floor hallway, my quads aching. At the door to the computer lab, I paused. I reminded myself that I wouldn't have to interact with Jimmy Frye. If he tried to talk to me, I'd just ignore him. All I had to do was write one email. It would take two minutes. That's what I kept telling myself as I lingered outside the computer lab, trying to psych myself up to go in.

The computer lab door opened and Christopher stepped out. There was no way he could miss seeing me, but he pretended not to notice me and walked right past me.

As Ms. Spider would say: the hell with it. The email was suddenly not my priority. I grabbed the strap of Christopher's backpack and held on hard. "Please don't run away," I said. "I really need to talk to you."

Reluctantly, he turned to face me. Up close, I saw dark circles under his eyes. I kept my grip on his backpack strap. He nodded, resigned.

"Okay," he said. "I guess it's time."

FAY

Devi encouraged me to go home. "I know the musical was important to you," she said. "If you just need to lie down, I'll excuse your absence."

"I think Theo Severyn is taking the day off too," said Glenn.

I unhesitatingly assented—but I was still in the company of my parents, which introduced an awkward question into an already awkward situation. I had left that morning from my father's apartment; I was scheduled to spend the weekend with my mother. Should I consider the morning extended and return to my father's, or treat this as the beginning of the weekend and decamp to my mother's?

"I leave it to you," said my father. "I won't be offended if you go home with your mama."

"Or you can go with Daddy," said my mother. "It's one hundred percent your choice."

I chose not to choose. "I'll just hang out at Starbucks for a while," I said. "Then I can hang out with Nell when she gets out of class."

My parents saw me to the Starbucks on the corner of Fifteenth and Third. I stood on line, or pretended to, while monitoring my parents through the window. Though they were most likely headed to the same destination—their respective homes on West Twenty-third—they hailed separate taxis. Once their cabs were a safe distance away, I left the

Starbucks line. I left the Starbucks. I walked south down Third Avenue. At Cooper Square, I turned right and walked west. As long as I remained in motion, I could avoid thinking about the musical or lack thereof, college or lack thereof, boy-on-boy kissing or lack thereof, Nell or lack thereof, my future or lack thereof.

From half a block away, I spotted the rainbow flags of the Stonewall Inn. I wanted to go up and look—even just at the door, at whoever might pass in and out of it—but I was conscious of appearing to others as a gawking tourist of a straight girl. In a paroxysm of self-disgust I strode past the bar, pretending not to notice it, and descended into the Sheridan Square subway station. There was a northbound 9 train roaring to a stop on the platform. I swiped my MetroCard and managed to leap into a car right before the doors closed.

All the way uptown, I thought only two thoughts. The first: *I'm not going anywhere in particular.* The second, which alternated with the first: *Just to see. Just for a second.*

I got off at Eighty-sixth Street and walked west again. The street sloped downward, and my pace quickened as I gained momentum. It was a cool, cloudy day. The farther west I walked, the harder the wind blew. My heart beat wildly when a slate-gray snatch of Hudson River revealed itself on the horizon, whitecapped and sparkling at the end of the corridor of buildings. *Just to see. Just for a second.*

I turned left on Riverside Drive and tracked the descending building numbers until I reached 125.

It was even lovelier than I'd imagined. It was ornately constructed of cream-colored brick, all curves and curlicues, no hard angles or sharp edges. Its old-fashioned, soot-stained stateliness made me think first of pen-and-ink illustrations in midcentury children's books—*Eloise*, perhaps, or *Stuart Little*—and then of *Rosemary's Baby*. I counted the rows of windows up to the tenth floor, wondering if I could see Theo and Christopher's bedroom window from where I stood. If Theo, reportedly staying home from school today, was in there right now.

Seized by the same self-consciousness that had propelled me past the Stonewall Inn, I didn't stop. I circled the block and passed 125 Riverside Drive again, trying to gaze at it using only my peripheral vision. I hummed "On the Street Where You Live" (see *My Fair Lady*, Lerner & Loewe, 1956). The sidewalk was so sparsely populated that I dared to sing aloud, softly and then less softly. *"I have often walked down this street before,"* I sang, though I had never walked down this street before today; I had wanted to but never gone through with it, sensing that it would be the start of something I would not be able to stop.

I was on perhaps my fifth or sixth circle of the block when I approached the building and saw Theo leaning against its outer wall. In contrast to its cream-colored curves and curlicues, he was all hard angles and sharp edges in black. I turned on my heel and tried to walk away quickly, casually, but I was too late. He'd seen me. "Hey, bitch." His voice was languorous, unsurprised.

Reluctantly, I turned around. What explanation for my presence here could I possibly formulate on the spot? I was visiting a relative. I was going to the dentist. I was—

"Don't lie. I've been watching you out the window for like half an hour." He was strolling unhurriedly toward me. "I know you're doing some kind of stalker shit. Whatever. I guess you heard."

I relaxed, as I always did when Theo so casually acknowledged my obsession with him. He accepted it so readily, with such unsurprised entitlement, that it forestalled any shame on my part. "That's why I cut school," I said. "Out of respect for the Friday night show. Why are you cutting?"

Confusion swept over his face for the briefest moment, then vanished. "To get my beauty rest," he said. "But Dorothy called me on the phone to tell me the bad news." The weather had warmed to the high fifties, so he'd shed his charcoal peacoat in favor of a slim-fitting black leather jacket. Faux, surely? But it flattered him, made him look like—the word flickered teasingly in my mind—*trade*. Even in spite of everything, my heart fluttered. I forced myself to look him in the eye, lest I fixate on the jacket's black leather collar against his pale throat. "Actually," he said, "she was worried about you."

"About me?" I was only half-listening. Was he wearing eyeliner? Perhaps he hadn't fully washed off his stage makeup from the night before.

"Yeah. She was like"—he shifted into an uncharacteristically well-observed parody of Ms. Spider's Brooklyn accent—"*Oy, Fay's gonna jump off a goddamn building.*"

"She said that?"

"No. She said, *I hate to think of her alone right now. Maybe you could pay her a visit?*" The riverside breeze ruffled his hair. He lifted a hand to smooth it. "Like you were dying or something."

Against my will I visualized his hand running through Christopher's hair the night before. His mouth against Christopher's mouth. I was looking at his mouth right now. I forced myself to stop. "That's a bit dramatic."

"Says the girl who just cut school and traveled all the way uptown to see where I live. I bet you're hoping I invite you upstairs and show you Christopher and I's bedroom."

That was, indeed, what I was hoping. "*Christopher and I's?*" I said. "You know that's not grammatically correct."

"Just for that, you don't get to see it." He flung out his leather-jacketed arm as though to block me from taking another step toward the building. "Restraining order. You can't come within fifteen feet."

I held his gaze for a moment, wondering if he was bluffing. But he made no move toward letting me any closer. "Fine," I said. "I guess I'll see you . . ." Not at the show tonight. Not at rehearsal, ever again. How many more Invert Society meetings were left in the year? Was the Invert Society even still extant, post–*On the Town*?

Theo laughed at me. "You *guess*," he said. "*Maybe* you'll come to school, even when there's no musical."

"Maybe," I said. "Or maybe you'll never see me again." I intended that as a joke, but it felt like less of one as I spoke it.

Theo looked at me so sharply that I expected him to respond with his own joke about how that outcome would be preferable. A second later, however, his makeup-smudged eyes softened. "Okay," he said. "Let's make this the best day ever."

NELL

Christopher wanted us to go somewhere private, where no one would overhear us. The rehearsal room, the library, even Starbucks felt too risky. We were going door to door down the fourth-floor hallway, looking for an empty classroom, when I had a better idea.

"Duh," I said. "The Meetinghouse."

Sure enough, no one was in the Meetinghouse, and the space was big enough to give us lots of advance warning if anyone walked in. My heart hurt at the sight of the *On the Town* set, towering and rickety and inexplicably pink. Christopher didn't know yet that we would never perform on it again.

"Let's sit on the stage," I said. "That gives us the best angle to keep an eye on all the entrances." This was true, but the real reason was that I didn't want to *look* at the stage.

Christopher and I walked down the center aisle and sat awkwardly, side by side, on the front edge of the risers. Even through my jeans, the metal was cold and uncomfortable.

I didn't know where to start. "I heard what Theo said to you last night."

"I know."

"I heard him say *Marble Faun*."

"Yeah."

He was giving me nothing. "Tell me," I said. "Who's the Marble Faun?"

Christopher squeezed his eyes shut and began to talk very fast, like he was trying to get it over with. "He's this sexy manipulative demon boy with, like, mind-control powers or something? He and Christopher are stepbrothers, and they have to share a bed for some random reason, and the Marble Faun sort of tricks Christopher into doing sex stuff. And then there's this, like, flash forward to the future, when they get drafted to the war in Iraq." He opened his eyes. "Um, I think that's all there is so far."

Blood was pounding in my ears. So they really had read it all. I forced myself to ask, "How did you find it?"

Christopher looked sideways at me. "How do you think?"

"I hate her," I said. It came out almost in a shout, but the Meetinghouse, designed to muffle acoustics, swallowed it up. I said it again, louder. "I hate her, I hate her, I hate her."

"Whoa, whoa, whoa." Christopher lifted a hand toward me, like he was going to touch my shoulder—the way he sometimes did to calm down Theo—but then he changed his mind and pulled it back. "You mean Fay?"

"Who the fuck else could have sent it to you?"

Christopher looked genuinely confused. "I mean, anyone could find it," he said. "It's public."

"Public?" Now I was lost. "What's public?"

"Your LiveJournal," he said.

My head spun. So this was *my* fault? But how? I'd been so careful. "It's *not* public," I said. "It's friendslocked. No one else has access to it."

"Nuh-uh," he said. "It comes right up if you go to, what is it, livejournal.com-slash-users-slash . . . uh, it begins with an O."

"No, it's—" My LiveJournal username was on the tip of my tongue. Christopher talked over me. "You know. The word on the Invert Society fliers."

I froze, trying to put it all together in my head. "*Omi-palone?*"

"Is that how you say it? Yeah, omi-palone Alone. All one word."

All at once I understood: This whole time, Fay had her own secret LiveJournal. Fay had her own secret LiveJournal and never bothered to lock it, just like she'd never bothered to put curtains on her bedroom windows. Fay had her own secret LiveJournal and she hadn't friendslocked it and she'd *posted our entire Faunfic on it.*

"But it was kind of random how we found it," said Christopher. "Me and Theo were in the computer lab one day, and Jimmy called us into his office. He said he had something funny to show us."

"Jimmy Frye? How did *he* have it?"

"He said it was in a school computer's browser history." (A *school* computer? Jesus Christ, Fay.) "But he wouldn't show us the actual website. He had a printout."

"He printed out the whole thing?"

"Yeah, and he'd gone through it with a highlighter."

"What did he highlight?"

"The sexy parts. It was pretty weird, to be honest."

The idea of *Jimmy Frye* going through my homemade porn with a highlighter . . . no, I couldn't break down. Not at school. I had to stay focused on facts. "When was this?"

"No idea. After *Othello*, I guess, 'cause I remember Jimmy telling us why Wanda got fired."

Even with everything else going on, I felt a wave of guilty relief. So it *wasn't* my fault that the whole school found out. It could have been, but it wasn't. That was a freebie.

"Actually," said Christopher, "do you know when Jimmy's birthday is?"

"Why the hell would I know that?"

"Well, whenever it is, it was about a month after that. He kept bringing it up, how his birthday was a whole month ago and no one remembered. Theo went out and bought him a tiramisu just to shut him up."

A random phrase popped into my head: *which was a MONTH ago, by the way.* Jimmy's angry email. Though even I hadn't realized he was *that* angry. "Whoa," I said. "Jimmy Frye is kind of a psycho."

"Yeah, pretty much," said Christopher. "He still emails us every time a new chapter goes up. It's kind of pathetic. He keeps saying he's our *friend*. Like, 'As a friend, I have to let you know what they're saying about you.'"

I would have laughed at that, if it weren't so horrible. More than anyone else at Idlewild, Jimmy Frye was obsessed with befriending the cool kids. Like Christopher, I'd always found it funny how desperate Jimmy was for the approval of teenagers. Until that second, it had never crossed my mind that it was also fucking scary.

"Theo thinks Jimmy has a crush on him," Christopher was saying. "But Jimmy's straight, right? He's always talking about Kendra Kwok and how hot she's gonna be."

Outside, in the Peace Garden, a bunch of kids burst out laughing. They were probably peeking under the tarp to look at the spray-painted dicks, but I imagined that they were laughing at me, that all of Idlewild had been laughing at me for months. It was time for the question I dreaded most. Weakly, I asked, "Does everyone know?"

"About his thing for Asian girls? Yeah, he's pretty open about it."

"No, about the—" I stopped myself from saying *Faunfic.* "The story."

Christopher shook his head so forcefully his curls bounced. "Theo wanted to keep it a secret. Thank god, because I would *freak out* if anyone else saw it." He shuddered at the thought. "I've had nightmares, actually, about people finding it and picturing me doing all that stuff."

That made me feel worse than anything he'd said so far. I'd been so fixated on what people would think of *me* after reading the Faunfic, I hadn't even thought about it from his point of view.

"And anyway," he said, "for a long time, we didn't have a way to share it. Jimmy wouldn't let us take home the printout, and he wouldn't tell us where to find it online. We couldn't find it on Google, either. So we just kept visiting Jimmy in his office to read every new chapter. It was like he was blackmailing us to hang out with him."

"I'm really sorry," I said, and I meant it. "That sounds horrible."

"For me, yeah," he said. "But Theo loved it. He was, like, addicted to it. That's why he came up with a plan to make Jimmy give us the website address. He kept saying, *I'm gonna make him an offer he can't refuse.*" He imitated Theo imitating Marlon Brando as the Godfather, which was like a bad Xerox of a bad Xerox of a mistake. (Marlon Brando doesn't even say that line.) "Basically, he came up with a . . . what did he call it? What's it called in Latin when you trade a favor for another favor?"

"Quid pro quo?"

"A quid pro quo, that was it."

"Jimmy loves those. What was the favor?"

Christopher ignored the question. "Yeah, it worked. Jimmy gave us the link. And then we knew for sure it was you and Fay, because of the *omi-palone* thing. And that created a monster in Theo." He rolled his eyes. "I mean, even more than usual. All he wanted to do at home was reread the story and check for new chapters. I'd go into my room to get away from him, and he'd trick me into opening the door for him and then come in with a printout and do a dramatic reading of the sex scenes, just to piss me off."

That sounded like Theo, all right. Except . . . "I thought you guys shared a room."

"No," said Christopher. "In real life he sleeps in the guest room."

"But you *said.*" I was sure of this one thing, if nothing else. "You've talked about sharing a room."

"Yeah." Christopher buried his face in his hands. His voice was muffled through his fingers. "That was Theo's idea."

"What?"

He lowered his hands. "Theo is, like, obsessed with the idea of being the Marble Faun," he said. "He's like, 'They *get* me. They *saw* me.' But I think he just wishes he were like that. I think he started acting more like the Marble Faun in real life just so you'd write more about him."

Numbly, I thought back on the last few months in the context of this new information.

"And I helped him out," said Christopher. "I played along. I hated the story, and I felt bad about lying to you, but . . ." He dropped his eyes guiltily. "He was being so flirty with me," he said. "I mean, he was before, but the Marble Faun thing put him into, like, overdrive. Well, obviously, you saw. I knew it was just pretend, but I thought maybe . . ."

In spite of everything, my stupid gay heart went out to Christopher. I said, "Last night didn't look so pretend."

Christopher looked up at me. "I don't know. Maybe. When we got home, I thought, like, maybe I could get through to him? So I told him you overheard, and now there probably wouldn't be any more chapters, and we could take down the . . ." He trailed off.

"Take down the what?"

"That pro quip thing—sorry, what's the word again?"

"The quid pro quo?"

"Yeah, that. But he wouldn't let me take it down. Like he physically held me back and wouldn't let me go on the computer. So I thought I'd do it when he wasn't around. But I tried just now, in the computer lab, and he changed the password. And I couldn't guess the new one. I tried like a million times."

"The password to *what?*" I prodded. "Are you gonna tell me, or . . . ?"

The bell rang, signaling the end of second period.

The sound seemed to jolt Christopher. "Sorry. I . . . I can't. Sorry." He shook his head anxiously and jumped off the edge of the stage. "I need to go to history."

And I needed to go to English. But I needed this more. I didn't move from the edge of the stage. "Come on, dude," I said. "You can't just *not tell me.*"

He slung his backpack over his shoulder. "Maybe later?" he pleaded. "I'm so stressed out. Let's just focus on the show for now, okay?"

"Oh," I said, and then it was my turn to deliver bad news.

FAY

Theo and I walked down Riverside Drive and east uphill to Broadway. We walked in the cloudy cool across the Upper West Side and all the way down past the park, wormed our way through the sluggish tourist crowds of Times Square. He dragged me into the Times Square Sephora and challenged me to a perfume fight. We grabbed free perfume samples and chased each other up and down the aisles, spraying each other until we dripped and reeked. A store employee finally kicked us out and we walked on, through Chelsea and the cobblestoned Meatpacking District. In the rippled aluminum tunnel entryway of the Comme des Garçons store we sang "Carried Away" to hear our own metallic echo. In the Jeffrey boutique we touched all the white Chanel items with our dirty fingers. We ran our hands over suede and cashmere and ostrich leather, stuck our noses deep inside thousand-dollar shoes and inhaled deeply, played hide-and-seek in the clothing racks and changing rooms until the security guards kicked us out. We moved from store to store, migrating southeast into Soho. By the time we got kicked out of the Prada store on Prince Street and Broadway, we were ravenous.

"I want sushi," he declared and led us to M2M, an Asian grocery store with a lunch counter. It was on Eleventh and Third, close to Idlewild, but it was late enough in the day not to matter. "I can't believe you've never been here," he said as we took our seats at the counter. "I come here all the time with Christopher. He'll be so pissed off when he finds out I brought you."

"I won't tell him," I said.

"Oh, *I'll* tell him. Just to fuck with him." He popped off the plastic lid of his boxed sushi. "You know how I am with him."

This was not entirely accurate. Even after all this time, the dynamic between Theo and Christopher continued to baffle me. But I was flattered by Theo's assumption that I understood it. "You're like that with everybody," I said. I thought of the bomb threat. "You like to fuck with people in general."

"Yeah. I do." He cracked his wooden chopsticks apart, peeled off a dangling splinter, flicked it onto the floor. "I like to find someone's weakness," he said. "Everyone has a weakness."

"What's yours?"

"Everyone except me." He poked his chopsticks against the rice underbelly of his sushi. "I have no weakness." He stabbed at the sushi harder. He failed to spear it.

I laughed with delight. I'd never met anyone who didn't know how to use chopsticks. I never would have guessed it of Theo.

"Shut up." He failed to stab the sushi again. "Okay, fine. I have *one* weakness." With his bare fingers, he picked up a ruby slab of raw tuna, detaching it from the rice. It glistened and wriggled in his hand as he turned to look sideways at me. "Seriously, though," he said, "I think my weakness is the same as yours."

"I know how to use chopsticks."

"No," he said, his voice suddenly low. "I mean the dollhouse thing."

Feigning nonchalance, I popped open the plastic lid of my take-out box and ran my fingers through cold edamame pods. "The dollhouse thing?"

"You know," he said. "The thing where nothing feels real." He dipped his head closer to mine. In a hushed, urgent voice, he said, "I have that too. I always thought it was just me."

Hard crystals of salt clung to my fingertips. I brought them to my mouth and gave them a surreptitious lick. The shock of salt on my tongue, the metallic Japanese pop on the radio, the delicate boy-smell of Theo beside me—all of it felt vividly real to me. If anything, the only unreal part of the scene was me. I mentally rounded down the difference and persuaded myself that this feeling was what Theo meant. "It's not just you," I said quietly.

Theo bit, at last, into the red tuna. "I know," he said, chewing. "We're the same." He swallowed. "Want to know a secret?"

Holding myself as still as possible, as though a hummingbird had landed on my finger, I nodded.

"When I first met you, back during *Othello*," he said, "I was, like, morbidly curious about your whole deal. You kept saying Iago was gay, but I couldn't figure out if *you* were gay, or if Nell was your girlfriend, or what. I mean, who cares, right? But Christopher wanted to know too, and it's not like we had anything better to do, so we joined the Invert Society, to try to figure it out. But we couldn't, and I didn't want to ask you, so . . . I asked Jimmy Frye."

The name alone nauseated me. I pushed away my edamame box. "Oh, no."

"It's okay." Theo waved a hand dismissively. "I don't care that you and Nell hooked up on 9/11."

I opened my mouth to explain that we hadn't, that I'd lied. But then it occurred to me that Theo believed this about me. I paused, considering the implications of this.

"I wasn't gonna tell you this," he continued, "but I'm pretty sure Christopher's gonna tell Nell. I told him not to, but he's an idiot." He gazed out the window at the Third Avenue traffic. I seized the opportunity to study him in profile—the metal studs on the lapels of his faux-leather jacket, the angle of his jawline, the dark flop of hair over his forehead. "Me and Christopher . . . we basically wrote a story about it. Just as a stupid inside joke."

"A story?"

"Yeah, about you and Nell hooking up on 9/11." He picked up another piece of sushi and stuffed it whole into his mouth. "Whatever," he said with his mouth full. "I don't even care what you think."

I was light-headed, physically dizzy with glee. This was too good to be true. "You wrote fanfic about me and Nell?"

"It's not fanfic," he insisted. "It's like . . . a writing project. A fake diary. Like Devi made us do for that *Wuthering Heights* project."

"My fake diary?"

"Nell's fake diary. You promised you wouldn't laugh!"

I'd promised no such thing, but I tried to collect myself. "Can I read it?"

"Not with that attitude."

We finished our sushi and walked west again. It began to rain, so we took shelter in a dark upstairs café on Greenwich Avenue. Theo drank chai and ate a slice of flourless chocolate cake; I drank Earl Grey and ate coconut sorbet out of a coconut shell. "The best day ever isn't over yet," said Theo. He reached across the table, grabbed my sorbet spoon, and licked its underside. "What should we do next?"

"We could walk down Eighth Avenue," I said, "and try to sneak into the gay sex shops. Or"—I laughed as though thinking of it for the first time, rather than confessing a deep and persistent fantasy—"a gay bar, even."

"We'd have to go deep undercover," said Theo. "As a gay couple." He sucked thoughtfully on my sorbet spoon.

I pushed my coconut-shell bowl toward him, indicating that he should finish my sorbet. "If we were a gay couple," I said, "I would be this sad, ugly old queen, and you'd be my arm candy."

Something beeped in his pocket. He pulled out his cell phone—brand-new, slick shiny silver with a clamshell cover that he flipped open like a switchblade, revealing a digital screen that glowed ice-blue. He studied it. "Text message from Maddy," he said. "Cast party tonight."

"Still?" I said. "Without the show?"

"*Instead* of the show. So it's starting, like, now. Should they go?"

"Who? Maddy and Kendra?"

He pointed to me, and then to himself. "The sad pervy old man," he said, "and his arm-candy boyfriend."

For a moment I was too overcome to speak. "I'd take you everywhere," I said. "I would shower you with presents, to make you stay. But it wouldn't work."

"Nah, I'd still leave you," he agreed. "But I'd miss you after." He swiped a fingertip through the powdered sugar on his cake plate. "Not at first," he said. "But the years would go by, and I'd keep randomly thinking about the first man who ever loved me."

My heart clenched. "He loved you madly," I said. "He would let you do anything."

He licked his sugar-dusted fingertip. Then he reached across the table and slapped me hard across the face. He did it so quickly, and so casually, that it went seemingly unnoticed in the dark café and took me several seconds to integrate into reality. To be hit in the face is a shockingly intimate experience. It wakes you up, even as it dazes you into docility. It makes your cheek go hot and red as if you're sunburned or drunk or in love.

"Even that?" he said.

It took me another moment to comprehend this as a response to *He would let you do anything*. At last I nodded, slowly. I was feeling many things at once, not least among them fear, which I tried to mask. "Sure," I said. "That was nothing."

NELL

"They can't even postpone it?" Christopher wasn't in tears, but he looked pretty close.

I didn't have time to soften the blow or deal with his feelings about it. "No. There's no show. So you can tell me about the quid pro quo now."

He looked around nervously. The Peace Garden was crowded with kids, many of whom were peeking behind the tarp and giggling. "I don't want to say it where people can hear."

"Can you show me in the computer lab?"

"I don't want other people to see."

I grabbed his arm. "Then you're gonna show me at my house," I said. "And we're gonna go there *right now*."

I was maybe 60 percent bluffing. I'd never cut school in the middle of the day. I could probably get away with it today—I was a second-semester senior, I'd already gotten into college, and teachers felt sorry for me because of the musical—but I hadn't been planning on it. And I definitely didn't expect Christopher to come with me. Why would he?

But when I tugged on his arm, he followed glumly after me like a dog on a leash. I led him back through the Meetinghouse, out the exit, east down Fifteenth Street, and he kept in step with me. He glanced over his shoulder as we walked away from Idlewild. "What if someone sees us leaving?"

"We're allowed to leave the building," I reminded him. "We do it multiple times a day."

"Oh, yeah."

He was actually letting me do this, I realized. He was cutting school in the middle of the day, just because I told him to. Christopher was a wimp, a total fucking pushover.

The thought gave me a guilty little thrill, an almost sexual sense of my own power. I wondered if this was how Theo felt around Christopher all the time. Then I wondered if it was how Fay felt around me.

The thrill curdled in my stomach. I walked faster, and Christopher matched my pace.

It felt very weird to have Christopher in my house. He took off his shoes before he came in and placed them neatly by the door. I couldn't decide if that was polite (he must have been raised in a strict shoes-off household) or presumptuous (I would have preferred not to see or smell his socks). My mom was at work, so Christopher and I had the place to ourselves, and we were both so nervous it felt like a bad gay parody of a high school hookup.

I booted up the computer. "Do you want, like, a snack or something?" I asked as it creaked awake.

"That's okay." He watched me log on to the Internet. "Wow, you still use dial-up?"

Once we were online, I stood up and motioned for him to sit in the computer chair. He sat down and typed *thevalueofn.blogspot.com* into the browser. Then he jumped up. "Actually," he said, "can I have a glass of water?"

"Get it yourself."

He fled to the kitchen and stayed there for a very long time while I looked at the website.

It was a plain-looking blog, black sans-serif text on a white background with a pale blue border. The most recent entry was dated Friday, March 21, 2003—that was today. It was titled "Devastation" and just two lines long:

The Friday night show got canceled.

I'm heartbroken but more than that, I'm worried about Fay.

The tag at the bottom said it had been posted at 10:30 a.m., just half an hour ago.

In the sidebar was an Archives list showing that the entries went back to September 2001. How was that possible? Theo and Christopher didn't know me then. Theo wasn't even at Idlewild yet. I clicked on the September 2001 link. The entries displayed in reverse chronological order, so the first one I saw was dated Saturday, September 22, 2001.

I cant stop thinking about it and remembering more detials. I forgot to write this before but when we were playing Truth or Dare, Fay kept callign me "good girl." Like when it was my turn and I chose Dare and Fay said "I dare you to take off your shirt" and I did, Fay whispered "good girl." It made my nipples hard!! I think she could see them thru my bra cuz she laughed when she looked at me. I thougt she was laughing at me and I was embarrased but embarrased in a way that made my pussy wet

It kept going, but I stopped reading there and scrolled down in a panic. The previous entries, dating back to September 12, were all along the same lines. I clicked randomly through the archives. After September there weren't that many entries, maybe one every other month. Every few months, I guess for realism, there was some generic entry like *Happy Hanukkah!* or *I'm soooo screwed on my bio test tomorrow, I haven't studied at all.* The rest of the entries were porny descriptions of sleepovers. It was like I was peeking into a parallel universe where Fay and I had been hooking up this whole time, and also I was worse at spelling.

I heard Christopher approach behind me. I didn't turn around. "I'm sorry," he said.

"How?" was all I could say. "How did you do this?"

"Blogspot lets you customize the dates," he said. "We actually did most of it in one night. But we showed it to Jimmy like it was a real thing we found."

I turned around in the computer chair. *"We?"*

He flinched and took a step back. "Theo did most of it," he said quickly. "It was his idea and everything. I just helped a little with the writing. Only because he asked me to."

"Yeah, *only.*" My voice came out as a snarl. "I bet you fucking *hated* that. I bet it *sucked* to curl up with him and write your own porn together."

He backed away a few steps more. "I don't want to be mean," he said uncertainly, "but how is this different from what you and Fay did?"

It wasn't, and I knew it. That was the worst part. "I think you should go," I said.

Christopher shuffled from one foot to the other. His socks whispered against the rug. Even though he towered over me, he looked like a little kid. "Should I go back to school?" he said. "Or just go home?"

"Are you *kidding* me? You need me to *decide* for you?"

Christopher's face crumpled, and I felt that little thrill of power again. It was so easy to take things out on him. It was almost like he set himself up for it on purpose. Or maybe I'm just projecting my own people-pleasing issues onto him.

"Just go home," I said, and I guess he did.

I tried to distract myself from the fake blog. I half-watched the war coverage on TV. I ate stale Tostitos plain out of the bag. I tried to call Fay on the phone. I alternated between calling her dad's (where it rang and rang because the phone was unplugged) and her mom's (where it went to voicemail). Periodically I went to the computer, where I logged on to AIM to see if Fay was online (she never was), gave into temptation, looked at the fake blog again, and felt so sick I had to eat more Tostitos about it.

No, *sick* isn't the right word. I felt dirty. Dirty because Jimmy Frye thought it was real. Dirty because I wanted it to be real. Dirty because Theo and Christopher knew it—they could tell this about me just from looking at me. Everyone could.

Around three-thirty, late enough in the day that my mom wouldn't know I'd cut school, I called her office and told her the bad news about the musical. By now that felt like the least of my problems, but as I talked, I began to cry.

"Oh, honey," my mom said. "I'm canceling all my sessions for the rest of the day. I want to come home right now and give you a hug."

"You don't need to do that," I said, but I was sobbing as I said it.

"I'll stop at the Second Avenue Deli," she said. "You and Fay can have a feast."

"Fay's not here."

"Oh. Do you want to invite her over?"

I hesitated. "I don't know where she is."

My mom could tell something was up, even apart from the show getting canceled. Over our deli dinner, which I listlessly picked at after all those Tostitos, she bombarded me with questions about Fay. "So she wasn't in school today? And you haven't heard from her at *all*? Not even an Instant Message? That's pretty unusual for her, right?"

I shrugged. "It's a pretty unusual day."

"What about last night? Did anything unusual happen last night?"

I almost laughed. Where to begin? "I don't know," I said and busied myself spreading mustard on my uneaten pastrami sandwich.

"Hey," she said quietly.

I slathered on even more mustard. The rye bread was now so thoroughly soaked in mustard that it would have been inedible even if I was hungry. "What?"

"Is there something you want to tell me?"

"Oh my god." I put down my sandwich. It plopped wetly onto the plate, splattering mustard on the coffee table. "We're not, like, in a fight."

My mom widened her eyes in a wounded way. "I'm not saying that," she said. "I just don't think she's being a very good friend to you right now."

"You hate her," I said. "You've always hated her." I knew I was being overdramatic and unreasonable, but the phrase *good girl* was rattling around in my brain and yelling at my mom was one way to drown it out.

"I don't *hate* her. I just think it's a little unhealthy how attached—"

"*Unhealthy?*" I said. "Why don't you just say *unnatural?* Say it, Mommy."

"Sweetie—"

"You wish I were straight."

That was a low blow, I knew. Adrenaline rushed through me as I braced myself for a yelling match.

But my mom just lowered her eyes.

My stomach sank. I got up, leaving my sandwich uneaten on the coffee table. I walked over to the computer and sat down in the computer chair. As I logged online, filling the living room with the beeping and screeching of the dial-up modem, my mom said nothing about me tying up the phone line. She said nothing at all.

It was around seven o'clock when Juniper Green messaged me on AIM.

Strumpet19: hey sorry about the musical :(
Strumpet19: cast party is still on tho
Strumpet19: and YES it's at my place, i would never let anyone else host :)
Strumpet19: my parents are away at an ethnomusicology conference in new zealand so its gonna be off the hook
Strumpet19: u should come
Strumpet19: u and fay are like the only ones who havent been on my roof
m k fantastico: we don't go to parties.

Even referring to myself and Fay as *we* felt dirty now.

I took my eyes off the computer screen and let my gaze wander. My mom was still on the couch, watching the news on TV. Behind her, the newscasters were reflected in the dark glass of the window. I could see raindrops starting to sprinkle against it.

The computer chimed with Juniper's response. I looked at the computer again.

Strumpet19: lmao fay is coming actually

I took a sharp breath. From across the living room, I felt my mom's eyes on me.

Strumpet19: 272 e 10th btwn 1st and a
Strumpet19: buzzer 5
Strumpet19: when i buzz u in just go all the way upstairs to the roof
m k fantastico: you talked to Fay?
m k fantastico: where is she?
Strumpet19 has logged off.

I scrolled back up through the conversation, perplexed. I looked at the word *roof.* I remembered the most recent entry on the fake blog: *I'm worried about Fay.*

I was.

I swiveled around in the computer chair. My mom looked at me tentatively from the couch. "Was that Fay?" she asked. A peace offering.

"No," I said. "Jennifer Green just invited me to a party."

My mom's face lit up.

FAY

Dread overtook me as Theo and I ascended the five flights of stairs toward Juniper Green's roof. I had never been to a high school party. The prospect of navigating indefinite unstructured time among a crowd of my peers, much like the prospect of college, made me feel as though I'd forgotten to put on something crucial—my pants, perhaps, or my actual face—whose absence would shock everyone else. Noticing that Juniper's fifth-floor apartment door was ajar, I told Theo, "I'll just use the bathroom first." He ascended the sixth flight without me, and I let myself into the apartment.

I hadn't been to the home of Juniper Green since middle school. I dimly recognized the exposed brick walls mounted with exotic stringed instruments, but I couldn't recall where the bathroom was, nor how to turn on the hall light. The darkened hallway had four closed doors, two on each side. I took a guess and opened the first door on the right; it was a closet. I guessed again and opened the second door on the right. My desire to stall for time was stronger than my physical need for a bathroom, which accounts for my apparently quiet slowness in opening the door, as well as my willingness to linger long enough to notice the following:

1. It was a small bedroom, with a small bed.

I'd guessed wrong again.

2. There were two people lying on the small bed.

In the dark, I couldn't immediately discern anything about them except that they were both clothed.

3. They were kissing.

Making out, I suppose, would be the proper term. I heard it before I saw it: the juicy sounds of suction and saliva, moaning exhalations and a feminine *"Oh."*

4. One of them was Juniper Green.

She was on top, her small frame obscuring the body beneath her. Her bleached ponytail bounced slightly as she lifted her head, breaking the kiss with an audibly wet pop. She transferred her oral attentions to her partner's neck, by which point my eyes had adjusted to the dark and the exposed face became visible to me.

4. The other one was Daylily Jones.

She was sprawled out beneath Juniper, her voluminous hair cascading in every direction on the pillow. Bracelets clattered all along her arm as she lifted a hand and placed it gently on Juniper's back. "Can I take off your shirt?"

Juniper laughed. "In the middle of the party? What if someone walks in?"

Daylily slipped her hand under the hem of Juniper's shirt. "Maybe I want them to see."

Juniper swatted Daylily's hand away. She rolled over (her back to me) and propped herself up on one elbow. "What about Sergio?"

"I'll break up with Sergio," Daylily said earnestly. "I love you."

"Shut up. You're drunk."

"So what?" Daylily pulled Juniper close again.

I took the opportunity to back out and slip away as silently as possible, down the hallway, out of the apartment.

If Theo and Christopher kissing the night before had made me feel nothing, Daylily and Juniper kissing made me feel as though something was being ripped out of me. The rage it ignited in me was physically annihilating—breathtaking, bone-breaking. The idea that Daylily Jones and Juniper Green, of all people, had a better claim than I did to homosexuality—it was unbearable. Unsurvivable.

I walked up the final flight of stairs and outside onto the roof. Though it was still lightly drizzling, the rooftop was crowded with partygoers. I greeted none of them. I saw Theo—in conversation with his underclassgirl compatriots Maddy and Kendra, the three of them standing beside a wooden picnic table laden with Smirnoff Ice six-packs—but didn't go to him. I lingered by the door in a psychological state akin to the brief moment when Wile E. Coyote, unaware that he's run off the edge of a cliff, takes several impossible steps in midair: I felt myself to be floating, and while I was distantly conscious that this portended a crisis, there was nothing I could do but wait for the law of gravity to catch up with me.

Then Juniper Green was wrestling her way through the heavy door behind me. "Fay? Why are you, like, lurking in the corner?"

I turned to face her. She was unaccompanied. I wondered where Daylily was, and why they'd stopped kissing. My mind spun itself into a tail-chasing frenzy (they were *gay*, authentically so, and I loathed them for it because I was a pathetic impostor and perhaps even a homophobe who hated them because they were *gay*, authentically so). I don't even know if I spoke in response.

"You're making me look like a bad host," she said. "Go smoke or drink or something."

I nodded dumbly and followed her to the picnic table, under whose umbrella Theo and Maddy and Kendra were stationed. "We have more in the kitchen," said Juniper, indicating the dwindling Smirnoff Ice supply. "Lily's boyfriend bought us a whole bunch yesterday."

"That's *so* cool," said Maddy.

"Is it true he's a professor at NYU?" Kendra asked.

Juniper rolled her eyes. "He's not a *professor*. Just a grad student." Wielding a bottle opener with a sprezzatura that was almost butch, she cracked open a Smirnoff Ice and handed it to me.

I took a sip. It tasted dreadful, I'm sure, but sensory perception was beyond me right then; I barely felt the sprinkling rain on my face. I looked at Theo and found him looking back at me. "Theo," I said. "That thing you told me about." I felt myself to be speaking from very far away. I took another sip. "The . . ." I decided, on impulse, not to say the word *fake*. ". . . diary?"

"Yeah." Theo studied me. "Do you want to see it right now?"

I regarded him in surprise. "You have it with you?"

"It's online." He turned to Juniper. "Can we use your computer?"

"Can we come?" asked Kendra.

Theo looked at me with a cautious smile. "I'm okay with people seeing it," he said, "if you're okay with people seeing it."

"I don't care who sees it." As I heard myself say it, Daylily's soft, sweet voice echoed in my head—*Maybe I want them to see*—and I spoke louder, trying to drown it out. "Let the whole school see it. I don't give a shit."

NELL

The rain had stopped by the time I left for the party. It was a straight shot down First Avenue, just a ten-minute walk, to 272 East Tenth Street. I stalled on the sidewalk, scared to ring the buzzer. I could smell stale cigarette smoke wafting out the door of the bar across the street. (People still smoked in bars back then.) I wondered if Fay was here yet, or if she'd already left. I wondered if I should tell her everything I'd just learned from Christopher, or if this was the worst possible time. I wondered if it was crazy of me to come here looking for her when she didn't seem to want to talk to me at all.

"Nell! Fancy meeting you here!"

I turned around to see a woman climbing out of a taxi. She wore cat's-eye glasses and dangly earrings and patterned scarves, which made her look a lot like . . .

"Wanda?"

"What are you doing out here?" She bustled over to me, her scarves trailing behind her. "Can't you buzz in?"

Before I could come up with an excuse for standing forlornly outside the building, someone else came out of the taxi behind her. It was Bottom, holding a yellow legal pad.

"Hey!" I ran up to him, confused that he was arriving in a taxi with Wanda, but mostly just relieved to see him. "How are you feeling?"

Bottom pointed to his throat, then held up the legal pad. In neat, careful block letters, he'd written: I HAVE LARYNGITIS, SO I'M ENJOYING THIS PARTY IN SILENCE.

"You can't talk at all?"

His mouth formed the words *not really*, but only a hissing sound came out.

"Now, now, you mustn't do that," Wanda scolded. "It strains the throat, you know. We need you in tip-top shape next week."

"Next week?" I asked, confused again. Had the musical been postponed after all?

"Oh, dear," said Wanda. "I thought Nell was inner circle. Well, with any luck, Nell, you'll find out soon enough." She pressed a button. The intercom buzzed. Bottom pushed the door open and held it for us, mouthing *Ladies first.*

"Have you been to Jennifer's house before?" Wanda pointed to the steep marble stairs. "No elevator, I'm afraid, but it's jolly good exercise."

As the three of us started up the stairs, I wondered how many times Wanda had been to Juniper's house.

"What a pity," said Wanda, "about the Friday night show. I heard Thursday night was splendid." She sounded sincere, but she must have been at least a little bit smug. "But I'm chuffed," she added, "to see you at a cast party for once!"

"Do you always come to the cast parties?" I asked.

"I do like to put in an appearance. But tonight I'm here in an unofficial capacity. Jennifer's been such a comfort to me during all my recent troubles. Lily, too—and Peter, of course," she added, beaming at Bottom. "Oh, it's been such a joy to get to know my former students as friends. Let's be friends, Nell, shall we?"

I was too winded to answer. She hadn't been kidding about the stairs being exercise.

"It quite nearly broke my heart, being exiled from Idlewild—cast out of Eden!—but I've come to think it might be for the best. The universe works in mysterious ways, you know. I've been trying my hand at writing a play of my own. It's about a lonely young girl who's befriended by the ghost of Joan of Arc. I'm hoping to workshop it in the fall with a cast of Idlewild alumni. Oh, Nell, the lead role is just tailor-made—"

She paused for breath. In spite of everything, I perked up hopefully.

"—for Lily. I know she'll be terribly busy at Tisch, but I do hope she can find the time to participate. There's a role in it for Peter, too, but touch wood, he'll be too busy in Hollywood."

"Hollywood?" I jerked around. Bottom closed his eyes in frustration and took a breath.

Wanda laughed. "There I go again! What a terrible blabber I am."

On the fifth floor we were met by Daylily Jones, who greeted Wanda with a squeal and a hug. She hugged Bottom too. Then she saw me and didn't even bother to hide her shock. She turned around and shouted into the apartment. "You guys! *Nell's* here!"

Trying to hide my gasps for breath, I asked, "Where's Fay?"

Daylily blinked slowly. It took her a long time to answer. "I'm not sure," she said. "I've been on buzzer duty, buzzing people up." She was drunk, I realized. I could smell it.

Bottom had been writing something on his legal pad, and now he held it up: CAN WE SIT DOWN? I shot him a grateful look.

Daylily brought us into the apartment. There was no else one around that I could see, and I wondered who, if anyone, she'd been shouting to when she announced I was here.

Wanda settled into an armchair. Bottom sat in the middle of the couch, and Daylily and I sat on either side of him. Daylily rested her head against Bottom's shoulder. "I miss your voice," she said sleepily. "It's such a nice voice. Will you have it back in time?"

Bottom shrugged, jostling her head. Even not knowing the context, I was annoyed on his behalf. "I'm sure he's wondering the same thing," I said.

Daylily lifted her head to look at me. "Oh," she said. "You know about the movie?"

Bottom shook his head furiously, just as Wanda said, "I'm afraid I may have let the cat out of the bag."

"I did a screen test too," Daylily told me. "Did you know that? They told me I was perfect for the lead, but the producers wanted a bigger name."

Bottom flipped to a new page on his legal pad. As he scribbled, Wanda said, "That's show business, dear. But one day *you'll* be the bigger name."

As casually as possible, like maybe I already knew the answer and just forgot because I didn't care, I asked, "What's the movie?"

"A high school comedy film," said Wanda. "Written by that woman from *Saturday Night Live*—what's her name? The clever lady with the glasses."

So this was a *real* movie. I tried not to let my jealousy show. "So you're, like, an agent now?"

"My friend Clara's the agent," said Wanda. "It all came together rather serendipitously. She came to the Friday night performance of Othello and scouted Peter and Lily."

"And Jen," said Daylily. "Because Jen is talented, and gorgeous, and hot. She liked Jen."

As Emilia, I thought—the role I'd shared with Juniper. What if Wanda had put *me* in the Friday night cast? It was getting harder to hide my resentment. "So all three of you auditioned for this movie?"

Daylily shook her head. "We all went to the casting call, but only Peter got an audition. A bunch of auditions."

"I sat in on one," said Wanda. "Quite a fascinating process."

Bottom had been scribbling on his legal pad this whole time, and now he held it up to me. I peered down at it. This time it wasn't in block letters, but his usual neat penmanship.

Please don't spread it around. Even my parents don't know. They want me to go to Yale, but if I get the part, they can't stop me. I'm 18

So here was yet another reason he'd been so uncharacteristically uncommitted to the musical: he'd gotten a bigger offer. And he got it thanks to Wanda, back before she got fired, which shed some new light on his loyalty to her. He must have felt so conflicted about it. I was suddenly overwhelmed by how big other people's lives were, and how little I knew about them at any given moment.

"WANDA!" Juniper Green burst into the living room. "You made it!" Then she saw me, and her face fell in horror. "Nell! Jesus Christ, how long have you been here?"

I wasn't expecting that reaction. Hadn't she invited me herself? Had I misinterpreted or something? I shifted awkwardly on the couch, feeling like I weighed a thousand pounds. "I just got here," I said. "Have you seen Fay?"

"Oh, yeah. She's on the roof." Juniper came over and thumped me on the back, hard, urging me off the couch. "You should go look for her."

As she herded me to the door, I knew she was trying to get rid of me. But I could worry about that later. I had to find Fay.

FAY

Juniper Green's computer monitor was translucent, its electronic innards faintly visible through the raspberry-pink plastic of its casing. It sat on a desk beside the small bed. I imagined I could smell the traces of Daylily and Juniper's embrace, raspberry-pink in its feminine essence. I imagined the same smell wafting off the computer screen as I scrolled through the blog entries Theo had pulled up.

Then it was my turn and I was scared to choose Dare agian so I said Truth and Fay said "Truth, is your pussy wet?" I opened my legs to show her I was soakign thru my panties. I wanted to dare her to put her fingers inside me but on her next turn she chose Truth. I said seductivley "Truth, what do you want to do rihgt now?" she said "I want you to lick my pussy"

That was the point past which I could read no further. My revulsion was visceral, primal, sloshing through my system along with the sickly-sweet Smirnoff Ice, the bottle of which I'd half-consciously depleted while reading. It didn't cross my mind in the moment to be angry with Theo. It wasn't his fault that the word *pussy* made me light-headed, that I experienced the very concept of pussy—anyone's, but especially my own—as Cronenbergian body horror.

Juniper, Daylily, Maddy, and Kendra hovered behind me, reading over my shoulder. "Oh my god," said Daylily.

"Hot," said Juniper.

"Is it real?" asked Maddy.

"I don't know," said Theo, who was leaning against the doorframe. "I just found it." I was distantly impressed by how smoothly he'd picked up and run with my impulse to pretend the blog was real. His puzzled sincerity was so convincing, I half-believed him.

"Did this really happen, Fay?" asked Kendra, and I felt five pairs of eyes boring into me.

I glanced to my left, at the small bed where Juniper and Daylily had so recently achieved homosexuality. I looked over my shoulder at the girls' expectant faces. I looked at Theo in the doorframe, his eyebrows raised in curiosity both feigned and genuine. I said, "No comment."

A slow smile spread over Theo's face. In spite of everything, this warmed me.

"So you're both dykes?" said Juniper. I winced at the word, and then took comfort in the casual aggression with which she threw it at me. It felt like a return to the natural order of things.

"No," I said. But this was a lie too: Nell was. *Nell.* My guilt at planting a rumor about her was secondary, in that moment, to my knee-jerk jealousy of her. "Well, maybe," I added and hated myself for it. I stood up from the computer chair, too fast. My head spun. It was hot in this crowded little room. "I'm going back to the roof," I mumbled, and I fled.

Back on the roof I helped myself to a second Smirnoff Ice and drank it while leaning against the roof railing. I had the thought, as I drank, that it would behoove me to be seen drinking. Should my classmates think back on this party and remember, after the fact, that I had been leaning too heavily on the roof railing—not climbing over it, not bending my knees as if to jump, merely leaning a few inches past the point of common sense such that my center of gravity might shift at any second from one side of the railing to the other—they would remember me with a bottle of Smirnoff Ice in my hand. Witnesses would attest (I thought, as

I drank), and people would be able to say (I thought, as I looked down), *She'd been drinking. She was on the roof. What a terrible accident. Poor Fay.*

Then Theo was at my side. In a low voice, he said, "You gonna jump?"

His tone was interpretable as edgy sarcasm. I responded in kind. "We're not that high up."

"When I was here for the *Othello* cast party," he said, "I went exploring, and I found something cool. Can I show you?"

Gazing down on the street six stories below, I wordlessly considered whether I wanted to move.

"It's higher up than this," Theo added.

At that, I followed him.

NELL

I stepped out onto the rooftop. The rain had stopped, but the air was damp and windy, and the rough tar was wet. The crowd was bigger than I expected—the party had definitely metastasized into something bigger than a cast party—but at a glance, I could tell Fay wasn't in it. I hesitated at the door, wondering what to do next.

A tall guy in a tattered black beanie ambled up to me. I didn't recognize him; he must have gone to another school. "Are you from Cartoon?" he asked.

"Am I what?"

"Aw, man," he said. "You're not from Cartoon. She's not from Cartoon," he announced to a nearby cluster of art kids.

"Yeah, no shit," said Kevin Comfort. "She goes to Idlewild." He shuffled up to me. "'Sup, Nell?"

"What's Cartoon?" I asked.

"Cartoon Network," said Kevin. "It's a delivery service."

"Just weed, though," said Kevin's friend. "Which is *bullshit*. We should be fuckin' *skiing* right now."

"What's bullshit is Cartoon is late," said Kevin. "I called them at seven. Look." He showed me his digital watch. "It's nine now. They should have been here at nine-thirty."

I thought about that for a second. "Wait, what?"

Kevin's tall friend boomed out a laugh. "Bro," he said, "you are so fuckin' wasted."

Nirvana Cavendish-Epstein walked up and nuzzled Kevin's shoulder. "I just heard Wanda's here," she said. "She's downstairs. Do you think she has another bomb?"

"Don't worry, babe," said Kevin. "I'll protect you." He cuddled her against his chest and wrapped her up in his oversized coat.

"Have you seen Fay?" I asked.

Nirvana was so bundled up in Kevin's coat that only her head stuck out, right under his chin, which he rested on her fuzzy blond dreadlocks. "Oh," she said. "She was wrestling with that boy."

"Here?" I said. "Just now?"

"No," said Nirvana. "Before. When we were building the set."

"In the House of God and shit," said Kevin, remembering. "That was wack."

"Yes," I said, trying to be patient. "I remember. Are they here now?"

"Over there," said Kevin's tall friend. He pointed across the rooftop. In the corner, a bunch of people were standing in a circle and cheering. "They're wrestling."

I crossed the rooftop and shoved my way through the cheering crowd.

But it wasn't Fay and Theo wrestling. It was Oliver Dicks and Eddie Applebaum. Oliver had Eddie pinned against the tar, and Eddie was squirming and protesting while Oliver pinched him in different places. "You fat fuck," said Oliver. "Who'd hook up with *you?*"

"I told you," said Eddie. "It was at summer camp."

"Either tell us who she was, or admit you're full of shit."

"Stop it!" Eddie was laughing, sort of, or trying to laugh, but I could tell he was struggling for real. "Let me go."

"Hit him in the nuts," said a voice in the crowd. Eddie yelped. The boys laughed.

I'd never seen anything like this at Idlewild. Up till that moment, I'd believed that nothing like this ever happened at Idlewild because it was an artsy hippie Quaker school. But maybe I didn't know the first thing about Idlewild. Maybe, after four years here, I knew nothing and no one. Not even Fay.

One thing was for sure: Fay wasn't on the roof. Maybe Juniper had just been messing with me when she said Fay was here. Or maybe, I thought, Fay *had* been on the roof earlier. I tried not to imagine the worst. I tried to think instead about what to do next.

"Have you seen Theo?"

I turned around to see Christopher. His hair was a frizzy mess, like he'd gotten caught in the rain, and he was panting like he'd run here. I was instinctively relieved to see him, and then I remembered I was mad at him. "No," I said curtly. "Have you seen Fay?"

"No, I just got here." He hadn't calmed down since I last saw him. He actually seemed more freaked out than ever. "I've been trying to find Theo for, like, eight hours."

I instinctively wanted to reassure him, which overrode my anger. "Fay's been missing all day too," I said. "They're probably together."

"Where?"

That was a good question. I motioned for Christopher to follow me away from the noisy crowd. "You saw him this morning, right?"

"When I woke up, yeah. But he wasn't there when I got home."

"What about your parents?" Eddie Applebaum's squeals faded into the crowd noise as we walked to the far corner of the rooftop. "Did you ask them?"

"Yeah. He didn't tell them anything."

"What about *his* parents?" I stopped to avoid a puddle on the concrete. "Oh, watch out."

I was too late. He stepped right into it. "Oh, crap." He looked down at his sneakers in dismay. "Well, they were already wet."

"Did you call Theo's parents?"

He shook his head. His hair was so wet that his curls didn't bounce. "His dad lives in France," he said. "And he doesn't talk to his mom."

"Are you sure?" I said. "Maybe today he did."

"It's more like . . ." He rested his elbow on the rusty guardrail. "She doesn't talk to him."

"Really?" I couldn't help being distracted by this. "Why not?"

He didn't answer for a while. When he did, he spoke to the Tenth Street sidewalk six stories below. "Because she's scared of him," he said. "And Fay should be too."

FAY

Theo and I climbed the low concrete wall that separated Juniper's rooftop from that of the building next door. We crossed the empty neighboring rooftop. The next building on the block was taller, but Theo, undaunted, climbed its fire escape to the top. I did the same.

This rooftop had a water tower—one of those picturesque old water towers commonly silhouetted against the New York skyline, a great cylindrical barrel of weathered wood with a conical roof. Bolted onto it was a spindly black ladder, the kind designed to accommodate mainte-nance men and frighten off everyone else. With feline fearlessness, Theo began to climb it. I hesitated only briefly; then I followed him up, and up, and up.

By the time I reached the top of the ladder, Theo was sitting on the water tower's conical roof, leaning back on his elbows and looking up at the night sky. I crawled gingerly onto the roof and stretched myself out beside him. Trying to hold myself in place, I pressed the palms of my hands against the wooden planks beneath me. Their slant was steep, but their rough texture provided enough traction for us to sit. For balance, I kept my feet firmly planted on the topmost rung of the ladder.

I could no longer hear the party at Juniper's over the wind in my ears. I could see the crowd, two stories down and two rooftops away, but it looked laughably small and distant. All of lower Manhattan stretched out twinkling before us. East Village rooftops surrounded us in every direc-tion, graffiti-streaked and ivy-choked. Beyond them, wrapped around the horizon, the skyline glittered harshly against the night. Uptown was the cloud-shrouded Empire State Building, illuminated in a soft shade of gold. Downtown was a blank negative space that still provoked a double take. I looked away from it.

"You can see the East River." I pointed. "And the Con Ed power plant."

"You can see something else too." Theo leaned close to me, bumping his shoulder against mine so that our bodies shifted dangerously on the steep slope. He spoke in my ear, his breath warm against my neck, as he pointed to the west. "Look."

The wind blew. My eyes watered. I blinked back tears, and then I saw it. There it was—the peaked roof of the Meetinghouse.

I had never seen Idlewild from such a distance, let alone from a bird's-eye perspective. The school looked too small to contain my life, yet my life up to this point had taken place entirely within its red brick walls. I had a sense of my whole existence shrunk into a snow globe.

"Do you see?" Theo was looking at me intently. "Do you get it?"

I nodded. We spoke at the same time.

"It's a dollhouse."

He smiled. "I knew you'd understand."

I laughed into the wind. The water tower's wooden planks creaked with my movement. I closed my eyes and the water tower seemed to tilt beneath me. "Darling boy," I said. "Let's wrestle."

NELL

The wind had picked up. I hugged myself to keep warm. "Scared of Theo?" I said. "Why?"

Christopher looked up from the guardrail and turned to face me. "Do you know why he moved in with me?"

I started to nod automatically. Then I realized we'd never confirmed it for sure. "Something to do with breathing problems?" I said. "From the Ground Zero dust."

"That's the story, yeah," he said. "But he was mostly breathing okay at home for the first year. He didn't move in with me till summer." He cast his eyes down at his wet shoes. "Can I tell you something I've never told anyone?"

Part of me felt like I'd already heard enough of Christopher's secrets today. But I nodded and stepped closer so he could speak more softly.

"So, you know, I met Theo last year, when he was a Stuyvesant refugee. He sat next to me in Morning Meeting that one time, and we just kept hanging out. Mostly we hung out at my house. I got the feeling he didn't want to be at home much."

It was hard to hear him over the wind. I angled my ear toward his mouth.

"On Memorial Day weekend he came with me to my family's beach house on the Vineyard. Me and Theo had to get back for school, so we left earlier than the rest of my family, and it was sort of complicated to figure out how to get us home from the ferry. There's no train that goes to Woods Hole, you know." (I did not know, but whatever.) "So we made a plan for Theo's mom to pick us up in Woods Hole and drive us back to New York."

This story was threatening to become boring. I looked out over the edge of the building, across Tenth Street. The roof of the building across the street was covered in graffiti. I wondered in the back of my mind how the graffiti artist got all the way up there.

"We took a late ferry, so it was night when she picked us up. Theo sat in the front and I sat in the back. Once we were on the highway, Theo and his mom got into an argument. I forget what started it, but Theo turned up the music really loud, to be annoying, and his mom asked him to turn it down, and he ignored her. So she reached over to turn it down herself . . . and he hit her."

I snapped to attention again. "He hit her hand?"

Christopher shook his head. "Her face."

I gasped. "While she was driving?"

"Yeah. He didn't even seem mad or anything—he just calmly reached over and slapped her. She swerved and . . . well, basically we got in an accident. No one was hurt or anything, but the car got all messed up and it was a whole thing. But the weirdest part was, he wasn't sorry. Or even scared. He actually thought it was funny. He still jokes about it sometimes."

"About hitting his mom?"

"No, about her crashing the car." He hunched his shoulders and lowered his head. In a rushed mumble, he added, "It wasn't the first time I saw him hit her."

I was getting a little freaked out too. I took a deep breath. "Okay," I said. "So she didn't want him to live with her. But why did *you* want him to live with you? Weren't you scared of him too, after that?"

"No," he said—too quickly. "I can handle him. I'm really good at predicting what's gonna set him off."

I looked him hard in the eye. "Has he ever hit you?"

"I told you, I can handle him. As long as I'm around, he's—"

That was when Eddie Applebaum came up to us. "Help," Eddie gasped out. "Oliver's chasing me. He keeps hitting me in the . . ." He doubled over and made a gagging noise.

I jumped away from him. "Not on me!" I shrieked. "Over the railing! Over the railing!"

Hearing me, people in the crowd hooted and cheered. Christopher jumped away too, just in time. Eddie leaned over the guardrail. I turned away so I wouldn't have to see him throw up.

That was when I saw. On top of a water tower, two rooftops away, there were two people moving around.

Behind me, Eddie retched. Some girls in the crowd screamed. Way down on the sidewalk, a man yelled faintly. "Fuckin' A!"

The people on the water tower were so far away, so high up, I could see them only as silhouettes. They could have been anybody. If I'd thought about it for a second, I might have decided to ignore it.

But I didn't think. I just knew.

I broke into a run.

FAY

I shrugged off my army jacket. The wind chilled my bare arms. Holding the jacket by one sleeve, I dangled it off the side of the water tower. I let it fall. I chose not to watch it land.

Theo watched me in mounting disbelief. "You crazy bitch," he murmured. "I'm obsessed with you."

I lay back, propping myself on my elbows. The wooden planks were damp and cold against my skin. "Count us down," I said.

Just when I thought he wouldn't move toward me, he did. He straddled me with his knees and looked down at me. His eyes, in the light-polluted darkness, looked almost black. His mouth opened slightly, and his breath hitched, as if from a rush of intense emotion. It looked like awe, or gratitude. In the years since then, I've wondered if it could have been a kind of love.

"You're so pretty." He blurted it out rather suddenly. Then, as if embarrassed, he placed his hands on my shoulders with impersonal briskness. He began to count down.

"Three."

NELL

I ran and ran. I don't know how I managed to get over the concrete wall that separated Juniper's roof from its neighbor, or how I made it across that rooftop so fast, or why I wasn't scared to run up the fire escape to the roof of the taller building after that. All I could think was *Fay, Fay, Fay*.

But then I got to the water tower.

Its wood was worn and splintered and wet from the rain. Maybe it was rotten—maybe it would crumble to bits the second I touched the little ladder bolted into it. And that ladder! It was so rickety and spindly, each iron rung the width of a Frappuccino straw. Its black paint was peeling. Some of the rungs looked rusty enough to snap in two.

I looked down. That was a mistake. There was no guardrail on this rooftop. The East Tenth Street sidewalk was hundreds of feet below me.

Something fell out of the sky and landed softly on the tar beside me. I jumped away, my heart jackhammering—a body?

No: a jacket, fallen in a rumpled heap from the water tower. A green army jacket.

I took a deep breath. I wrapped both hands around one of the rusty rungs. I began to climb.

FAY

All he had to do was push. All I had to do was roll. It would be so easy, so quick, the whole thing over in seconds. *She'd been drinking. What a tragic accident. She had her whole life ahead of her.* I closed my eyes and waited for . . . something. Rapture. Peace. Joy.

"Two."

But instead, what seized me was mere terror—an animal will to live. I heard, or imagined I heard, Nell's voice calling my name. My eyes flew open. "Wait," I said.

"No," said Theo. Still straddling me with his knees, he pressed my shoulders against the damp plywood and held me down. "One."

I screamed and automatically began to thrash, fishlike, in his grip. His hands clenched into my shoulders, as if to flip me over. He was stronger than I—the thought registered dully in the back of my mind—because he was growing into a man, and I was not, and in the end there was no way around that.

NELL

I forced myself not to look down. I pulled myself up carefully, from one rickety rung to the next. I thought I heard a scream, but I wasn't sure.

I called out, "Fay?" The wind was so strong I could barely hear myself.

There was just one more rung above me on the ladder. I grasped it tightly and hoisted myself up. Gripping that last rung for dear life, I stood there perched at the top of the ladder.

The wind blew my hair over my eyes and into my mouth. I prayed it wouldn't blow me off the ladder, or blow down the whole water tower. I spat the strands out of my mouth and shook my head back and forth, trying to get my hair out of my eyes. "Fay," I said again, and then my vision cleared and I saw her.

FAY

Theo wrenched my shoulders upward, bringing us face-to-face. In the dark and the wind and my own terror, my eye for detail was unreliable, but I remember his set jaw and stony expression—a look that went beyond determination into an almost animal hunger. In that moment I was certain he was about to throw me off the edge. It shocked me, the ferocity of his desire to see me fall. Theo and I weren't the same after all; this empty-eyed boy was alien to me. I was alone. I had always been alone.

I heard it again: Nell's voice. "Fay!"

Theo heard it too. His grip on me softened. I jerked away from him, causing the wooden planks to groan beneath me, and saw that she was really there. I wasn't alone.

"Let's all come down." Nell spoke evenly, carefully. "Okay?" I could have dissolved in the warmth of her. I was liquid with relief.

"You got here just in time," said Theo. His tone was light, sardonic, only slightly breathless from exertion. "Fay was gonna jump."

I couldn't bring myself to speak, and so I didn't dispute this claim. To this day, I'm unsure whether to categorize it as a lie.

NELL

I carefully climbed back down the ladder. Fay came down after me, and then Theo. As I found my footing on the tar surface of the rooftop, I saw Christopher running toward us. Following close behind him were a bunch of other people from the party. I realized, belatedly, how much attention I must have attracted by running over here.

Theo jumped off the last rung of the ladder and took a theatrical bow. Someone called out, "You're insane."

Theo trotted toward the others, cupping his hands around his mouth to be heard across the rooftop. "It was Fay's fault," he called back to them. "She dared me."

His tone was so light and jokey, so *normal*, I was suddenly unsure of what I'd just seen. Maybe it was nothing. Maybe I'd overreacted. I looked over at Fay, wondering if she was laughing it off too.

She was shivering—she was in just a T-shirt with the sleeves cut off—and her eyes were huge. I couldn't tell if she was looking at me, or Theo, or the edge of the roof, or nothing at all. But I'd never seen her look so scared.

I noticed her army jacket near my feet, right where it had fallen. I picked it up. It was wet in some spots, but not soaked. Like my mom used to do for me when I was a kid, I held the jacket open for Fay. Limply, she slipped her arms into the sleeves. In a strangely flat voice, she asked, "Would the show be over by now? If we were still doing it?"

In that moment, I think, I loved her in a different way than I'd loved her before. I had no idea what was going on with her, but I didn't need to know. I just needed her to be alive.

I checked my watch. "Not quite," I said. "We'd be deep into Act Two. Maybe in the middle of 'Some Other Time.'"

"That's my favorite part," she said. Her teeth were chattering. "Because we're together."

At first I was touched. But then, as I followed her gaze across the rooftop, I wondered what she meant by *we*. Just the two of us? All four of us? Her and Theo?

There was another gust of wind. A raindrop fell.

FAY

I remember thinking *thank you* with such obliterating force that I'm uncertain if I said it out loud. Sometimes I remember bleating it continuously—*thank you thank you thank you thank you thank you*—as Nell guided me back down the water tower and helped me into my jacket. Other times I remember being so overwhelmed with gratitude that I was unable to express it at all. But surely, I thought, Nell would understand it regardless of whether I said it. She'd found me. She'd saved me. She knew me. She had to understand me. She *had* to.

NELL

Rain began to sprinkle. Fay and I made our way back across the roof-tops, catching up with the group that had broken off from the party to follow me to the water tower. Theo was in the middle of his hag-gling routine. "Please? I'll give you five dollars. No—three dollars. Nothing. It's free."

Christopher saw me and Fay approaching. He met my eyes for just a second, then turned back to Theo. "Fifty," said Christopher. "It'll cost you fifty dollars to borrow my jacket."

"Fine. You win. Negative fifty dollars—you give *me* fifty dollars. And your jacket."

The crowd laughed. Even Christopher laughed—a little shakily, but he was obviously determined to act normal. He took off his loose denim jacket and handed it to Theo, who put it on over his own leather jacket.

Just as we reached Juniper's roof it started pouring, the kind of rain that gives you two choices: run through it and get soaked, or take cover and wait it out. Theo and Christopher and their entourage chose to sprint. Shrieking, they all dashed across Juniper's roof and disappeared through the door. But Fay sank to all fours and took shelter under the wooden picnic table, so I crawled in after her. We were the only ones on the roof now; the rest of the party had gone inside. The rain hammered on the table above us, splattered onto the concrete so hard it splashed us. Through the table's slats, cold water dripped onto my head.

"Maybe"—I raised my voice over the roaring rain—"we should just make a run for it."

"No," said Fay. "The rain will let up soon."

It didn't. I'm not sure how long we crouched there, shivering, but after a while Juniper Green showed up. She was maneuvering her way toward the picnic table, holding a flimsy pink umbrella, when she saw us. "What the *fuck*?" She almost dropped the umbrella. "You guys scared the shit out of me! What are you still doing here?"

Peering up at her from under the table, I deadpanned, "I found Fay."

"We'll come out when the rain stops," said Fay.

Juniper snorted. "Yeah, it's not gonna stop," she said. "I just came back for the Smirnoff. But I'm not gonna leave you guys trapped under a table all night."

It was a bit of a logic problem to figure out how the three of us could share Juniper's small umbrella. The only solution was for Juniper to walk us inside one at a time. I let Fay go first.

A minute later, Juniper returned for me. But before I could come out from under the table, Juniper squatted down and crawled under it to sit with me.

"I actually wanted to talk to you alone for a second," she said. She closed her pink umbrella and shook it out. "I just want to say, first of all, I think you're brave."

"Oh," I said, surprised but pleased. "You saw me climb the—?"

"You don't care what people think of you." Instead of looking directly at me, she examined her jeans. They were too long for her, and their hem was frayed and filthy. "It's cool." She yanked a stray thread. "I wish I could be like you sometimes."

That confused me. Caring what people thought of me was pretty much all I ever did.

"But can I give you some advice?" Now she turned to face me. "I know Idlewild is a bubble, but in the real world, people can be really weird about sex. Lesbian stuff, I mean. Even if you're, like, *out* or whatever, it's not a good idea to put it on the Internet."

My heart stopped. I couldn't answer. I couldn't move.

"So you should probably take down your blog," she said. "At least before college."

In hindsight, I'm sure she was relishing the drama of it all. But her face was so serious, I almost believed she was sincere.

Through her rain-spattered glasses, Juniper's eyes widened. "I'm guessing Fay didn't mention she showed it around?" She whistled. "Yeah, you *really* need to take it down."

Fay. I scrambled out from under the table. I didn't bother to grab the umbrella. The rain hit me like a cold shower as I ran across the rooftop. By the time I made it to the door, I was drenched from my hair to my sneakers.

Fay was waiting for me inside. She took one look at me, turned her back to me, and began to walk down the stairs.

"It's not real." My voice, breathless from running and panic, echoed through the stairwell. "I didn't do it. Theo and Christopher made it."

Fay didn't turn around. "I know."

I followed her down the stairs. My socks squelched inside my shoes. "You *know?*"

"Theo told me." She was walking very fast. "I guess Christopher told you."

"But—" My wet sneakers slipped on the marble steps. I grabbed the banister just in time. "Juniper thinks it's real."

Fay kept walking and didn't answer me.

At the fourth-floor landing, I asked, "Did you tell her it's real?"

She ignored me.

At the third-floor landing, I said, "She's gonna tell *everyone* it's real."

She continued down the stairs. I chased her down the last three flights and caught up with her as she was crossing the lobby. She pushed open the front door, but the rain was lashing down so hard she closed it again. The two of us stood side by side in the vestibule, watching the rain pound against the glass pane.

Finally she spoke, in a small voice. "Can't we just pretend it's real?"

I turned to her in disbelief. Her eyes flickered hopefully toward me.

When I replay this in my mind, I come up with a million different answers. In my head I tell her she has no idea what it's like to be me. That she's been using me like a prop, like a little lesbian doll she carries around to play gay make-believe, and I'm sick of it. Sometimes, reliving it in my head, I get angry enough to fantasize about hitting her. In my imagination I slap her the same way she slapped me, proving to her— proving to myself, really—that I exist outside her mind. I'm a *person*. What do I have to do to make her see me as a person?

But in the moment, I couldn't summon up that anger. Not yet. All I felt was drained, literally, like she was draining the life out of me and there was no amount of myself I could give her that would make her stop. I was so tired.

Ignoring her question, I pressed my forehead against the window. Through the smeared blur of the rainy glass, I spotted a taxi with the roof light on.

I pushed open the front door and ran out into the rain, arm extended, to flag it down. The rain pelted down on me again, but it barely mattered; my clothes were already soaked through. The cab rolled to a stop. I thought about opening the passenger door and climbing inside. I thought about how warm and dry it would be in there. I thought about driving off without even a look back at the vestibule, where Fay was still waiting for my answer.

Seeing me hesitate, the driver rolled down the window. "Where you going?"

"Twenty-third between Ninth and Tenth," I said. "It's for my friend."

It was a stupid martyr move, letting Fay have the cab. I couldn't find another one and ended up walking home in the rain. But of all the stupid ways I martyred myself for Fay, I don't regret that one so much. It was the last thing I ever did for her.

FAY

On nights when sleep eludes me, I often pretend to be in the company of Nell. I close my eyes and attempt to recreate from memory her voice, her laugh, her verbal mannerisms, the shape and scent and warmth of her body. I draw from every memory of her that I've retained over the years, right up to this one, the final one: Nell running into the rain, arm extended toward the taxi.

But tonight that image is superimposed by Nell as I saw her today on the street outside the Meetinghouse. I see Nell wearing a long-sleeved shirt beneath smartly tailored scrubs. I see Nell with her sandy hair professionally tapered and faded. I see Nell as a nurse, capable and competent and butch. I see her from behind as she moves away from me.

In the taxi that Nell had hailed for me, I thought again about Daylily and Juniper. How fearlessly they'd touched each other. How easily Daylily had said *love*. All along, then, there had been others like Nell at Idlewild, sitting in the Meetinghouse and going to class and performing onstage alongside her. She had never needed me at all.

Of all the ways I let her down, this one haunts me especially: I could still have told her. But I couldn't bear for her to know.

What I felt in that taxi was not precisely self-loathing, but grim self-knowledge. I knew myself to be an impostor in Nell's world. I knew that I had tried and failed to attach myself to her queerness—which existed independently of me, even as mine was contingent on hers—and that I'd hurt her in the attempt. And I knew, even then, that I would spend the rest of my life trying to outrun the shame of it. An escape route was already forming in my mind.

The cab carried me crosstown, sluicing through streetlight-shimmering puddles, its windows so wet I could see little past my own faint reflection. The whole way home, I planned.

NELL

The fake blog got taken down over the weekend. By then, though, I figured everyone at Idlewild must have seen it.

On Monday morning, when my mom came in to check on me, I said, "I don't feel good. Maybe I should stay home."

She felt my forehead skeptically. "Is this about Fay? What's going on with you two?"

I considered telling her. I really did want to talk about it. I imagined explaining to my mom that everyone in school would be graphically picturing me performing oral sex on Fay.

"Never mind," I said and dragged myself out of bed.

When I got to school I noticed that the Peace Garden wall mural had been repainted over the weekend. The dicks were gone. So was the *On the Town* set. And Fay was conspicuously absent too.

She didn't show up all day. I was hugely relieved, if not surprised. I drifted solo through Meeting and Chorus and English and history, wondering miserably how I would be able to avoid her when she wasn't cutting school. What was I going to do, give her the silent treatment in front of everyone? Every day, for the next two and a half months? Could I somehow fake it with her until graduation without making the rumors worse? I didn't know which would be more horrible.

As the day went on, I came to a bitterly funny realization. I'd been right about one thing: I *was* different from Daylily and Juniper with their fake-lesbian act. Nobody made a show of being cartoonishly horny over me and Fay playing in a room by ourselves. Nobody even mentioned it to my face. If I hadn't kept catching classmates staring at me and quickly looking away as soon as I met their eyes, I might have convinced myself nobody cared. I almost wished someone would accost me in the stairs, or whisper *dyke* behind my back, or ask me a rude question about how two girls did it—just as proof that I wasn't imagining the attention. But as I already knew, Idlewild wasn't the kind of school where kids got bullied for being openly gay. Idlewild was the kind of school where theoretically it was okay for kids to be openly gay, but no one was dumb enough to test this in practice except me, and now I would never be known or remembered as anything but Nell the Lesbian.

But that had always been true, hadn't it? It just hadn't mattered, not with Fay by my side. That was why I'd loved her: I was so excited to be gay, and she was the only one who really got that. What a stupid irony that she also ended up being the one to make me feel ashamed.

Fay was absent the next day, too, so there was an empty space next to me on the Meetinghouse bench in the morning. It was the only empty space remaining by the time Eddie Applebaum showed up. "Are you saving this seat?" he asked.

"Yes," I lied, because I didn't want to talk to him.

"For who? Fay?"

"Yeah."

He raised his eyebrows. I tensed in anticipation of some comment about how she was my girlfriend. Maybe a double entendre about saving my seat for her. (I cursed myself for setting him up for that one.) Instead he said, "She's coming to school?"

"I have no idea," I said. "I'm not her secretary."

Out of the corner of my eye I saw his face fall. Then I felt shitty. It was so easy to be mean to Eddie Applebaum, but I didn't actually want to hurt his feelings. Or maybe I did a little, but it was less satisfying than I expected. I scooched over to let him squeeze into the bench beside me. "She's probably cutting again," I said. "She has senioritis."

"Oh, you don't need to pretend with me." He settled into the bench. "I know she's suspended."

I turned to face him. He wasn't wearing his Yankees cap, for once. After years of getting scolded by teachers, he'd finally learned to take it off in the House of God. His head looked bigger without it. His hair was dark and curly, a Jewfro.

"I overheard yesterday," he said. "Mr. Prins sent me to Skip and Trudy's office because I was late and I missed Meeting. It wasn't my fault—there was a problem with the N train—but he was pissed." He grimaced. "It was my third late in a row since my last detention, so I have to go before StuDisc again."

The Meetinghouse had filled up. The big Meetinghouse clock was at nine o'clock exactly. Silence was going to fall any second.

He saw me looking at the clock. "Anyway," he said quickly, "Fay was in the office when I got there, so I waited outside the door, and—I wasn't eavesdropping or anything. I just heard." He squinted at me, incredulous. "You don't know?"

"Don't know what?" I had to say it quietly. All around the Meetinghouse, voices were trailing off.

Silence fell.

Eddie Applebaum committed sacrilege for me. He whispered in my ear.

FAY

Getting in trouble at Idlewild was a ten-step procedure laid out in the Idlewild student handbook, the 2002 edition of which I still have in my possession.

Step 0: Determine that the incident in question is worthy of initiating the disciplinary process.

Step 1: Gather the student members of the StuDisc committee, which must consist of two elected representatives from each Upper School grade.

During the 2002–2003 school year, the StuDisc representatives from the senior class were Oliver Dicks and Bottom.

Step 2: The student members of the StuDisc committee shall select two faculty members, preferably acquainted with the accused student, to serve in an advisory role.

The two faculty members selected for my case were Glenn Harding and Deenie Mellman.

Step 3: The accused student shall select one peer advocate and one teacher advocate from outside the StuDisc committee.

Everyone on the committee expected me to choose Nell and Ms. Spider. The collective surprise was palpable when I announced that I waived my right to any advocate at all. I wished to represent myself.

Step 4: The accused student shall go before StuDisc and make his or her own case.

The hearing was conducted on Wednesday afternoon, during Activity Period. It took place in the Meetinghouse, newly roomy in the absence of the *On the Town* set. If I had clung to any shred of hope that the aborted second performance might be rescheduled for a future date, that hope vanished along with the set. When my turn came to take the floor, I did so on gray carpet still marked with indentations from the recently removed stage risers. My statement was brief.

"On February thirteenth," I said, "I called the Idlewild front desk from the pay phone on the corner of Sixteenth and Third. I imitated Marlon Brando in *The Godfather* so no one would recognize my voice, and I made a fake bomb threat. It was me. I did it."

Step 5: After the student has told his/her side of the story, StuDisc may ask questions.

Bottom asked me if I had acted alone; I asserted that I had. Oliver Dicks asked me if I'd considered that the recent memory of 9/11 meant that a bomb threat would be received with a high degree of alarm; I replied that I had, and that my intention had been to sow panic. Glenn asked me why I chose to confess now; I said I wished to be punished. Deenie asked me what punishment I believed I deserved. I told her.

Step 6: After the hearing, StuDisc shall hold a confidential Meeting for Business to form a consensus on the appropriate consequences for the student.

Step 7: Concurrently, the student and the student's parents will meet with Skip and Trudy.

Step 8: Having reached consensus, StuDisc shall make a recommendation to Trudy.

Step 9: Taking the StuDisc recommendation into account, Trudy shall make a recommendation to Skip.

Step 10: Skip and Trudy shall deliver the ultimate judgment.

Steps 8 through 10 often provoked complaints from Idlewilders that the whole StuDisc system was a mere formality, a Potemkin village of Quaker egalitarianism that served no real purpose beyond burnishing the extra-curricular résumés of its student members. My parents, banking on the same idea, appealed to Skip and Trudy's authority.

"I'd be happy to make a donation to the school," my mother said. "On top of what I already gave at the fundraiser this year."

"I thought Quakers were all about forgiveness and second chances," my father said.

"She has just two months till graduation," my mother said. "Think of her future."

"Unfortunately," said Trudy, "with her grades the way they are, it's not clear if she can make it to graduation as it is."

I mouthed *bathroom*, slipped out of the office, and fled to the Peace Garden.

Aware that I might never enter the garden again, I tried to memorize every inch of it. To this day, I sometimes try to reconstruct the Peace Garden in my mind. I'm reconstructing it right now. Quiet as a cloister. Redolent of cold stone. Ivy lushly overgrown, creeping up the four walls, obscuring the repainted mural, cloaking and choking the crumbling brickwork.

I felt no regret—not then, not yet. I was anxious, I suppose, but it was only the anxiety I felt backstage before my final scene. I was not burning, but glowing. I was radiant with resolve.

I believed then, and I want to believe now, that I was doing Nell a favor. By removing myself from Idlewild, disappearing from her life, I was set-ting her free. But mere altruism seems insufficient to account for the twisted triumph I took in the prospect of my own expulsion. Of claiming

Theo's crime as my own, accepting the punishment that would have gone to him.

I can see now, from fifteen years' distance, what I was really doing. In my own secret way, in the only way I knew how, I transformed myself into Theo Severyn.

The Meetinghouse door opened. The committee hearing was over. Consensus had been reached.

NELL

Gossip traveled fast at Idlewild. By Wednesday morning, the whole school knew. I overheard people talking about it in the hallway.

". . . going before StuDisc today."

"Is it true she turned *herself* in?"

They didn't seem to notice me as I passed, and I realized the fake blog had essentially been bumped from the headlines. I wondered if that was part of Fay's motivation. I kind of hoped not, so I could stay uncomplicatedly mad at her.

At one point I passed Theo and Christopher on the stairs. I ignored them. They ignored me. For the rest of my time at Idlewild, we would act like we didn't know each other.

I dragged myself through the day. Sixth period Chorus ended and the underclassgirls cleared out, leaving me and Bottom and Ms. Spider alone in the Meetinghouse Loft. It was time, theoretically, for Senior Musical Theater Seminar.

For a minute or two, the three of us just sat there in miserable silence—Ms. Spider on the piano bench, me and Bottom on opposite ends of the semicircle of black plastic chairs. In Fay's absence the rehearsal room felt huge, cavernous. At the same time, it looked newly dinky and shabby to me. It was hard to believe how happy it used to make me just to walk into it.

The bell rang. Seventh period had officially started.

"I don't feel much like singing." Ms. Spider was rocking slightly, like a sad haunted rocking horse, on the piano bench. Her body seemed tiny and fragile, and her face looked really old. "I don't suppose you do either."

Bottom and I shook our heads.

"We probably can't continue this class," she said. "But you two should still get credit for it. I'll see to that. We'll call it an independent study project."

Bottom and I mumbled our thanks.

Ms. Spider sighed. "I just don't understand," she said. "She had so much potential." She rose to her feet, or tried to. Her face tightened with pain. Her knees must have really been bothering her. For the first time ever, I thought of offering to help her up—but by the time I had the thought, it was too late. She shuffled slowly out of the rehearsal room.

Then it was just me and Bottom. To fill the silence, I asked, "When's the movie audition?"

"Friday afternoon," he said. "But I'm trying not to think about it." His voice was mostly back to normal. For the millionth time, I marveled at what a gorgeous voice it was—so rich and resonant and deep.

"I'm sure you'll do great," I said.

He shook his head. "Let's talk about something else."

"When's the StuDisc hearing?" I asked, even though I knew the answer.

"Activity Period," he said. "So, in about forty-five minutes."

I slid my butt across my chair and onto the one to my left, closer to him. "What's it like being on StuDisc? Holding people's fate in your hands."

"I wouldn't go that far." He slid, too, onto the chair to his right. Now there were only two chairs between us. "It's boring," he said. "Mostly we just deal with lates. Lates and absences. If there are no new cases, we spend the meetings rewriting the student handbook. We've been rewriting the student handbook sentence by sentence for about a year now."

I was genuinely amazed at how boring that sounded. "I'm sorry we got you elected," I said. "I didn't know we'd be inflicting *that* on you."

I expected him to wave this off and say, *Oh, it's no trouble.* Instead he said, "Well, you did, and here we are." He sat up straighter, correcting his posture, which had almost slumped for a second. "That's all to say," he said, "I've never dealt with a major disciplinary infraction before now."

"So you've never had to expel someone," I said.

"Well, StuDisc doesn't do the expelling. We make a recommendation to Trudy, and . . ." He rolled his eyes like the sentence was too boring to finish. "But everyone's expecting us to recommend expulsion, yes."

I scooched once more, so there was only one chair between me and him. "Will you?"

Bottom looked me right in the eye. "Do you think I should?"

His eyes were so big and dark. They sparkled in the sunlight coming through the window. I had the funny thought that I loved his eyes, just like I loved his voice. I loved *him*. Not in the same way I loved Fay. But I wanted to know him better. I wanted to be his friend.

I wondered what my time at Idlewild would have been like if I hadn't spent it all in Fay's shadow. Maybe I'd have been close with Bottom. (I wouldn't still think of him as Bottom, that's for sure. He would be Peter to me.) Maybe, instead of the Invert Society, I could have done something legit with the Gay-Straight Alliance. I could have taken Christopher under my wing. We could have been two gay kids looking out for each other. The two of us—or more of us, even, who knows?—could have gone together to gay youth group meetings in the city. I might have found a girlfriend.

"I think she wants to be expelled," I said. "She's not going to college anyway. She didn't get in anywhere."

His eyes widened. "She didn't get in *anywhere*? How is that possible? She's so smart."

"She's not *that* smart," I said. "She just uses a lot of big words and her parents are rich."

I had never said that to anyone before. I'd never even thought it.

"You're mad at her," said Bottom. "Did you two . . . ?" He trailed off awkwardly.

I felt a squeeze of anger that he was too squeamish to ask directly. "We didn't *break up*," I snapped, "because we were never dating. That blog thing was fake. Theo and—"

He put up a hand to stop me. "It's none of my business," he said. "I was just going to say, that makes two of us. Being mad at Fay."

This distracted me from my anger. Of course, I thought: he blamed the two of us for spreading the rumor that his parents got Wanda fired. "That wasn't her fault," I said urgently. "I know that for a fact."

"I know it wasn't her *idea*," he said. "But that was rather cold comfort, I have to say, when she was hitting me."

I paused to take this in and recalibrate. It took me a stupidly long moment. This sounds hard to believe now, but I had honestly never considered that Bottom might have resented Fay for that at the time—let alone months later.

"But that was just pretend." I was trying to convince myself as much as him. "Did she actually hurt you?"

"Not physically. She made contact a few times, but that's more on Wanda for being untrained in fight choreography. Theo was the one I had to watch out for." He rubbed his neck, remembering. "He got a real kick out of that prologue, I think."

He paused, and I wanted to tell him he was right. I wanted to tell him about Theo's Marble Faun act, and his mom crashing the car, and what I saw up there on the water tower. I was so close to blurting out that Fay was lying, that Theo was the one who called in the bomb threat. I think, if Bottom had let the silence build for one second longer, I would have told him everything. I've often wondered how that would have changed things.

But then he went on. "Fay, though—she only did it because Wanda told her to. Of *all* the times for Fay to do what she was told." He laughed bitterly. "The whole time I've known her, she's acted like rules were just suggestions and she didn't have to do anything she didn't want to do. Which she *didn't*! She could get away with murder here. She could have said no to Wanda anytime. I kept thinking she would, eventually." His hands were clenched on his lap. "Even on opening night. The curtain went up, and part of me still hoped . . ."

I wanted to comfort him, but I couldn't think of a single comforting thing to say.

"Sorry," he said, like he'd just remembered I was there. "I think about this a lot."

"I'm so sorry," I said. "I had no idea you felt that way." This, at least, was true. "I thought you and Wanda were cool. I thought she was making you into a movie star."

"Oh, that." He unclenched his hands. "I'd be lying if I said I didn't appreciate that. If I get cast in the movie, I'll always feel grateful to Wanda."

He said it so mechanically, I didn't believe him. "Really?" I said. "You won't feel like, I don't know, like she bought your loyalty?"

"It's possible to feel two things at once," he said dryly. "Anyway, she didn't buy *your* loyalty, so I was surprised when you sided with her during the Meetinghouse incident."

"I didn't side with Wanda!"

He just looked at me.

"I mean," I said, "I didn't take sides." Even then, I could hear how lame that sounded. "It was . . . complicated."

"Was it about Yale?" he asked. "Were you jealous I got in? That's what Lily thinks."

The question was too uncomfortable even to think about, so I turned it around on him. "Lily sided with Wanda more than anyone," I said. "Why do you give a shit what she thinks?"

"Because she cares about me," he said.

I snorted. "Does she actually? Or do you just have a crush on her?"

He looked me hard in the eye. "I could ask you the very same question about Fay."

I had that coming, I guess.

I stood up and walked over to the window. I pressed my hands against the dusty dove-gray windowsill and looked out at the Peace Garden. I saw the wall mural, with its stick-figure kids holding hands around planet Earth. I saw the bed of ivy where we'd found the can of black spray paint last Thursday night. I half-expected to see it now, gleaming on the ground in the afternoon sun—but of course it was gone, and so were the empty Frappuccino cups Fay and I had littered with, because the whole garden had been cleaned up along with the mural. There were pale green shoots poking out of the dirt, and a couple of crocus buds so vibrantly purple I could see them from all the way up here.

Behind me, Bottom said, "I'd better get ready for the hearing." I heard him stand up to leave.

I turned around. "Wait."

He paused in the middle of the room, illuminated in a shaft of sunlight from the window.

"It's just high school," I said. "All this"—I waved my hands around—"it feels like a big deal right now, but you're gonna be a big movie star and never think about any of this again."

Once again, I expected him to demur modestly—something like *Oh, Nell, you think too much of me*—but he didn't. "That's what keeps me going," he said, and walked out.

"You won't even remember this place." As the door swung shut behind him, I called out, "You're gonna be like, 'Idlewild? What the hell was *that*?'"

The question echoed through the empty rehearsal room.

EPILOGUE

FAY

I am not telling this story from beyond the grave. It's only in a metaphorical sense that my life ended at Idlewild in the spring of 2003, and only in a metaphorical sense that I've existed for the last fifteen years as a ghost.

I never left New York. I never even left 465 West Twenty-third Street. After my expulsion, my mother purchased the studio apartment downstairs from her three-bedroom on the pretext of one day combining the two units into a duplex. Though it was as a stopgap measure that she invited me to live rent-free in the studio, I understood that I could do so indefinitely under the tacit condition that I make myself scarce. This arrangement, which mirrors my parents' separation agreement, is still in effect. I see them about as frequently as they see each other.

A few days after my expulsion, I visited my local video store and asked Calvin if his Cavern was hiring. He employed me on the spot. I swiftly realized my naïveté in expecting the work to suit my interests and abilities. Video store clerking was retail labor through and through: window washing, inventory logging, receipt sorting, sore feet from standing for eight hours a day, obsequious politeness toward middle-aged women who shouted at me when a title was available on DVD but not VHS or vice versa. My parents assumed that I would quickly tire of such a life, get my GED, and reapply to college, but every time I considered it, I failed—just as I'd failed in Deenie Mellman's office in the fall of 2002—to see my future self as anything but an empty silhouette surrounded by a corporeal crowd. At least I could picture myself as a video store clerk.

Besides, the job offered one redeeming perk: renting out gay porn videos to the aging neighborhood men. How I loved the store's discreet system! I loved acting blasé whenever a gentleman took a pencil and slip of paper from the candy dish on the counter. I loved the covert intimacy of taking the paper slip from his hand and reading filthy words in his handwriting. I loved disappearing into the dusty shelves behind the counter in search of the pencil-scrawled title. I loved handing him the video in a plain black case, smiling the same smile I gave to customers who rented non-pornographic films, his secret safe with me. I prayed that such men would never find out that gay porn was available for free on the Internet. It was my favorite part of my job. It was my favorite part of my life.

It was also my only interaction with gay culture after Idlewild. I never rented any gay porn videos for myself, nor any other gay-themed films. I even managed, after several late-night relapses, to swear off slash fiction. Painful memories aside, I was afraid of what it might reawaken in me.

For the same reason, I avoided gay people. This was a good deal easier than avoiding gay shit. After Idlewild, the only gay person left in my life was my father's friend Gareth. Still, he proved awkwardly difficult to shake. For months, he kept dropping by Calvin's Cavern during my shifts, chatting me up despite my repeated hints that I was too busy to talk. Even after he moved out of my father's apartment and left New York, he periodically emailed me gay porn clips that reminded him of me. I deleted each message without replying. Once he sent me a package in the mail, with a return address in Providence, Rhode Island. I opened the package; it contained a hardcover book (*Tab Hunter Confidential: The Making of a Movie Star*, Tab Hunter and Eddie Muller, 2005). I threw it in the trash. Hours later I recognized how disproportionate my reaction was, and I wondered for the first time if I was angry at Gareth.

In the summer of 2008, Gareth died. The *Providence Journal* obituary reported the cause as a heart attack, my father reported the cause as methamphetamine abuse, and neither source is necessarily reliable. I found out too late to attend the funeral, though I like to think I otherwise would have gone. When I look back now on my teenage friendship with

Gareth, I'm unsettled in a way I struggle to interpret. Sometimes it feels like resentment. Other times it feels like gratitude.

I worked at Calvin's Cavern for eight years. The store managed against all odds to survive well into the Netflix era—it shuttered for good in the fall of 2011—but its financial straits grew more dire with each passing year. In 2009, Calvin cut my hours. Though my own resultant financial problems were solvable in the short term by a phone call to my mother, and solvable in the long term by a college degree, I instead posted an ad in the jobs section of Craigslist offering my services as an SAT tutor. I had only one credential—my perfect 800 verbal score—but I made much of it, as did the parents who responded to the ad. So began my current career.

From SAT tutoring I expanded into college application essay coaching, and from there into college application essay ghostwriting. In the last few years, between Craigslist and word of mouth, I've amassed a self-regenerating client base of New York private school kids who pay me handsomely for my application essays. Yes, I get rich kids into college for a living. The irony.

If I was hoping, on some level, to relive my high school years by professionally surrounding myself with high schoolers, this hope was dashed. Today's teenagers are culturally alien to me. I don't mean that they listen to unfamiliar pop music or use unfamiliar slang or any of the other bellwethers of youth culture for which I myself had no affinity as a teenager; I mean that the very nature of teenhood seems to have changed in the last fifteen years. The teenagers I meet are kinder and gentler, less sarcastic and more sincere than any of us ever were at Idlewild—and they are all, as far as I can tell, some flavor of queer. I don't know if this demographic increase is attributable to a passing fad, New York private school selection bias, or social progress on which I just barely missed out. Whatever the cause of this cultural shift, it fills me with a jealousy so intense that I can't reliably mask it.

To wit: in the summer of 2014 I was hired as a college essay coach (the aboveboard kind) for a rising Saint Ann's senior named Sam. Sam's mother, who brokered the arrangement, avoided gendered pronouns throughout our email exchange, and even in person I was initially unsure of the gender of this androgynous beauty. Bleach-haired, eyeliner-smudged, and husky-voiced, Sam wore studded leather bracelets and spoke enthusiastically of a favorite anime series, none of which clarified things for me. I hoped the answer would reveal itself organically, and it did, halfway through our first session, in the context of essay brainstorming. "I could write about my transition," Sam suggested. "Like how I always felt like a boy, but I thought I couldn't *be* a boy, because I was attracted to boys. But then at theater camp I met this guy Eric, who's gay, and I was like, oh right, gay guys exist! And now Eric's my boyfriend." His shy laugh trailed off. A melancholy air overtook him. "But that would be kind of a sad essay," he said. "Because I wasted so much time. I didn't even start transitioning until I was sixteen."

I had, at that point, nearly thirty years of practice maintaining a façade of Brechtian detachment, but my powers nearly failed me in that moment. My jealousy was compounded by anxiety that Sam would perceive my reaction and interpret it as transphobia—or, worse, that he would interpret it correctly. I dropped Sam as a client after that first session, knowing that this would only contribute to the impression of my bigotry, but unable to bear even the thought of another hour in his presence. To his irate mother, I apologized and blamed my physical health. This explanation wasn't entirely false: my physical health was increasingly compromised by drinking.

It was a few months after this incident that the Lyric Theatre on Broadway mounted its revival of *On the Town*. Late one night in December, drinking alone in my apartment, I impulsively went on StubHub and found a single orchestra ticket, available for $17, for the following night's performance. I bought it.

I attended the show. It played, and then it ended. The houselights went up. I remained in my seat while the audience murmured and shuffled toward the exit. I blew my nose and wiped away the tears I had wept for the duration of the performance. Slowly I stood, slowly I turned—and suddenly I saw, amid the slow-moving and largely elderly crowd, Theo

Severyn and Christopher Korkian. They had been seated, and were now standing, two rows behind me. They looked, in that initial glimpse, exactly as I remembered them.

It was a shock that surpassed shock, registering instead as a dreamlike lack of surprise. "Over here," I called out, as if they'd been searching for me. "Theo and Christopher!" Hearing their names, they looked toward the stage and saw me.

In an adolescent surge of energy, I climbed over my seat to stand one row closer to them. Leaning over the empty seats that separated me from them, I threw out my arms for a hug. I'd never been a hugger. I was performing the role of a woman greeting a couple of beloved old friends from high school. In the presence of Theo and Christopher, performing came easily to me again.

I embraced Theo first. It was, I suppose, the first time we'd ever embraced as such, though the physical closeness was familiar. His fragrance was eye-watering but, to my nose, designer. His black coat felt expensively soft under my fingers. His body was stiff in my arms. I let go.

From across the row of red velvet seats, Theo looked me up and down. He spoke the first words he'd spoken to me since that night on the water tower twelve years before.

"What the hell happened to you? Cancer?"

The words made no sense in my ears. Laughing automatically in reaction to the joke I assumed he was making, I moved over to hug Christopher, who was still staring at me. "This is freaking me out," said Christopher. "You haven't aged at all."

I heard this a lot from clients, bartenders, doctor's office receptionists, and anyone else who had occasion to learn my true age. "But you look like you're in *high school!*" And then, off my reaction: "Don't worry, that's a good thing!" I knew it wasn't. Sometimes, glimpsing myself in a store window—cropped hair, apple-cheeked face, slouching around in the same army jacket I'd been wearing since I was fourteen—I wondered if I was cursed, magically stunted at the age I was when expelled from Idlewild. A monkey's-paw wish, cruelly granted, to remain forever in high school.

"Seriously, you look the same." I remember Christopher saying it several times. "Like, *exactly* the same."

"In every other way, yeah," said Theo.

It was only as Christopher's arms encircled me, in a more committed performance of long-lost friendship, that I realized what Theo meant.

I'd dropped Sam as a client several months ago, but not before observing that he wore a cloth binder to flatten his chest. Since then, in a series of late-night online impulse purchases, I had acquired several for myself. I was, on that night, sporting my tightest binder for the occasion. I was breathless, light-headed from the pressure on my lungs, which may have played a role in my dreamy slowness that night, and surely accounted for my delay in understanding that Theo was commenting on my apparent lack of breasts.

I pulled away from Christopher and said to Theo, "Really?" I performed sarcasm, coolness; it all came back to me instinctively. "That's the first thing you notice?"

"I barely recognize you without them," said Theo.

"Without what?" said Christopher, earnestly confused.

"Her one good feature," said Theo.

The floor of the Lyric Theatre was tilted downward toward the stage. Standing one row ahead of Theo and Christopher, I had the illusion of being much smaller than them. I suppose it wasn't entirely an illusion. Christopher was very tall indeed, his shoulders square and broad, his manicured hands quite large. Theo remained shorter, but his body had filled out, his boyish slenderness hardened into wiry power. His angular face was shadowed with dark stubble, and his hairline had receded ever so slightly, just enough to reshape his forehead with masculine breadth. But what struck me most about Theo was not how he'd changed, but how he hadn't. Theo had always looked at me the way he was looking at me now—with lacerating recognition.

Before I could formulate a response, an usher ushered us out of the theater through the back exit. The three of us paused (or, really, the two of them paused and I paused alongside them) in the crowded cold on Forty-second Street. Times Square lights flickered and glared. Taxis honked. Cigarette smoke wafted around us from among the milling theatergoers. "I hate this," said Theo. He was grinding his teeth, I noticed; I was studying his sharp stubbled jaw and saw it working slightly. "This is the worst street in New York. Christopher, get an Uber."

"All the way to Williamsburg?" said Christopher. I heard a slight sibilance in the *s*. His curls were voluminous and defined, his face tanned golden even though it was December. He'd grown even gayer in the last twelve years, blossoming into the club-scene beauty he was born to be.

"Yeah," said Theo. "I'm not getting in the Times Square subway." Theo, I thought, had *not* grown appreciably gayer in looks or mannerisms. Was he straight? Even after all these years, I couldn't tell. I wondered if he and Christopher had ever kissed again.

As Christopher swiped at his iPhone, I said, "You live in Williamsburg?"

"We just moved there." Theo was scrolling idly through his own iPhone. "We got a loft."

We? "You and Christopher?"

"We've been roommates since college," said Theo. "He's, like, barely housebroken, but he's always good for the rent." He looked up briefly from his phone, jerked his thumb in Christopher's direction, and stage-whispered, "Trust fund baby."

Roommates? I was dizzy, breathless from the binder and the wafting cigarette smoke. *What's the deal with you two?* I wanted to ask. It seemed that Theo was daring me to ask. I didn't ask. "My boyfriend lives in Brooklyn too," I said. "Crown Heights." This was a half-truth: he wasn't my boyfriend but a married man with whom I was occasionally sleeping. He was a community college professor who'd posted in the Craigslist Casual Encounters section in search of a mistress who liked it rough.

"Crown Heights." Theo smiled for the first time, baring his teeth. "That's nice."

Christopher looked up from his phone. "What's nice?"

"Crown Heights," said Theo. "Heard of it?"

Christopher nodded. "Crown Heights has some good Caribbean restaurants," he said. "Someone told me that in Turks and Caicos. I think he said Crown Heights. Or maybe—"

"No one gives a shit," Theo snapped, so harshly I jumped.

Christopher looked at his phone. "Our driver's here."

This was the point in the interaction at which one was supposed to say, "Let's hang out sometime," even if one didn't mean it. I didn't say it, and neither did Theo or Christopher. They didn't even say goodbye.

If at any point during that encounter a stranger had asked me my age, I believe I would have said, "Seventeen." Not until later would I feel wounded by Theo's hostility. Not until later would I wonder if he felt shame or discomfort at the sight of me, or if this was just his personality now, or if it always had been. Not until later would I wish I hadn't seen him at all. In the moment, I couldn't judge or even react emotionally to his behavior; I could only observe it, hungrily and uncritically, memorizing it for later study. Mentally, I was back at Idlewild.

For the same reason, my first instinct was to call Nell. I pulled my phone out of my jacket pocket and was actually beginning to dial her home phone number (I still have it memorized, though God knows whose number it is now) when I came to my senses. Instead, as I walked home to West Twenty-third Street, I had an imaginary conversation with her. No one had ever replaced her in my life as the person with whom I shared everything, and so I never lost the habit of organizing my thoughts with Nell as their anticipated audience.

That night, in my head, I explained to her about my binder. *I don't do it for the same reason that Sam does it,* I told her. *It's an aesthetic thing for me.* The Nell in my head understood this, as I'd already explained it to her multiple times. She responded the same way she always did: *Welcome to the BOOBLESS League!*

When I got to the grand reveal, the Nell in my head was gratifyingly amazed. *They're roommates?* I could almost hear her saying. *Like actual roommates? Or, like, old-school quote-unquote "roommates"? Where are they living, 221B Baker Street?*

No—that last thing was something I would say, not Nell. I still struggle, at times, to distinguish her from myself.

I can't believe they stayed best friends and we didn't, Nell said in my head— and then, the fantasy collapsing in on itself, she vanished.

After that night, I found ever more excuses to pass through the vicinity of East Fifteenth Street. Eventually I gave up the pretense that these visits were accidental, and nowadays I walk past Idlewild at least once a week, making a game of seeing it without being seen. I keep to the opposite side of the street, face forward, and walk briskly. So long as I appear to be going somewhere in a hurry, no one looks at me long enough to notice that I'm going in circles.

All the while, I talk to Nell in my head. I tell her that this was the only place I was ever fully myself. That I've never really existed except as a teenager at Idlewild between 1999 and 2003. That I wish I were younger, born later. If only I'd known as a teenager what today's teenagers know! But I didn't know it then, and it's too late for me to act on the knowledge now. To do so would be tantamount to crashing a child's imaginary tea party, crouching clumsily at a too-small toy table and insisting that everyone join me in my game of make-believe. *Make-believe?* she echoes. I clarify that it's not make-believe for others, only for me. I'm too old, and the desire is too recent. *What desire?* she asks. Our mental conversations generally take the form of Socratic dialogue. *You mean the desire to be a gay dude? That's like your whole thing.*

Yes, I concede, but a sexual fantasy isn't an identity. It would be disrespectful and perverse to define myself publicly by my fetish for (here I slip into our old vernacular) two dudes doing it.

Isn't that literally what you did in high school?

Yes, and look where that got me.

Good point. Like her real-life counterpart, the Nell who lives in my head usually ends up agreeing with me. Unlike her real-life counterpart, she has little to contribute to our conversations, which tend to be fairly one-sided.

But the woman I saw on the street today was not the Nell who lives in my head.

The woman I saw today on East Fifteenth Street was Nell, no doubt. But when I recognized her, it was not by her sandy hair or her hunched posture or any individual traits; I recognized her in the preconscious way that one recognizes a person one knows intimately. And yet I didn't really know her. I wonder now if I ever did. I loved her as I loved myself—uneasily, protectively, sometimes not at all—but perhaps I didn't know her.

The woman on the street today was thirty-three, butch, a nurse, a person who's lived a life without me for fifteen years. When she peered at the

Meetinghouse through the sawed-off wrought iron fence, I couldn't guess what she felt. I had no access to her thoughts. My impulse to call out to her, to run to her, was forestalled by my inability to predict her response to the sight of me. Would her face light up, or fall? Does she remember me fondly, or bitterly, or just barely?

I believe that for a year and a half, Nell loved me more than anyone else ever has, ever will, or ever should. This is a belief I dare not subject to reality testing. I want to remain the girl Nell loved. And so I didn't reveal myself.

But now I wish I had. It's three o'clock in the morning and I am still drinking alone in the dark and thinking of Nell. I wonder what would have happened had I called out *Nell! Hey, Nell!* and crossed the street to greet her. I imagine extending my hand and introducing myself, as if for the first time. I imagine saying that I'd like to get to know her. That we have something in common, though we're not exactly the same. I imagine telling her something I've never told anyone: I'm—not a gay man, exactly, but I want to be. I want to be—I want to *become*—not just gay, not just a man, but a *faggot*. I WANT TO BE A FAGGOT I WANT

TO BE A FAGGOT I WANT TO BE A FAGGOT and I want to be friends.

NELL

Smith is a small school, but after Idlewild it felt overwhelmingly huge. I was hoping my shyness would magically disappear once I was surrounded by other lesbians, but it turns out shyness is a built-in part of me. I spent most of freshman year in my dorm room, torrenting old *Buffy* episodes and using subnetwork-based file-sharing software to download music from the computers of dormmates I never talked to. I don't even want to say how much time I spent on the phone with my mom. Let's just say it was more time than is considered normal or healthy for a college student.

But then, at the end of freshman year, I met Kiley. I'd seen her around campus before; she was this really cute combination of muscular jock and awkward nerd. In the spring of 2004, "TheFacebook" came to Smith, and the first thing I did after signing up was look up Kiley's profile. I noticed she listed "Willow and Tara" under Interests, so I "friended" her and wrote on her Facebook wall saying I loved Willow and Tara too. She wrote back inviting me to her dorm room to watch *Buffy* DVDs. That's how I lost my gay virginity.

We hooked up a few times before going on an actual date. When she told me she was on the crew team, I got excited and told her about my holding-hands-in-a-rowboat fantasy—and she actually arranged for us to go in a rowboat together. Of course, it was hard to hold hands and row at the same time, and I was too out of shape to row effectively, so I just let her row me around for an hour or so. "This is fun," she said. "Do you want to be my girlfriend?"

I was so happy, and so scared. I called my mom the second I got back to my dorm room. "Mommy, guess what," I said, and in one babbling burst I told her about the rowboat date. "And then," I said, "she asked me to be her girlfriend."

There was a pause on the other end of the line. Finally my mom said, "Is that good?"

"Yeah! I think so? I said yes."

"Oh, okay," said my mom. "Hey, did I tell you Grandma's having cataract surgery?"

It wasn't a homophobic response, exactly. It wasn't a response at all. It rattled me so much I avoided mentioning Kiley to my mom after that. I talked to my mom less in general. A couple of times I spent the holidays with Kiley's family instead of going home.

Kiley and I were together for three years; we broke up right before graduation. She was about to start a neuroscience PhD program in Arizona, and the relationship had run its course anyway. But I regret that I never made the effort to introduce her to my mom. That's the only long-term relationship I've ever had. Unless you count Fay, which sometimes I kind of do.

I never did any theater at Smith. You basically had to be a theater major, and I couldn't justify a theater degree. Besides, after Idlewild, theater made me sad. Still, I missed it a lot. I majored in psychology instead. At first I thought I'd follow in my mom's footsteps and become a therapist, but I cooled on that idea as I grew more emotionally distant from her. After graduation I got a tech support job. Long term, I thought I might go to grad school for psychological research.

Then my mom developed a tremor in her right hand. She went to the doctor and got diagnosed with Parkinson's. My grandparents had both died by then, and they'd left some money, but not enough to cover everything my mom would eventually need: a wheelchair, a specialized shower setup, help around the house, other kinds of help as her condition got worse. She didn't explicitly ask me to provide any of those things—and she definitely didn't ask me to live with her permanently—but who else was going to do it? There was only me.

So I moved back in with my mom and went to nursing school at Columbia. There, of all places, I started doing theater again: Columbia has a drama club for medical and nursing students, and I got super involved in it. I was in the ensemble of *Crazy for You*, I ran the sound board for *Footloose*, and I even played the Nurse in *Romeo and Juliet*. The productions were surprisingly professional, which really made me realize how shitty Idlewild's theater program was. Still, there was something about high school theater that I continued to miss.

In 2014 I got certified as a Psychiatric Mental Health Nurse Practitioner. I've been working since then at the VA clinic on East Twenty-third Street. That was a pragmatic choice—it's a five-minute walk from home—but the job turned out to be a pretty good fit for me. I see about a dozen patients a day, all veterans, mostly Afghanistan and Iraq with the occasional Vietnam. They all have PTSD, and the women—I've basically never seen an exception to this—have extra PTSD from being sexually assaulted in the service. A lot of the vets have addiction issues. Sometimes they're suicidal. The first time I lost a patient (a tattooed motorcycle guy who had a service dog I was obsessed with, a fat yellow lab named Lola), I couldn't sleep for three nights in a row. I've gotten better at handling patient death since then, but I still cry about it at night. It really haunts me—all the time, but especially on those nights—that I never went to any of the antiwar demonstrations. I know I was only seventeen, and it's not like it would have changed anything, but I still should have gone. Even at the time, I knew I should have gone. That's what bothers me most: I knew what was right, and I chose wrong anyway.

I haven't stayed in touch with anyone from Idlewild—with just one exception.

Three years ago, Eddie Applebaum posted on Facebook that he had a Groupon for a guided walking tour of the Met. The theme was "Gay Secrets of the Metropolitan Museum." He was looking for someone to go with him, and on a total whim, I volunteered. It was a strange, out-of-character move for me. We were Facebook friends, but we hadn't interacted since high school. I hadn't thought about him in a decade. But the tour sounded genuinely cool. It was the kind of thing I always wanted to do but never actually got around to doing—partly because I was so busy and exhausted all the time, and partly because I didn't have anyone to go with.

So I took a gay tour of the Met with Eddie Applebaum. It was a two-hour tour that turned into five hours of hanging out—Central Park, dinner at Shake Shack, after-dinner drinks at a bar with board games. We played some intense rounds of Connect Four, plus a game of hangman where

I tried to stump him with COCKSUCKER but he guessed it right away. He'd grown up to be a self-described "bear," a big chubby guy with a black beard and a warm smile. I thought he was cool as hell, and we had so much to say to each other. "Why weren't we friends in high school?" we kept exclaiming. "Why did it take us so long to do this?"

"Honestly?" I said. "It's because I've always kind of blamed you for 9/11."

"That's fair," he said. "Sorry I did 9/11. I was young and stupid."

"Hey, we all were."

Ever since then, we've been meeting up for Shake Shack and Connect Four every few months. I don't have any friends I see more frequently than that, so by process of elimination, Eddie Applebaum might technically be my best friend now.

He's a math teacher at Idlewild. They hired him right out of college (SUNY Rochester), so it's the only job he's ever had. I couldn't get over it when he told me. "You basically never left," I said. "Your whole life is one of those back-to-school dreams."

"Yeah, it's kind of surreal," he said. "If you'd told me in high school that I'd still be here in ten years . . ." He shuddered. He had a rough time in high school, he told me. He wasn't physically bullied—that weird beatdown at the party was apparently a one-time thing—but the boys picked on him a lot. "Some girls too," he said. "Even a few teachers had it out for me." (I remembered that, actually. Teachers were always yelling at him. I just assumed he deserved it.) It wasn't only because he was fat, or because he was gay—both of those things played into it, he said, but it was more because he was working-class. He attended Idlewild on scholarship, and he never had the money for Starbucks or movie tickets or lunch at Joe Junior or any of the other hidden prices of admission for Idlewild social life. Before high school, he'd barely even visited Manhattan. He lived in Coney Island, and his commute on the N train was over an hour each way. That was why he was always late.

He told me this so matter-of-factly. I don't think he was trying to make me feel bad. I'm not sure he even knows I was one of the kids who made fun of him. It keeps me up at night sometimes, the fear that he'll find out.

"But it's not so bad to be back," he said. "The school has changed so much, it barely feels like the same place." He described all the renovations and expansions Idlewild has undergone since 2003: an elevator, a fitness center, a dance and yoga studio, a rooftop vegetable garden for the Lower

Schoolers, a new gymnasium with an eighty-foot climbing wall, two extra stories (hence the elevator) devoted to STEM labs, and all blackboards replaced with interactive touchscreen whiteboards. Every student receives a personal iPad. Every visitor has to have their picture taken and wear a visitor badge ID. There are security cameras everywhere. "The only thing that still looks the same," he said, "is the Meetinghouse."

I live for Eddie's gossip about our old teachers. Not all of them are still there, of course. Skip and Trudy have been replaced by a new principal and head of Upper School. Dorothy Schneider, alias Ms. Spider, retired when we graduated. (Apparently she's still alive. She must be a hundred and fifty years old.) Wanda Higgins, alias the Witch, moved back to England. (Allegedly. But that's exactly what a regular American faking a British accent would *want* you to think.) Her first original play, *Joan of Arc Is My Prefect*, was staged in 2011 at the Edinburgh Festival Fringe.

Incredibly, though, most of my teachers are still there. (Eddie says it's not that incredible. Idlewild offers a good benefits package.) Glenn Harding—alias Glenningrad, United Colors of Glennetton, Glennifer Glaniston from *Glennds*, etc.—still teaches history. I asked Eddie if the poor guy had gotten more confident over the years. In response, Eddie told me the following story.

It was a warm spring morning in 2009, and the whole Upper School was gathered for Meeting for Worship. In the middle of Silence, Glenn stood up. He spoke—in that same old monotonous drone—about how much he'd changed since he first came to teach at Idlewild in 2002. "I was only twenty-two then," he said. "I've grown so much in my time here. I've learned my own values, and how to live by them. I've learned that sometimes you have to open your heart and take risks, even if it scares you. And most of all, I've learned that life is better with someone you love by your side." Then he turned to face the English teacher Devi Saxena (alias Devi the Dove), who was sitting next to him on the bench. He pulled a ring box out of his shirt pocket. "Devi," he said. "I love you. Will you marry me?"

Not since the "I stand with Wanda" incident, said Eddie, had Meeting for Worship gone so fully off the rails. There was so much screaming and clapping, it took the new principal a good five minutes to restore order. Just as Silence was finally re-descending, Glenn yelled, "She said yes!" and the Meetinghouse exploded again.

Glenn and Devi had their wedding in the Meetinghouse, in summer. Ms. Caputo and Mr. Prins both gave readings at the ceremony. Eddie, who was there, swears up and down that Mr. Prins cried, but I don't believe him.

Deenie Mellman is still the college counselor, and Eddie still can't stand her. "It's not personal," he told me. "I know it's her job to get kids into fancy colleges. I just hate seeing my students so stressed about it. I don't think it's good for their mental health. Or their sense of social justice." He paused and added, "Okay, and maybe it is personal. In my first Deenie meeting, I told her I was only looking at SUNY and CUNY schools—and, like, you could *see* the light going out of her eyes. She basically never looked at me again until I started working here."

Jimmy Frye is no longer the IT guy. He was fired in 2008—not for any of the reasons I'd have expected, but because he got caught torrenting *Dead Poets Society* on a school computer. Though I never gave this a moment's thought when I was torrenting *Buffy* in college, torrenting copyrighted material is illegal, so not only did he lose his job, he was charged with copyright infringement and had to pay a fine. "Couldn't have happened to a nicer guy," I snarked to Eddie, and Eddie laughed knowingly, which saved me from having to get into the whole story. I guess I wasn't the only one who had reason to hate Jimmy Frye.

Here's what I know, thanks to Eddie and the Internet, about the class of 2003.

Lily Day-Jones, alias Daylily, went to Tisch at NYU to study acting, but dropped out to pursue a career in modeling. She ended up becoming—plot twist—a *singer*. She's released two albums under the name Lily Day (I don't know why she dropped the Jones). When Eddie told me this, I thought he was joking. There were two things I thought I knew for sure about her: she was beautiful, and she couldn't sing. But later I listened online to her first single, "Maybe I Want Them to See," and grudgingly had to admit she had a pretty voice. It's wispy and ethereal and relies heavily on that I'm-about-to-cry cracking sound that white girl singers love to make. It's not a musical theater voice, but it's good in its own way. I can't believe I'm saying that.

Jennifer Green, alias Juniper, went to Wesleyan. There—according to Eddie, who saw her at the 2008 reunion—she gained "the freshman fifteen. And the sophomore sixteen. And the junior, uh . . . well, she got fat, is what I'm saying." I cackled, and then I felt bad—but Eddie declared that "as people of fat-kid experience," we're allowed to be smug when skinny girls join our ranks. Anyway, she became a reporter. At first she contributed celebrity gossip and pop culture content for Gawker and Thrillist, but then she moved to the labor beat, and now she reports on unions and strikes and migrant worker conditions. She won some kind of journalism award for a long-form Buzzfeed article about fast-food workers organizing to raise the minimum wage to $15. Sometimes her tweets go viral. She has a rainbow flag emoji in her Twitter display name, and I'm annoyed by it every single time I see it. "That's biphobic," Eddie teased me when I mentioned this to him. But I bet she's not even bisexual. Or at least I don't want her to be.

Speaking of annoying people: Oliver Dicks went to Princeton, and then to Harvard Law. (Eddie, who hated Oliver Dicks even more than I did, was pleased when I told him that Harvard isn't considered the most prestigious law school. Yale is better.) Now he's an attorney in Washington, D.C. He's married to some bland-looking lady, but Eddie insists he once saw Oliver on Grindr using a fake name and a shirtless mirror selfie. It was just a brief glimpse—he recognized Oliver's face, panic-swiped away, and couldn't find him again later—but he's sure it was Oliver. I don't know if I believe it. Oliver Dicks seems way too boring to be gay.

Nirvana Cavendish-Epstein no longer has dreadlocks. She went to RISD and now sells handmade ceramics on Etsy. She lives in Austin with her husband, and she recently had a baby. The baby's name is Jane Brown.

Kevin Comfort didn't go to college. He went to rehab, and then he went to rehab again. For a while it looked like he was getting his life together, but two years ago he took heroin laced with fentanyl, and he died. I found out on Facebook, and I was shocked by how upset I was. I barely knew him. But I keep randomly remembering him at the party on the roof—how he wrapped up Nirvana in his coat and promised to protect her.

Peter Baptiste, alias Bottom, did not end up getting cast in *Mean Girls*. He's never gone to an Idlewild reunion, so Eddie doesn't have any intel on him. He's not on Facebook, either, which is frustrating but not surprising—of course he wouldn't be a social media guy. He does have a LinkedIn page, though. That's how I know he graduated from Yale with a double major in music and history, and then he went to Howard University for a master's degree in music education. Today, assuming his LinkedIn is up to date, he's the program director for a nonprofit that gives music lessons to at-risk kids in Philadelphia. He must be a great music teacher. I bet kids adore him.

For a long time it hurt my heart that he didn't become a professional actor. I imagined he must be so sad about it. But recently I Googled him again and found his name listed in the caption of a YouTube video. It was a New Jersey community theater production of *Carousel*, starring him as Billy Bigelow. The whole first act was uploaded. It's filmed on someone's phone, so it's hard to look at and the audio is shitty. The ingenue Julie Jordan looks about forty, old Nettie looks about fifteen, and most of the cast speaks with a Jersey accent. It's clearly not a good production. Even so, when he holds the final note of "Soliloquy" ("*I'll go out and make it or steal it or take it or DIIIIIEEEEE!*"), I get goose bumps. For those few seconds, he shines with happiness.

Theo Severyn and Christopher Korkian were class of 2005, not 2003. Eddie didn't know them in school, and he doesn't know anything about them now. I'm not Facebook friends with either of them. I try not to Google them too often. I don't want to say how often I break down and Google them.

I've never told anyone about Theo—not even Eddie—because I don't know how to explain his whole deal, and his Internet presence contains zero trace of it, which makes me feel insane. According to his LinkedIn, Theo went to Duke. He majored in French Studies and minored in Finance, and his extracurricular activities included a sketch comedy group called No Offense. He got an MBA at a place called HEC Paris, which seems to be an English-language business school in Paris, and then he went into luxury real estate. These days he's a business development manager at one of the big New York brokerages. There's a picture of his face on the company website, and he looks like a completely regular guy.

Christopher's life trajectory is weirder. He seems to have gone to Oberlin after Idlewild—there's an *Oberlin Review* article from November 2005 ("A Picasso on Your Dorm Wall: Six Obies on What the Art Rental Program Means to Them") that quotes "Christopher Korkian, class of 2009." At some point, though, he must have transferred to Duke. He's

listed in an online PDF of the Duke 2009 commencement program—
the same list where I found Theo Severyn's name and honors—under
"Bachelor of Arts." No honors, no mention of a major.

I don't know for a fact that he transferred just to be with Theo. I have
no proof of that. I have no proof of anything at all. Christopher Korkian
has no Internet presence outside of an Instagram account that makes his
whole life look like a beach vacation. I have no idea what his job is, or
if he even has a job. All he posts are shirtless beach photos, Fire Island
party photos, tropical resort vacation photos. He seems to be having fun,
or at least he's smiling in all the pictures. He's attractive like a Ken doll,
all abs and hairless pecs. I described him to Eddie as a "twink." Eddie
looked at the photos and said, "He's more of a circuit boy."

Theo appears in a few of Christopher's Instagram photos. The most
recent one, from New Year's Eve 2015, is a grainy low-light selfie whose
caption just says #nofilter. The two of them are standing against a brick
wall. Their heads are touching. Theo, who has a five o'clock shadow
and dark circles under his eyes, is pouting or glaring at something out
of frame. Christopher, the one taking the selfie, is smiling, but . . . am I
just imagining that his eyes look scared?

I have no logical reason to worry about him. We were never friends,
in the end. If I feel sick and panicky when I look at that New Year's Eve
selfie, that's not a meaningful sign that Christopher needs help. It's just
the vertigo of knowing two things at once: that Fay and I cared about
Theo and Christopher so much, it altered the course of our lives; and
that these two men are strangers to me.

It's 3:00 a.m. and I have to get up for work in three hours, but I can't
sleep. I keep thinking about the last time I hung out with Eddie
Applebaum.

It was in February, right after the Parkland shooting, so he was an
emotional mess. We'd promised beforehand not to talk about it. We've
been making promises like that ever since Trump got elected, but we
can never stick to the agreement. We were still standing in line to order
when Eddie brought it up. "There are all these platitudes going around,"
he said, "about how, you know, teachers are *more important now than ever
before!* Especially at Idlewild. The importance of Quaker values, peace and
equality and community, blah blah blah. But to be honest . . ." He looked

around to make sure there was no one in the Shake Shack who knew him. "I don't know any teacher who actually feels that way," he confessed. "At Idlewild or anywhere. We all feel so fucking useless right now."

Shake Shack was so crowded we couldn't find an empty table, so we took our food outside and ate on a bench at the edge of Central Park. Even though it was February, the weather was humid and warm. As we unwrapped our cheeseburgers, Eddie tried to change the subject to something more cheerful. "Did I tell you," he said, "Idlewild did *Othello* this year?"

I exclaimed, "Again?" Then I laughed at myself, realizing how long it had been since the last one. "It's weird," I said, "to picture other kids doing *Othello* in the Meetinghouse."

"It wasn't in the Meetinghouse, actually," he said. "Idlewild has a contract with the Vineyard Theatre off-Broadway. It's pretty cool. They have professional lighting and sound. Oh, and body mics, so you can actually hear the kids say their lines. There were six performances over two weeks."

I groaned with jealousy.

"But your version was good too," he said quickly.

"Oh, Christ, you don't have to say that." Then I couldn't resist asking, "How was their Emilia?"

"That's the best-friend character? That was one of my advisees," he said proudly. "She played her very tough, very self-controlled. I got the sense that her character was an angry person, and she spent the whole play trying to swallow her rage and control her temper until it was too late. Which I thought added some interesting tension to the peace-and-love theme—oh, they set it during the Summer of Love. All the girls were dressed like hippie flower children, and Othello was dressed like Jimi Hendrix, and Iago was this sort of Charles Manson figure who ruins it for everybody."

I was about to ask sarcastically how they squared the hippie theme with the fact that the play is set entirely in the military, but Eddie was still talking.

"Anyway, your Emilia was different," he said. "You played her in a more openhearted way. I could tell your character was motivated by her love for Desdemona, which made her more emotional and expressive from the beginning. So your arc was more about not having the courage to stand up for yourself until it was too late."

I stared at him. I'd been about to bite into my burger, but I had totally forgotten it and my mouth hung open uselessly.

"What?" he said.

"You saw me?" I said. "You actually came to the Thursday night show?"

"Well, sure," he said. "You were in it."

Not knowing what to say, I took a big bite of my burger. I had no memory of seeing Eddie in the audience or talking to him afterward. Had I not noticed he was there? Or did I see him and just fail to register him as a person worth noticing?

"I came to every show you were in," he said. "I was obsessed with you, you know."

With my mouth full, I mumbled, "Why?"

"What do you mean, *why*? Why do you think? You were the first openly gay person I ever knew. I fucking worshiped you."

To my horror, I felt tears forming in my eyes. I hoped he didn't notice.

"You and Fay," he said. "I was dying to be friends with you guys. But . . ." He shrugged self-deprecatingly. "You were too cool for me."

I swallowed and said, "Fay wasn't gay." He knew that. We'd talked about it before. I just didn't know how else to respond to what he was telling me.

"Well, whatever her deal was," he said, "I thought she was the second-coolest person in the world. After you."

"Oh, come on."

"Have you heard anything about her?"

He often asks me that question. The answer is always *no*.

Not for lack of trying. I search "Fay Vasquez-Rabinowitz" on Google almost as often as I did on Yahoo in 1999, except now it's bizarre that a thirty-three-year-old woman with such a distinctive name would have no Internet presence at all. Maybe she changed her name.

I don't know exactly what I'm hoping to find when I Google her. I know what I'm hoping *not* to find: an obituary. That's my one comfort, the only thing I can be reasonably sure of, when I search for her and find nothing. Wherever she is, she's still alive.

The Internet does contain one record of Fay's existence, but it doesn't come up when you Google her and it probably won't exist for much longer. In 2007, LiveJournal got bought by a Russian company, and since then a lot of old LiveJournal pages have auto-deleted—especially if they had sexually explicit content, especially if that sexual content involved minors, and *especially* if it was gay. But Fay's not-so-secret LiveJournal—formerly www.livejournal.com/users/omipalonealone, now auto-reformatted to omipalonealone.livejournal.com—is somehow still up, Faunfic and all. I guess she never found out that Theo and Christopher knew about it, or maybe she knew and didn't care. I check it every few months, just to see if it's still there. I can't bring myself to read it. I hate looking at it. And I dread the day I discover it's gone forever.

I've never told Eddie any of that. That February evening on the Central Park bench, I just said, "I told you. She fell off the face of the earth." I took another bite of my burger and tried to think of a way to change the subject.

"You used to be so close," said Eddie. "I hope this isn't a fucked-up thing to ask, but do you ever miss her?"

I chewed, thinking about how to answer.

Here's the thing: I've never forgotten how it felt to love Fay. For a year and a half, my brain merged into hers until I had no idea where she ended and I began. I know if I tried to explain that to anyone, it would sound scary. Like I lost myself to her. At the time, though, it felt like just the opposite. I knew exactly who I was. I was Fay's best friend. We loved theater and gay shit and ourselves. We went to Idlewild.

I regret who I was back then. At the same time, I don't know if I'll ever be happy in the same way again. And I don't know what to do with that.

"I don't know," I said to Eddie. "It was a long time ago."

Eddie took the C train home that night. I had to get to the 6 train. I walked west to Riverside Drive so I could catch the M79 crosstown bus at the beginning of its route and get a good seat. I managed to snag a double seat on the sidewalk-facing side. I looked out the mist-fogged window as the bus began to move.

And I saw her.

She was walking east up Seventy-ninth Street, toward Broadway, her hands crammed into the pockets of a green army jacket, her head bent down so her short hair hid her face.

It was foggy. It was dark. The bus was moving. It made no sense, when I thought about it later, that she would still look exactly the same—same haircut, same jacket—after all these years. It must have been someone else. She'd been on my mind, that was all.

Still, in that instant, I knew. I saw her, and I knew her, and my insides turned into pure light. *Fay*, I thought. *Fay!*

But then I wasn't sure.

The bus kept moving. Whoever that person was, they receded into the distance before I could get a better look.

ACKNOWLEDGMENTS

At my Quaker school, teachers wouldn't accept homework assignments if you didn't include acknowledgments at the end. So this isn't my first rodeo, but it's by far the biggest yet. *Idlewild* took shape over five years, and it would not exist without an enormous amount of assistance, encouragement, and support from the following people. From the bottom of my heart, I am so deeply grateful:

—to Abby Muller, my brilliant editor, and the team at The Overlook Press. Abby, I cannot imagine *Idlewild* being edited by anyone but you, and I am overwhelmed with gratitude that it found its way to you. Thank you for turning it into a book.

—to Ayla Zuraw-Friedland, my wonderful chaotic pixie pit bull of an agent, and the Frances Goldin Literary Agency. Ayla, you were the best choice I ever made.

—to the McIntyre Fellowship and everyone who facilitated my residency at the New Mexico School for the Arts, with special thanks to Dee Ann McIntyre, Jane Van Voorhis, and the formidable Denise Hinton.

—to the Iowa Writers' Workshop and the Iowa Arts Fellowship, with forceful thanks to Connie Brothers, Jan Zenisek, Deb West, and Sasha Khmelnik.

—to the City College of New York, with endless thanks to my professors Václav Paris and Robert Higney.

—to Paul Harding and his spring 2018 novel workshop, which changed my life in more ways than one. Paul, you were right about everything, and I do mean everything. Thank you for teaching me how to read myself.

—to Lan Samantha Chang. Sam, where do I even begin? Thank you for taking a chance on me. Thank you for that first phone call (and for the second, longer one after I'd recovered from the shock). Thank you for being my first instructor at Iowa and forbidding us, on the first day of workshop, from dismissing anything as *sentimental* or *grandiose*. Thank you for being my thesis advisor and giving me the single most useful note I received at any point in the writing process: "The *friendship* is what's making me turn the pages." Thank you for all those cozy Sunday tea parties with Alexa and Tai. Thank you for reading my manuscript and giving me notes when I needed them most. Thank you for believing in me as a writer, teacher, and friend. Thank you for being in my life.

—to all my Iowa friends, classmates, and "aesthetic cousins" (as Sam puts it), with special thanks to the above-and-beyond Alexa Frank, Mark Prins, and Sarah Thankam Mathews.

—to Stephen Ira, Liam O'Brien, Danny Lavery, Peyton Thomas, and Kyle Lukoff. I couldn't have finished *Idlewild* if I hadn't transitioned, and I couldn't have transitioned if you hadn't shown me the way. I'm so happy to know you.

—to my friends, with special love for Jaya Saxena, Laura Kilberg, Carrie Rosen, Danny and Peyton again, Abigail Carr, Mattie Lubchansky, Harry Bogosian, David Tay, and Art Mohr.

—to Adam Schlesinger and Kit Cali, with *eros* and *philia*.

—to Shapiro, duh. I'd tell you how much you mean to me, but as you wrote in my high school yearbook: "Dude, you already know it."

—to Jeni Wischmeyer, the High Ground Café, Alexes Hazen, Callen-Lorde, Ian Tattersall, and Twitter.

—to Friends Seminary.

—to my family, with so much love for Anya Bernstein, Anna Simmons, Alexander Bernstein, Nina Bernstein Simmons, Rudd Simmons, Evan Thomas, and Melba and Herbie.

—to my mother, Jamie Bernstein. In a very literal sense, I would not be here without you, but you are (in Shapiro's words) "special even amongst moms." Your support—emotional, financial, and even physical—has carried me through the last few years, which, *dayenu*, but you also happen to be my favorite person in the world. I'm literally obsessed with you. It's the joy of my life to dine at Le Zie with you, to go to the theater with you, to play LearnedLeague with you, to exchange books and gossip and cute animal videos with you, even just to walk to the mailbox with you. I love you *so much!* Thank you for loving me. I know you'd still love me even if I never wrote or published anything, but I hope *Idlewild* makes you proud.